Barrow King

King

Book One of the Realms

by

C.M. Carney

Barrow King - Book One of The Realms by C.M. Carney

www.cmcarneywrites.com

Cover by Lou Harper.
https://coveraffairs.com/

Dedication

To my father, Kevin Carney.
I could not have written this book without you.
I miss you, Pop.

1

The shadows crept in from the corners, stretching, grasping at Brynn as she walked down the dim hallway past dozens of secure doors, trying to ease calm into her frayed nerves. Sweat chilled her. The small hairs on her arms stood on end, leaking heat into the cool air.

There wasn't much time. *Let it be enough. Please be enough.* She cursed her clacking heels, advertising her presence to anything with even the most dullard of ears. She rounded a corner, forcing calm into her nerves and the smile that had charmed millions warmed her face. *This is it. This is the last chance. It goes to shit if I fail.*

Reynolds looked up from his desk. Brynn's grin grew wide and warm. She liked Reynolds. Better still, he liked her. A deep breath brought calm to Brynn's mind, but all Reynolds saw was the way the silk of her blouse expanded.

"Good evening, Miss Caldwell," he said, shifting his gaze to her eyes in embarrassment. "I didn't expect to see anyone in the Dungeon, tonight of all nights."

"How many times have I told you to call me Brynn? At least when we're alone." Brynn grinned, a crooked smile bringing a flush to the burly man's face. Her touch to his arm, such a simple gesture, so easily missed, became Reynolds's entire world.

Damn. How easy deception comes these days. Brynn swallowed her doubts. There was too much at stake for guilt to turn her course.

After a moment, Reynolds's regained his professionalism. Brynn saw the man bury his desires under a veneer of responsibility. "I thought everyone was up at the gala?" His tone hovered on the border between curiosity and suspicion. Brynn had to ease those thoughts back.

"You know Mr. Bechard, always some last-minute tweak."

To heighten her authority, she held up the pulse drive, forcing her hand steady. It was a perfect copy of the one that Alistair carried at all times. A master key to the Realms.

Reynolds nodded and sat upright. Brynn didn't think the ex-military man could be more at attention. Even he knew the tiny device was the literal key to power. Brynn inserted the pulse drive into a slot on Reynolds's security desk. A tense moment hung heavy in the air before a panel swooshed open on the blast-grade metal door. A biometric scanner powered to life, the green glow adding a sinister hue to the room. Reynolds stood and held his hand over the scanner.

Reynolds hesitated, and Brynn saw his shoulders tense. She could almost see his thoughts. Why would the VP of public relations need access to the room behind this door? He paused, palm hovering over the sensor as doubt thrashed through his brain.

Brynn's mind was lightning, seeking an out. "And here I thought I was higher up the corporate ladder," Brynn said, adding a sexy pout to her voice. "It should be Schechter down here, not me." Brynn paused, finger to lip. "But Mr. Bechard said I'm the one he trusts, so I guess that's something."

Reynolds's shoulders relaxed. He too thrived on the approval of Alistair Bechard. Reynolds's reverence was almost religious, akin to being chosen by God.

Brynn heaved a silent sigh of relief as Reynolds activated the sensor pad and turned with an intense stare. He held the handle in a fierce grip, muscles tensing and releasing as his mind battled.

"Typical Alistair. I'm sorry, Mr. Bechard," Brynn said, mustering schoolgirl embarrassment at her calculated faux pas. "He probably decided the Dragon's Claw Inn needed cream-colored curtains instead of eggshell."

A smile crossed Reynolds's face. Everyone at Sacrosanct Integrative Networks knew the big boss's obsession with perfection. Bechard had a literal army of programmers, but they had only the smallest input on the project. Bechard handled all the core coding. Reynolds chuckled a tad. "That's what makes him the best. Always willing to go that extra inch."

"Paint the underside of the drawers," Brynn said,

repeating one of Alistair's favorite mantras.

"Paint the underside of the drawers," Reynolds said in response as if it were a religious phrase. He pulled the door open with a fluid motion. Brynn flowed past, tracing his arm with a light touch as she passed.

This has to work, Brynn thought, forcing calm with a measured and confident pace. She neared the corner. One more turn and her quarry was hers. Reynolds's sharp voice called out.

"Miss Caldwell."

Brynn took a slow calming breath as she turned back, remembering the man's history, the man's training. Brynn knew the things he could do. She smiled as he came into view.

"Don't take too long," Reynolds said. His intense stare chilled Brynn. Had she conned Reynolds, or had he been playing her? Seconds became hours before a grin eased Reynolds's face. "If anyone deserves the party upstairs, it's you."

Brynn masked her relief under a veil of embarrassment. "I'm just a girl who talks to people, Reynolds. I'm the least important cog in this machine."

"You're much more than that, ma'am. Much more." Reynolds smiled and eased the door shut with a *hiss* and a metallic *clang*. Brynn's heart raced. Locked in a literal dungeon. Cool and dark with no way out.

Brynn turned the corner and entered the Nexus Chamber. The long room pulsed with heat despite the frigid air pulsing from the vents. Long rows of linked quantum cores shot into the distance. The quantitative power in this one room was staggering. Brynn walked up to the control dais as a large holo-vis projector came to life.

Brynn inhaled, gripping the pulse drive in her fist. Reynolds feared the small device as much as she did. It was the key to a new world. A world unaware of what was coming. She shook with the full understanding of the desperate gamble she was taking. One that may very well cost her life. A gamble that might save millions more.

Brynn plugged the pulse drive into the slot on the desk. Swirls of light pulsed inside the small device and, a moment later, a calm voice rose in the room.

3

"Access granted. Welcome back, Mr. Bechard."

Brynn glanced over her shoulder one last time, knowing she was alone but still needing to look. She pulled a second pulse drive from her bra and knelt. Gentle pressure against the dais caused a panel to slide open. Brynn plugged the second drive into the backup access port and stood.

Brynn's fingers sped across the keyboard, seeking the hidden directory Sean had installed. His risk was as big as hers, bigger even. If Alistair knew what Sean had done, what she did now, both would disappear. Brynn was sure of that.

A prompt shone on the holo-vis.

UPLOAD PATCH?

A blazing **YES** blinked in time with her thundering heart. Her finger hesitated over the panel. *Thump, Thump.* Blink, Blink. *Thump, Thump.* Blink, Blink. Her finger spiked down, and the patch cycled into the quantum core. It wormed its way into the billions of lines of code, altering the tiniest fraction of their purpose.

A moment later, the upload finished, and the second pulse drive ran a purge, erasing any evidence. Only Reynolds knew she had been here, and he was so in awe of Mr. Bechard that he would never speak to the man unbidden. The risk was minimal. It had to be.

Brynn allowed herself one last look into the infinite worlds contained in the room. *I have no choice. Alistair Bechard must be stopped.*

Brynn pulled the pulse drive from the core. A deep sigh released pent up tension. The release that comes with knowing whatever happened now was out of her hands.

"It's up to you, Finn," Brynn said to the empty room. "I'm so sorry."

2

Finn's mind found solace in the menial task of emptying the bar's dishwasher. The gentle hum, the sluice of warm water, and the waves of steam rising from the spinning contraption was a salve to his nerves. He was so lost in this rare moment of calm he didn't hear Doc.

"Earth to John. Hello, John."

Finn looked up and gave the haggard man an embarrassed grin. He still wasn't used to being John. His training and experience usually made slipping into an alter ego as simple as pulling on a pair of socks. It troubled him that this time was different.

"Sorry, Doc. Didn't sleep so well last night."

"Yeah, you look like shit, buddy," Doc said with a grin and a heft of his empty pint glass. Finn grabbed it, held it up to the spout, and flipped the tap open. Amber liquid flowed into the glass. "Got a lady friend keeping you up all night?"

Finn chuckled. He liked Doc. He was a kindred spirit. A man who'd screwed his life up as much as Finn had. Yet, as he set the fresh pint in front of the older man, Finn couldn't help wishing that his demon was as simple as alcoholism.

"No such luck, Doc. The ladies aren't scrambling to get with lowly bartenders."

"Stop playing coy. I may be a drunk, but I'm no idiot. You've got many a hidden depth to you."

Panic rose in Finn as he eyed Doc. The man had been a McHenry's regular years before Finn bought the place, so the likelihood of him being a plant was slim to none. Yet professional paranoia had helped Finn live this long.

"Don't be so uptight, lad. A man is entitled to his secrets. Especially in this world. I have a few dark ones I keep to myself, too." Doc raised his pint in a knowing salute before taking a sip.

But you don't, Finn thought.

Doc's once a week ritual, fueled by guilt and alcohol, was to regale Finn with the tale of his downfall. The man had once been a brilliant surgeon, but alcohol had seeped into his soul and a mother had died on his table. Doc didn't even fight the inquiry. He'd forfeited his medical license the very next day. Now he spent his days at Finn's bar, watching soccer and trying to drown his demons.

Finn started cutting fruit for the day.

"Can I turn on the news?" Doc asked.

Finn nodded. He had long ago given Doc access to the large holo-vis behind the bar. It popped to life and CNN came on.

"This is Snapper Carr, reporting from outside Sacrosanct Integrative Technologies," a young man with a winning smile said. A crowd of angry protesters gathered in front of the stunning modern skyscraper. "Today, after a successful six-month beta test, the Realms was set to go public. The world's first Neuro Integrated Massive Multi-Player Online Role-Playing Game has wowed critics and beta players alike. Industry experts expected it to be a multi-billion-dollar money maker for Sacrosanct Founder and CEO, Alistair Bechard."

"I never understood these games," Doc said.

"Never been my thing either," Finn said. "But I get it. Who doesn't want an escape from the drudgery and pain of the real world?"

Doc nodded and hoisted his beer in salute. Screams of anger and pain brought his attention back to the newscast. The crowd pushed forward against the wall of riot cops as rocks flew over the shield wall. An improvised Molotov cocktail exploded against the building. The cops pushed into the crowd, riot shields smashing and advancing.

"Jesus," Doc said, drawing Finn's eyes to the holo-vis.

"It's just a game, isn't it?" Doc asked, stunned.

"Things have become violent here," Snapper Carr said, ducking as a rock whizzed a bit too close to his head. "All because this morning, instead of opening the Realms to the public, Sacrosanct cut off all access. A short press release from Sacrosanct blamed the shutdown on a temporary glitch, but rumors swirling on gaming forums claim that access to the game has been blocked, perhaps permanently. The Sacrosanct leadership has been silent, unseen since the beta launch, giving some credence to the rumors. The question on many lips: What is Alistair Bechard hiding?"

"The world is going to shit," Doc said.

"It's always been shit, Doc."

"True that." Doc switched the channel to a soccer game.

The calm voice of the announcer melded with the task of cutting fruit, lulling Finn's mind. His repetitive deftness with the knife eased the task into a meditative state. Once more, he pushed the world away. He didn't look up when he heard the door open or the scrape of a stool, but he sensed the man sit in front of him. There was a whole bar, why did people always have to invade this one small haven?

"Hello, Finn," a familiar voice said through a haze of pain. Finn gripped the knife harder, awareness surging to the fore. "Easy, buddy. I'm just here to deliver a message."

Finn's training took over and his eyes eased up. A haggard face surrounded the controlled smile of a man whose every aura suggested competence and ability. He was pale and hunched in pain. One hand hidden by the bar, Finn stared, eyes filled with demand.

Lex, is he transmitting? Finn silently asked his banner, the semi sentient artificial intelligence that shared his mind. Sometimes Finn was amazed at how quickly the public had become used to the idea of banner technology. Essentially banners were seriously advanced personal assistants akin to Siri or Alexa from decades before. But unlike those technologies, banners melded with the user's nervous system. The old internet had been ill equipped to handle that level of bandwidth and had led to the invention of the lattice, an ever-present field of information.

Nope, no electronic signals of any kind. In fact, I'd say he's put his banner into standby. He is not connected to the lattice, Lex responded. Finn wondered why Lex was more *alive* than his old Army issued banner.

Let me know if that changes.

Right-O.

"My banner is offline and I'm not recording or transmitting. But you already knew that."

7

"Dalton," Finn said, his grip tensing up on the knife. The gesture was pointless. If Dalton wanted him dead, he would be. This was something else. "How did you find me?"

"I'm just that good, kiddo." A subtle shift in Finn's eyes caused Dalton to lean back with a grunt of pain. The older man nodded and put both hands face up on the bar, showing Finn he meant no harm. It was a classic technique, and Finn knew he couldn't trust it. "Don't worry, I'm the only one who knows. I'm not here in an…official capacity."

Finn's eyes widened in shock when he saw the blood covering the man's hands. A hurried and clinical examination told Finn that Dalton was in bad shape. Finn rushed around the bar and caught his old mentor as the older man slipped from the barstool.

"Doc," Finn said in an urgent tone. Despite the alcohol fuzzing his mind, old training jumped to the fore of Doc's mind. He leapt from his stool, helping Finn. They eased Dalton onto the ragged couch near the pool table.

Doc knelt and pulled Dalton's jacket aside, revealing a large wound in the man's side. "Gunshot," Doc said, "at least two."

"Three," Dalton bragged with humor before a coughing fit pulsed bloody foam from his mouth.

Lex lock the front door and activate the closed sign. And keep an eye on the external sensors. We may soon have company.

Sure thing, bud.

"Who shot you, Dalton?"

"Not the right question," Dalton said with a wry smile. Finn flashed back to a time years ago when Finn was a newbie and Dalton assigned as his mentor. A day Finn now marked as the first step on the road that had led to his ruin.

He was recruited the day after his discharge from the Army when Finn's world was full of anger and regret. The discharge was classified as top secret. The Army wanted no details of the botched op getting out. Public sentiment against the war was already critical. The exposure of a massacre would have tipped the scales. To this day, Finn did not know how his last employers had known who he was, known he was available. Known he was willing and that he burned for the chance to make amends.

Forcing the memory back into the dark recesses of his mind, Finn asked the correct question. "Why are you here then?"

"Can't an old friend pop in and say hi?" Dalton said with a grin, pleased that Finn knew the *right* question.

"We're not friends."

"That's where you're wrong, pal. I may be the only friend you have left," Dalton said, his grin buried under another fit of bloody coughing.

"Do you have a med kit?" Doc asked.

"Under the bar." Finn indicated with a nod of his head.

Doc retrieved the kit and motioned for Finn to ease the wounded man back on the couch. "Grab me that knife," Doc said.

"And your best whiskey." Dalton smiled through gritted teeth.

Finn grabbed both. Doc snatched the knife and sliced Dalton's shirt up the middle. The wounded man took a swig from the bottle Finn handed him. Doc opened the med kit and got to work on Dalton.

"I have a message."

"I'm not interested."

"Oh, you are. You just don't know it yet." He set the bottle onto the side table with a *thump*. He wiped an errant drop of whiskey from his lip, smearing a crimson streak across his face that gave him the visage of an insane clown.

"May I?" Dalton asked, his hand hovering over the pocket to his jacket. After a moment of locked eyes, Finn nodded. Dalton removed something from his jacket pocket. He extended his hand to Finn. A pulse drive rested on his palm.

"I'm not going back, Dalton."

"It's not from Central."

"Who then?"

"Brynn."

Finn's eyes went wide and his hand snapped around the pulse drive. "Brynn?" he said without realizing he had spoken. He pulled his hand back and eased the drive into his pocket like a mother handling a newborn, all fear and gentleness.

Finn's mind flashed to the last time he'd seen his sister.

Misty eyed under the black umbrella as their father's coffin was lowered into the ground. Brynn, always so kind, so sweet, and so brave. Alone in the world. Perhaps that is why he allowed her to see him. A moment of weakness. A moment of kindness. The guns were still echoing as Brynn excused herself from the small crowd. Feigning a desire to be alone, she found Finn sitting on a bench.

"I knew you were still alive," she said, tears welling in her eyes. "Why did you leave?"

"I had no choice."

"There's always a choice, Finn."

"Tell that to the colonel," Finn said, idly rubbing a spot on his chest. A spot marred by scar tissue.

Brynn held back a sob and took a small box from her purse. She handed it to Finn.

"What's this?"

"Something to help you remember. Something to help you not be alone."

With that, she had pecked him on the cheek, stood, and walked away.

Finn's mind came back to the present. He pulled the pulse drive from his pocket and fear ate at his guts, twisting it harder than the worst bar rot scotch. What could scare Brynn enough for her to enlist Dalton's aid? How did they even know each other?

Old training, deeply ingrained in his mind, took control. His mind analyzed the available data and one conclusion jumped to the fore. *The colonel*, Finn thought. He was still mucking up his children's lives, even from the grave.

"John," Doc said with controlled alarm, "we need to get him to a hospital."

Finn pulled himself from his thoughts and looked to Doc. The old surgeon's eyes told Finn all he needed to know. Dalton didn't have long.

"It's okay, kid. I always knew it could end this way," Dalton said, "but maybe this will help wipe some of my ledger clean."

Boss, we have company, Lex chimed in his mind. *Four men, two teams of two. Back and front. Heavily armed.*

Finn's eyes hazed as he accepted the feed from Lex. Two

men, armed with silenced automatic rifles, took up positions on each side of the front door. A quick check told him there were two more at the back door.

"We've got company. Four total. Two at the front. Two at the back."

"Shit, I thought I'd ditched them." Dalton grimaced as he attempted to rise.

Finn told Lex to dim the lights, then rushed to the bar and grabbed a hidden pistol. He returned to Dalton and Doc.

"Doc take this and lock yourself in the bathroom. Don't come out until I tell you it's okay." He palmed the pulse drive into Doc's hand.

"What if you don't tell me it's okay?"

Finn shrugged, and with a resigned nod, Doc rushed to the bathroom. Finn turned to Dalton. "You armed?"

Dalton pulled a pistol from his jacket and checked the magazine and safety. "Help me up."

Finn eased Dalton to his feet. The man grunted in pain, but the old bastard was tough. Finn helped position Dalton behind the bar where he'd have some measure of protection. Finn then rushed to the gap between two antiquated stand-up video game consoles. He noted with a sense of irony that one involved shooting ducks with an orange plastic rifle.

Hopefully, we won't be the ducks, Finn thought.

11

3

They're gonna breach, Lex said.

Finn accessed the external feed only to see one man raise his silenced weapon. A sharp flash and the feed turned to fuzz. The backdoor camera was down as well. Finn saw the men pull night vision rigs over their eyes. The darkness was not their ally.

Finn made eye contact with Dalton and held up four, then five fingers, hoping his estimation was right. He considered opening a direct channel to Dalton's own banner AI but suspected the link was hacked. Time for old-fashioned methods.

He pointed to the lights and opened his hand like an expanding sun. Then indicated ten-seconds by pulsing his spread hand twice. Dalton nodded and aimed his pistol towards the door. Finn did the same, knowing the team at the back would need more time to reach the bar.

Finn's mind counted down. The air was heavy with anticipation as the seconds passed. The dull *thud* of a focused explosion punched his ears as the door flew off its hinges. Several smoke canisters skittered into the room.

A moment later, shadowy forms moved through the door. Dalton opened fire with a quick three shot burst, and Finn heard a grunt of pain as one figure fell to the ground. Finn fired at the other target and earned another grunt of pain. Both attackers sought cover behind the host stand as smoke filled the entryway.

They're wearing Mark IV tactical body armor, Lex said. *Your weapons will just annoy them.*

Mark IV tactical armor would easily block small-arms fire but had the appearance of a well-tailored suit. A standard issue for spec ops agents, high-end bodyguards, and anyone else who desired both protection and fashion.

I'd shoot them in the head. Boom, boom. Oh God, there are brains everywhere.

Keep the comments to a minimum, Lex. And preferably keep them useful. Not for the first time, Finn wondered about his banner. Lex was a gift from Brynn. She'd warned him that Lex was different. Perhaps she knew her brother better than he knew himself. Maybe he'd needed the sarcastic dickhead AI to keep him engaged in life when he was close to giving up on it.

Early critics of banners raised fears that the technology could be used to alter people's thoughts. The fear had long ago been debunked, but Finn couldn't stop a thought from popping into his mind. *He can't read my thoughts, can he?*

Finn's mental countdown reached zero, and he hoped Dalton was ready. Finn squeezed his eyes shut and ordered Lex to power the lights up to maximum. A blazing surge banished the darkness. The sudden illumination was murder on Finn's eyes, but the attackers fared much worse.

Triumph surged into Finn's mind as he heard the surprised grunts. The pain caused the closest attacker to spasm, exposing his head. Finn squeezed the trigger three times fast and a bloody third eye welled up in the center of the man's head, a posthumous gift of enlightenment to a man who no longer needed it.

The other attacker recovered quicker than Finn expected and opened fire. Finn dove behind the arcade machine. A torrent of bullets tore into the ancient tube monitor. Spouts of gas exploded with a pop. The wood frame of the machine provided crap cover. The gunshots grew closer as the second gunman advanced towards Finn's position.

This won't end well, dude, Lex said.

Shut up, Finn ordered, but he knew his prick of a banner was right. He had a few seconds before he'd be dead. There was no way he could risk finding a clear shot with the rapid-fire bullets coming his way.

Dalton fired several quick shots from behind the bar, and the other attacker went down. Finn risked a look and saw another corpse draining onto the floor. He looked at Dalton and nodded. Dalton nodded back. A quick *pop* of silenced weapons fire announced the second team had entered the fray. Dalton fell with a scream.

Finn spun, found his target and shot quick, timed bursts. Time slowed as it always did for him. One of his shots hit the attacker in the neck and the man fell in a spurt of blood. But Finn was now exposed, and the other attacker opened fire. He dove behind the half-wall that separated the main bar from the walkway to the bathrooms. A bullet took him in the shoulder as he fell. His head smacked against the wall and stars shot through his vision. With a grunt of pain, Finn assessed the damage.

Just a flesh wound, Lex said.

Didn't I tell you to be quiet? But Finn had to agree with his irritating banner's opinion.

I thought you were being rhetorical.

More bullets tore into the wall above Finn's head, and he rolled and leaned around the wall's edge, firing blindly. Volleys fired with neither party hitting the other. But Finn understood his enemies' tactic. Finn was nearly out of bullets.

Lex show me the feed from the register camera.

Now you feel like talking, Lex said, but the camera feed popped into Finn's vision. It wasn't designed to show the bar, but rather to make sure the shady folks Finn hired weren't ripping him off. It was pointing towards the register, but a blur of motion reflected by the filthy mirror behind the register showed Finn the enemies' location. *I need to clean the glass more often*, Finn thought and chuckled grimly. He knew regardless of what happened next that his days of tending bar were over.

Finn sprinted towards the man's position, using his last few rounds to lay down cover fire. The bullets forced the attacker to hide inside the door to the unused kitchen. Finn knew his plan to rush an enemy without ammo was insane, but he didn't see any other option.

As the man's rifle emerged once again from behind the door, Finn grabbed the barrel with his free hand and twisted it away from him. The rifle fired. Vibrations surged up Finn's arm, and the agony in his wounded shoulder forced him to release the rifle.

Finn smashed the butt of his pistol into the man's face. The *crunch* of bone was muted by the man's scream. Finn wrenched the gun from the man's hands. Finn was shocked the man still stood and outright stunned when he smashed a forearm into the side of Finn's head, dropping Finn to one knee. The gun fell from his hand and skittered under a nearby table.

The man grinned in triumph as he pulled a combat knife from a sheath at his waist and stabbed at Finn. Desperate, Finn thrust his left hand upward, and the knife pierced his palm. Finn screamed as the blade emerged from the back of his hand, midway between his middle and index fingers.

The man pushed, and with his better leverage, the knife crept closer to Finn's face, becoming his entire world. Within moments, it was hovering mere inches from his left eye. In a desperate motion, Finn moved to the left and pummeled his right forearm into the side of the man's knee. The knee buckled with a wet *crunch*. The man collapsed with a grunt.

Finn brought his right hand up, palm to the fleshy part of the man's wrist. Another *snap* and the man lost his grip on the knife. Finn yanked the combat blade from his hand. Before he could bring it to bear on his enemy, the man knocked it from his hand.

His opponent twisted and rolled, drawing Finn into a pincer between his legs. Finn punched at the man's injured knee, drawing grunts of pain but little relief. Finn was suffocating and knew he wouldn't last much longer. He was about to die, and Brynn still needed him.

Dude, you forgot you have a knife on your hip, didn't you? Lex said.

Finn's oxygen deprived brain almost didn't believe it was Lex. Was it his subconscious? His pain in the ass banner wouldn't jest about his imminent death, would he?

Finn struggled to reach the sheath at his waist. The bar knife wasn't the best weapon, but it was pointy and sharp, and he'd used worse. He brought his knee up and into his assailant's kidneys. The man grinned down at him, thinking Finn was flailing as he neared death. But a few hits to the man's side moved the man enough to allow Finn to finger the knife free.

With one last burst of energy, Finn impaled the man through the ear. The violent power behind the thrust snapped the handle off, leaving seven inches of metal lodged in the man's head.

A look of shock crossed the man's face as his muscles went slack and his legs released Finn's neck. A coughing fit racked Finn's body as air rushed back into his lungs and awareness returned to his brain. He lay for a few moments recovering before he remembered he wasn't alone.

"Dalton?" he called in a hoarse voice. Nothing.

He got to his feet and hobbled to the bar. He found Dalton face down. A jagged exit wound had torn apart his shoulder and blood flowed freely. He turned him over, relieved at the moan of pain from his old mentor. His eyes opened, and with returning consciousness came pain.

"Fuck me," the old warrior grumbled. Finn found the entry wound low on his left shoulder, between the collarbone and his heart. Finn was no medical expert, but he'd seen enough gunshot wounds to know this one was fatal.

"You're going to be okay," Finn said.

"Liar," Dalton said with a bitter chuckle that spit up blood. "Did we get them, at least?"

"We did," Finn said, sadness staining his voice. "Who were they, Dalton?"

"Mercs. Contractors hired by Sacrosanct."

"Sacrosanct? That's where Brynn works." Panic ate at Finn. "What is going on? Where is Brynn?"

"I don't know. Nobody has seen her, or the rest of the Pantheon in months."

"Pantheon?"

A bitter laugh rumbled from Dalton. "Yeah, that's what they call themselves. Alistair Bechard and his cronies who run Sacrosanct. Pretentious assholes if you ask me. It's as if they think they're gods."

"Dalton, you're not making any sense."

"I'm dying, kid, so shut up and listen. Do you know what the Realms is?"

"Some kinda game or something. What does this have to do with Brynn? Or this," Finn said, waving his hand around the bar turned war zone.

"Brynn suspected something was off with the Realms and brought me in to help."

"How do you two even know each other?" Finn's mind

raced to find any source of contact. He could conceive of none. Finn had made sure not to mix his two lives.

Dalton laughed at Finn's puzzled expression. "Man, you're a naïve dullard. Did you think you were the only one your father recruited?"

Shock pummeled Finn. "Brynn worked for Dad? I don't believe it. I won't believe it."

"Your father had tendrils everywhere, kid. I'm one scary dude, and your old man terrified the shit out of me."

Finn's mind pushed aside the shock and refocused. "Where is Brynn?"

"I told you, nobody knows. Last I knew she was going into the Realms. She told me to find you and give you the pulse drive. Took me six months. Guess I trained you too well."

Mention of the pulse drive brought Doc rushing back into Finn's awareness. "Doc!" Finn yelled. "Doc, I need your help!"

"It's too late. You need to find Brynn." Dalton said, his eyes glazing. "Did you know I'm her godfather? I don't think even she knows that." Dalton's eyes went blank, and he was gone.

Shock pummeled Finn's mind. None of this made sense. Doc shoved him aside and performed CPR on Dalton. After a few minutes, Doc gave up. Doc spoke to him, but Finn did not hear. His world was a swirling vortex of muddled confusion.

Doc slapped Finn hard across the face, and Finn was back. He looked from Doc to Dalton as reality came rushing back. "Doc?"

"I'm sorry, he's dead." A look of sympathy crossed his face.

Finn looked down upon his old mentor, a man he both loved and loathed. "I don't understand any of this," Finn mumbled.

"That makes two of us Finn," Doc said with a stare.

Doc had used his real name. Finn looked up. "That's a long story, Doc. One you're better off not knowing."

Doc looked around the bar. "I believe you. This has the look of one of those I'd have to kill you if I told you situations."

"Something like that. I wouldn't know where to start, anyway."

"Let's start with an introduction. I'm Percy Winkelvoss." Doc extended his hand.

Finn gave Doc a sideways glance and reached out and shook his hand. The man had the firm and steady grip of a surgeon, despite the alcoholism that had destroyed his life.

"Finn, Finn Caldwell."

"Nice to meet you, Finn."

"Same." A few seconds passed in silence as Finn looked down on Dalton. "Now I know why you go by Doc."

Doc harrumphed. "Yeah, thanks Ma and Pa Winkelvoss. Lean back and let me have a look at those wounds."

At the mention of his wounds, the pain rushed back. Finn's adrenaline surge had worn off, and the pain had arrived. He eased back against a beer cooler with a grimace. Doc tended to the wound in Finn's shoulder first.

"Through and through on the shoulder. That's good. I'll stitch it up, but your range of motion will suck for a few weeks."

He removed a suture wand from the med kit and closed the wound with polymer staples. They leaked anti-inflammatory and antibiotic drugs into his body. In a few days, when they had done their job, they would melt away.

Next, Doc examined his hand. Again, the damage was muscular, not structural. His hand would also be useless for a few weeks.

His ministrations finished Doc pulled the pulse drive from his pocket and handed it to Finn. "I hope it's worth all this death," Doc said with a sigh.

"It never is, Doc."

"I'm gonna hit the head. Too much excitement is *no bueno* for my old bladder."

Finn nodded. "Thank you, Doc."

"You're welcome, kid." Doc grabbed a bottle of whiskey off the bar and took a big swig. "Consider this payment." Doc headed towards the bathroom, carrying the bottle under his arm the way other men hit the bathroom with a magazine.

Finn smiled at the old drunk and looked down at the pulse drive. His face turned grim. *What did you die for, Dalton?* Finn thought. *And what have you gotten yourself into, Brynn?*

Finn walked into the small office behind the bar and sat.

The desk held a computer that had been obsolete before Finn was born. It was slow. However, it had no built-in access to the lattice, making it untraceable. Finn inserted the pulse drive into an external port, a shiny bit of malplast that looked so out of place with the rest of the rig.

The ancient monitor powered up and the only file on the drive pulsed to life. It brought up a blinking password prompt. Finn stared for a few moments.

"Shit," Finn said aloud. Brynn was smart, which meant only Finn would be able to decipher the code. Which meant he already knew it. He racked his brain, trying to remember everything he knew about his sister.

Finn had always been the silent loner, while Brynn was always joyous, even as a child. Her mere presence lit up a room. It was no wonder she had thrived in life. He'd been so proud of her when she'd earned VP at Sacrosanct Integrative Networks. Sure, they were 'just a game company,' Brynn had said. But they were cutting edge and even had contracts with the US military.

Finn cursed himself for falling out of her life, both before and after his disgrace. His work had made real connections difficult, even with Brynn. He thought back to the last time he'd been happy.

He'd come to the family summer home after graduating from boot camp. It was Brynn's favorite place in the entire world. A wondrous and magical oasis nestled on Bow Lake in New Hampshire near where their Mom had grown up. Brynn, all of thirteen years old, dragged her big brother into an adventure around the lake. There they fought goblins and orcs and dragons and even saved a gryphon. A live action adventure based upon the role-playing games Brynn forced Finn the play.

Finn asked her why they saved the gryphon after slaying so many other monsters. Brynn got her intense look. That look that would someday shame everyone from big brothers to local police chiefs to the heads of Senate committees.

"Because the gryphon is noble and strong and always fights for what is right," Brynn said with the intensity only a thirteen-year-old could muster. "Just like you, Finn."

Brynn had always hated that their names rhymed, so from

then on, when it was just the two of them, she had called him Gryph. Finn's heart seized at the memory. He'd been her hero, but unlike the gryphon he had done many a thing that was not noble or right.

His amazing and strong sister, the best of the Caldwells, was in trouble. She needed him, and if he had any chance for redemption, he needed to become who she always thought he was. He needed to become the gryphon.

"G-R-Y-P-H," Finn realized. "The passcode is Gryph."

Finn's fingers sped across the keyboard typing the code. Then a video began to play. A video of Brynn.

4

Finn's heart thudded in his chest at the look of fear on Brynn's face. Several moments passed before his training took over. Finn watched every detail with detachment and precision. Brynn was in her office. It was night and the San Francisco skyline glinted through a window behind her. The room was dimly lit as if she was trying not to draw attention to herself.

She's at Sacrosanct, Finn realized.

"Hello, Finn," Brynn said, sneaking a glance past the camera as if fearing interruption. "I'm in trouble. We're all in trouble." Her small smile seemed forced.

She's terrified.

"I don't have the time to explain everything, and to be honest, I don't think you'd believe me if I did," Brynn said. She glanced around again.

She's afraid somebody will interrupt her, catch her.

"I'm about to go into the Realms, and I don't think I'll be coming back out. I don't have a choice. None of us do. He's become paranoid, suspicious. He may be onto us already. By the time you get this, I'll either be in the Realms or…" Brynn bit her lip and Finn saw the fear bubble to the surface as she tried to keep herself together.

What could scare her this badly? By the time I get this? Finn's eyes snapped down to the time code buried in the info feed at the bottom of the video. April the 4th. *Six months ago?* His mind reeled. *Six months?* Dalton had been right. Finn cursed himself. *Why was I so damn stubborn?* He should have known she was missing. He should have been searching for her all this time.

"The Realms are not what we thought they were. Alistair is not who he claims to be. My God, Finn, it's bad. I need you to come find me. Not here, but in the Realms. Finding my body in this world won't do me any good if you cannot rescue my mind."

Brynn held up a pulse drive, a small data storage device that used pulses of light to encode information. They were popular not just for their massive storage capacity but also for being nearly impervious to hacking. It was the same pulse drive Finn had docked in his computer.

"This drive has a map to a safe house. Dad made me memorize its location in case I ever got into any *boy trouble*. As if any boy would ever date me with the colonel lurking." A small smile curled her lips. "There you'll find a cutting-edge neural immersion rig that will get you into the Realms. Your banner already has the codes necessary to override Alistair's security protocols."

She grinned and, for a moment, she was the Brynn he remembered. Then as she leaned closer to the camera that Brynn was gone. Stress lines had aged her face. She was scared and tired and on the edge of a breakdown.

"When this video is over, you'll have two minutes to port the map and safe house access code onto your banner before the pulse drive self-destructs."

"I love you, big brother. Come get me. Come save me. Everything depends…" Brynn stopped cold and glanced up. Behind her, reflected in the window, was the silhouette of a man. "Shit, you scared me," Brynn said, and the video ended.

The screen went blank, and Finn tapped at the keyboard desperate to bring it back. There had to be more clues. The screen didn't respond but, a moment later, a countdown appeared.

2:00…1:59…1:58 …

Finn tugged the pulse drive from the dock and placed it onto his injured left palm. The organic circuitry tattooed into his palm activated and flares of sub-dermal light moved in intricate circular patterns as his banner attempted to connect to the pulse drive. The banner interface lit up and cycled but flared out.

"Shit," he said aloud, lifting and replacing the pulse drive in an attempt to connect. Once again, the cycle began, but it collapsed. The knife must have damaged the circuits.

Lex? Finn begged.

My interface is damaged, Lex responded in a calm voice.

No shit. What do I do?

Find another banner, Lex said smugly. *I'm okay by the way. In case you were concerned.*

Shut up.

So that's a no, I guess. Well, at least now I know where I stand.

"Doc?" he yelled as he emerged behind the bar and sprinted towards the back of the room. He slammed open the ratty door to the men's room.

"Doc?"

The disgraced surgeon stood in front of the urinal doing his business. The noise made him jump and piss sprayed everywhere.

"Dammit, Finn. Can't a man take a whizz in peace?"

Finn ignored the anger and grabbed Doc's hand.

"What the hell?" Doc sputtered pulling his hand from Finn's grasp. "I know I'm a casual kinda guy, man, but even I have boundaries."

"I need you to access this pulse drive," Finn said and grabbed Doc around the wrist

Finn slapped the pulse drive onto Doc's left palm. Doc opened his mouth to protest, but the desperate look on Finn's face must have convinced him. Doc closed his eyes and the interface of the older man's banner surged to life as a connection synced.

Finn folded Doc's fingers over the pulse drive, securing it. Time crawled as the file in the pulse drive merged with neural interface of Doc's banner. Finn's heart thundered away the seconds.

Doc's eyes opened, and he swayed, knees failing him. Finn caught him before he could fall to the floor.

"Jesus, Finn, what was that?" Doc reached up to rub his temples.

"Sorry, Doc, but I needed a banner, and I needed it quickly."

"Because yours is all cut up," Doc said, nodding his head.

"Did the file download?" Finn asked.

Doc nodded, regaining some of his equilibrium. "It's a map and some kinda passcode."

"Good. We need to go there. Now."

"What is going…" Doc began, before his eyes widened and his mouth erupted in a scream of pain. Finn felt the heat a moment before he smelled the burning skin. He still held Doc's palm closed, but now a fierce heat surged through their fingers.

"My hand is burning. Fuck Finn, I'm on fire."

"The self-destruct," Finn said.

"The what?"

"This is going to hurt."

Finn wrenched Doc's fingers back and charred flesh tore. Doc screamed in agony and his eyes widened at the burning shard of malplast melted into his hand.

Finn did the only thing he could think of. He dragged Doc into the stall and shoved his hand into the toilet. The heat died amidst a surge of steam. Finn pulled Doc's hand out of the toilet and wrenched the melted pulse drive from Doc's palm, tossing it to the ground.

Doc pulled back his undamaged hand and punched Finn in the face. It was a good punch. It hurt.

"Dammit," Finn said.

Doc remembered who he was dealing with and his natural calm returned.

"Sorry, just reacted."

"Understandable," Finn said rubbing his jaw. "That's some punch you have there, Doc."

"Harvard boxing champ, 2021." Pride beamed through the pain on Doc's face. "You're a dick by the way, and I really need that med kit."

I'm detecting tons of encrypted lattice traffic, Lex said.

Can you tell what are they saying?

You do know what the word encrypted means, right?

Finn felt the need to deliver serious violence to Lex. He knew it was stupid. Finn decided that he'd have to have words with his sister once he found her.

"We have to go, Doc."

"More bad guys?"

"More bad guys."

5

It would take them a few minutes to get out of the building. Ever mistrustful, Finn had long ago scouted an emergency exit from the bar. Despite numerous attempts to kill his past life, old training died hard. The colonel had begun grooming Finn very early for a life he'd never wanted. It had caused a rift between father and son, and as soon as he was able Finn had rushed to join the Army to get away from the old man. How ironic, that as an adult, Finn had unknowingly worked for the colonel. Now, it seemed, even Brynn had been unable to escape the colonel's web.

Finn forced the anger at his father down. He had no time to dwell on the past. He led Doc to an old ladder at the back of the kitchen, and they climbed to the roof. There, Finn placed a few planks he'd set aside ahead of time across the gap between buildings.

"You're nuts if you think I'm crossing that," Doc said, then noticed more armed men entering the bar below. Doc found his courage and eased himself across the makeshift bridge.

A terrifying jump from one rooftop to another and a few more ladders and they were back on the ground. Finn led them to a small door in the alley. He grimaced as he placed his left hand against the scanner pad hanging next to the door. The pad made an angry noise, blared red, and refused to open.

Finn scowled and pulled a small device from his sweatshirt pocket and inserted it into the keypad's data port. He'd grabbed the device, and the gun in his waistband, from a stash he kept under the floorboards of the storeroom.

"Pretty sure that's not legal tech," Doc said as the door *chirped* and clicked open. "But I guess that's the smallest felony I've been a party to this afternoon."

Finn gave him a glance that said, 'you sure you're up for

this?' A calm look crossed Doc's face, and he nodded. Finn pulled the door open and motioned for Doc to enter the small garage. Doc eased inside. A large mass covered in a tarp dominated the room. Finn pulled the tarp off to reveal a late model sedan.

Finn got behind the wheel, and Doc sat in the passenger seat.

Lex open the door.

The squeal of a long unused motor broke the silence and a garage door lifted into the ceiling. Finn started the car, rammed it into drive, and surged into the alley.

Half an hour later, sure nobody had tailed them, Finn pulled onto a service road. Dozens of identical buildings lined the street. They were near the port where hundreds of the structures created a maze. Finn killed the engine.

"This is it," Doc said, pointing to a squat two story.

Finn scanned the area, but they were alone. He pulled the pistol from his waistband, checked the safety and the cartridge and looked at Doc.

"Under normal circumstances, I'm not a fan of guns," Doc said, "but today has proven the exception."

Doc flexed his bandaged hand. Guilt wormed its way into Finn's guts, but he shoved it down. There was no time for that now. "How's the hand?"

Doc looked down on it. "Hurts like a son of a bitch, but I'll get proper treatment when this is all through."

Finn nodded, and both men exited the car. Spotlights illuminated the doorways up and down the long row of buildings. A few doors down, a light flickered and went dark. Finn's hackles rose. "Classic technique," he muttered. He stared into the murk, seeking hidden opponents.

Lex, are you sensing any active lattice links?

Nothing but the normal passive security links for the warehouses. This place is as dead as disco.

You are one weird bastard, Lex. Finn shook his head and wondered again why the hell Brynn had given him Lex.

That hurts my feelings.

Doc had walked up to the building indicated in the map. A high-tech lock secured the door. A quick survey of nearby doors told Finn that the new lock was abnormal.

What did you get yourself into, Brynn?

Doc looked to Finn, who nodded. Doc sent the code from his banner into the lock and, after a few seconds, a happy *chirp* and a pleasant green glow rewarded them. A moment later, the sound of heavy bolts retracted from the doorframe and the door opened.

Finn motioned for Doc to stay back as he hefted his pistol and entered the dark building. Dim lighting came on as Finn entered, tripped by motion sensors. The room was a simple 20x20 square. A small bed and fridge lined one wall. A couch sat towards the back of the room facing a holo-vis. A small kitchenette rounded out the luxury. Another door was set into the back wall. On the wall next to the door was a small security monitor showing a long hallway of nearly identical doors.

At the center of the room sat a large crate on a raised dais. It reminded Finn of a coffin in an ancient vampire movie…if the vampire had been an alien. The crate was modern malplast and held a banner panel at its center. Cool air suggested the room was climate controlled. Another door at the back led to a hallway bearing dozens of identical doors. After assuring himself that the place was safe, Finn returned to the front.

"It's safe, Doc."

"So, what's all this then?" Doc said as he entered. Finn flipped the main power switch. More lights came on and a low hum rose from underneath them. Finn saw a metal grate in the floor near the far wall. He lifted the grate, revealing a small fusion generator. Cables snaked from the generator up into the floor below the mysterious crate.

"That thing puts out a crap load of power," Finn said. "What the hell is in that crate?"

"Only one way to find out," Doc said, raising his hand again.

Finn nodded and Doc sent the code to the banner panel. The crate powered up, and the surface parted as if it were undergoing a controlled melting. Inside sat another coffin of glass, plymetal and malplast.

"It's a neural immersion rig. This technology was tested at my old hospital when it was still in the prototype phase. It was a program designed to help vets with PTSD through direct neural interface. They commercialized the technology for the NI helmets the beta players used to get into the Realms. But this unit looks more advanced than any I've ever seen." Doc tapped at the interface.

"This is how Brynn wants me to go into the Realms?"

"Makes sense. It has built in biosensors and life support. Quite an advantage."

Finn nodded. "Time to open her up." Doc moved towards the NI rig and placed his hand atop it.

Finn, I'm sensing an encrypted lattice link, Lex said.

Then they were no longer alone.

6

A few hundred meters away, Milena Ortiz Yung, or Mo as her friends called her, stared through the scope of a sniper rifle. She could hear the entire conversation through sensors hidden in the safe house walls. She didn't know who this man Doc was, but Finn seemed to trust him, so Mo would as well.

Mo grabbed a towel and wiped the sweat and blood from her face. She took a moment to inspect herself. She sighed. Thankfully, the blood was not hers.

Mo switched to the internal surveillance. Finn and Doc were examining the crate. She moved in on Finn, biometric readings popping into her banner display. His heartbeat was steady and even, in stark contrast to the thundering pulse of the doctor who stood next to him.

Mo watched Finn and a worm of doubt burrowed into her mind. Brynn better be right. If her faith in her brother was misplaced… Mo shivered at the thought. Everything depended upon him. She glanced down at her own NI rig, open and ready to receive her. Mo had lost count of the hours she'd spent in that small coffin over the last six months.

Mo dreaded and loved the Realms. The danger of an untamed world and the freedom to remake herself as she always wanted to be. The adrenaline surges of combat, new knowledge, and terrifying truths.

She brought her attention back to Finn. He did not understand what he was getting involved in. Mo at least had been able to grind and level inside the Realms for the last six months. She'd uncovered enough of the mysteries of the Realms to know the danger was real. She hoped the aid she'd secured Finn was enough. He was a noob in the strictest sense of the word, and he would be taking on a god.

Mo stripped down, the chill of the room biting into her. She sent a silent prayer into the universe, pleading that the override Brynn had built into her banner would still grant her access. It wasn't just a job any longer. Mo loved the Realms. She understood the public rage at Sacrosanct all too well.

Despite her training, she was nervous. She glanced around the city, the twinkling lights calming her. The world sat on a knife edge and she was one of the few who knew. It was not a burden she wished on anyone. She climbed into the cushioned coffin and powered up her holo transmitter. With a calming breath, she activated the transmission.

Doc removed his hand from the NI Rig and stumbled back. The woman appeared out of nowhere. One moment there was an empty space, the next moment, there she stood. She was five-foot two, with raven black hair, deep brown eyes, and olive skin. Despite her small stature, her bearing suggested a capable woman who gave crap but took none. She smiled and met Finn's gaze.

"Hello, Finn," she said, eyes locking onto his.

Finn leveled his gun on her before the words were from her mouth. His heart pounded inside his chest. Doc fell over, startled, a yelp of alarm escaping his lips.

"I'm Mo, and I'm a friend of your sister," the woman said, and despite his alarm, Finn lowered his gun. Doc grumbled, and Finn extended a hand and helped the older man to his feet.

"She's a hologram," Finn said.

"Smart boy," Mo responded and ignored Doc's angry stare. "We don't have a lot of time, so listen up. Brynn's in trouble. You know that already. But it's worse than you know. And you are the only one who can help her. This..." Mo placed her hand on the NI capsule, "Will get you into the Realms. Once inside, you must survive long enough to find her and help her escape. She wasn't able to tell me much, but I know one thing, the Realms is much more than a game."

Her phantom touch sent a code into the capsule, and it opened with a low hiss. It resembled a comfortable coffin covered in readouts, sensors, and ports. A malleable, reactive gel lined the interior. He would be comfortable.

"Strip down and get in," Mo said.

"Excuse me?"

"Listen, man, time is short. From our perspective, Brynn and the Pantheon only entered the Realms six months ago. But for them it's been nearly fifty years."

Finn exchanged a look of doubt with Doc. "Bullshit," he said.

"Just hear me out. When Bechard cut access to the Realms, time inside the game jumped forward."

The looks of doubt turned to confusion.

"Look, I don't get it either. I just know what I know."

"You're saying that time is moving faster inside the Realms?" Finn asked.

"No, I'm saying that there was a jump. Bechard shut down access and time jumped forward fifty years"

"Why would he do that?" Doc asked.

"Like I know. All I do know is the longer you wait, the worse it gets in there."

"Why should I trust anything you say?" Finn asked.

Mo sighed, her impatience bubbling to anger. "Brynn told me you were a pain in the ass."

Finn just stared.

"Fine. She told me to tell you that the gryphon always did what was right. Whatever the hell that means."

Finn's eyes went wide, and he stripped down. Mo looked him up and down in admiration, and Finn felt a rush of heat in his cheeks.

"Hmmm, nice," she said. Finn eased himself into the NI capsule, and the inert gel chilled his body. As his skin made contact, the gel warmed. Mo and Doc looked down on him.

Bio readings normal. NI rig synchronization sequence on standby. Lattice connection steady, Lex muttered in a bored tone.

"What's so special about the Realms? Why send mercs to kill me? Why is Brynn so scared?"

"Because the Realms is not a game," Mo said, the jest in her eyes disappearing. "It is a real place, as real as Earth. And

Alistair Bechard used the Betas to conquer it."

Finn stared at Mo in shock.

"Holy Shit," Doc said.

"Real, as in an alternate dimension?" Finn asked, disbelief painting his face.

"I'm no scientist, but something like that. I've been there, and it's real, as real as the room we are standing in. But it has its own rules. Our universe relies upon physics. The Realms are controlled by the game mechanics."

"I have no idea what that means."

"Damn, you really are a noob. Don't worry, you'll learn. Your banner will get a patch as you enter the Realms, and he'll explain everything."

"You're telling me Brynn is part of Bechard's army? I don't believe it. She would never be a party to such an abomination."

"She didn't know what the Realms were at first. Nobody did. Once she found out, she knew she had to do something, no matter the risk. So, she played along, never giving Bechard any reason for suspicion."

"She always was the bravest Caldwell."

"Funny, she said the same thing about you," Mo said. "There's something else you should know. She's one of the gods. One of the Pantheon."

A deep-rooted fear invaded Finn's mind. "Brynn, what did you do?"

"She didn't have a choice. Bechard has killed for this. He won't hesitate to do so again."

"Why me?" Finn asked. He knew he would do as this woman asked. But he needed all the intel he could gather.

Mo took a deep breath. "Brynn said you were the only one she could trust with what's to come."

"What's to come?"

Mo shrugged. "Guess you'll find out." She tapped at a non-existent watch on her wrist. "Time's up. No more dilly dallying, hun."

Finn looked at Doc, whose shoulders popped up in a 'don't look at me pal' shrug. Finn's heart pounded. *Odd, that.* He's been in serious combat situations and kept himself under control. Why did this send chills up his spine?

Your heart rate is increasing. You freaking out, boss?

"Can I get a new banner first?" Finn mumbled.

Now that's just hurtful, Lex said. Finn could almost hear the pout in the AI's voice.

"No time for that. And Brynn said Lex was different, special."

See, I'm special.

Not sure that was meant as a compliment.

"I'm sending you a map." Mo said. "Get to your starter village, gear up, and hit up the locations tagged in red. They're dungeons, and they'll give you some easy grinding opportunities. Trust me, you'll need the experience and the loot."

"Grinding?"

Mo shook her head and didn't even bother saying noob this time. She gave him one last appreciative up and down glance. "I'll see you in the Realms. I go by Eris." She tapped the top of the NI rig.

Finn glanced one more time at Doc, who nodded.

"One last thing. I don't think Brynn remembers who she is. I approached her once, and she didn't recognize me. So, for now, don't trust her."

"Why wouldn't she remember who she is?"

Mo shrugged. "What better way to control someone than to take their memories and make them believe they're a god?"

Finn sighed, worry digging deeper into him.

"This will feel a little weird," Mo said as the top of the NI rig closed.

Finn closed his eyes and tried to relax as the micro fiber filaments wormed their way into his body and mind. His mind expanded and exploded.

7

Finn's body was his mind, and his mind was infinite.

He rushed down a tunnel of light. A wormhole connecting two universes never meant to touch. Time stretched to eons as mere moments passed. His mind and soul were cataloged. He would have screamed, but he had no body, was no longer a physical entity.

Memories and flashes of who he had been pulled from him in iridescent strands. They coiled and bundled into a swirling mass of entwined tendrils. The mass spun and condensed and collapsed into a singularity. Just as Finn knew he was forever trapped in this state, he was somewhere else.

He stood on a flat plane. Whiteness stretched in every direction. The sensation was both disturbing and disorientating. How could something so empty be so vast?

A tall and powerful man appeared, clad in gleaming armor of metal that absorbed and reflected light like flowing mercury. From within the intricate horned helm, eyes radiated power. This man was a god.

A warm smile crossed the god's face, and Finn knew him.

"Alistair Bechard," Finn said in a low voice.

Bechard drew a large sword from its sheath. Undulating patterns of stars and nebullaic ribbons of primal energy swirled along the length of the black blade. Finn tried to back away, but no matter how many steps he took, his distance from the unmoving god remained constant.

"Welcome, player," Bechard intoned. "I am the High God Aluran, Prime of the Pantheon, and I welcome you to the Realms." He turned his sword point down and gripped the hilt with both hands. With a powerful flourish, he drew the sword up and smashed it down into the nonexistent nothingness of the floor.

Color and space exploded around Finn. Green grass grew

from the point of Aluran's sword and spread in every direction. A low rumble built under Finn's feet, and he fell to one knee. The ground erupted beneath him. He stood atop a mountain peak as it surged towards the forming heavens. Stars and planets popped into existence above him and sped away to take their rightful place in the sky. Below him, mountains, rivers, lakes, deserts, and oceans burst and bubbled from the ground. Finn was witness to a world being born.

"This is the planet Korynn, one of many in the Realms," Aluran said. He waved a gauntleted hand wide, somehow encompassing all that was and all that would become. "It is an ancient place of power and struggle, of good and evil. And I have brought you here because I need your help."

As Aluran spoke, cities rose and fell around them. Massive armies of man and beast crossed the lands and battled. Destruction flared and life grew. Aluran drew a distant mountain fortress to the fore.

"This is Avernia, the Shining City, home base of the corrupt New Gods who rule this world with despotic fervor. Under their tyrannical reign, the people of the Realms suffer." Visions of men, elves, and dwarves toiling under the whip of reptilian humanoids flashed.

"The New Gods know they are unassailable. That their reign is eternal. I am here to prove them wrong. You are here to prove them wrong. Will you join me in this fight for freedom? Will you stand by my side player?" Aluran presented a gilded scroll to Finn.

Finn had heard this speech many times. The words Aluran spouted were full of lies. Humankind had followed many a great man, god, or cause into battle and death always followed. There were no noble crusades and there never had been.

If Mo had told the truth, then this world was as real as Earth. A Realm of incredible wonder, danger, and intrigue. Somewhere in this world, Brynn was a prisoner in her own mind. She needed him. He would find her.

Finn grasped the scroll, but Aluran held firm. Finn looked into the god's eyes.

"Fight well for me and I will shower you with rewards.

Together, we can accomplish anything." Aluran stared into Finn's eyes and a sense of unease rose in him. Those eyes pierced to the core of his being. They were more than lines of code processed by a computer. Somehow, they knew. Somehow, *he* knew.

Finn's heartbeat jumped, and he felt sweat trickle down his back. This was wrong. Panic rose in Finn as the shining eyes of this god bored into his soul. As Finn felt his secrets laid bare, Aluran let go of the scroll. Finn stumbled back in surprise but stayed on his feet. A wry grin crossed Aluran's face, then disappeared. A doorway of light split the universe to Finn's left. The other side showed a room that could have been at home in any coastal Irish pub. The large window looked upon a calm sea.

Aluran indicated the doorway. "Enter and choose your path. Once you have finished, I will give you a final blessing and send you on your way. Greatness awaits you, player." With that, Aluran disappeared.

"Well, he has a flair for the dramatic," Lex said in a voice that Finn could now hear.

Finn jumped. He had forgotten all about the banner AI. A few rocks dislodged from under his feet and rolled off the edge of the mountain peak. The thin air bit at him.

"Jesus don't do that," Finn said.

"Sorry, dude," Lex said. "Don't wanna kill us before we even get our characters made."

Finn gazed around the world. From this vantage point, he could see for thousands of miles in every direction. The cold, thin air bit into his bones.

To the west lay a near endless desert dotted with an occasional oasis around which towns and cities thrived. Deep in the burning sands, a complex of gold tipped pyramids shone like beacons along a knife thin lake. The surrounding city looked capable of holding hundreds of thousands of citizens. In the distance, sprawling sands broke against a forested range of mountains. Across them lay a thin ribbon of land along a shining ocean. Large cities lined the coast, built around well-protected ports.

To the north, the range of mountains delved to a plain, dotted by old forests and lakes. The plains became tundra that reached to the top of the world. Glaciers and flows of ice dominated. A spider web of rivers fed the plains. It reminded Finn of the Midwestern United States. This would be the breadbasket of this world.

To the east lay a large expanse of ancient forests fed by rivers that came from the north. Where the north met east, jagged mountains tore at the sky, a gaping maw biting at the world. Near their center, a fiery glow of magma showed active volcanoes. Further east lay another ocean. Dozens of cities dotted the coast, built around river deltas or ports.

A range of mountains dominated the south, and the forests turned to jungle. The size of the green expanse dwarfed the Amazon rainforest of Earth. The tributaries pouring from the north merged to form a river so wide that few bridges spanned its girth. The river emptied into a gulf that was a sea unto its own. The city that guarded the river mouth made the others seen small towns. Finn knew the place was a seat of power.

"Time to get this wagon on the road," Lex said, sensing his mood.

With a nod of assent, Finn walked towards the shimmering doorway to another place.

8

Finn felt a slight pressure as he passed through the slice in reality, and then hard-packed earth lay beneath his sandaled feet. He looked himself up and down and realized he wore the dingiest of rags. A beggar at the whim of a god.

Finn smiled at that classic bit of psychological warfare. Bechard, or Aluran as he now called himself, knew how to play the game. So did Finn, and Aluran did not understand who he was, nor what he could do.

A fireplace warmed the room. It reminded Finn of the cozy inn he'd spent time in on the southern coast of Ireland during a pre-college trip to Europe. The fire crackling away in the hearth felt real and chased the chill from Finn's bones. A fragment of flame leapt forward and hung in mid-air spinning. It spun and condensed into a singularity, his singularity. It pulsed and flexed, tearing dimensions. Finn stared at the vortex of unknowable potential.

The sphere flickered and calmed and expanded into a perfect glowing sphere an inch in diameter. Time was meaningless here. Finn did not know if he stood there for moments or eons when the sphere rushed at him, penetrating his chest with tingling brilliance.

His vision exploded with prompts. Images and information appeared in a virtual display that hovered in front of his eyes. The information was semi-translucent, allowing him to see the world through a haze of words. It was nearly identical to one of the functions of his banner, and Finn wondered if Lex would serve a similar function inside the Realms as he had in the real world.

You have learned the skill SMALL BLADES.

Level(s): 1-5.
Skill Type: Active.

You have shown proficiency in wielding small blades. These include knives, daggers, short swords, and their variations.

To Hit Bonus: +10%.
Damage Bonus: +10%.
"Stab, stab, kill, kill."

You have learned the skill STAVES/SPEARS.

Level(s): 1-5.
Skill Type: Active.

You have shown proficiency in wielding staves and spears. These include bo-staves, quarterstaffs, short spears, and long spears.

To Hit Bonus: +10%.
Damage Bonus: +10%.
Attack Speed: + 25%.
"Longer stab, smash, kill, kill."

You have learned the skill UNARMED.

Level(s): 1-5.
Skill Type: Active.

You have shown proficiency in hand-to-hand combat. You can cause damage, disarm and incapacitate opponents with just your hands and feet.

To Hit Bonus: +10%.
Damage Bonus: +10%.
Chance to Disarm: 10%.
Attack Speed: + 25%.
"You learn quickly grasshopper. And kill, kill."

Finn paused the prompts, shaking and nauseous. The amount of information that assaulted his mind was insane.

"Lex, what is all this?"

"Skill prompts. Every game has a set of skills that measure your ability to perform certain actions. The Realms is different from the games that came before it in one totally badass area. As the NI rig integrates your mind into the game, it also extrapolates and imports your inherent real-world skills."

"That sounds like mind reading," Finn said, concerned.

"Yeah it does, doesn't it? So cool."

"You and I have very different definitions of the word cool."

"Trust me in the game you'll be happy you were a real-life Rambo."

"What?"

"Great movie. You need to watch the classics, bro."

Finn shook his head at his oh so odd banner and returned to the prompts.

You have learned the skill DISARM TRAPS.

Level(s): 1-5.
Skill Type: Active.

You are able to disarm traps.

Disarm Traps: 20% chance.
Acquire Traps: 10% chance
Understand Traps: 5% chance. (For use with the CRAFTING skills).
"Pick, tinker, no exploding shrapnel in face."

"Quit adding commentary to the skills Lex

"I have no idea what you are talking about," his banner said with feigned annoyance.

If Lex had had a physical form, Finn would have smacked him. A part of his mind, the one trained to see subterfuge and danger everywhere, wondered if he could trust Lex. Brynn had been working with their father. Could the colonel have gotten his hands on Lex, or worse, had engineered the delivery of the odd banner to Finn?

Despite the red flags, there was nothing he could do about his suspicions at the moment. He returned his attention to the prompts.

You have learned the skill ALCHEMY.

Level(s): 1-5. Skill Type: Active.

You can mix various ingredients to form useful potions, tinctures and poisons.

Potency: +10%
Chance to Understand Recipe: 10%
"Mix, mix, yay, herbal Viagra."

"Why are some stats listed as active and some as passive?"

"Active skills require not only focus but *Stamina*, usually at a point per second cost. Passive skills are always active so do not need concentration or a *Stamina* cost. For example, *Stealth*, ya know, 'sneak, sneak, hide, hide,' is an active skill and sneaking about is more tiring than walking around all normal like. Then there are the knowledge skills such as *Perception*. There's no active participation in that, you just know what ya know. That's a passive skill."

"You do realize you just outed yourself on the skill commentary, right?"

"Crap," Lex whispered.

Finn chuckled to himself, getting an odd pleasure from ribbing Lex.

"Why do all the skills level out at five?"

"Yeah, that one blows. The designers capped any real-world skills at five to balance the scales somewhat. They wanted to make it so nerdy losers who smoked pot and ate Doritos all day could compete with badasses like you. And let's face it, there's a lot more of them type than love children of Jason Bourne and James Bond."

"Quit making stupid movie references, Lex."

"Pffft. You just ain't cultured enough to appreciate my references."

The skill prompts ended, and another slice in reality opened. Beyond was a grand chamber of tall windows and massive arches.

9

The chamber was a gothic cathedral, but circular, like the massive Orthodox churches that dotted Eastern Europe. Thirteen alcoves held ornate statues, surrounding a raised dais on which a throne rested. Finn knew that this was the Pantheon, the new cadre of gods led by Aluran. Each god stood rigid, shrouded in shadow, but the power possessed by these beings held heavy in the air.

"Well, this is a little much, don't ya think?" Lex asked. "Awesome, but over the top."

Finn nodded and looked from one statue to another. They stood six to a side, and at the center stood the larger form of Aluran, standing tall. His sword held point down, tip piercing a coiled serpent that lay dead at his feet. While Aluran's statue was as lifelike as the god he had met moments ago, the others were shrouded in robes of deep, undulating shadows. None of their features were visible. Only differences in stature suggested they were different beings.

Was one of these Brynn? Finn's eyes came to rest on a smaller figure in the third alcove to the right. It felt right somehow.

"Which of the gods shall you fight for player? Which of the gods will you worship?" boomed a voice that could have been Aluran's. "Gaze upon the Pantheon. Let your mind find freedom and your heart will choose."

Finn didn't know what to make of it, but a nagging feeling tugged at the corner of his being. He suspected picking Brynn would put her at risk. His gaze moved along the line of immobile gods. None of them felt right and none could be trusted. So, Finn made the choice to choose none of them.

A thin god to Aluran's left came to life and walked towards Finn. A sharp metallic beak protruded from his hood. He gazed upon Finn with eyes the color of blood diamonds. Incredible power emanated from the god and Finn took an involuntary step backwards.

The god continued towards Finn and pulled his hood down to reveal the metallic beak was part of a mask. Finn took another step back as the regal figure came close. His crimson gaze pierced Finn from a height of at least seven feet. With a wave of his hand, the mask disappeared, revealing a thin face and a bald head.

"Welcome Child of the Crusade, I am Zeckoth, the God of Knowledge. You have taken the unusual step of refusing to select a deity. So, I will aid you and help you learn. Together, we will discover the truth of your nature and make you anew. To help set you on your path towards destiny."

Zeckoth gazed upon Finn with black eyes, and Finn's mind expanded with knowledge as if the god were downloading information directly into his mind. Around him, a variety of bipedal figures stood, and Finn knew that he had to choose his race. As he focused on each figure, they moved to the fore and information about each race came to the fore.

His gaze passed over the assembled figures. A tall and regal sea elf stood next to a pale, almost silver, skinned wood elf. An albino white fell elf scowled next to a haughty human known as an Eldarian. A tanned desert dwelling human known as an Aegyptian scoffed at a burly Ordonian, a human race that dwelled in the northern wastes. Next were a pair of dwarven races, the stocky and dour mountain dwarf warily eyed his hill dwarf cousin. Lastly, standing apart from the others was a fierce half orc.

Finn assimilated all the information and cast his gaze back and forth along the assembled races. He knew that this decision was one of the most important he'd make in the Realms. And despite his misgivings, he knew he needed some advice. Question is, could he trust his odd banner?

"Lex, any thoughts?"

"Hmmmm," the disembodied AI mumbled. "Well, let's analyze what you hope to do here. Since your main mission is to find…"

Finn gave a sideways glance at Zeckoth and cleared his throat, causing Lex to pause. He assumed that this was a recorded intro message. But had no wish to put Brynn in further danger by letting Lex blab like some muahahaha villain.

"To…find wealth and fortune and glory for the Pantheon. All hail to thee," Lex continued, much to Finn's relief. "So, it would behoove you to get along with others, or at least not be hated on sight."

"So, that eliminates the fell elf and the half orc," Finn said.

"Yeah, they're both usually pricks," Lex said.

Finn examined his current skills and knew that to survive he would need to maximize their early efficiency. "My skills are skewed towards being lean and agile, with a quick strike capability."

"So, I'd say that eliminates the dwarven races," Lex agreed.

Finn's eyes came to the Eldarians, Aegyptians, sea elves, and the wood elves. All four held some appeal.

"Wood elves are snobs," Lex said with distaste as if he was struggling to recall a half-forgotten memory. "And the Aegyptians think they're the god's gift to Korynn."

"And how do you know that?"

"Not sure," Lex said sounding bewildered. "Just a feeling I guess."

"And I'm supposed to accept these feelings?"

"You must get over your trust issues, buddy, or your time in the Realms will be short and sucky," Lex said, a hurt tone to his voice.

Finn sighed, once again wishing he'd been able to debug Lex before entering the Realms. Despite being his constant companion for a year, Finn had always thought the banner was a bit odd. Now, suspecting his father may have had a hand in the AI's creation, his suspicions intensified. *How can I trust him? He's so…off.* After a moment, Finn shelved the thought. He knew he had no choice but to trust the quirky AI. *But I've got my eye on you.*

Finn looked at the sea elf. He was tall and lean and bore a spark of keen intelligence behind his eyes. The race's style of fighting favored Finn's own, and he pulled the figure forward with a motion of his hand. As he did so, the man's features morphed into a visage like his own, except for the pointed ears.

"Whoa, a handsome hipster version of you," Lex said.

"'Course, you could always go as a woman. Nudge, nudge, wink, wink."

It was then that Finn noticed a shadowy form behind the male sea elf and with a flick of his wrist, she came to the fore. She was shorter but no less lean and graceful than her male counterpart. The woman was stunning, and the idea of experiencing life as a woman held some appeal.

"She looks like your sister," Lex said.

Well, that ruins that, Finn thought with a scowl and spun back to the male sea elf.

Finn drew the figure forward and adjusted his features. Lex was right, the man did look like him. Likely the same technology that extrapolated skills from his mind. He needed to be incognito in this world and hoped that Aluran had no way of knowing who he was. He had only met the man once, and that was in passing. He had no idea if this Aluran had any connection to the real one or if he was simply a computer-generated avatar, but in Finn's experience, no risk was too small to ignore. Plus, while he wasn't overly vain, even he had a few things he'd like to change about himself.

Finn nudged the nose stronger, changed the eyes to a pale blue, and turned his dark brown hair to a deep black. He couldn't help but add a few inches to his height, bringing him to six-foot two. He knew he wanted speed and mobility, so he didn't bother to add any bulk.

Finn examined his avatar and smiled. He approved the sea elf. Zeckoth stepped forward.

"As a purchaser of the Deluxe Beta Preorder, you are awarded the Ancestor's Boon Perk," the God of Knowledge said with a tone of wonder. "You are upgraded to an El'Edryn, the legendary high elves of yore, from whom all elven races devolved."

Finn's sea elf morphed again, becoming taller still. The eyes turned a wondrous blue with flecks of silver. His cheekbones sailed higher on his face, giving him a regal appearance. His skin darkened to a well-tanned hue and his dark hair transformed into a cascade of flowing platinum.

A prompt popped into his vision.

You have been awarded RACIAL GIFTS.

El'Edryn are stronger, smarter, faster, wiser, and longer-lived than their descendants. You have also been awarded three Racial Gifts.

- *+10 bonus Attribute Points (for a total of 30) to distribute as you choose.*
- *Night Vision up to 120 feet.*
- *Quick Mana and Health Regeneration: Mana and Health regenerate 25% faster.*

Sweet, Finn thought, before realizing that the system had essentially ignored his selections and preferences. But the high elf's perks more than made up for any cosmetic irritation Finn felt. He sent a silent thank you out to Brynn, his eyes drifting to the hooded figure he imagined represented his sister.

"Are you done selecting and modifying your race and gender?" Zeckoth prompted.

With only the slightest hesitation, Finn nodded.

10⊕

Finn became a stream of energetic particles that launched into the sky. In moments, he reached superluminal velocity and moved through all existence. The particles that were Finn screamed through space-time and then sprung back as if pulled by an elastic band. Then he was back in the room with Zeckoth.

A prompt blinked in the corner of Finn's vision, and he tapped it open. His inventory screen opened. On the left was a slotted grid where he imagined items could be stored. The right side was dominated by an avatar. The tall, regal elf bore a look of fierce determination and endless potential, despite being dressed in rags. Finn barely recognized himself in this new being. Nothing but the eyes. The eyes were still his, and they held a fierce determination.

I will find you, Brynn, Finn promised.

A new round of prompts filled his vision.

You have 30 *Attribute Points* to distribute between your five base attributes. They are…

ATTRIBUTES.

----- Strength -----
Measures the characters physical power. Determines damage bonuses with melee weapons, encumbrance, Stamina, and the AC (armor class) bonus for heavy armor.

----- Dexterity -----
Measures the characters agility and speed. Determines damage bonuses with ranged weapons, the chance to hit bonuses, speed, and AC bonuses for light armor.

----- Constitution -----
Measures the characters endurance. Determines Health, Stamina, speed, Encumbrance, and the AC bonus for wearing heavy armor.

ATTRIBUTES.

----- Intelligence -----

Measures the character's ability to solve problems and use logic. Determines mana. Intelligence also partially determines the pace at which skills are learned and leveled.

----- Wisdom -----

Measures the character's common sense, spirituality, and willpower. Determines spirit, and ability to withstand spells and prayers that affect the mind.

"Lex, any thoughts?"

"Based on your personality and existing skill set, I'd suggest you play an agile warrior who augments his abilities with magic," Lex said. "So far, you have no magic skills, but once we're in the game, we'll find some wussbag caster and make them teach us."

"We're not mugging people for knowledge."

"Have it your way," Lex said with a definite pout. "Anyway, with 30 *Attribute Points* to spend, you have a lot of flexibility. I'd say up your physical stats until we learn some magic, and then we'll go from there. But I wouldn't completely ignore *Intelligence* since it has tons of less obvious benefits."

Finn studied the *Attribute* descriptions again and decided Lex's theory had merit. He put 10 points into *Strength*, 7 each into *Dexterity* and *Constitution*, 6 into *Intelligence*. He ignored *Wisdom* for now.

"It is now time to complete your character and choose a name," Zeckoth said. "Be warned once you choose a name it cannot be changed."

A field popped into his vision with a blinking prompt that reminded Finn of an old word processing program. He knew what name he would choose. "Gryph," he said, and the name appeared in the spot. It hung there blinking for a few seconds until Finn accepted it. From that moment forth, he was no longer Finn Caldwell. Now he was the high elf warrior mage Gryph.

Gryph's *Character Sheet* came up, and he checked it over one last time before continuing.

Gryph - Level 1	Stats
High Elf (El'Edryn) Deity: None Experience: 0 Next Level: 2,000	Health: 134 Stamina: 137 Mana: 132 Spirit: 120
Attributes	**Gifts**
Strength: 20 Constitution: 17 Dexterity: 17 Intelligence: 16 Wisdom: 10	Health Regeneration: +25% Mana Regeneration: +25% Night Vision: 120 Ft. Master of Tongues

"Lex explain these *Stats* to me."

"*Stats* like *Health* and *Stamina* are measurements of your overall wellbeing. *Mana* measures the amount of magical power you have to cast spells, and *Spirit* measures the amount of divine energy you can call upon to cast invocations, which are basically spells using the power of your god."

"I'm guessing I have no access to my *Spirit* because I've refused to worship any of the gods?"

"Right. Since *Spirit* is the energy of belief and you're a heathen, atheist, unbeliever, you don't get none."

"Right," Gryph muttered.

Zeckoth stepped forward again. Gryph had forgotten he was there as much as you can forget a seven-foot bald god. This time, he walked right up to Gryph and, before he could react, grabbed him by the head. Gryph panicked until Zeckoth spoke up.

"It is time to awaken your magic," the god intoned.

Tendrils of energy wormed their way into Gryph's brain. It started as one filament but then branched and split, becoming thirteen distinct strands. He saw as much as felt pops of light explode in the various parts of his mind. Some were large, some so small as to be mere pinpricks in a star filled sky.

There was no pain, but for reasons he could not quantify, Gryph screamed. Time became still, and Gryph lost all sense of place. Then, suddenly, he was back in the cathedral surrounded by the hooded deities.

"There are thirteen spheres of magic," Zeckoth intoned.

"I got this chum," Lex said. Then added under his breath. "You're likely to bore the dude to death." He continued with his normal snark filled tone. "So, Old Baldy here is right, if dull. Magic is the ability to rewrite the underlying code of the Realms. It manifests itself in thirteen spheres. Each sphere represents one of the primal building blocks of reality.

"Now long ago in the primal blah, blah, blah of creation, the spheres came into being during a massive battle between aether and thought. Life and death came into the Realms for the first time. These four spheres became known as the four primal magics."

"Okay, that sounds...logical," Gryph said.

"Next came the four elemental spheres of fire, air, earth, and water. These are all self-explanatory. Fire mages will blast enemies with fireballs. Kaboom, kuuurrshhh, burn, burn, oh no, I'm scarred for life. No maiden will wanna bed me again. The children will run in fear."

"Lex, just the facts," Gryph said, and he saw what may have been the hint of a smile cross Zeckoth's face.

"Jeez, tough crowd," Lex whined. "Anyway, air guys can make shields, knock people on their asses with big gusts of wind, and hurl bolts of lightning. So, zap, singe, singe, oh no, where'd my eyebrows go. Earth folks are usually stodgy grumps who talk way too slow. Water wizz-ards," he paused for effect. Gryph refused to take the bait. "Um, well they can breathe underwater, create ice, and control water. They're essential first picks if you ever get into a snowball fight."

Gryph sighed and almost asked Zeckoth if he could get a new banner.

"Yo, pay attention," Lex muttered in annoyance. "This is some good shit."

Gryph rolled his eyes and made the 'get on with it' hand motion.

"Fine, jeez. I hope everyone else in the game ain't as grumpy as you. Anyway, then we have the so called higher magics. These spheres are empyrean, beloved of people who believe in angels and celestial trees and crystals and junk. The chthonics, now they're more fun in my book. Demon summoners who love wearing dark robes and talking in funny voices they think are intimidating. *Life* and *Death Magic* are self-explanatory. Healers and killers."

Lex stopped his rambling, and while Gryph found the silence welcome, he had only counted twelve spheres of magic. "And the thirteenth?"

"*Soul Magic.* Can't say I know nuthin' about that one. Affinity for that one is ultra-rare."

"Affinity?"

"Everyone in the Realms has an affinity and an antipathy for every sphere of magic. An affinity of 100% means that you can learn that magic up to level 100, the maximum measurement of proficiency in the Realms. 50% means a max of level 50, etc., blah, blah.

"Affinities and antipathies are connected. If you have 100% affinity in *Life Magic* for example, not only will you be some kinda boring do-gooder, but you'll also have a 100% antipathy, or 0% affinity, for *Death Magic.* It's an oil and water kinda thing."

Gryph nodded. Despite his childish methods, Lex was a fountain of information. He supposed he was lucky to have the annoying banner with him.

"So, when Chuckles here laid hands on you, he opened your affinity and your antipathy. Open your *Skill Sheet* and you'll see what's what."

Gryph did as bidden.

Magic Skills: Level (Affinity) (Tier).
Fire: 0 (25%) (Base)
Air: 0 (75%) (Base)
Water: 0 (75%) (Base)
Earth: 0 (25%) (Base)
Chthonic: 0 (0%) (Base)
Empyrean: 0 (100%) (Base)
Chaos: 0 (75%) (Base)

Magic Skills: Level (Affinity) (Tier).
Order: 0 (25%) (Base)
Life: 0 (75%) (Base)
Death: 0 (25%) (Base)
Thought: 0 (75%) (Base)
Aether: 0 (25%) (Base)
Soul: 0 (50%) (Base)

Martial Skills: Level (Tier).
Unarmed: 5 (Base)
Small Blades: 5 (Base)
Staves/Spears: 5 (Base)
Thrown Weapons: 5 (Base)
Stealth: 5 (Base)
Light Armor: 5 (Base)
Dodge: 5 (Base)

Knowledge Skills (Tier).
Alchemy: 5 (Base)
Perception: 5 (Base)
Lock-picking: 5 (Base)
Traps: 5 (Base)
Perk Points: 0
Divine Perk Points: 0

Gryph closed out his *Skill Sheet* and nodded in appreciation. He was eager to try out magic. Chortles of laughter broke his reverie.

"Ha, ha, ha. Of course, you're an empyrean. Bet you'll get your halo any day now," Lex said, continuing his fake laugh several seconds too long.

"You done?"

"Not quite yet," Lex started his fake laughter again.

"Well, be done," Gryph said. Lex stopped, but even though his banner was still a disembodied voice, Gryph could sense his pouting. "Why don't I have any magic skills?"

"Did you know any magic on Earth?" Lex said in an irritated tone.

"Um, no. But I have an affinity in several"

"Affinity is potential not actual. Affinity means you have the potential to master a sphere of magic, but you still have to learn it."

"And how do I do that?" Gryph said through gritted teeth.

"A master of any sphere can teach you if they wish. They'll lay hands on you like Lean Mr. Clean here did to awaken your affinities. Or you can use a spell stone to learn a spell along with the requisite magic skill needed to cast the spell."

"If I have an affinity for that sphere of magic?"

"Hey, using that brain for smart making. Good on ya, pal. As long as you don't have an affinity of 0%, you can learn a sphere of magic. But your advancement is limited by the affinity. In your case, you will not be able to rise above level 25 in *Order Magic*."

Zeckoth stepped forward again with a blessedly welcome interruption.

"Our time together has ended," the tall god said. With a flourish of his arm, another slice in reality opened. "It is now time for you to visit the armory where you will receive your starter equipment."

"Oooh, swag," Lex said. "Love me some swag."

"In addition, Crusader," Zeckoth continued, "now that your character is complete, your banner will take physical form as your personal banner NPC. Your NPC's race, skill set, affinities, and physical form will be auto generated. This will help balance any of your deficiencies."

Gryph wasn't sure he would enjoy a flesh and blood Lex being his constant companion. He was irritating enough as a disembodied voice. What would he be like in real life?

"You better not screw me, dude" Lex said with trepidation.

11

Gryph passed through another slice in reality and emerged onto a massive shelf carved into the side of a tall mountain. A range of smaller mountains split the sky as far as he could see. Sweat pooled on his body and an intense glow came from behind him. He turned to see a huge forge fed by red-hot magma. With a jump of panic, he realized he was standing inside the cone of an active volcano. The sound of clanging metal rang in his ears, jarring his nerves.

He turned and saw a lithe red-haired woman banging away on an anvil. The large hammer she wielded seemed far too heavy for someone her size to lift, much less swing with such ease.

Her rhythmic work sung to Gryph. Her timing was perfection, and Gryph hesitated to interrupt her. He waited and after a few more moments the woman laid her hammer down and turned towards Gryph.

Tanned by fire and forge and covered in sweat, she was still stunning. She smiled at Gryph. He felt his heart jump. She walked up to him and held her hand out.

"Welcome, Crusader. I am Heleracon, Goddess of Artifice and the Forge. Blah, blah, blah."

Gryph stared.

"Well, don't leave me hanging cute thing," Heleracon said with a smirk.

Her manner was so different from the other gods he'd met so far that he didn't know how to respond.

"Lex?" Gryph said, his eyes squinting down in suspicion.

"No, sweetie, I told you, Heleracon, the Goddess of Artifice and the Forge. Try to keep up. I make cool stuff for the other gods, and sometimes for you mere mortals. If you make it worth my while."

She walked around Gryph, analyzing him like he was a

prized breeding stallion. Gryph was starting to become uncomfortable when Heleracon smacked his ass and bit her lower lip.

"Um, do you greet every player this way?" Gryph asked.

"Of course not. Do you think I'm some kinda floozy?"

"Ah, well?"

"Just kidding, handsome. Relax. To answer your question, yes, I greet every player this way. This aspect of me is programmed to be a tad spicier than those other fellas." She did a dance that was far more appealing than it should have been. "Market research shows that players, even the female ones, like saucy minxes. I do so enjoy the role."

"Um," Gryph said.

"You're the first high elf I've seen come through here. And I gotta say, *rowwwr*. How's you manage that one? Buddies with Aluran?"

"Not exactly," Gryph began.

"Yeah, I don't really care. Just making conversation. Something you should work on. I like conversation. I also like not talking if you catch my drift? If you ever find yourself near the real Source Forge, look me up. I'm a girl who works hard and likes to play harder." The goddess' eyes lit with an internal flame as she ogled Gryph up and down.

Gryph just stared in bewilderment.

"OK, you're a bit slow, but I can work with that. Anyway, guess we should get to it. I bet you're excited to meet your banner NPC in the flesh?"

"I'd say anxious," Gryph said.

"Oh, he's one of them types. I get it. Well, good luck, honey, because once your new buddy is made there ain't no refund."

"Great," Gryph muttered and turned with Heleracon towards a large set of gilded doors.

"Drum roll please," Heleracon said in a loud announcer voice, and the sound of deep bass drums emanated from nowhere and everywhere. "Lexicon, banner NPC of Gryph of the Tasty Glutes, come on down."

Gryph sent a sideways glance at the fiery goddess, but a loud *clang* of metal brought his attention back to the gilded entrance. A red light split them in two, and the massive doors opened.

Illuminated from behind was a powerful figure of muscle and brawn. Shadows masked Lex's features, but the NPC strode forward with purpose. The new Lex seemed impressive. He was a broad-shouldered man dressed in flowing robes and carrying a large metal hammer. A long beard swung side to side as he approached.

As the space between them diminished, Gryph realized that the distance had not been as large as it first seemed. As Lex got close, he could see his NPC's swagger diminish. Lex strode up with a scowl and smashed his hammer on the floor of the forge. His head barely came up to Gryph's chest.

"You have gotta be fricking kidding me," Lex said with a growl. "What the hell is this?"

Gryph shrugged and tried to keep the grin from his face.

"Hey, short stuff," Heleracon said. "How's the weather down there?"

Lex raised his hammer, ready to crush her pretty red skull. Gryph stepped in and put a hand on Lex's shoulder. He bent down to get eye level with his NPC. Lex noticed.

"Uh, buddy," Gryph said in the soothing tone one uses on a drunken friend. "I wouldn't do that. Goddess." Lex relaxed, lowering his hammer with a low grumble. "So, you look…good. What are you, a hill dwarf?"

"I'm an effing Ordonian."

"Wait aren't those the Viking dudes. Tallest race on Korynn?"

"Yes!" Lex howled in a rage.

"Well, that's an average," Heleracon said. "You may be on the lower end…height wise."

"Lower, I'm only five-foot two," Lex raged.

"I'd say more like five one and three quarters."

Lex glared up at Heleracon, his face as red as her hair.

"Hey, love muffin, don't blame me, I just build stuff. I'm not responsible for whatever this is."

Lex bellowed and hefted his hammer over his head. He swung it down several times, smashing a crate of coal, a barrel of water, and a table covered in metal ingots. Gryph sent a nervous glance at Heleracon, but she seemed more amused than annoyed.

"I see you like the hammer, though," she said. "I did make that for you." She held her hand palm up and a golden apple appeared in a flash of light. A paring knife appeared in the other hand.

Lex eyed her a moment before turning his gaze on the hammer. "Yeah, it's pretty good."

Gryph walked up and put his arm around his NPC's shoulder. The sad look in Lex's eyes was hard to take. The banner had been his constant companion for over a year, and for the first time, Gryph thought of him as human, with actual feelings. He made a promise to himself to treat the little guy with more respect.

"Wanna go get drunk?" Lex said.

May have to rethink that respect thing, Gryph thought. "Let's have a look at you," Gryph said.

Lex's eyes blanked as he turned his gaze inwards analyzing his *Character Sheet.* "Hrrmmmm," Lex grunted in a tone that didn't sound thrilled.

"What is it?"

"It looks like I'm some kinda priest. My main affinity is for *Thought Magic,* and I worship some dude named Cerrunian, whoever that is."

"He's dead," Heleracon said as if it were nothing. She sliced a piece of the apple and eased it past her full lips.

"Dead?" Lex squealed in alarm.

"Yeah, dead."

"What do you mean dead?" Gryph asked.

"As in dead," Heleracon twitched her neck to the side, closed her eyes, and pulled up on an imaginary noose that made her tongue loll out of her mouth. "No longer of this world. Pushing up the daisies. Gone to meet his maker."

"How can I worship a dead god?"

Heleracon shrugged. "Got me, never met one."

"Great. So, I'm a midget priest of a dead god."

"Technically a midget is four-foot ten or less. And I do believe that term has fallen out of favor," Heleracon said, slipping another slice of apple into her mouth with a *crunch.*

Lex glared and hefted his hammer again.

"Let's not get caught up in semantics," Gryph said. "Is there a way we can fix him?"

"Fix me?" Lex raged. "There's nothing wrong with me."

Gryph wasn't about to get into that debate and looked at Heleracon, repeating the question.

"Nope. I told you, no returns, no exchanges."

"Okay, buddy," Gryph said stooping down to get eye level with Lex. "There's gotta be a reason for all this."

"Always is," Heleracon said. "The Source always has its reasons."

Gryph didn't know what to make of that and kept his attention on Lex. "You and me against the Realms. Right, buddy?" Gryph held out his hand and, after a moment, Lex grumbled and took it. Gryph's massive hand swallowed up Lex's.

"This isn't helping," Lex said. "Nor is the kneeling thing you got going on."

"Sorry," Gryph said, standing back at his full height.

"Or maybe it was," Lex muttered.

Gryph sighed and returned his attention to the goddess. "You said you had some gifts?"

"Oh yeah, good memory you got, honey." She shook her shoulders and much of the snark seemed to drain from her. She cleared her throat and started a speech that seemed both pre-written and filled with user agreement style language.

"Congratulations, player," Heleracon said. "As a purchaser of the Deluxe Beta Preorder, you have been awarded an Upgraded Starter Pack. This includes a minor magic weapon, a minor piece of magical equipment, and a bonus potion pack. These items are influenced by your skill set and *Attribute Points* distribution trends. Note, in game treasure and loot awards are also influenced by your skill set and *Attribute Points* distribution trends."

Before Gryph had time to miss the real Heleracon, her old personality came back. "Cuz getting a kick ass war hammer when you're a knife and spear guy would just be no fun, now would it?" She winked at Lex, who scowled and gripped his hammer with white knuckles.

Prompts filled Gryph's vision.

You have been awarded an El'Edryn Swift Spear.

(Staves/Spear)
Item Class: Base.
Item Category: Active.
Base Dmg: 12 (+2 Base Item Bonus).

The preferred weapon of high elf warriors, the swift spear is lightweight and imbued with powers that make it a weapon capable of dealing quick and deadly attacks.

Active Powers.
Power (1): Quick Strike. 1% chance per point of mana spent to gain a second attack that automatically hits.

Mana Limit: 1%
Cool Down: 5 minutes.

You have been awarded a Soul Bound Satchel of Holding.

Item Class: Base.
Item Category: Passive.

This fine leather satchel is, in fact, a portal to a pocket dimension. It can hold a vast amount of inventory and is useful for hauling loot and treasure.

Passive Powers.
Power (1): Weight Reduction. Reduces the weight of stored items by 95%.
Power (2): Stasis Field. Items will remain in their current state for as long as they remain in the satchel.
Power (3): Soul Bound. This item is Soul Bound and cannot be lost or stolen.
Power (4) Auto sort. This item will automatically sort and categorize anything put into it.

You have been awarded a Belt of Deftness.

Item Class: Base
Item Category: Passive.

This fine leather belt was cured with an oil infused with Quickvine Sap.

Passive Powers.
Power (1): +3 to Dexterity.

You have been awarded a Bonus Potion Pack.

Two Potions of Minor Health (50 points to Health).

Two Potions of Minor Stamina (50 points to Stamina).

Two Potions of Minor Mana (50 points to Mana).

One Potion of Cure Disease.

"Sweet toys, dude," Lex said.

He glanced into his satchel to see he also had a coil of rope, five standard rations, a torch, a locksmith kit, and a bag that contained ten gold coins, whose value he did not understand how to calculate in real-world terms. Gryph smiled down on him but had to admit the equipment was pretty impressive.

"Your very own Boy Scout survival pack," Lex said.

"Now that you've both got your gift basket, it's time for you to move on. The boss wants to give you a nice send off."

The world around Gryph and Lex faded and a dim new one came to the fore. It was as if they transitioned to a new scene in a movie in a dissolve. Gryph watched Heleracon sway away. She must have felt his gaze because she looked back over her shoulder and gave him a wink. Then Heleracon and the Source Forge disappeared, and Gryph was back atop the mountain overlooking the world.

"Are you ready, player?" a familiar and unwelcome voice boomed.

12

The booming voice caused Lex to jump in surprise, nearly toppling off the side of the peak. Gryph grabbed him by the scruff of his robes and held him secure. The diminutive NPC grunted his thanks.

"Thanks, man. I don't like being this high up," Lex said before realizing he'd just mocked his small stature. He gave Gryph a 'don't say it' look and Gryph stifled a smile.

"Are you ready, player? Ready to serve me? Ready to rid this world of evil?"

Gryph and Lex turned to see the avatar of the High God Aluran once again. The experience with the other gods had done nothing to diminish the power and potency of this man turned god. Part of Gryph still knew that he was merely Alistair Bechard, CEO of Sacrosanct Integrative Networks, but here and now, he knew that if he wished it, Aluran could crush him like the smallest of bugs.

"I am ready to do what is necessary to protect those who cannot protect themselves and to rid the Realms of evil," Gryph said, forcing defiance into his vow.

Aluran turned his head an inch, his gaze boring into Gryph's eyes. Did he detect a hint of suspicion in the High God's face? Was his assumption right? Was this man simply an avatar and not the real thing? After a moment, Aluran nodded.

"Your pledge is accepted and archived," Aluran said before turning his gaze on Lex. Lex just grinned until Gryph nudged him.

"Um, yeah," Lex said giving a wink and a hearty thumbs up. "Ready to serve. Excited to thrash evil and junk."

"Your pledge is accepted and archived," Aluran said again.

The High God waved his hand, and a doorway appeared

and opened. On the other side lay a pleasant village. People walked to and fro, buying and selling wares in an open-air market. Smoke rose from the chimney of a pleasant inn carrying the smell of cooking food to Gryph's nose. His stomach grumbled, and he realized he was starving.

"Don your armor, equip your weapons, and prepare to enter the Realms. Adventure and glory await."

Gryph opened his inventory and surveyed the contents. On the left stood a representation of him. It was a crude avatar that allowed him to see what he looked like with various clothing, armor, and weapons equipped. In a world with few mirrors, was this the way people in the Realms checked themselves before going out for the day?

His avatar wore a rough-spun tunic, pants, bracers, gloves, and a hat. Each provided him with a measly 1 point of armor class (AC), but he supposed they were better than nothing. He buckled his Belt of Deftness around his waist and felt more energized as his *Dexterity* jumped by three points.

Gryph sheathed his dagger and hooked it to his belt next to the coil of rope. He equipped his El'Edryn Swift Spear and his avatar did a few test spins and a thrust before settling back. Each potion stacked in a single spot based upon type, no matter how many he had. *Nice perk,* he thought.

He reached up to close his inventory window when something at the bottom sparkled and caught his interest. The mote of energy came into focus and a prompt filled his vision.

Prime Godhead.
Tier: 0.
Item Class: Mote of Creation
Item Category: Unknown.
Base Dmg: Unknown.
Base AC: Unknown.
A Prime Godhead is a mote of creation.
Active Powers.
Unknown.

"What the hell?" Gryph said in shock.

"What the hell what?" Lex said, idly digging something from his beard.

"I found something weird in my inventory?"

"Weird how?" Lex sniffed the mystery item, his nose scrunching up in distaste.

"Have you ever heard of a Prime Godhead? It says it's a Divine Artifact, whatever the heck that is."

Lex's eyes widened in panic, and he shot a glance at Aluran. The High God's avatar seemed to pay no attention. Lex cast an odd smile at the god and then pulled Gryph aside.

"It looks like I can equip it," Gryph said, his eyes still glazed from examining his inventory.

"No, no, no," Lex yelled in panic and moved to slap Gryph across the face to force his attention.

The world slowed as Gryph moved the Prime Godhead. It

clicked into a glowing slot in the middle of his forehead, the home of the third eye in some ancient mythologies. His mind exploded in a supernova of expansion.

Thin filaments expanded from the Prime Godhead and wormed their way into his body. They traversed and replaced nerves and enhanced neural connections. Gryph screamed.

Time slowed to a crawl. Lex's hand hovered mere inches from Gryph's face, but at the pace it would take an hour to find its mark. Aluran's eyes came alive and widened in shock as they moved to look at Gryph.

But Gryph was elsewhere.

He became the Source at the beginning of time. Thought erupted from nowhere into the endless expanse of aether that was all of creation. Eddies and whorls of potentiality popped in and out of existence. The War of Creation had begun.

Gryph's small mind couldn't understand the experience. His consciousness unraveled as it sought solace, a safe zone amongst primal energies giving birth to reality. A mote of energy, the tiniest fraction of the Source, beckoned and Gryph's mind fell into it.

Gryph fell into ease, and he stopped screaming. His eyes opened as the *Prime Godhead,* a Mote of Creation itself completed its integration. He saw Lex's wide eyes and outstretched hand. He also saw Aluran's gaze on him. Not the empty shell that had directed his character creation. This was the real Aluran, Bechard himself. He was also something else, something more ancient than both, and terror filled its eyes.

Time returned to normal, and Lex's hand slapped across his face. The pain barely registered. Aluran had all of Gryph's attention. Gryph's body surged with energy and he knew what must be done. With all his strength, Gryph shoved his NPC through the doorway into the Realms. As Lex stumbled through the threshold he screamed.

"No!"

Once Gryph was sure that Lex would make it through the portal, he charged after him. But Aluran moved quicker than he could have imagined and blocked the doorway. The High God raised his sword and swung a blow that would have taken Gryph's head clean off had he not predicted the move and tucked and rolled past the enraged god.

Gryph was past Aluran and sprinted towards the door. The High God raised his sword and pointed the tip at Gryph's back. With a word in some ancient language, a bolt of multi-chromatic energy erupted from the tip. Gryph dove, hit the ground hard, and slid towards the portal. On the other side, Lex sprawled on his back, his short legs upended. A scene that would have been hilarious under different circumstances.

Gryph's skid would take him through the portal, as well, and he cheered in triumph. Then Aluran's bolt hit the surface of the doorway. It pulsed and morphed and changed to a stark desert, then a deep ocean, and then a camp in the mountains. Then back to the village with Lex back on his feet, yelling soundlessly. When Lex saw Gryph he tried to jump back through the portal, but as he touched the threshold energy coursed through the short Ordonian's body and knocked him to the ground.

Another bolt of energy hit the floor near Gryph, and his body seized in pain. He felt as if he'd been electrocuted and the bolt hadn't even hit him. Gryph saw his red *Health* bar dip by nearly 30% as he stood and ran towards the portal, his muscles tightening in spasms.

Gryph jumped as the air became heavy with energy again. He passed through the threshold just as the portal switched to somewhere dark.

13

Gryph's mind warped as he sluiced through an aperture into another universe. He felt a heart that was not his own pounding. The real Aluran had seen him. The being who attacked him was not some computer-generated welcoming committee, but a powerful avatar filled with malevolent intent.

It had to be the *Godhead*. Lex had freaked when he heard the name. The fear that showed in his amiable and immature NPC's eyes had been downright terrifying. That look, bereft of any humor or jest was the most unnerving sight of Gryph's new life. Even Finn Caldwell, who had seen many a horrible deed in his life, rarely experienced such terror.

Gryph was trapped. He feared he would be in this weightless, bodiless state forever. Then he hit a stone floor with enough force to crack ribs, expel air, and bruise muscles. For a few seconds, Gryph couldn't breathe and his entire world was pain.

Gryph's lungs burned. To say the wind had been knocked out of him was like saying decapitation was a mild inconvenience. He believed he'd never draw breath again. A few moments passed before he pulled in a short burst of air full of pain, relief, and an awful stench.

"Ouch," Gryph said through gritted teeth.

Gryph's *Health* bar flashed in alarm, and he discovered that he had lost another 50% in the fall.

"What the hell was that?" he grumbled, and the pain of broken ribs took his breath away. He moved to grab a *Health* potion but discovered that he couldn't move.

Gryph stared as the debuff clock counted down in the corner of his vision. He tried to turn his head to find Lex.

"Lex," Gryph said in a strangled voice. "Hey, Lex, over here."

There was no response, and Gryph wondered if his NPC was dead, smashed on impact. *Perhaps that wasn't a bad thing,* Gryph thought and immediately felt guilty. Lex might be the most irritating banner of all time, but he had always been loyal. Maybe his personality would improve now he was a flesh and blood person and a wandering preacher to boot.

Face down in grit and muck, Gryph realized he was in a cave. A dark, dingy, and stinking cave.

In the corner of his vision, his prompt icon blinked. With nothing else to do until the debuffs disappeared, he checked his prompts.

WELCOME TO THE REALMS.

You have arrived at the starter village of ERROR.

You will have a few hours to acclimate to your surroundings, become familiar with your new skills, and purchase any additional equipment you may need before joining the Great Quest.

Congratulations player. Endless adventure awaits you.

"What the hell?" Gryph grumbled at the blazing red ERROR message. *I'm not where I'm supposed to be.* Gryph struggled to move, willing his damaged body to ignore the debuffs. Nothing.

Then he heard a scratching, a scritching of not so tiny claws digging into the rock of the cave floor. It was coming from behind him. Gryph attempted to turn, but his traitor body refused to obey his commands. The barest tingle in the fingers of his right hand, like the painful pins and needles rush one gets after sleeping on an arm all night, hinted that feeling was slowly returning.

"Shit," Gryph said aloud, and the scritching stopped. Had he scared the scritcher with his outburst, or was it examining him, waiting and wondering? Was he prey?

The scratching got closer, and Gryph did the only thing he could think of, he made lots of noise. Grunts and howls and expletives of anger poured from Gryph's parched lips, and he realized just how thirsty he was.

The burning pain of returning sensation moved up his arm, and he made the clumsiest of movement towards the knife at his belt. He'd forgotten it until feeling returned and the pommel dug into his side.

Something the size and weight of a mid-size dog stepped up onto his booted foot and a low growl rumbled through the cave. With tentative steps, it crawled up Gryph's back getting closer and closer to his face. And still, he couldn't move.

The numbing burn of returning blood tore at Gryph's shoulder, and he was just able to grasp the hilt of the blade with his trembling fingers. The hiss of steel greeted Gryph's ears as he eased the dagger from its sheath. No sound was ever so welcome.

A cool breath exhaled onto his face. The stale stench he'd noticed earlier grew to a horrid carrion smell. Gryph knew that it came from whatever now lurked on his back. It was a carnivore, ready to take a bite out of him.

A long snout came into sharp focus. Beady eyes that glowed with a dim green light sat atop the muzzle. Gryph made eye contact, and the foul creature opened its mouth to expose row after row of needle-sharp teeth. A low, evil hiss flowed from the creature's mouth.

Gryph stared at the creature. Information rushed into his mind. A new prompt popped up unbidden in Gryph's vision.

Undead Barrow Rat.

Level: 2.
Health: 35.
Stamina: :20.
Mana: 0.
Spirit: 0.

Barrow Rats are larger, more disgusting cousins to normal rats and while they prefer carrion, they have been known to take bites out of easy prey when the opportunity presents itself. This barrow rat was reanimated after death. Cowardly and easily spooked, Barrow rats' real danger comes from the disease Barrow Rot that fills their foul mouths.

Strengths: Unknown.
Immunities: Unknown.
Weakness: Unknown.

You Have Learned the Skill ANALYZE.

Level: 1.
Tier: Base.
Skill Type: Passive.

You have shown an ability to identify creatures you encounter. You can now identify basic creatures (Levels 1 - 5). You can now access the skill perk tree that will allow you to know their strengths and weaknesses. Each level will unlock the ability to identify creatures of an additional 5 levels.

The barrow rat climbed onto Gryph's shoulder and sniffed at his face. Gryph knew the debuff clock would last longer than this stinking beast's fear. It would take a bite out of him. He would get Barrow Rot, which sounded horrid. So, he did the only thing he could.

"Raaarrrgghhh!" Gryph bellowed at the top of his lungs, tearing at his parched throat.

The rat jumped back in fright, before hissing in anger, and perhaps embarrassment. It took just a few seconds for the creature to regain its courage and climb back onto Gryph's shoulder, ready to take a bite out of him.

DEBUFFS CLEARED.

Gryph thrust the dagger up with all his might and impaled the rat through the mouth. The point erupted from the back of the stinking creature's head, destroying its small brain before the signals of pain reached it. The creature died in a spasm of blood and gore.

You have scored a CRITICAL HIT.

5X normal damage.

You have received EXPERIENCE POINTS.

You have earned 175 Experience Points (XP) for killing Undead Barrow Rat.

"Well, that sucked," Gryph said getting to his feet. He was in a small cave. He looked around but could see no way out. "How'd you get in here?" he said to the dead rat, nudging it with his toe.

"Lex? You around, buddy?"

As expected, he got no answer. The room was dimly lit by a luminescent fungus clinging to the walls and fed by a slow trickle of water that came from a small crevice near the ceiling. Was that how the rat got in? The sight of water reminded him how thirsty he was. He girded himself and then slurped at the trickle, half expecting to get some horrid disease. It took him nearly ten minutes, but soon he'd drank his fill.

Gryph brought up his internal map, hoping to discover where he was. The world was a black mass of nothingness, aside from the small cave he occupied. The tag on the map read The Barrow: Level Three.

"Well, that's no help," Gryph grumbled, wincing at the pain from his broken ribs. He eased himself into a sitting position forcing the fear and claustrophobia into the deep recesses of his mind. It wasn't gone, it was just submerged. So far, his experience with the Realms had not been pleasant.

Yet people enter this place by choice.

Gryph knew he wasn't where he was supposed to be. Aluran must have altered the system in some way. He was alone, God only knew where and no closer to saving Brynn. Maybe he should log off and reboot. The Realms may be real, but the game used to get players into the Realms was, at its heart, still a computer program. And what did you do when your computer went wonky? You rebooted it.

Gryph brought up his interface again and tapped at the **LOG OFF** button. He felt it depress and prepared to return to the real world. Nothing happened. Not even another **ERROR** message. He hit it again. Nothing.

Never one to resort to bitching, Gryph assessed his situation. His *Health* was still low, and he was in pain. He pulled a *Health Potion* from his inventory. He examined the vial of swirling red liquid for a few moments before shrugging and downing it in one gulp.

Instantly, heat flowed through his body and his pains soothed away. First, the minor scratches and bruises disappeared. The pounding in his head, he suspected was a concussion, lessened and eased. He felt his ribs snap back into place and the bones knit together again.

"Holy crap," Gryph said, his mood perking up. *The US Army would kill for this technology.*

Gryph stood and did a few jumping jacks to force feeling back into his arms and legs. After stretching he noticed a small wooden chest hidden in a nook. It hadn't been there a few moments ago, Gryph was sure of it. Where had it come from?

Gryph walked up to the chest with caution. It couldn't have just magically appeared, could it? Was the concussion worse than he thought? Maybe he was hallucinating. He'd hit his head pretty hard when he fell.

With that thought, Gryph looked up at the roof of the cavern a mere dozen-feet above him where stalactites jabbed down like fangs. He felt like he was inside the maw of a massive stone beast. He expected to see a hole in the roof. Something he had fallen through. Something that would explain all of this. But the ceiling was solid.

"None of this makes any sense."

Gryph walked up to the small chest. Made of simple planks of wood bound by tarnished bands of iron. A rusty latch bore a keyhole, but the latch itself was bent, suggesting that the lock had long ago failed its purpose.

Gryph's hand hesitated above the lid. A faint red glow pulsed around the keyhole. His hand stopped, and he focused his attention on the glow. It intensified, and he knew he was looking at a trap.

TRAP DETECTED.

Use the Disarm skill to avoid pain and death.

"Well, that's helpful," Gryph grumbled.

He grabbed his locksmith kit. Opening the small box, he saw various tools designed for intricate detail work. His mind flashed back to his time in the army where he'd learned how to disarm a claymore mine and gave thanks to the US Army. He suspected it would not be the last time he'd be thankful that the Realms imported real world skills.

Gryph inhaled, calming his hand and his mind and slipped the thin pick into the lock. After careful probing, he felt a *click*, and the red glow disappeared. He replaced the tools and eased the chest open. Inside was a small bag of coins, a small shield, a dagger in a sheath, a bandolier bearing six throwing knives, and a small silver ring with a row of sapphires.

You have found TREASURE.

3 gold coins.
12 silver coins.
22 bronze coins.

You have found a Banded Wooden Buckler.

(Block)
Item Class: Non-magical.
Base AC: 6.

This small shield attaches to the forearm and is a great complement to staves and spears.

You have found a Fine Steel Dagger.

(Short Blade)
Item Class: Non-magical.
Base Damage: 6.

This finely honed dagger is sharper than a normal steel dagger.

You have found Ring of Minor Air Shield.

Item Class: Base.
Item Category: Active.

Active Powers
Power (1): Creates a sphere of solidified air that will protect the user from damage. The air shield can absorb 5 points of damage for each point of mana spent. It will last for 5 seconds per point of mana spent. The air shield will collapse once damage limit is reached or time expires.
Power (2): Each level of Air Magic mastery reduces Cool Down by 5 seconds.
Power (3): Each tier of Air Magic mastery ups total daily usage by 1.

Mana Limit: 10%.
Cool Down: 5 minutes.
Max Uses: 3x Day.

"Not a bad haul," Gryph said as he pulled the bandolier on and slipped the ring onto his finger. Part of him wondered why he'd received such a bounty for slaying so simple a foe. *Maybe due to the paralysis?* He realized his excitement was rather foolish. What good would any of this stuff do him if he was stuck in this damn cavern?

The stirrings of panic and despair built up in him when another dim glow appeared inside the chest. A small blue square glowed at the top left corner where the walls of the chest joined.

He eased his hand in and pressed down on the blue glow. He heard a small *click*, and then the rumble of rock scraping on rock. Behind him, the cave wall rose into the ceiling, revealing a dark passageway.

14

Deep in the darkest parts of the Barrow, on an ancient altar sat a skull as old as the world. Its eye sockets were pits of primal darkness. Along the wall, braziers glowed with emerald fire.

It was enough light for the barrow rat to see by as it sniffed for bugs and grubs among the ancient refuse that littered the floor. A low hum, lower than human hearing rose, and the rat twitched. The braziers along the walls erupted into gouts of green flame, and the rat squealed in terror as the hum became the grinding of bones.

Pinpricks of murky green light came alive in the empty eye sockets of the skull and the Barrow King wakened from his slumber. His energy reserves remained low. It was too early. His mind reached out seeking the source of his revival.

Something is different. If anyone else had been there to hear his telepathic voice, a fear unlike any known since the primal days of the world would have gripped them. Few could hear the voice, but all life in the Barrow could sense a change had come.

The skull floated off the altar and darkness spread from it, forming an ethereal body made of solid smoke. The Barrow King had returned to the world of the living.

A tendril of energy erupted from the gaping maw of the skull and enveloped the barrow rat. The rat spasmed and opened its mouth to shriek in horror, but no sound came out. Instead, pulses of light flowed up the tendril from the rat's body and into the mouth of the Barrow King.

The barrow rat's drained and desiccated corpse collapsed.

Foul tasting beast, the Barrow King said as he sat on a throne behind the altar. *Why have I awakened?* The glowing eyes of the Barrow King winked out as the ancient fiend concentrated and looked inward.

The Barrow King extended his perception outward through the passageways and rooms of the Barrow. The swirling form of darkness was not his true body, nor was the Barrow itself, but he influenced both. His true body, murdered by his apprentice, had long ago turned to dust. Now he was a soul trapped in this half-life of hate and the need for vengeance.

The Barrow was a massive underground complex. Millennia ago, it had been a gleaming tower on the surface. There he'd conducted a search for truth others deemed evil, as they feared the unbridled power of *Soul Magic*. The Barrow King thrived on the fear of others.

He saw the Barrow. The passageways and rooms, the traps and the false paths. As his awareness wormed through this surrogate body, his mind noticed bright pools of energy.

Life, he said with greed. Tendrils of his mind flowed over the motes of light with desire.

Life birthed souls, and he fed on souls. There was a time when he did not slumber. A time when his Barrow was full of life. A time when adventurers came to the Barrow in search of wealth and power. Then he had never been hungry. But these last centuries were a famine. Something had changed in the world above the Barrow. A once mighty city destroyed. The life in the Barrow reduced. His stock of souls pared down. He was hungry now.

To preserve his existence, he spent most of his existence in slumber. Each time he woke, his reserves were further depleted. Yet, this time, something was different. He expanded his awareness, knowing that even this small exertion of his powers cost him greatly.

There were pockets of life of various shades and intensities. Foul creatures were common, filled with rancid, bitter souls. His minions, once dead creatures given false life to act as extensions of his will, still slumbered.

There was far too little life. He had gorged before his last slumber, preparing for a long sleep. He'd consumed many a sentient soul that day. Over time the Barrow would capture more souls, and he would feed again. But his Barrow had not had enough time to restock. The number of souls in his Barrow was insufficient. Panic surged in the Barrow King's mind.

There is not enough.

Then he felt it, towards the edge of his being in a part of himself long abandoned. A light stronger than any since the ancient days. There was something familiar about this light. It was beyond sentience. His mind touched the edges of it, a nexus of potentiality, unlike anything he'd felt since…

In a flash, his betrayal came back to him. The hidden power brought to bear against him that day was like nothing experienced before or since, and he knew what had become trapped by his web.

A Godhead, the Barrow King thought in both fear and reverence, snapping his tendrils back from the light as if burned. *Has the Betrayer returned?* Fear ripped claws through his mind, and he felt a desperate need to return to his slumber.

But the Barrow King was no coward and his hunger was great. He reached out again and sampled the edges of the light. It was potent and pure and primal.

"And different," the Barrow King said aloud. Renewed confidence and desire flowed through his ethereal body. He poured more of his stored energy into the tendrils and reached out to touch the light. The tendrils melted in the glory of the light, but the Barrow King was now certain that this was not the Betrayer returned.

He needed to know more. He gazed upon the corpse of the dead rat and an idea formed in the revenant's mind. He stretched his will into the Barrow and found another barrow rat close to the *Godhead*. He pushed a small amount of power into the rat and possessed its small mind.

The rat found the light of the *Godhead* locked in a cave with no entrance and no exit. *How did it get there?* the Barrow King wondered. He spent too much energy opening a small crevasse in the side of this mystery room and his scout entered.

It was an El'Edryn. "A high elf," the Barrow King said bewildered. That race had left Korynn millennia ago. His scout gazed upon the elf. He was face down and damaged. The Barrow King extended his *Analyze* skill through his surrogate and read the newcomer.

The elf suffered from several broken bones and a paralysis debuff as if he'd fallen a great height. That made no sense. The cave's ceiling was only a dozen feet above the man's prone form.

The elf was also a paltry Level One and had zero experience. How had it come to be there? Why was it here? The Barrow King ordered his scout forward. He needed a closer examination. The man was aware of his scout, but was unable to move, despite the twitching of his finger near the dagger at his belt. There was time.

The Barrow King poured more of his dwindling power into the rat and there it was, the *Godhead*. The blaze of energy it put off flowed through the rat's eyes. The *Godhead* was undetectable to those ignorant to its presence or its purpose. Yet the Barrow King had felt one's touch before.

The Barrow King imagined himself filled with the divine power of the *Godhead*. He would never be hungry again. The vast potential contained in this mote of creation surged through his poisoned mind.

A vast army of the dead rose and marched in front of him, the foul energies leaking from them drawing clouds across the sky. Astride a skeletal dragon, the Barrow King moved across the land.

An army of the dead rose in the ruined city to the South. Ancient corpses that lay where they'd fallen in battle centuries before stumbled to their feet, weapons held aloft in worship of their new god. They marched through the villages that still dotted the hills and valleys around the dead city, pillaging and adding more to their numbers.

Then he turned his forces towards the mountain kingdom of the dwarves and plundered it for weapons, wealth and warriors. With each conquest his army would grow, for the dead served only him.

His army laid waste to all the lands of Korynn. Then he would turn the dead gazes of his million strong army against the Shining City itself and lay the Betrayer low.

The Barrow King pulled himself from his foretelling and looked at the man. He was weak. The *Godhead* would be easy to take. A plan formed in the Barrow King's mind. He would draw this adventurer further into the Barrow, kill him and absorb him, body and soul. The *Godhead* would be his.

He would be reborn and remade and have his vengeance.

The elf stabbed up with his dagger, killing the rat. The Barrow King's scout died, and the view of the man blinked out. No matter, the greed of mortals was their great weakness.

The Barrow King let flow a twinge of mana and gifts appeared. A small chest containing tools to survive his Barrow. It was an irresistible invitation that would inexorably lead the elf deep into the Barrow.

Exhausted, the Barrow King withdrew most of his tendrils. He let one slither through the passages of the Barrow, seeking. He needed power to challenge the man with the *Godhead*.

It was time to feed.

15

The door seemed too convenient. As did the long passageway beyond it. Gryph attached the small buckler to his left arm, hefted his spear and entered the passage. Fearful of what lay beyond, he slipped into *Stealth*.

The passageway was long and gave Gryph time to think on the absurd situation he was in and the long list of things that had gone wrong.

What had Aluran done to him? What was the Barrow?

Aluran had been acting normal as far as Gryph could tell. He was just the same start up game avatar that greeted every new player. Nothing odd there. Sure, it showed how egocentric Aluran was, but arrogance was never a real threat.

Then his entire demeanor had changed. It had to be the *Godhead*, whatever the hell that thing was. The way it had freaked Lex out suggested that it was powerful. Aluran had only *noticed* Gryph when he'd equipped the odd artifact. Gryph had seen a look of fear in the god's suddenly aware eyes.

The *Godhead*. He pulled open his inventory. The icon for the mysterious artifact was hazy this time. When he'd equipped it, the icon had been bright and shiny. Gryph attempted to unequip it but discovered that he could not.

He tried a few of the other icons. His tattered boots, worn shirt and ragged trousers glowed and fell away from his avatar. With a start, he discovered he also stood naked. He re-equipped his avatar.

He looked back at the icon for the *Godhead* and focused. Other than the *Gift of Tongues* ability, the description was not at all helpful. Yet, the name *Divine Artifact* and the fact it was the only magical item he possessed with a *Tier* suggested that its power could evolve.

That is what drew Aluran's ire. I'm a threat to him.

Somehow, it had bonded with him. Whatever it was, his possession of it had pissed off a god. That meant it would be a powerful tool in his quest to save Brynn. He had to make unlocking its abilities a priority.

Without Lex to guide him he would have to figure out everything on his own. He was surprised how much he missed his irritating banner turned foul-mouthed priest. He was sure that sooner or later he would have punched Lex in the mouth, but now, alone in the bowels of this wretched dungeon, he missed the company.

According to Mo, or should he be calling her Eris, he was meant to spawn in a pleasant town with ample places to grind. The lingo was still new to him, but he understood enough to know despite his impressive list of imported skills, he was still inexperienced and weak.

Gryph hefted his spear, stretched his muscles, and moved down the passage. He kept his pace steady, thankful that the El'Edryn had night vision up to 120 feet. A dull glow appeared up in the distance out of the gloom. It took Gryph a moment to realize it was much further away than any human eyes would be able to register. He forged ahead, and the corridor eventually ended in a large cavern.

The cavern was the size of a high school gymnasium. The area was filled with huge mushrooms that glowed with a dull silver light. Though they stood taller than he, Gryph was able to see beyond them and spot another entrance on the opposite side of the cavern. The continuing passageway appeared to head down.

The stench in this chamber was a notch beyond awful. It was the smell of carrion and decay. Bones of every shape and size littered the floor of the cavern. It was a feeding ground, and one for a creature none too concerned with cleanliness or hygiene.

Gryph scanned the cave for a few moments before assuring himself that he was alone, then he moved forward. He was careful not to step on any of the innumerable bits of bones or shards of rusted metal that lay scattered between the mushroom's stalks. After a few minutes, he had made a circuit of the room confirming that he was alone. He'd even stabbed into the base of one mushroom to assure himself that the things wouldn't jump to life and take a bite out of him. The mushroom leaked a silver sap, but otherwise showed no ill effects.

Gryph made his way to the other exit and confirmed that the tunnel went down further into the Barrow, but it turned a sharp corner after a few dozen feet, so he couldn't see much else. Gryph remembered Lex's conversation telling him to leave no stone unturned.

He returned his attention to the room and checked the remains for treasure.

The work itself was both disgusting and sacrilegious. Gryph wasn't a fan of looting the dead, but he was also practical. Whatever had turned these into dust and bone must be a deadly foe.

Gryph began his search, finding a variety of useful items.

You have found Treasure.

24 gold coins.
38 silver coins.
56 bronze coins.
*3 **Non-Magical Jewelry.***

You have found a Basic Alchemist's Kit.

Item Class: Non-magical.
Item Category: NA.

With this kit you can collect alchemical and crafting ingredients and make Base Tier potions.

You have found an Animate Rope Spell Stone.

(Air Magic)

This enchanted stone will allow you to learn a spell.

You have found Padded Leather Jerkin.

(Light Armor)
Item Class: Non-magical.
Item Category: NA.
AC Bonus: +8.

A standard padded leather jerkin provides decent protection from attack.

You have found Padded Leather Pants.

(Light Armor)
Item Class: Non-magical.
Item Category: NA.
AC Bonus: +4.

A standard pair of padded leather pants provides decent protection from attack.

You have found Scaled Leather Boots.

(Light Armor)
Item Class: Non-magical.
Item Category: NA.
AC Bonus: +5.

A fine pair of scaled leather boots provides above average protection from attack.

```
┌──────────────────────────────────────────────────────┐
│           You have found Banded Leather Bracers.        │
├──────────────────────────────────────────────────────┤
│                                                        │
│                    (Light Armor)                       │
│              Item Class: Non-magical.                  │
│               Item Category: NA.                       │
│                 AC Bonus: +5.                          │
│                                                        │
│   A standard pair of leather bracers enhanced with     │
│   small iron plates provides above average protection  │
│              from attack.                              │
│                                                        │
└──────────────────────────────────────────────────────┘
```

Gryph was most interested in the *spell stone*. Even a newbie like him understood that in the Realms magic was the true power. He held the jewel in his hand. It was a blue gemstone, a sapphire perhaps. Gryph stared, drawn in by a swirling glow of white light deep inside the crystal matrix of the gem.

He focused on the light and his vision swam, and he felt the beginnings of a headache. Then he felt a rush of air snake up his arm into his chest and then up into his head. His brain pulsed with the sudden influx of knowledge and he fell to his knees in surprise.

```
┌──────────────────────────────────────────────────────┐
│        You have learned the spell ANIMATE ROPE.        │
├──────────────────────────────────────────────────────┤
│                                                        │
│                 Sphere: Air Magic.                     │
│                   Tier: Base.                          │
│                                                        │
│   Allows the caster to animate rope (or chains, vines, │
│   or anything that can be considered a rope). The rope │
│   will obey basic commands and can tie, entangle, trip │
│   or squeeze opponents. The rope's AC and HP derive    │
│   from the quality of the rope. Each Tier mastered     │
│   adds one rope to the total control limit.            │
│                                                        │
│                 Mana Cost: 50.                         │
│          Damage (Squeeze): 5 points per sec.           │
│   Duration: 1 minute + 5 seconds per level of Air      │
│                  Magic mastery.                        │
│               Cooldown: 5 minutes.                     │
│                                                        │
└──────────────────────────────────────────────────────┘
```

> **You have learned the skill AIR MAGIC.**
>
> _Level:_ 1.
> _Tier:_ Base.
> _Skill Type:_ Active.
>
> You can now wield the power of Air Magic. Air Magic allows the user to manipulate the wind, the air around us and other gases. Air Magic is used for offensive and defensive purposes but can also summon or create creatures made of air and is useful for animating a variety of inanimate objects. Spells that make use of electricity are the province of Air Magic.

Despite the headache, the inrush of information punished him with, Gryph was ecstatic. He had just learned his first magic spell and the accompanying skill. Even though _Animate Rope_ sounded rather silly he could not wait to cast it.

It turned out he'd get his chance sooner than he thought. Gryph struggled to pull the _padded leather jerkin_ over his head when he heard the heavy thud of footsteps coming from the unexplored tunnel.

16

Even hunched over, the beast was near seven feet tall and muscled like a gorilla who'd failed a steroid test. It had a large mouth, which it was gracious enough to show Gryph as it chomped down on what appeared to be a child's arm. The casual *crunch* of bone told Gryph a tale he wished he'd never heard.

The large beast passed him by, its small beady eyes never once glancing his way. It was likely near blind, which made sense this far underground. Its splayed nostrils suggested its sense of smell would be the inverse of its eyesight.

After a few moments, the horrible crunching noise stopped and Gryph gave thanks for small miracles. With the cacophony of its meal ended the beast paused as if sensing the interloper in its living room. The massive head swung to the left and to the right, nostrils flared. Gryph hoped that the god-awful smell of the room overpowered whatever stench he exuded.

A few tense heartbeats later the beast lifted the body in its right hand. It wasn't a child, but a tiny man with striking green hair and an outfit that featured nearly every bright color of the rainbow including the crimson stain of blood.

The beast eased back onto its haunches and with a fibrous tear of muscle and skin being wrenched apart the beast shoved another arm into its mouth.

Then things got worse.

At that moment, Gryph's nose decided that playing hide and seek was a bore. A huge sneeze erupted followed by a stream of tears. The sound tore through the cave. Gryph ran.

He staggered and slipped and bounced off another mushroom stalk as he ran blindly through the cavern. Behind him the beast bellowed and tore off after him. Reaching down to the bandolier on his chest, Gryph pulled one of the throwing knives and pitched it wildly behind him. The knife bounced off the beast, unable to penetrate its thick hide.

Gryph sensed the beast's swing and did a duck and roll as the massive body rumbled past him. He spun up to his feet and thrust his spear towards the beast. The point took the creature high in the thigh and sunk in several inches.

With a howl that pierced Gryph's ears, the creature stumbled and fell to one knee. A meaty fist swiped back at the offending spear before Gryph could retrieve it, snapping the shaft a few inches below the spearhead.

The beast spun and swung a fist. Gryph ducked, lost his balance and fell to his rear, scrambling backwards as fast as his frantic legs and arms would crab walk him, the broken haft of his spear clutched near useless in his hand.

The monster tugged the broken spearhead from its leg and flung it at Gryph. It sank deep into the hard-packed dirt of the cavern floor an inch from his crotch. The spearhead vibrated and hummed from the impact before falling silent. Gryph looked at the beast to see the gash in its leg close and knit before his eyes.

"What the hell?"

The beast dropped to all fours and charged. In a panic, Gryph scuttled back further until he bumped into the stalk of another mushroom. There was nowhere else to go. The beast got close, and Gryph held the broken spear shaft in front of him, a pathetic defense against the onrush of a locomotive sized bull. The beast must have sensed the easy prey as it ducked its head and increased speed. Gryph noticed the two curved horns on the beast's head.

Perfect, Gryph thought and braced the broken spear against the base of the mushroom. He held it at an angle, gripping it with every ounce of strength. It was a desperate move with surprisingly concrete results.

The beast, full of stupidity and rage, charged ahead, paying no heed to the pathetic weapon. It lowered its head, preparing to batter Gryph to a pulp. Pain exploded in the beast's head. Gryph's desperate last attack, braced against the base of a mushroom stalk sent the broken shaft deep inside the beast's left nostril, where it buried itself in the soft flesh of its brain. The beast did not fall, did not die.

"Come on," Gryph said in disbelief.

The beast reared on its hind legs and bellowed. It stumbled, flailing back and forth, straining to find the source of the excruciating pain.

That has to do it," Gryph thought.

The beast howled again, arms spasming back and forth as it sought the spear shaft. Its eyes opened and closed as it lost control of parts of its body.

"Die, die, die!" Gryph yelled at the top of his lungs. The sound drowned by the monster's rage. Not wasting the opportunity, Gryph stood and his hands found the throwing knives at his chest. He took careful aim and threw one, two, three, four of the small enchanted blades.

Two bounced off the thick hide of the monster's face, but two more found their mark. Tiny eyeballs ruptured, and a viscous mix of ocular fluid and green blood flowed down the beast's face.

Another howl exploded from the beast. One of its massive mitts found the spear shaft and yanked it free, drawing a fountain of blood, snot, and what may have been brain matter out. The beast tossed it aside and roared again.

Gryph moved quickly and silently, attempting to make his way to the exit which led further down into the Barrow. He had no clue what awaited him below, but there was no way it was worse than his current situation.

But the beast's sense of smell, even with one ruined nostril, was incredible. It looked right at him, metal shards glinting in the dim glow. Gryph made himself as rigid as a statue and held his breath. After several thunderous heartbeats, the beast turned away, cocking its head to the side.

Gryph was sweating and knew the stench pouring off of him had to be an easy mark for the beast's sense of smell. A thought hit him. *The smell of the dust.* That earthy smell. It covered him, mixed with and masking his sweat.

Maybe I'll get out of this after all, Gryph thought, realizing that, until now, he had accepted his imminent death. The beast slowed and turned its head from side to side, nostrils expanding and contracting as it sought its prey. The damage to the left nostril had healed. Whatever this thing was, it regenerated quickly.

He had to move silently; a task far easier imagined than executed on a floor littered with bone. He took a slow step back, foot landing with a *crunch*. The sound, so small, drew the attention of his enemy. The blinded beast turned to him, and a low growl rose from deep inside its chest.

Shit, Gryph thought. He grabbed what he guessed was a large femur and hurled it towards the back of the cavern, opposite the exit. The bone clattered against the wall, and the beast's head snapped towards the sound sniffing.

Gryph eased himself up onto a moss-covered boulder, struggling against the slick wetness and saw a path out. He grinned as the plan coalesced in his mind. *This will never work*, he thought. Then he jumped from the rock to the top of the closest mushroom. He swayed for a moment on the spongy cap, forcing himself to fight for balance. Then he leapt from one mushroom to another, and then to another, like that guy Mario from an ancient video game he and Brynn had played at his grandfather's house as a kid. The irony of playing a game in a world he'd accessed via a game was not lost on him.

He'd traversed the top of a dozen mushrooms before the beast tracked him. It howled and Gryph laughed in triumph. He knew he'd reach the other side of the cavern long before the beast reached him. All he had to do was leap the last few caps and sprint down the tunnel to whatever lay in store for him down its dim passage.

Then a large bone smashed into his back, knocking him forward and off the mushroom. He hit the ground with a *thud*, his breath forced from him like a fist to the gut. His face landed in a heap of moldy clothing, shards of bone and rusted metal. Blood welled up from a dozen tiny nicks along his face and neck. *Do they have tetanus in the Realms?* he wondered, but the sound of the beast's howl pushed the idiotic thought from his mind.

The monster charged. Gryph scrambled to his feet, rocks skittering underneath him. The beast's rage induced speed was tremendous and within mere seconds it was upon him. Gryph attempted to leap towards the entrance of the tunnel, remembering how stooped over and slow the beast had been as it emerged. If he could only reach it, perhaps he would be fast enough to get away.

A few feet from the entrance, the beast caught him by the ankle and dragged him backwards. A desperate howl of fear filled the room, and Gryph realized it had come from him and not the monster. He kicked with one foot, the heel of his boot smashing into the tender flesh of the beast's damaged eye.

The beast roared again and pulled Gryph back, tossing him against the base of a mushroom. Gryph gasped for breath as the beast charged, mouth open wide like the maw of hell.

On instinct, Gryph shot his left arm up to protect his face and the beast's mouth came down hard on the small buckler attached to Gryph's forearm. The beast chewed like a dog on a bone, all slobber and intensity. The wood and iron of the small shield splintered and cracked.

Gryph was about to die. Again, he was resigned to this fate. The human brain does odd things when it has accepted death. We examine our regrets and sometimes think on those we love. Gryph's thoughts drifted to Brynn and the look of fear on her face in her video. He wanted to see her again, her face split by a smile instead of darkened by fear and worry. He was going to die in a realm of magic and wonder and hadn't even had a chance to use magic.

You idiot, Gryph thought. He set his mind to casting *Animate Rope* and the fingers of his right hand, as if commanded by an outside force, moved through a series of motions. A cool rush of air shot down his arm as he grabbed the loop of rope. The rope throbbed with power, and Gryph tossed it at the creature.

The rope moved like a snake and coiled around the beast's legs. It slithered up its torso, pinning one arm against the creature's bulbous head. The rope was cheap and Gryph suspected that it would not last long, but he had bought himself a few moments.

He had seconds to act, so he pulled the dagger from his waist with his right hand. He thrust up and into the beast's open mouth, sinking the eight-inch blade into the roof of the creature's mouth just as its teeth bit into Gryph's forearm.

Gryph's *Health* bar dipped by 25%, and he screamed in agony. A prompt popped into his vision.

Debuff Added.
You are bleeding. *5pts of damage per second.*

Both elf and monster howled in pain. The beast opened its mouth and bellowed. The bottom row of teeth still skewered Gryph's wrist, trapping his arm. Time slowed. Gryph's life was now measured in seconds.

Gryph ordered the rope to coil tighter trying to pull the beast away from him, or at least making it harder for the beast to bite down again. The monster strained, fury and pain enhancing its strength.

Time slowed as Gryph heard the rope snapping. Rotten gobbets of flesh sprayed from the creature's teeth. Blood poured down Gryph's arm. A large tooth stuck through his wrist. Then he saw the sapphire glint from the ring on his finger.

Despite the agony of impending death, Gryph smiled. "Sayonara, fucker."

17

Gryph sent a mental command to the *Ring of Minor Air Shield* and in a fraction of a second a sphere of solid air exploded from the ring. It expanded and took the beast's head with it. Gryph thought he saw a look of stunned incomprehension cross the beast's face, but then the beast had no head and so, no face.

To Gryph's irritation, the shimmering sphere of air blinked out. The force of the beast's skull losing to the sphere of solid air had used up the shield's *Health* points. Gore, blood, brains and far too much mucus cascaded onto Gryph, followed by the beast's body. The weight hit him, causing ribs to crack and lungs to expel air. He lost another 10% of his *Health* and it continued to dip.

Gryph sensed the prompt in the corner of his vision and ignored it. *Yeah, debuffs added, I know.* He'd defeated the beast, but its leaking, fetid corpse was crushing the life out of him.

He was suffocating as his *Health* ticked downwards, approaching zero. He heaved and lifted a small edge of the beast's corpse. Just enough for him to wriggle to freedom.

He inhaled to satiate his burning lungs, but also inhaled the rancid slop that covered him. The taste and smell made him gag, and he coughed, rolled onto his side and vomited.

I am alive, he rejoiced before his thoughts once again dwelled on the idea that people entered this hellish place for fun. He pushed the thoughts away and leaned against the stalk of a mushroom and downed a *Health Potion*. Warmth pulsed into him as his *Health* filled. Closing his eyes, he inhaled. In the corner of his vision, his prompt indicator blinked.

You have earned Experience Points.
You have earned 15,600 XP for slaying a Baalgrath.

You have reached Level 2, 3, 4, and 5.
You have 24 (20 Base + 4 Godhead Bonus) unused Attribute Points. *You have 5 unused Perk Points.*

Your Skills have Levelled.
You have reached Level 2 in AIR MAGIC. *You have reached Level 3 in ANALYZE.*

That was a lot of prompts, Gryph would have smiled, except being covered in stinking gore was a mood killer. He now knew the disgusting beast was a baalgrath. He wasn't sure if it was because his *Analyze* skill had leveled or if it was a prompt given because he had slain the beast. Apparently killing a high-level creature enabled a basic identification. Convenient, if odd.

He stood and kicked the headless corpse several times. He knew it was stupid, but it felt amazing. After a few moments his rage calmed, and he laughed. He stared at the beast and used *Analyze*.

Baalgrath.
Level: 21. *Health: 320.* *Stamina: 520.* *Mana: 0.* *Spirit: 0.*

Baalgrath (Con't)

Baalgrath are not natural beasts. They are the product of ancient magical experimentation, which combined the ancient wyrmynn race of lizard people with mountain trolls. Baalgrath are not the most intelligent or cunning creatures but are tough and difficult to kill. Their extensive regeneration abilities allow them to heal nearly any wound in time. Baalgrath are omnivores, but they rather enjoy feasting on the smaller sentient races that live on the surface. Solitary creatures in the wild, their wyrmynn cousins often keep baalgrath as pets.

Strengths: Unknown.
Immunities: Unknown.
Weakness: Unknown.

Gryph noticed the metal collar around the thick, headless neck. The collar had a thick ring attached scored with metal-on-metal abrasions.

"This thing was a pet?" His eyes went to the tunnel heading further into the Barrow. "Shit." What lay down that tunnel? Wyrmynn? Whatever the heck those were? Gryph sighed in resignation knowing it was his only option.

He retrieved his throwing knives and the tip of his broken spear from the corpse. Maybe it could be repaired. He suspected that magic items were not common in the Realms. He wiped the blood from the knives when he got a prompt.

You have harvested Baalgrath Blood.

This rare and valuable ingredient has many uses in both Alchemy and Crafting. You suspect it could make a Potion of Health Regeneration and other unidentified effects.

You also get the sense it could craft an item that increases Health regeneration and other unidentified effects.

Level: 1.
Skill Type: Active.

The Realms are full of amazing ingredients that Alchemists, Crafters and Artificers can use to create wondrous potions, healing salves and deadly poisons.
The Harvest skill allows you to identify and harvest these ingredients.
50% chance to harvest ingredients. Every ingredient has four or more effects.

At the Base Tier you are able to identify the Base Effect.

"Sweet," Gryph exclaimed as he pulled his *Alchemy Kit* from his inventory. It was a leather box the size of a briefcase. It contained a variety of alchemical equipment and a hundred small vials he guessed were for collecting and storing ingredients.

He pulled a pump used to extract liquids and attached an empty vial to the end. He spent the next ten minutes siphoning the thick green black blood from the baalgrath's corpse. His 50% chance to harvest was annoying as he failed half the time. He had collected a nice haul. He even leveled *Harvest* which increased his success rate by 2%.

You have reached Level 2 in HARVEST.

Gryph considered trying to make a few potions with the kit. Then reconsidered. He didn't know what ingredients combined well with others. Surviving the huge beast only to drink a poison cocktail of one's own making was not a dignified way to go.

He stuffed the kit back into his inventory, again amazed by the weight and space reducing powers of his satchel. On Earth it would be the greatest invention of all time, but here in the Realms they gave it to every Tom, Dick and Sally. It was time to finish looting. If he were to survive facing the wyrmynn he needed better weapons.

He pulled a torn and tattered cape from an ancient
skeleton of some knight errant that had faced the baalgrath
and lost. Like everything in the cave, it glittered with a fine
layer of mushroom spores. Gryph wiped most of the gore and
goo from him, but he now sparkled like a woo party girl on a
whoop it up night.

He spent the next half an hour gathering everything of use
he could find in the cavern.

You have found Treasure.

24 gold coins.
34 silver coins.
10 bronze coins.

3 Minor Potion of Healing.
2 Minor Potion of Stamina.
1 Minor Potion of Mana.

You have been awarded a Fine Steel Spear.

(Staves/Spears)
Item Class: Non-magical.
Item Category: N/A.
Base Damage: 10.

A finely crafted steel spear.

You have found Padded Leather Helm.

(Light Armor)
Item Class: Non-magical.
Item Category: NA.
AC Bonus: +5.

*A standard padded leather helmet provides decent protection from
attack.*

The loot thrilled him, but there was one final task. A task he was dreading. He walked up to the armless corpse of the small man.

Gnome Corpse.

Gnomes are small humanoids whose love for mischief, song and tinkering is famous, or infamous. Gregarious and jovial, gnomes are natural wanderers. They are fond of adventure and will take up difficult and dangerous tasks if they believe the rewards will benefit them or their clan.

The description of the small gnome tugged at Gryph's heart. Nobody deserved the fate this little guy had suffered. After a moment's hesitation, Gryph searched the body, hoping to find something that told him the gnome's identity. He found a sack of coins, a beautifully crafted dagger, a diamond ring on a chain, and a small book.

You have found Treasure.

56 gold coins.
65 silver coins.
12 bronze coins.

You have found an Ordonian Ice Dagger.

(Short Blade)
(Air/Water Magic)

Item Class: *Base*
Item Category: *Active.*
Base Dmg: *7 (+2 Base Item Bonus).*

Ordonian Ice Dagger (Con't).

Active Powers.
Power (1): Cold Strike. 1 point of damage per point of mana spent.
Power (2): 10% chance to freeze an opponent for 10 seconds, paralyzing them.

Mana Limit: 5%
Cool Down: 5 minutes.

This dagger was forged using a piece of enchanted ice from the northernmost reaches of Korynn. It is a traditional weapon of Ordonian chieftains and is on rare occasions given to outsiders who have performed a great service to the tribe.

You have found Gnomish Ring of Promise.

(Life Magic)
Item Class: Base.
Item Category: Passive.

Passive Powers.
Power (1): +2 to Charisma.
Power (2): +50 to Health.

This ring is one half of a pair given to two Gnome lovers who have committed to spend their lives together. As long as the commitment is honored, the powers stay active. If one lover dies, the other ring is reduced to half power. If the fallen lover's ring is returned, the surviving lover will get the power of both rings.

You have found Jebbis's Journal.

A basic leather journal used by the people of the Realms to record the events of their lives.

Gryph took a deep breath and opened the pages of the

journal.

Dearest Rehla,

It has been barely a week since we parted ways, but the caravan has already reached the mountains. We will traverse Long Pass and then we will be in the desert. I miss you dearly, but I will not lie and say that seeing the endless sands and the ancient pyramids of the Aegyptians has me more excited than I have been since the day you agreed to bear my ring. Laughter and jokes fill the air around the caravan. As you would expect of any group filled with so many gnomes. Even Thaaardik the mountain dwarf and Zelyanna that stuck up wood elf have been surprisingly agreeable. I must go now my love. Tifala is insisting I teach cousin Wick how to dance. I understand why you dislike him but trust me he is family and a misunderstood soul.

My Heart is Your Heart,
Jebbis

Gryph read several other entries, each increasing the tear in his heart. This gnome, this Jebbis was a beloved husband who had left his love to build a better life for them both, but here, in the depths of this accursed Barrow, he had lost his life. Gryph flipped to the last entry and forced himself to read.

Dearest Rehla,

I have little time. It has been nearly a month since we became trapped in this evil place. Wick discovered this foul dungeon in an old tome. He insisted it was a place rife with treasures, but all we have found is evil and death. It is no normal dungeon my love. This Barrow is alive. It sounds insane, but the walls and the tunnels, sometimes they move and shift during the night. And the beasts. It's their eyes, Rehla. Foul and primal, but sometimes they look upon us with a keen and nefarious intelligence. I've become separated from the rest of the group and I suspect that soon I will be dead. My greatest regret is that you will feel the moment I am gone. You will feel it and I fear it will destroy you. I am sorry, my love. This will be my last entry.

I Love You,
Jebbis

Gryph held back a tear, and then saw a message meant for him, scrawled inside the back cover in a ragged and rushed hand.

To Whoever Shall Find This Journal and This Ring,

I implore you to find my kin, my cousin Wick and bring my journal and my ring to him. He will get them back to my love if he is able. I do not know who you are or if you even exist, but I have faith in the goodness of the gods and hope you can help this small part of me find my way home. If Wick is also dead, please consider making the journey to Erram, my village, where you will find my beautiful Rehla.

Thank You,
Jebbis

You have been offered the Quest Soothe a Broken Heart.

Two lovers have been torn apart by death and uncertainty. Deliver this ring and this journal to the gnome known as Wick. Or if Wick is also dead, bring it to the gnome woman Rehla in the village of Erram.

Difficulty: Moderate to Difficult.
Reward: Unknown.
XP: 5,000 - 10,000.

Without a word, Gryph accepted the quest. He placed the ring and the journal into his inventory. Then he buried Jebbis.

"I hate this fucking universe," Gryph muttered.

18

Gryph returned to the pile of loot he had collected right before the baalgrath attack and equipped all the armor. His AC leapt up to 38. He even felt a bit more solid. He also had *Attribute Points* to spend.

The points he put into *Intelligence* had already paid off, but the baalgrath had only landed a few hits and nearly killed him. Perhaps it was time to increase his physical prowess.

He put eight points into *Constitution* and eight more in *Dexterity* and was rewarded with leaps in *Health, Stamina*, AC bonus and speed. He decided to put three more into *Strength*, both for the extra damage capabilities and the increase in *Stamina* Who knew when he'd find a place to offload his loot.

He thought about dumping the last five points into *Intelligence* but decided to keep them in reserve instead. His magical capabilities were still limited, and the Army trained him to always keep something in reserve for unexpected situations.

Gryph - Level 5	Stats
High Elf (El'Edryn) Deity: None Experience: 15,775 Next Level: 7,225	Health: 154 Stamina: 156 Mana: 145 Spirit: 126
Attributes	**Gifts**
Strength: 23 Constitution: 25 Dexterity: 28 (25 +3 Bonus) Intelligence: 16 Wisdom: 10	Health Regeneration: +25% Mana Regeneration: +25% Night Vision: 120 Ft. Master of Tongues

Gryph smiled. He was progressing nicely for a dude who had no damn clue what he was doing. He hated to admit it, even in the privacy of his own head, but he missed Lex. The banner AI turned grumpy NPC priest may have been obnoxious, but he knew his stuff.

Now it was on to his *Perk Points*.

It appeared that each skill had six tiers, and they each required a specific level in the requisite skill before that tier becomes available. Each tier opened up better perks.

Tier Levels.

Base: Level 1.
Apprentice: Level 20.
Journeyman: Level 50.
Master: Level 75.
Grandmaster: Level 100.
Divine: Level 101+.

Based on his current skill set he liked the idea of focusing on spears. He opened the *Staves/Spears Perk Tree* to see what kind of goodies it offered. There were three branches. He focused on each in turn.

Staves/Spears Perk Tree.

----- Impale -----
An aggressive attack that can be initiated upon a successful attack. Impale does 2X damage with a spear. Impaled opponents cannot move or counterattack for 5 seconds.

----- Stun -----
An aggressive attack with a staff that can be initiated upon a successful attack. Stun does 1.5X damage and prevents an opponent from moving or counterattacking for 10 seconds.

----- Quick Strike -----
An aggressive attack with a staff or spear that can be initiated upon a successful attack. Quick Strike has a chance to land a second attack for the same amount of damage as the first.

Staves/Spears Perk Tree (Con't).
----- Parry -----
Staves and spears provide good defense. When an attacker lands a blow, Parry can be initiated. If successful, Parry blocks the attack resulting in no damage.

The *Stamina* cost to use the perks was high, but their intelligent application could be the difference between life and death. He also noted that there were six distinct tiers to each perk tree and that anything above his current Tier was unavailable. He guessed that he'd need to get to the appropriate level in each skill to hit the next tier, but when he did, oh boy, would it be worth it.

All the branches sounded amazing but *Impale* and *Parry* were the ones that truly caught Gryph's eye. He dumped one *Perk Point* into each and admired the increased potency they brought to the skill.

Staves/Spears Perk Tree.			
Tier	Impale	Quick Strike	Parry
Base	20%	15%	20%
Apprentice	30%	25%	30%
Journeyman	40%	35%	40%
Master	50%	45%	50%
Grandmaster	60%	55%	60%
Divine	75%	75%	75%

He looked through his other skills and while all of them would be useful. He knew he had to get the most bang for his buck. His eyes gleamed as he read the perks for *Dodge*.

DODGE PERKS.

----- Counter-Attack-----
Upon a successful Dodge the percentage listed is the chance to land a Counter-Attack. This ignores all other attack bonuses and defenses. Damage is applied as normal. The weapon skill used must be equal to or greater than the opponents Dodge skill.

----- Enter Stealth -----
Upon a successful Dodge the percentage listed is the chance to enter Stealth. The user's Stealth skill must be of a higher level than the opponents Perception skill to enter Stealth.

----- Push Off -----
When Dodge is successful, a specialty attack that provides separation from the attacker.

Gryph dumped a *Perk Point* into *Counter-Attack* and grinned at the possibilities. He loved *Enter Stealth* as well, but at his current tier the percentage chance was so small he didn't think it was worth the cost. Yet, at later levels, he could load the branch with points and quickly power up. In the end he put another point into *Push Off.* Sometimes the best defense was distancing oneself from an enemy. *Push Off* could literally put space between him and death.

Dodge Perk Tree.			
Tier	Counter-Attack	Enter Stealth	Push Off
Base	20%	15%	5 feet
Apprentice	30%	25%	10 feet
Journeyman	40%	35%	15 feet
Master	50%	45%	20 feet
Grandmaster	60%	55%	25 feet
Divine	75%	75%	50 feet

This left him with a single *Perk Point* to spend. *Light Armor, Air Magic* and *Small Blades* all had their appeal, but it was *Stealth* that made him feel like a kid on Christmas morning.

His real-world experience had taught him that being upon an enemy before they knew you were there was an amazing advantage. He greedily read the perks.

STEALTH PERKS.

----- **Backstab** -----
A sneak attack launched while Stealthed. The attack automatically succeeds and does multiple times damages depending on the tier. The attackers Stealth skill must be higher than the opponents Perception and Dodge skill to land this attack.

----- **Invisibility** -----
While in Stealth the percentage chance to become invisible. While invisible a character can still use Stealth to initiate a Backstab or other attack, but the attack nullifies Invisibility.

----- **Speed** -----
A character can move at a percentage of their normal movement speed while in Stealth. The normal max is 20%.

He debated both *Backstab* and *Speed*. Each was incredibly powerful. An automatic hit that did twice as much damage sounded fantastic even though Gryph didn't think of himself as an assassin. Moral qualms aside, the *Speed* perk was likely to be far more useful, if less sexy. He dumped his last point into *Speed*.

Stealth Perk Tree.			
Tier	Backstab	Invisibility	Speed
Base	2X	15%	50%
Apprentice	3X	25%	60%
Journeyman	4X	35%	70%
Master	5X	45%	80%
Grandmaster	6X	55%	90%
Divine	10X	75%	2X

Satisfied with his choices and feeling like a guy who'd just spent all his Amazon gift cards, Gryph closed out the perk sheet.

19

Life is a stubborn force and even here, in the Barrow, it thrived. Perhaps thrived was too strong a word. It would be more accurate to say even here beings of all kinds clung to life. From mosses to rats, creepers to insects, wyrmynn to human, life was everywhere. One just had to know where to look.

Wick looked down from the hidden outcropping nearly fifty feet above the floor of the large chamber. From this high up, the reptilian humanoids scuttling around their settlement seemed no bigger threat than an anthill. But Wick knew differently. Wyrmynn had long been a scourge in the darker realms under the surface of Korynn. He remembered tales told to him as a child. "Behave, Wick, or the wyrmynn will take you away," his mother always said.

Wick had learned that no matter how badly he behaved, the wyrmynn never came for him. That had just egged on his bad behavior, heightening his youthful arrogance and smugness.

Perhaps this is Mother's revenge, Wick thought. The idea that he would likely never see his mother's head of purple hair again filled him with sorrow. *You sure screwed your life up, bud.* He gripped his staff in white-knuckled hands as thoughts drifted to Tifala and the rest of his group. He hadn't just screwed up his own life this time. *I'll get us out of this, Tif.*

He wished he believed his inner voice. Something had changed. Everything in the Barrow knew it. A surge of malevolence had risen, covering the entire area in an oily miasma of evil. Something had awoken. Were the legends true?

The wyrmynn sensed it, too. Their village, if a collection of muck covered tents, fire pits and cesspools could be called a village, had been a hive of frantic activity all morning. Random outbursts of violence, so common in the cold-blooded creature's world, had increased. Wick adjusted the lenses of his *maker goggles* and the largest wyrmynn came into sharp focus.

The huge reptile hissed at his fellows. Wick could sense the massive creature's fear, and it knotted up Wick's guts. Thick muscles rippled under the wyrmynn's skin, and he towered over his fellows, reaching nearly six feet in height. On his back, he carried a huge two-handed sword of questionable quality but obvious deadliness. A mouthful of sharp teeth barked orders to his cowering underlings. The large wyrmynn snapped a taloned hand out and grabbed his smaller brethren by the throat.

Wick did not understand the beast's words. There was no way he could know their language. Until recently, the wyrmynn had been a myth. Wick knew one thing, though. Something was happening, and it was bad.

The wyrmynn leader, who Wick dubbed Scarface due to the jagged white line that bisected his face from the fringe of horns to his mouth, barked orders with a whip snap of his tail. He pushed and shoved his people into a line near the entrance to the passageway leading further down into the Barrow.

A welcoming committee, Wick thought. *What are they welcoming?*

Wick felt it long before he saw it. A chill crept into him, starting from his bones and flowing outward. The hair on his arms stood on end as if his body was desperate to expel the unnatural sensation.

Scarface felt it too and a low, guttural bark erupted from him. The wyrmynn knelt as one. Even Scarface lowered his head in supplication. Wick's heart thundered in his chest as darkness flowed from the tunnel. The flowing blackness moved with purpose and intelligence, swallowing any nearby light. The Barrow was always dark, but this was something altogether new.

Wick adjusted the lenses again as a shadowy form emerged from the tunnel. Spectral energies flowed around the creature. The oily black of *Death Magic* mixed with a silver shimmer that Wick did not recognize. His heart jumped at this. *I've seen most types of magic*, he thought. *So, what is that?*

The cloaked form stopped and said "rise" in the common

tongue. The voice sounded like old bones scraping together. Scarface shot to his feet. He was much taller than the apparition before him, but there was no doubt who was in charge.

"Something new has entered my Barrow," the apparition said. "You will find him and bring him to me." As the apparition spoke it walked up and down the line of kneeling wyrmynn, small squeaks of fear and involuntary jumps and spasms trailed in its wake.

"Yes, master," Scarface hissed, his tongue struggling to form the words so unsuited to his physiology. "I will send my best warriors."

My Barrow? Wick thought. *This is the Barrow King?*

The apparition paused and stared down upon one of the wyrmynn, a wyrmynn scout. It lightly caressed the side of the scaly creature's face and Wick felt the beast's fear. The bone white hand eased the wyrmynn's chin up to face it and a tendril of silvery energy erupted from the shrouded hood of shadows. The energy speared the wyrmynn's mouth and its body stiffened. Globules of white energy gilded by sheens of silver flowed from the beast back into the apparition.

Are my maker goggles malfunctioning? Wick wondered. His father had spared no expense on Wick's Day of Choosing gift. His father knew, as did the rest of the clan, that Wick would follow in his footsteps and become a Master Tinker. The look of betrayal on his face when Wick announced he would pursue the path of *Chthonic Magic* was one he would never erase from his mind's eye. His arrogance that day led him on the erratic path to the very spot he now stood.

Below, the apparition finished what Wick could only guess had been some kind of feeding, and the corpse of the scout collapsed in a heap. The husk fell to the ground like old tinder and the lizard folk trembled.

"Find this newcomer and bring him to me," the apparition said, turning to Scarface.

"Yes, massster," Scarface said, his tongue battling his teeth as it forced the words from his mouth.

"Do not fail me," the shadow said.

It was then that Wick saw the tendril of energy, silver mixed with black and white pulsing from the apparition back

110

into the tunnel that led deep into the bowels of the Barrow. The energies drained from the wyrmynn were being siphoned somewhere else, to something else. Soon the pulses slowed and then stopped altogether.

The shadows surging around the apparition dissipated revealing a bone skeleton. The skeleton trembled for a moment before collapsing into a clattering pile. Whatever malevolence had animated the ancient bones had faded.

With a relieved exhalation of air, Scarface stood and nudged the pile of bone with a tentative foot. Satisfied that it was just a pile of bone, Scarface hissed at his people, and the entire tribe rushed into motion.

Wick pulled the goggles up to his forehead and exhaled, not realizing he'd been holding his breath. He needed to get back to Tifala. Whatever was happening, whatever the Barrow King wanted, no good would come of it.

Wick eased back into the tunnel behind him and gripped his staff. He closed his eyes. He spoke in barely heard murmurs as magical energy surged inside of him as he began a summoning.

Pulses and shimmers split the air as a rift to another place opened. Wick formed an image in his mind. The rift expanded to the deep crimson color of blood and a small demonling stepped from the portal.

The imp stood a foot high. Its skin was the color of a furious sunburn infused with veins of crimson fire. Its body was rail thin, all ribs and gangly limbs. A prehensile tail slid back and forth, cutting the air with knifelike movements. Atop an unnaturally thin neck sat a triangular shaped head. The head was mostly mouth, and the mouth held more teeth than logic suggested was natural. Beady, hungry eyes glared up at Wick.

"Watch the wyrmynn camp," Wick commanded with precise words. "Stay quiet and do not move from this spot until they move out. Then come to me and tell me all you have seen. Only then will I release you."

The imp hissed in annoyance and held a hand out. Wick pulled a slab of meat from his pack and passed it to the imp.

"Human?" the imp said with a hopeful screech.

"Rat," Wick said.

The imp's face went from joy to anger and it spat venomous words of the chthonic realm at Wick. Wick ignored the imp's ire. He had dealt with this foul creature on many occasions.

"Xeg want a something more tasty."

"The bargain is sealed, Xegreb Kurhrn Zaqaai," Wick said, forcing the imp's true name past his lips with a sneer. The language of the chthonic realm was not meant for mortal tongues. Speaking the words always made Wick's stomach surge with acid. "Now do as I command."

The imp hissed at its true name but nodded in assent. It shoved the rat meat into its mouth and tore a chunk off, swallowing it nearly whole. It took a seat on a small rock and looked down upon the wyrmynn camp. With one last glance, Wick pulled his cloak around him and moved into the tunnel.

"Xeg maybe taste gnome soon," the demonling muttered to itself as Wick disappeared. "Roasted. Grilled. Raw," the imp said, a forked tongue snaking from his mouth to pick bits of rat flesh from his teeth.

Wick dipped into *Stealth*, ears straining for any sound. It would take some time for the wyrmynn to get anywhere near his current location, but he wasn't stupid enough to drop his guard, ever. He might stumble across a wyrmynn hunting party, run afoul of an umber beast or get caught in a trap. And the Barrow held worse things than wyrmynn.

It was just over a month since Wick and his group had first become trapped in the Barrow. What started as an adventuring group of six was down to two. Wick blamed himself for the deaths. He'd been the one who found the ancient map among the brick-a-brack in the mage's lair. A few of the others weren't convinced that the Barrow was any different from any other run-of-the-mill dungeon.

Wick's mind drifted back to the fateful conversation that led him here. Led his group to death.

"If it is as rich as the map claims, won't it be picked clean by now?" Zelyanna, a regal wood elf archer said in her melodic voice.

"Not if it's been lost these last thousand years," Tifala countered. "It used to be on a major trade route near Ryneeria, here." Tifala pointed to the Barrow's location on a map.

"Never heard of it," Hugarn, a half orc barbarian said.

"I'd be surprised if you had," Wick said.

"You calling me dumb?" Hugarn said with threat in his tone.

"No, he isn't," Tifala said, a hand resting on the massive warrior's arm. "The city was razed by zealots who worshipped one of the New Gods. If nobody remembers the city, it is highly unlikely that they'd remember the Barrow."

Hugarn nodded and his anger abated.

"I dislike entering a dungeon so ancient. Who knows what devils may call it home," Thaardik, the mountain dwarf priest countered.

"Isn't that the point?" Jebbis said. "According to the map it was home to a wizard known only as the Barrow King. The only reference to the name is in an 8,000-year-old text."

"I don't put much stock in books," Hugarn grumbled.

Wick held back a snarky response. Hugarn was more than twice his height and he'd seen the barbarian slay a dozen enemies all by himself. He was a raging inferno that could not be contained, only pointed. Wick was not dumb enough to point the barbarian at himself.

"You remember the last wizard lair we plundered?" Wick said. Everyone nodded, and their eyes filled with gleams of greed. Hugarn even hefted the axe he'd acquired on that dive. "Well, that dungeon was barely 400 years old." The greedy looks multiplied. "This will be our biggest payday ever."

The group agreed with little more persuasion.

So far, they'd found very little treasure, yet quite a bit of death. Only Tifala and he still lived. Wick had been right about one thing. The Barrow was unlike any other dungeon they'd ever encountered. Once they'd entered, they learned that there was no way out. It wasn't a dungeon so much as a prison.

20

Gryph descended deeper into the Barrow. He dreaded the entire idea, but he knew sometimes you need to go down to go up. He reeked like week old roadkill and despite his Stats being at 100%, he didn't feel much better.

Low-level light infused everything. His high elf racial ability *Night Vision* amplified ambient light, a magical version of the night vision goggles he'd used on Earth. True darkness would likely blind him, but iridescent moss spotted the walls like streetlights on a lonely road providing ample light to fuel the ability.

The tunnel was large and descended at a comfortable angle. Every few feet he had to step over a shard of bone, a reminder of the beast that had called this place home. Ten minutes later his *Stamina* bar started blinking. His constant use of *Stealth* was draining his reserves quicker than it was regenerating.

Gryph continued downward. He brought up his map and saw it gave him an advantage. The map generated the area within the range of his vision. Not a line of sight, mind you, but a sphere of sight. Details illuminated the explored areas. The unexplored areas remained shrouded in shadows but gave hints of what was to come, like a virtual fog that retreated with each step.

Now, if I can only find a full map of this place. Accurate intel was often the difference between life and death on Earth. The Realms would be no different, Gryph thought, making a mental note to search fallen foes for maps.

He hurried down the hallway with renewed confidence, almost letting *Stealth* drop. As he approached the junction he paused, ducking behind a boulder. Something was coming from the right-hand tunnel. The confined space made fighting with a spear difficult at best, so he eased the long-shafted weapon to the floor and drew his daggers. If he needed it, the spear was within reach.

He fidgeted, spinning the daggers in his hands like a gunslinger. He slowed his breathing and waited. A few moments later, he could sense more than see a shadow pause in the darkness at the edge of his *Night Vision*. Gryph froze, willing every muscle in his body to pause. *Was this what seeing a Stealthed opponent looked like?*

Eyes passed over him several times as the moments stretched to eons. Then a small figure emerged into the dim light of the junction. It was a small man, maybe three and a half feet tall. He was wiry and gripped a short staff topped with a red jewel. A crazed frock of electric blue hair plumed upwards at an improbable angle. Fierce gold hued eyes scanned the area. Gryph used *Analyze*.

Gnome.

Level: Unknown.
Health: ?
Stamina: ?
Mana: ?
Spirit: ?

This is a gnome.

Strengths: Unknown.
Immunities: Unknown.
Weakness: Unknown.

Gryph's thoughts drifted to the gnome he'd buried. Was this gnome his kin? Was this Wick? How would he react to the news of his cousin's death? Would he shoot the messenger? *Analyze* had given him no information, so the gnome was at least level sixteen. After weighting all the options, Gryph decided it was better to stay solo and safe than risk exposure and enmity.

After a few tense moments, the gnome crept past Gryph and down the other tunnel. Gryph waited a full five minutes and was about to follow the small man when the quiet shuffle of many feet held him up. He checked his *Stamina* and ducked into *Stealth*.

The shuffling noise grew louder, accompanied by an exchange of irritated hisses. Gryph eased the daggers to the ground at his side and drew two throwing knives.

Several large figures emerged into the junction. They were bipedal reptilians as if a Komodo dragon had decided that walking around on all fours was boring and decided to stand upright, wear rags and carry rusted weapons. He used *Analyze*.

Wyrmynn Scout.

Level: 6.

Wyrmynn are medium sized reptilian humanoids. They hate most other sentient races and travel in rigidly hierarchical packs. Their society prizes strength and violence over all things. They often serve more powerful creatures as battle fodder.

Strengths: Unknown.
Immunities: Unknown.
Weakness: Unknown.

One scout dropped to all fours and sniffed the ground. Gryph eased further back into the darkness. *Shit. No way he won't be able to smell me.* Gryph thought, before remembering he was slathered in baalgrath filth.

The wyrmynn's eyes went wide in fear and it barked and hissed to his fellows. The others cast nervous glances in Gryph's direction. *Analyze* revealed all eight ranged from levels six to eleven. The odds were not in his favor, so he remained hidden.

"Jyrrysssis erth un baalgrath," the lead wyrmynn [*Wyrmynn Scout; Level 6*] said pointing in Gryph's direction.

The leader [*Wyrmynn Skirmisher; Level 11*] cuffed the smaller scout, pointing to the heavy iron chain at his belt. "Ytthiss wergal control ferdyss."

The wyrmynn argued among themselves, and Gryph realized he could now understand bits of their language.

"Gthissgry which way did thyyrrdss?" the leader said in an angry voice.

"I thssdrr tell," the scout said. The leader smashed an iron clad fist into the side of the scout's head. The scout cowered and then pointed the direction the gnome had taken. "This way."

Gryph realized that the more words he heard the more he understood the wyrmynn. It had to be the *Master of Tongues* ability. *Will I be able to understand any language I hear?* The idea was intriguing and Gryph considered the tactical uses of such knowledge.

The wyrmynn continued down the tunnel the gnome had taken. The debate raging in Gryph's mind triggered a quest.

You have been offered the Quest Gnomish Team Up.

You have discovered that a troop of wyrmynn is stalking a lone gnome. Team up with the gnome to defeat the pack of lizard folk.

Difficulty: Moderate.
Reward: Unknown.
XP: 5,000.

Gryph was certain that the way out of the Barrow lay to the right but knew that death stalked the gnome. A few moments of indecision battled inside Gryph's mind, before he followed after the wyrmynn.

After several minutes of quick but stealthy progress, Gryph heard the sounds of battle coming from around an upcoming bend. He rushed forward and peered around the corner to see a large cavern. The wyrmynn had caught up with the gnome and had him surrounded.

The body of one wyrmynn lay crumpled on the ground. Smoke spiraled from a fiery exit crater in the creature's back. The other wyrmynn were stabbing inwards with their spears and swords. The gnome was agile and avoided the strikes while sending bursts of black-red fire from his right hand and parrying strikes with the staff in his left.

One wyrmynn went down screaming as dark flame enveloped its head. Eyes boiled and scaled skin sloughed off its face. The sound and the smell were horrendous and the other wyrmynn backed away in fear.

Another volley of fire flew from the gnome's hand. This time at the wyrmynn leader, who raised the buckler on his forearm preventing the flames from finding its mark. The gnome's hand glowed again as he prepped another spell. The wyrmynn leader thrust his spear forward, catching the gnome with a glancing blow to the side. The energy around the gnome's hand faded.

Gryph knew the foul beasts would soon overwhelm the gnome. It was time to decide. With an irritated grunt, Gryph pulled his last remaining loop of rope from his inventory and tossed it towards the closest enemy [Wyrmynn Skirmisher; Level 6]. He then cast *Animate Rope* and drew a few throwing knives.

The rope slithered with the silent grace of a hunting viper as it eased up behind the wyrmynn. On Gryph's mental command, it surged up and around the reptile's legs. The startled creature yelped in surprise as the rope took him down and constricted. The spell didn't do much damage, but it immobilized the wyrmynn. Hopefully, the loop would hold the weaker opponent longer than it had the baalgrath.

Gryph stood and threw both throwing knives at the second wyrmynn [*Wyrmynn Scout; Level 5*]. Both found their mark and sunk into the wyrmynn's neck. Their anatomy may be nothing like humans, but he figured no creature enjoyed metal blades sunk into their spine.

His aim was true, and a *Critical Hit* notification popped into the corner of his vision. The wyrmynn went down. Gryph hefted his spear and rushed forwards. He used *Impale* on another wyrmynn [Wyrmynn Skirmisher; Level 7], but the creature turned and swung a large sword at him. Gryph activated *Dodge* and jumped to the side, narrowly avoiding the strike.

The wyrmynn's sword sped in a downward arc. Gryph activated *Parry* and blocked the successful attack. He quickly

Counter Attacked and landed a blow to the beast's side. Green blood flowed from the wound and the creature grunted. Its sword lashed out again and Gryph dropped his spear and rolled, lest he lose his head. Gryph came back to his feet, drawing his daggers from his waist. He crouched in a defensive position and waited for the wyrmynn to make a move.

Evidently the creatures were not as dumb as they looked. The wyrmynn took advantage of the reach of its sword and eased back into a defensive position. Gryph feigned left, then right and surged forward, landing a glancing blow on the wyrmynn's sword arm.

The other wyrmynn noticed Gryph's arrival. The wyrmynn leader ordered his subordinates to rush Gryph as he returned his attention to the gnome. The gnome did not sit idle but used the brief distraction to leap and climb onto a raised ledge. He ducked behind a boulder and disappeared from view.

"Damn coward," Gryph bellowed. He could not believe the gall of the gnome. He was only alive because Gryph had been stupid enough to engage the wyrmynn. Now he'd been betrayed, abandoned and left to fight three wyrmynn with only a pair of daggers.

"Great," Gryph muttered and braced for the attack. The wyrmynn rushed forward with no tactical sense, emboldened by the superior numbers.

Gryph activated his *Ring of Minor Air Shield* and a bubble of solid air formed around him with a snap. The first wyrmynn smashed into the invisible shield and bounced off, shock crossing his face as he fell back in a heap.

The others hacked at the shell and it soon began to blink. Gryph prepared himself. Soon, the shield would fail. With a final, frantic blink, the shield disappeared with a *pop*. The first wyrmynn was upon him in seconds.

Gryph sidestepped the lizard man's attack, spinning past the stabbing spear and slashing down with his left-hand dagger. He felt the metal bite into the creature's calf, and it went down with a scream, hamstrung.

Gryph turned and parried a sword strike from the second. The jarring thud of metal on metal forced Gryph down to one knee. Damn these things were strong. The wyrmynn pulled back for another strike and Gryph decided he needed to be elsewhere.

He rolled forward and past his foe and flipped the dagger in his right hand while spinning. The blade now faced downward and Gryph used his momentum to thrust the blade into the beast's back. It sunk deep with a crunch of bone. Gryph twisted the blade and yanked it free. He felt the creature's spinal column snap. The wyrmynn went down. It wasn't dead, but it wouldn't be getting back on its feet anytime soon.

Gryph got to his feet just in time to lock his daggers and parry a crushing blow from the leader's massive two-handed sword. The force caused Gryph to collapse to the ground again, and the wyrmynn brought his knee up into Gryph's face. His *Health* dropped by a third as he felt his nose break. The blow caused his eyes to water and his vision grew blurry.

Debuff Added.

You have received a Disorienting Blow.

Attack and Defense reduced by 25% for 1 minute.
Unable to cast spells for 1 minute.

In a panic, Gryph's mind scrambled for a way out of his situation. The two-handed sword connected again, and his *Health* dropped below half. Gryph needed space and activated *Push Off.* He climbed onto the wyrmynn's chest and pushed off with both feet, flipping head over heels and landing about five feet back. The wyrmynn sprawled onto the ground, taking minor damage.

Gryph pulled a *Health Potion* from his pack and went to drink it when another wyrmynn threw a spear at Gryph. He dodged the hasty throw, but the potion fell from his hand. *I need to up my Health,* he thought, forcing his panic down.

With no other idea he dumped his last five *Attribute Points* into *Constitution,* hoping the small increase they provided would allow him to survive long enough to escape. His *Constitution* shot up to 29 and not only did his total *Health*

120

bump up by eight points, his entire *Health* bar refilled.

What the hell? A life hack, Gryph thought to himself amazed. *I wonder if it works for my other stats as well?* Unfortunately, he wasn't able to test that theory since he had no more points. He grinned to himself, laughing at the absurdity of being unhappy that he was healthy. Already the game mechanics were messing with his mindset.

He had no time to brag as the wyrmynn he'd knocked over was back and swinging. Gryph staggered and fell back onto all fours to avoid the attack. The dagger in his right hand skittered away, knocked free by the fall to the ground. He tugged a throwing knife from the bandolier and tossed it at the leader's face. Gryph's aim was true, but a quick swipe of the leader's sword deflected the knife before it found purchase. Gryph had just witnessed the *Parry* perk used against him.

The leader grinned and rushed forward. Gryph knew he was in desperate trouble but would not go down without a fight. He feigned left with his dagger and spun right, his right palm connecting with the reptile's ribs right below his armpit. Bones cracked, and the leader grunted, but he still managed a one-handed swing of his massive blade.

Gryph could smell the rust of the blade as it buzzed over his head, missing him by a few hairs. His defensive move caused him to fall onto his backside again. He held his one dagger out in front of him and almost chuckled at the lame deterrent. The wyrmynn outright laughed and brandished its two-handed sword.

One of the other wyrmynn rushed Gryph, but a barked order stopped the creature in its tracks. A strange quiet settled over the cavern as Gryph stumbled to his feet. The blood flow from his nose had slowed and the debuff clock ticked closer to zero. *What is he doing?* Gryph wondered.

"Hold. Surround him. Then we will attack from all sides," the leader said in its odd, guttural language. Gryph's eyes widened. A moment later, the leader's did as well. "You understand me? How is this possible?"

Gryph knew every moment he kept his enemies off balance was another minute he got to live. "Because any simpleton could master your language. All you do is grunt and hiss and spit and drool," he said in wyrmynn.

The leader grinned a terrifying explosion of sharp teeth and chuckled. "Surface folk. You always underestimate us. My kind walked the surface of this world long before you warm-bloods. And we will reign long after the sun goes dark and you are all gone."

As the leader talked, his subordinates surrounded Gryph. The one he'd used *Animate Rope* on was back up, his bonds cut by one of his fellows. The beast tossed the rope on top of Gryph's lost spear. An idea popped into Gryph's head, and he checked the status of *Animate Rope*. He had a mere ten-seconds of cooldown left. Time for more distracting talk.

"Blah, blah, blah, we are mighty wyrmynn and we used to rule the roost, but then the meanie weenie warm bloods kicked our asses and made us live in a hole in the ground. Wah, wah, poor us," Gryph said in the wyrmynn's own tongue. The effort was almost painful and Gryph feigned a coughing fit. "Damn your language is uglier than you are."

The leader grinned wider, his head split near in two and he barked a horrific laugh. Gryph's right hand twisted and contorted as he cast *Animate Rope* again. A low chanting hum surged. *What the hell is that?* Gryph tried to find the source of the sound, but it was a barely audible hum and the cavern was a natural echo chamber.

More enemies? Gryph thought, his stomach surging with acid and fear. Then he saw the gnome peek up from behind a boulder on the ledge. The chanting was coming from him, and he stared intently at Gryph. *'Buy me time,'* the look said.

Gryph returned his attention to the wyrmynn just as he finished casting. The length of rope came alive and entwined itself around Gryph's spear. It raised up behind the wyrmynn like a cobra ready to strike.

The rope spun itself several times and threw the spear towards Gryph. The spear spun end over end and Gryph caught it in midair. He brandished the weapon in front of him. "Do you know what this is?" he bellowed. "Or are you too stupid to identify the bane of your species?"

The wyrmynn looked at the spear in confusion and trepidation and paused, confusion plastering their faces. The leader hissed and barked in laughter. "You are a fool. Tonight, we will dine on elf." The leader's long tongue eased out of his mouth and danced across his teeth. The effect was chilling and Gryph felt a trickle of sweat drip down his back. He laughed again and his cohorts joined.

"Any time now guy," Gryph yelled. This confused the wyrmynn who looked back and forth at each other. The leader was having none of it though and growled at his troops to focus. On his order the wyrmynn all ran at him full bore. "Shit," Gryph said bracing his spear for the attack.

Then a cacophonous boom of a single word split the air. "AVERNERIUS!"

Gryph looked up to see the gnome lift his staff above his head, the red jewel atop it glowing like a red dwarf star. The stunned wyrmynn also looked up, shielding their eyes from the brightness. The gnome brought the staff down with a thunderous crack.

"I CALL THEE!"

The gnome rumbled in a louder and deeper voice than should have been possible. He collapsed to one knee as his command echoed throughout the chamber. Then the world grew silent once more.

Confusion and uncertainty reigned for several heartbeats as Gryph and the wyrmynn looked around in confusion and expectation. Had the gnome's spell failed?

Then a pinprick bleed of red light appeared between Gryph and the wyrmynn. It sparked and spun and expanded faster than Gryph's eyes could follow. A tear split the fabric of reality open from ceiling to floor. It pulsed and expanded reaching a width of ten feet.

The crimson haze of a hellish realm of darkness, fire and movement blocked Gryph's view of the wyrmynn. A black sun hung in a sky of seething red clouds. Streaks of green lightning leapt from cloud to ground, casting jets of earth to spiral skyward. Each flash brought more focus to the hellacious realm. Gryph wished it hadn't.

The ground was awash in talons, horns, tails and teeth. Tortured bodies of red and black, green and gray roiled like an ocean of malevolence. It pulsed and spasmed and then parted like a literal Red Sea. A hunched demon sprinted, a sword of black flame clutched in a claw-tipped hand. It

lurched with purpose straight at the portal and towards
Gryph.

21

Gryph got ready to jump aside, but as the demonic beast crossed the threshold, the surface pulsed like a mirror breaking in slow motion and the horror emerged on the other side, facing the wyrmynn. It whipped its head back and screeched. The sound of a thousand eagles pierced Gryph's skull, and he fell to one knee, hands clamped to his ears. The portal winked out with a flash and a rush of air.

The wyrmynn covered their ears in terror and pain, but that was the best of what they endured. The creature's sword moved with a blue-black blur and the closest wyrmynn was without a head. The head bounced to Gryph's feet, still gazing upwards in surprise, a stupid expression now permanently scrawled across its ugly face. Its tongue lolled out with a final exhalation of air.

All the wyrmynn tried to run, except for the leader who Gryph had to admit, showed incredible bravery in the face of the demonic beast. Gryph took a moment to *Analyze* the creature.

Your Skills have Levelled.
You have reached Level 5 in ANALYZE.

Abyssal Terror.
Level: 24. *Health*: 554. *Stamina*: 420. *Mana*: 310. *Spirit*: 300.

"Unholy Shit," Gryph muttered as the abyssal terror swung its sword at the wyrmynn leader. The wyrmynn leader barely got his sword up to parry the blow, but it proved a small and useless victory. The ember of molten cobalt seared right through the rusty iron of the wyrmynn's blade and bit into the wyrmynn's shoulder, slicing down and splitting the cold-blooded beast in twain.

The demon tugged its weapon, but it remained lodged inside the corpse of the wyrmynn leader. The demon almost shrugged as it looked up at the remaining two wyrmynn. It struck out with one hand and grabbed the closest lizard by the throat. Flames surged from the demon's hands, and the wyrmynn's eyes melted. It squealed in horror and pain.

At the same moment the demon shot its tail out and impaled the other wyrmynn through the chest. The demon raised its tail, pulling the wyrmynn off its feet. The obsidian barb protruded several feet from the wyrmynn's back, covered in green blood and gore. The wyrmynn struggled for a few moments before going limp.

The demon shook its tail and flung the corpse against the cavern wall with a sickening thud. The demon paid it no heed as it pulled the other wyrmynn close. The saurian creature tried to scream, but its vocal cords were charred and useless. The eyeless sockets stared in horror as the abyssal terror brought it to its maw of needle-sharp teeth and chomped down on the wyrmynn's head, severing it with all the ease and interest of a sociopathic child tearing the wings of a fly.

The world went silent except for the sickening chomping of the demon's maw as it feasted on lizard flesh. Bones cracked, and tendons tore, and gore dribbled and splatted. Gryph backed into the corner. So far, the demon hadn't noticed him. That soon changed.

In his panic, Gryph backed into a pile of stone and gravel. The sound of skittering rocks drew the demon's attention and its head spun on Gryph, eyes burning from the inside with cold fire. It screeched, tossed the partially eaten wyrmynn aside and rushed at Gryph with a speed that defied its bulk.

Gryph raised his spear, wedging its base against a boulder and hoped. The abyssal terror was mere feet from adding Gryph to its varied buffet when an order in an odd language erupted from the gnome. In an instant the demon pulled up short, its bulk only a few inches from Gryph.

"Sorry, I forgot to designate you as a friendly," the gnome said.

"Forgot!" Gryph yelled. "What the hell is wrong with you?"

"I'd lower that spear. First, it won't do much on good ol' Avernerius here. Second, if you so much as prick his infernal skin, your status as friendly will become void. And that would be…well seriously ungood."

"You're a lunatic," Gryph sputtered, but he lowered his spear. He cast a hesitant gaze up at Avernerius and could see the hate in the demon's eyes. It still wanted to gut and feast on him and the beast's infernal presence penetrated his mind and his soul. It felt like an oily stain seeping through every fiber of his being with acid tendrils that burned away bits of him.

"Yeah, and I wouldn't stare in those eyes either. Bad things live in there."

Gryph pulled his eyes away, and the foul sensation dissipated.

"Call it off?"

"Not how it works, but don't worry his time in this realm is limited. He has about twenty seconds more before he's dragged back to his own realm."

"I have decided I hate you," Gryph said as he eased away from the abyssal terror and made his way closer to the ledge where the gnome stood. Gryph didn't look up, but

Avernerius' eyes followed his every move. The muscles in the creature's body strained as if it were fighting against itself to get to Gryph.

"You sure you have control of this thing?"

"Pretty sure. But no need to fret cuz in... 3...2...now."

A pinprick of fiery light punctured the veils between Realms again and dragged Avernerius backwards as if pushed by hurricane strength winds. A foul rush of sulfuric air sucked the demon through the portal. The smell made Gryph gag.

The gnome slid down from the ledge and looked around at the bodies of the wyrmynn. Gryph got to his feet and advanced on the small man with virulent ire. Before the gnome knew he was upon him, Gryph had him by the neck and hoisted the tiny man with ease, lifting him up to his eye level.

"You nearly got me killed," Gryph said in calm fury.

"I saved your life, man," the gnome said, gasping for breath.

"I saved yours," Gryph grumbled, but his anger was subsiding. He let the small man drop and felt shame pulse through him. Finn had never been one to let anger cloud his mind. Gryph refused to be victimized by it either.

The gnome coughed a few times as he forced air back into his lungs. He rubbed a hand against his throat as he stood. He walked right up to Gryph and held out a hand.

"The name's Wick."

So, he is the gnome from the journal, Gryph realized.

Wick held his hand out as the seconds ticked by and the air grew uncomfortable. Wick widened his eyes in a 'don't leave me hangin' buddy' gesture as Gryph continued to stare.

"And your name is?" Wick said in an irritating drawl that dripped sarcasm.

Gryph held the stare before grasping the small man's hand.

"Gryph."

"Nice to meet ya, Gryph. Thanks for the save there. I'd thought I'd given this lot the slip, but evidently my stealth skills aren't up to snuff." Wick grew uncomfortable as Gryph refused to release his hand. "Gettin' a little weird, pal."

Gryph pulled the little man closer and said, "Want to explain that demon lord of hell thing?"

"What's to explain?" Wick said with a nervous grin.

"Tell me why I shouldn't gut you now. You dredged that demon up from hell. What are you some kind of evil necromancer priest?"

"First off, I'm a chthonic summoner, not a necromancer. Necromancers hang out in graveyards digging up corpses. I summon beings from the chthonic realm. Second, I am not evil, I just make use of beings whose moral standards may be a tad looser than my own."

Gryph's withering look suggested that in his mind the two things were not all that different on the moral scale of things.

"You sound just like my dad," Wick grumbled. "Well, maybe you act like my dad, since you aren't really saying much. You've really mastered the strong and brooding thing."

Gryph just stared.

"Now look, do you think I asked for this? It's not my fault I have an affinity for the chthonic sphere. I sure as shit didn't ask for it. I would have been perfectly happy following in my dad's footsteps and become another in a long line of Flintspanner Master Tinkers. But no, the gods cursed me with this."

"Are you done?" Gryph asked.

After a shy moment of introspection, Wick nodded. Gryph let go and Wick lurched back at the sudden freedom. He smoothed out his wrinkled clothes, all the while casting a sideways glance of mistrust at Gryph.

"Yes, I believe I am."

Gryph's mind went to Jebbis' quest. This Wick was like the child who liked to play with fire. All fun and games until the neighbor's house burned down. Definitely someone not to trust. Maybe Jebbis and Rehla would be better off if Gryph completed the quest on his own. Not that he knew where he was, much less how to get to their village. After a few moments' consideration, Gryph decided to keep the quest a secret.

"Good, now how do I get out of here?"

"Out of the Barrow?" Wick snickered. "Are you new here?"

"Just answer the question Wick."

"Well, you don't. There is no way out." Wick laughed out loud at the crestfallen look that crossed the tall elf's face, earning a look of ire from Gryph. "I'm sorry, I don't mean to pile on your misery, but if there was a way out do you think I'd be hanging out here?" He waved his hands around with all the drama of a stage magician.

"I don't believe you."

"Yeah, well nobody ever does," Wick mumbled and almost sounded sad. "Listen, come with me. I have a safe place. Well, relatively safe since we're in a sentient dungeon bent on seeing us all dead."

"What did you say?"

"I have a place."

"No, a sentient dungeon. What does that mean?"

"Are you new to language too or maybe just dim?" Wick said and then gave Gryph a sideways glance. "How is it that you don't know anything about anything?"

"I'm not from around here."

"Yeah?" Wick said, a look of suspicion crossing his face. "Where you from then?"

"You won't have heard of it."

"Try me. I'm well-travelled."

Normally, Gryph would have said nothing. Years of training warned him not to hand out information that could give anyone an advantage. But, at this point, he didn't see any harm. Maybe he was getting soft. Maybe it was just loneliness.

"I'm from a place called Earth," Gryph said.

"Well, I'll be damned, you're a player?" Wick said, eyes going wide. "You are, aren't you? A little late to the party, aren't you?"

Shit, Gryph thought. "I don't understand anything that is coming out of your mouth."

"Yup, definitely slow. You don't seem to get any of this." Wick spread his hands around in a spastic gesture indicating all of creation.

"Why don't you explain it then," Gryph said through gritted teeth.

"Cool, man, chill," Wick said, giving Gryph a sideways glance. "The way my gramps tells the story is that a ways back, say fifty years ago, the Pantheon invaded the Realms. They came from some Realm called Earth that nobody had ever heard of. The Pantheon brought a bunch of buddies with them. They called these people players. Not sure why since, as you've seen, this place ain't no game. Anyway, they fought against the corrupt New Gods and defeated them. The Pantheon took over, ruling over Korynn with 'benevolence and justice.'" This last part he said with sarcastic air quotes.

Gryph, realizing how weary he was, sat down as Wick told his tale.

"So, after the Pantheon defeated the New Gods they sent all the players back home with thanks and well wishes. Nobody's seen a player since that day. Sure, rumors floated that a player was seen in this place or that, but I never believed it. To be honest, I always thought the tales were a bunch of poppycock. Yah know, stories made up to inspire children."

"Doesn't seem to have worked on you too well there, Little Demon Lord," Gryph said.

"Look, guy, we went over this. I'm not an evil wizard, I'm just a guy who got a bad rap."

"And summons demons from hell."

Wick stood up and turned away from Gryph. "Listen, I already thanked you for saving my butt. I'd be gnome stew if you hadn't come around."

Gryph said nothing.

"Seriously, dude, you need to work on your people skills. I said thanks. Now let me show you my appreciation. Come with me and I'll get you a hot meal of…" Wick's voice went low. "Rat stew."

"Did you just say rat stew?"

Wick shrugged. "What do you expect? It's not like there's a handy market right around the corner. We make do with what we got, and we survive."

Gryph stood, and Wick smiled.

"Good, finally showing some sense. Let's loot these bodies and then head back to my hideout."

"I'm not going to any hideout." Gryph didn't move. "I'm getting out of here."

"I already told you there is no way out of here."

"You're telling me that somebody built this place without an exit?"

"Not exactly."

"So, there is an exit?"

"There's an entrance. A one-way door. We could never reopen it once it closed. Wait, why don't you know this? How did you get in here?"

"Which way?" Gryph demanded. A few heartbeats of tense silence followed.

"Fine, man. Your funeral." Wick reached out his hand. Gryph just stared. "Well, take my hand, man. How else do you expect me to give you my map? You really don't know what the hell you're doing, do you? Gonna bode well for you."

Gryph extended his hand palm up, and Wick placed his hand on top. Wick closed his eyes, and Gryph felt a pulse of warmth spread outward from the gnome's child-sized hand. It pulsed into Gryph and moved up his arm and through his chest where it settled in his mind.

An extensive map of the Barrow filled Gryph's mind. It included a ton of notations, including the location of Wick's camp, the various warrens of the Wyrmynn and a place called Gray Haven, a network of caves and tunnels offset from the rest of the Barrow. But all that interested Gryph was the door marked entrance. It was a way up through a series of tunnels and caverns that intersected the wyrmynn held areas.

Gryph opened his eyes and nodded his thanks to Wick.

"Wow, was that gratitude? You're moving up in the emotional spectrum, man. Congratulations."

Gryph grinned and held out his hand to Wick. "Thanks for the help, and the info."

"You're welcome," Wick said, taking Gryph's hand. "You sure I can't talk you out of this?"

"No, I'm supposed to be somewhere else."

"We're all supposed to be somewhere else."

Gryph nodded. Maybe Wick wasn't all bad.

"Before you go, let's see what these lizard bastards have on them. You'll need every advantage you can get."

While Wick searched the bodies, Gryph checked out his prompts.

You have Completed a Quest.

You have earned 5,000 XP for completing the Quest Gnomish Team Up.

You have helped the gnome Wick and defeated the wyrmynn. Wick now has a friendly disposition towards you.

<u>Reward</u>: Partial map of the Barrow.

You have earned Experience Points.

You have earned 15,535 XP for slaying Wyrmynn (X6).

You have reached Level 6 and 7.

You have 12 (5 Base + 2 Godhead Bonus) unused Attribute Points. You have 2 unused Perk Points.

Your Skills have Levelled.

You have reached Level 3 in AIR MAGIC.

You have reached Level 6 in STEALTH.

You have reached Level 6 in LIGHT ARMOR.

You have reached Level 6 in DODGE.

You have reached Level 6 in STAVES/SPEARS.

You have reached Level 6 in THROWN WEAPONS.

Gryph put two points into *Constitution* and four into *Dexterity* and *Intelligence*. His stats received a nice boost. He kept two in reserve for his newly discovered game hack. Now for the tough and fun part.

Gryph - Level 7	Stats
High Elf (El'Edryn) Deity: None Experience: 36,310 Next Level: 14,690	Health: 165 Stamina: 166 Mana: 153 Spirit: 130
Attributes	**Gifts**
Strength: 23 Constitution: 27 Dexterity: 29 Intelligence: 20 Wisdom: 10	Health Regeneration: +25% Mana Regeneration: +25% Night Vision: 120 Ft. Master of Tongues

How to spend his *Perk Points*? Without hesitation he dumped one into the *Stealth* perk *Invisibility*, having already seen what the lack of that skill had nearly cost him.

Stealth Perk Tree.			
Tier	Backstab	Invisibility	Speed
Base	2X	15%	50%
Apprentice	3X	25%	60%
Journeyman	4X	35%	70%
Master	5X	45%	80%
Grandmaster	6X	55%	90%
Divine	10X	75%	2X

Now what to do with the other one? He opened his *Air Magic* perk tree and examined it.

AIR MAGIC PERKS.

----- Mana -----
Reduces the cost needed for any spell in this sphere to the percentage listed.

----- Effectiveness -----
Increases the effectiveness (damage, duration, heal, etc.) for any spell in this sphere to the percentage listed.

----- Resistance -----
The ability to resist a percentage of the effects of spells and weapons derived from this sphere of magic.

----- Item Power -----
Any magical item or weapon in this sphere has its effectiveness increased by 25%.

Gryph noticed that the perks for magic were generic as if every magic skill would have the same basic branches. It made sense as the perks increased the effectiveness and reduced the cost of casting. It was easy to imagine that one day, if he focused on one or two spheres of magic, that Gryph could grow to be incredibly powerful.

He started now. *Animate Rope* was so far his only spell, but it had saved his life on two occasions. He suspected if he were to live long enough to find Brynn that it would do so many more times. He put his last perk point into *Mana*.

Air Magic Perk Tree.

Tier	Mana	Effect	Resistance	Item
Base	80%	+25%	10%	+25%
Apprentice	70%	+50%	25%	+50%
Journeyman	60%	+75%	50%	+75%
Master	50%	+100%	70%	+100%
Grandmaster	30%	+200%	80%	+200%
Divine	20%	+300%	90%	+300%

Satisfied, he closed down his prompts and went to find Wick. He found the gnome next to a pile of loot. True to his word, Wick gave Gryph most of the loot he'd found.

You have found Treasure.

31 gold coins.
34 silver coins.
56 bronze coins.

1 Potion of Minor Healing.

You have found a spell stone for the Earth Magic Spell Flying Stalactite.

Most of the loot was unimpressive, except for the spell stone. As Gryph examined it he wondered why the wyrmynn hadn't used it. Why not learn what sounded like a kick ass spell? He asked Wick.

"Cuz wyrmynn are dumbasses with tiny brains," the gnome said as he knelt down near one of the wyrmynn and pulled a dagger. Without hesitation, he hacked into the neck of the reptilian corpse. Unnerved, Gryph wondered if he was digging for one of these *tiny brains*.

"This isn't bolstering my confidence you're not an evil wizard," Gryph commented as Wick dug into the necks of the lizard beasts with a dagger.

Wick dug a grisly bit of gore from the wound he'd carved. It was a gland of some kind. "Wyrmynn Adrenaline Glands," Wick said, as if that explained anything. "Look closer."

Gryph stared at the bit of gristle and his *Harvest* skill gave him a prompt.

You have discovered **Wyrmynn Adrenaline Gland.**

This rare and valuable ingredient has many uses in both Alchemy and Crafting.

Wyrmynn Adrenaline Gland (Con't).
You believe it could make a potion that will temporarily increase Stamina, Dexterity and Speed and other unidentified effects.
You also get the sense it could craft an item that increases Stamina, Dexterity and Speed and other unidentified effects.

"My girl will love these. She's an alchemist and great at this stuff," Wick said. "Among other things," he added with a wink. "Come with me, she'd be willing to train you up in *Alchemy* as a thank you for saving my sweet ass."

Gryph considered the offer for a moment, but he had to escape this place. He needed to find Brynn and defeat Aluran. Once again, he thought on the absurdity of his situation. Here he was, a lone guy who'd never played an RPG or MMO in his life, thrust into a world run by game mechanics, where he was tasked with defeating a god. Gryph inhaled and forced his mind to its task.

"I appreciate it, I really do, but somebody out there needs me. I can't fail her."

A look of understanding crossed Wick's face, and he extended his hand out to Gryph. "Best of luck my friend."

Gryph shook the gnome's hand. "To you, as well." With no further ceremony, Gryph turned and headed towards the tunnel that led towards the entrance. As he got close, Wick called out to him.

"Hey, Gryph."

Gryph turned back to the gnome.

"See you in your next life," Wick said with a melancholy look.

With that confusing comment, Wick disappeared down another tunnel. Gryph shook his head in bewilderment, but remembered the gnome was a summoner of demons. Who could say what else was wrong with him?

22

It had been nearly twenty minutes since Gryph had left Wick behind when the doubt wormed its way into his guts. Had he made the right choice to go it alone? What if Wick was right? What if there was no way out?

He pulled his new spell stone from his *inventory*. It was like the *Animate Rope* stone he'd found in his original *Inventory*, except where that one had been a sapphire filled with swirls of white light, this one was anthracite pulsing with sparks of brown energy.

Gryph held it in his closed palm and concentrated. Energy pulsed and flowed from the stone just as it had before, but this time as it flowed up his limbs it made them rigid and heavy as if his body was turning to stone. It flowed up into his neck and settled into his brain. He could hear the grinding and slow cracking of the earth and stone around him and then his mind expanded and filled with knowledge.

You have learned the spell FLYING STALACTITE.

Sphere: Earth Magic.
Tier: Base.

This spell will conjure a single spear of stone that will fly wherever the caster points. Base Damage: 20 points of Earth damage +2 points per level of Earth Magic mastery.

Mana Cost: 30.
Duration: N/A.
Cooldown: None.

You have learned the skill EARTH MAGIC.
Level: 1.   _Tier_: Base.   _Skill Type_: Active.   You can now wield the power of Earth Magic. Earth Magic allows the user to manipulate the earth itself. Earth Magic makes use of offensive and defensive spells but is also used in mining and to summon or construct creatures made of earth.

Well, that rocks, Gryph thought before realizing he'd made a horrible pun.

Gryph checked the map Wick had given him and took a tunnel that led west. If he was reading the map correctly, he was three hundred feet underground and over a mile of snaking tunnels from his goal.

Not too bad, Gryph thought. There were a ton of skull and crossbones icons of various colors littering his path. Gryph concentrated on a red one not too far from him and a prompt popped into his vision.

Pit Trap.
Punji Sticks.   _Poison._

A few minutes later Gryph found the trap. He could see a faint red glow outlining the pit. This was his _Perception_ skill in action. At level five he had a 25% chance of spotting traps. The dimness of the glow suggested to Gryph that had he not already known the trap was there that he may not have detected it. He made a mental note to be more careful.

Gryph eased himself by the pit trap but couldn't resist activating it. He applied pressure with the butt of his spear until the ultra-thin stone covering the pit fractured and fell.

The pit was nearly ten feet deep and lined with dozens of needle-sharp punji sticks. They were not wood, but stone stalagmites that grew from the floor. Their uniformity and even spacing were perfect like rows of corn, suggesting that they had been cultivated. Worse still the needle point tips of each stalagmite oozed viscous liquid.

Poison rocks. Perfect. Who the hell built this place? And why? Gryph wondered. He still didn't understand why the Barrow tossed death around so casually.

He moved onward. The tunnel took a slight left, and the gradient increased. If the map was accurate, he'd soon hit a large cavern that Wick had marked with half a dozen blue skulls. Gryph focused on a scroll icon in the corner of the room and another prompt emerged.

Wyrmynn Outpost.

Full of stank wyrmynn. At least ten. This is the base from which they patrol our area. I told Tifala that I could summon Avernerius into their midst and Bam, problem solved. She said no and gave me that look. Yah know, the one that says, 'I love you, but the things you can do terrify me.' Regardless, they are getting too close, and we must do something about them soon.

Who was Wick? Now, Gryph was the first to admit that he knew nothing about the Realms, but even he sensed the odd juxtaposition between the gnome's jovial personality and the things he could do. Gryph made a mental note to not put too much faith into the map or the gnome who made it. It could cost him his life.

Gryph plotted out another route. It was more circuitous and took him perilously close to unmapped territory, but it had less death's head icons. He had only seen a small sampling of the terrors this world held, and he was in no hurry to up his experience with them now.

After nearly half an hour, he had snaked his way upwards. He'd activated *Stealth* on three occasions. Twice as wyrmynn patrols went by and once as a snuffling beast lumbered past his hiding spot. His *Analyze* skill identified it.

Umber Beast.

Level: 17.
Health: 235.
Stamina: 230.
Mana: 0.
*Spirit:*0.

Umber Beasts are a foul mixture of a beetle and a gorilla. Their origins are shrouded in mystery, but most scholars believe the Umber Beast was the product of unnatural magical experiments.

Strengths: Unknown.
Immunities: Unknown.
Weakness: Unknown.

Gryph decided there was no need to tangle with the beast now, or ever. He gave the creature a few minutes before he continued up the tunnel.

Twenty minutes later he discovered a pressure plate trap that connected to nozzles built into the wall. The nozzles reminded Gryph of the flamethrowers he'd seen back on Earth. He eased slowly by the pressure plate, swearing he could smell an old odor of charred flesh.

He walked for another twenty minutes before coming to a fork in the tunnel. The left-hand tunnel descended, and he could hear the rush of moving water. The right tunnel eased up at a comfortable gradient.

Gryph chose the right-hand path. Not only could underground rivers be deadly with their uncontrolled surges, but the sound dredged up memories of the flash flood tunnels under Las Vegas. His unit had gone into the tunnels to track down a terrorist cell that was hiding among the city's homeless. One minute the tunnels were quiet and dry, the next a flash flood brought a wall of water at them. He'd climbed an emergency ladder, but several of his men were caught in the torrent. Their bodies were found several miles away, so battered that dental records had to be used to identify them. The terror of drowning still sat heavy in his mind.

Barely twenty yards up the passage, Gryph heard the sounds of approaching feet. He dipped into *Stealth* as another wyrmynn patrol came into view. A robed figure led this group. Gryph used *Analyze* and learned that it was a [Wyrmynn Priest - Level 12]. This priest seemed smarter than its kin as it paused and snapped an order to its underlings.

Shit, Gryph thought.

The priest was looking right at his hiding spot, beady eyes scanning back and forth. *Stealth* was holding, but Gryph decided it was time to test out his new *Invisibility* perk. He felt a shimmer pass through his body as if light were refracting off of him. Then the shimmer stopped, and a prompt popped into his vision.

Invisibility has Failed.

Crap, 15% sucks. Had he made a mistake in using a precious point on such an unreliable perk? Not only that, but the failed attempt had still drained thirty points from his *Stamina*.

A quick glance at his dipping *Stamina* bar sent a surge of worry through Gryph's stomach. *Move on, move on. Nothing to see here*, Gryph thought, forcing mental commands into the universe.

The universe ignored him, and the priest still stared. Gryph's *Stamina* bar flared like the pulsing lights of a police car. He forced his mind to calm. Panic would be deadly, but so would the sound of his body falling to the ground if he lost consciousness.

A eureka moment surged into his brain. He still had *Attribute Points* to use. He opened his interface and dumped a point into *Constitution* and his *Stamina* ticked up *a few points*, but the bar did not refill.

What the hell? Gryph thought in alarm and dumped the

second point into *Constitution*. Again, a small uptick was the only response. *Why didn't it work?* Gryph's mind scrambled for an answer. It must require five points for the game hack to work. That was a full level's worth of *Attribute Points*. A heavy cost for the game hack.

His *Stamina* bar pulsed. *Stealth* would fail any moment. What the hell was this priest doing? His fellows wondered the same thing as the low grumbling of complaints moved through the other wyrmynn.

"Silence," the priest hissed in their horrid sounding language.

Gryph's muscles ached with the strain of staying absolutely still. The priest's eyes moved away from Gryph's hiding spot and its body relaxed. Sensing the ease of tension, a wyrmynn scout mouthed off. A backhand strike from the priest's staff knocked the offender to the ground with a grunt of pain.

Gryph had his chance and eased back into the tunnel. If he could get to the next turn, maybe, just maybe he'd be able to sneak away. He moved back one foot, then another, slowly and silently bringing each boot to the ground. Never once taking his eyes of the wyrmynn priest.

He was doing it. He was almost out of sight when his foot came down onto a loose rock, and he slipped. The rock skittered down the decline behind him and the priest's eyes snapped up boring right into Gryph's eyes.

The priest grinned a mouthful of jagged teeth and raised its hand. A bolt of black energy blasted Gryph in the chest and his body seized in pain. His *Health* dropped by nearly a third as his muscles spasmed.

You have been hit by Necrotic Blast.

Necrotic Blast is a Base Tier Death Magic spell. It deals direct death damage and can cause temporary paralysis.

You have resisted temporary paralysis.

Thanking the small miracle, he turned and sprinted away from the wyrmynn. A barked order from the priest sent the foul creatures in pursuit. Another *Necrotic Blast* flew over his left shoulder, exploding against the wall of the tunnel. Several arrows and a spear clattered against the wall as he dipped and dodged and ran.

Gryph came to the fork again and considered heading back the way he'd originally come but suspected that the wyrmynn would catch up with him and even be able to summon their brethren from deeper in the Barrow.

Gryph turned into the left fork and the cacophony of rushing water drowned out all sounds of pursuit. He could no longer hear the wyrmynn and didn't know how close they were. The ground was wet and littered with rocks and patches of moss making the footing treacherous. He dared not glance back for fear of falling.

Another *Necrotic Blast* zipped past him, and he ducked on instinct. Shards of rock cut into his face but did no damage. However, the arrow that hit his right shoulder did plenty. Pain pumped into him, and he stumbled. His *Health* dropped to barely over half, and he wished that Lex had been there. His NPC's healing skills and a big ass hammer would have been welcome support.

The air filled with mist as Gryph rounded the corner. A fifteen-foot-wide torrent of white water bisected the tunnel. Two slime covered ropes, one just a few inches above the roiling froth, another about chest height, stretched across the river. From there the tunnel continued deeper into the Barrow. Calling the pair of ancient ropes a bridge was as much a joke as reality. Gryph knew what he had to do; he just had no desire to do it.

Another *Necrotic Bolt* flew overhead and forced the decision. Gryph eased a foot onto the lower rope while grabbing the other in his hands. The rope swayed, and Gryph nearly lost his balance. He was barely to the middle when the wyrmynn arrived.

The priest barked orders and the only words Gryph could make out above the din was "take him alive." He found this very sporting until his mind wandered to what being captured alive by these stinking beasts might mean. Would he end up in a cooking pot? Torture? Something even more awful?

He moved with agonizing slowness to the center of the river. The froth made seeing difficult, and he could hear nothing. Any second he expected metal from a spear or arrow would bite him, or the sting of the priest's *Death Magic*. Nothing came, and he risked a glance back. Two wyrmynn were clipping a rope to the end of a spear. An image of Moby Dick flashed through his mind. The barbed tip of the spear would be perfect. The bastards were making a harpoon. Gryph sped up and nearly fell as his left foot slipped.

His body dropped and pain from the arrow in his shoulder nearly caused him to lose his grip, but he held fast. He was getting close to the other side, but another glance back told him he would not make it. The wyrmynn had completed their makeshift harpoon, and the largest one a [*Wyrmynn Skirmisher; Level 9*] took aim.

Gryph knew he needed to jump for it. He turned, tensed his muscles and leapt. He landed hard, rib crunching pain bursting through him. He nearly slipped back into the raging water, but his outstretched arms found the strands of wet moss that clung to the far side. He pulled himself up when a deep sting bit into his left calf.

Gryph screamed at the agony surging up his leg. His *Health* dropped further, dipping below the 40% mark. Another pull dragged him into the water. The current pounded Gryph, smashing him against the bank before pulling him downstream. His mouth and nose filled with water, and he couldn't breathe.

Debuffs Added.

You are drowning; 5 points of damage per second.

You are bleeding; 5 points of damage per second.

Gryph didn't waste time doing the math, but he knew he'd be dead in under a minute if he didn't do something. Almost unbidden, he cast *Animate Rope*. Another violent jerk on the rope pulled his head above water. He would have screamed if he wasn't coughing voluminous amounts of water from his lungs. They dragged him like a limp fish onto the shore. As he finished retching bile and brackish water, he felt himself turned onto his stomach. His arms were wrenched behind him and ropes bound his hands.

Gryph finished casting, and the rope attached to the spear slithered with fake life. At first his captors were unaware of the serpentine presence until the rope snapped forward, coiling a loop around the neck of the wyrmynn who was tying Gryph's hands. The rope tugged hard and spun, tossing the surprised lizard man towards the river. The creature's head smashed against the roof of the cave and the wyrmynn disappeared into the water, sucked away like waste in a toilet.

Another lizard was tossed into the water, and the wyrmynn priest raged. The rope drew up like a cobra ready to strike. Gryph was cognizant to keep slack where the rope attached to the spear. He pulled a red *Health Potion* from his bag and downed it.

Warmth tore through him like whiskey on a cold day, and with it, life. His *Health* bar surged, topping out at 65%. He would not die, at least not yet. The priest was muttering under his breath and gesturing with his clawed hands. Whatever he was casting took longer than the *Necrotic Bolts* he'd been tossing earlier. Gryph was no magic expert, but he suspected that a longer casting time meant bad things were on the horizon.

Gryph went on the offensive and cast *Flying Stalactite*. He felt his arm grow rigid as the power of the earth itself flowed down his arm. With a crack a thin missile of rock erupted from his outstretched palm.

Gryph pointed his hand at the closest wyrmynn, a scout who'd raised his mace overhead and was ready to bring it crashing down onto Gryph. The stalactite punctured the wyrmynn's armor and impaled it through the chest. Gryph earned a *Critical Strike* for the range and the surprise. The wyrmynn was dead before the stalactite pinned it to the wall of the cave behind it.

The priest was reaching the climax of his dramatic chanting. Gryph had no idea what was about to happen, but he knew one thing, he had no desire to hang out and wait. Gryph hobbled to his feet. He turned to face the priest and extended the middle fingers on both hands. He had no idea if the wyrmynn understood the gesture, so he hissed and growled the meaning in fluent wyrmynn.

The priest's eyes went wide in fury, but he kept discipline and finished his chanting with a hiss of anger. The priest raised his hands above his head and silver energy coalesced. Gryph decided he needed to be elsewhere and dove into the rushing water. The river smashed him into the sides of the tunnel and his *Health* sank again. But a few moments later, the surge calmed as the water filled the tunnel. The good news, he was no longer being smashed against the sides of the tunnel. The bad, there was nowhere to find air.

He spun and sped and soon his breath was falling. Angry red light raged in his vision and he began to drown.

23

A surge of excitement pulsed through the Barrow King. His wyrmynn had cornered the elf and would bring the *Godhead* to him. Soon, he would have the power to escape this wretched half-life. Soon he would become a god.

He watched the battle through the eyes of the wyrmynn priest. While still relatively low level, this elf had proven to be incredibly resourceful, even creative. The Barrow King liked a challenge. As a master of the soul sphere, the Barrow King could assimilate the skills and knowledge of those he possessed. That was the way he had gained so much knowledge and power in his physical life. And he would have it again.

Nefarious joy exploded in the Barrow King's mind. *The wyrmynn have him.* The man was injured, but alive, just as he had demanded. The revenant made plans. He would consume the elf's soul and take his body as his own. With the *Godhead* he could gorge himself on all the life in the Barrow.

Then he would evolve the *Godhead.* It would take time and patience, but the Barrow King had suffered for millennia, so he was also a master of patience. The wyrmynn had his prize tied and ready for delivery when the man escaped his bonds and used them as a weapon. He'd used his limited magic in a most inventive way. The Barrow King would have been impressed if he weren't so angry.

Time to take control of this situation, the Barrow King realized.

He extended his will through his dungeon and placed himself into the small mind of the wyrmynn priest. The beast had just enough mana for this one spell. It would be a conduit for the Barrow King's casting. He knew it would burn out the priest's mind, but he cared less about that than a man who mistakenly steps on an ant while out for a walk.

The Barrow King started casting *Soul Portal*, a spell of his own creation. It required a lengthy casting time, but when completed, it would create a doorway between his location and the battle. Then he could drag the man through the portal and take his prize.

The man locked eyes with him and made a furious gesture with both hands that the Barrow King did not understand. Then the elf spoke in the wyrmynn's horrid language and the meaning became clear.

No, young fool, fuck you, the Barrow King thought. The casting was at an end when the elf added one last insult to gesture and words and jumped into the raging river.

The Barrow King howled, and his rage burned out what little remained of the wyrmynn priest's paltry mind. The creature collapsed, dead before it hit the ground. The pent-up energy of the Barrow King's spell had nowhere to go. It exploded and tore through the remaining wyrmynn, splattering the cave with blood and gore.

The revenant's mind tried to feel the *Godhead*. It could not see the man. He had no minion in the torrential river, but he knew where it would take the elf. To the cavern with the lake. The lake where the arboleth dwelled.

Fear gripped the Barrow King. There was no being in this dungeon who could challenge the Barrow King except for the arboleth. The arboleth was an ancient aetherial aberration that the Barrow King had drawn to this realm in his youthful arrogance. It had taken all of his power to trap the beast in the watery prison where it now lived. The watery prison the man with the *Godhead* would soon enter.

If the arboleth took possession of the *Godhead*, it would escape, and the Barrow King was far too weak to survive a battle with the immortal entity. He needed to stop that from happening.

He extended his mind into the underground lake. There on a small island he caused a chest to emerge, laden with the best weapons the Barrow King could provide. He glamoured the chest with a spell of seduction that would lure the elf to the island. It was not much, but perhaps it would be enough for the high elf to survive and to escape.

It would have to be.

24

Gryph's *Health* was playing a game called 'How Quickly Can I Plummet?' and it was putting up an MVP effort. He guessed he'd been in the water for a minute when a *Drowning* prompt popped into the corner of his vision. *Again? Dammit.* Flashes of light sparked in his vision ticking away the last moments of his life.

The torrent of water shot Gryph from the cave opening like a cannonball. A coughing, sputtering near dead cannonball. Gryph inhaled a ragged breath that burned his starved lungs as it nourished them.

It was then he realized he was falling. He'd emerged into a large cavern, dominated by a lake. The water from the river erupted into the cavern nearly one hundred feet in the air. Gryph shot like a cork exploding from a shaken bottle of champagne, tumbling head over feet as he plummeted towards the lake.

Gryph knew that pain was coming, but as he hit the surface of the water with an epic, skin smacking belly flop he suspected he might also die. The water felt like concrete and the small breaths he'd pulled into his lungs exploded on impact.

Gryph lost consciousness.

Deep in the lake, something stirred. Powerful thoughts reached outwards as a primordial body awoke from a deathlike slumber. Something was in its cave. Something that held a powerful potential. Something that would serve it.

When Gryph came to, he was several feet below the water and sinking. His sliver of *Health* flashed as it dipped to 10%. His *Health*, like his body, was sinking. He pushed through the agony and swam towards the dim light of the surface. His lungs burned like molten iron as he put the last of his life into a few more frantic kicks. His mind retreated to a place of comfort. A place from his past.

Brynn walked in the place she once loved most. The house at Bow Lake. The house that burned. The house that had taken their mother. Brynn looked back at Gryph and smiled. It was all wrong. It was adult Brynn who looked back at Gryph. Yet, he could see the fifteen-year-old girl whose life would soon shatter looking back at him. He had failed her then. He wouldn't fail her now.

Gryph broke the surface and his lungs burned as he inhaled.

He spent a few moments recovering when a sharp pain reminded him the spear was still lodged in his leg. The journey down the river had broken the shaft in two, causing the flow of blood to increase. He tried to pull the spear shaft from his leg but couldn't get a solid grip on the weapon.

Instead, he fumbled through his pack, grabbing his last *Health Potion*. His hand shook with pain as he struggled to keep the vial above water. He popped the cork and downed the liquid in one large gulp. Warmth and ease spread though his body and his *Health* bar shot up to nearly 60%.

The potency of the healing potions continued to amaze him. They didn't just restore *Health*, they knit bones and closed wounds. It was one of the many things in this world he couldn't wrap his head around. He made himself a promise. If he lived through this hellhole of a dungeon, he would learn how to make them. Lots of them.

He caught his breath and surveyed his surroundings. The lake was large, half a mile across at its widest. It was surrounded on three sides by the high walls of the cavern, but the fourth side had a beach and better yet a solid metal door. There was a way out.

Then he felt a tingle at the back of his mind and his gaze turned to his left like iron to a magnet. Two hundred yards off was an island of rock and sand. A large metal and wood chest sat at the center of the island. A swell of desire rose in his mind. He wanted the chest, wanted it more than he'd ever wanted anything. Somewhere in the recesses of his mind, he knew it was foolish. He needed to get out of the Barrow, not detour for a few trinkets.

Gryph concentrated and swam towards the beach. He focused his mind, ignoring the lure of the chest clawing at his mind. After a few minutes of swimming he was stunned to realize that he had drifted and was now swimming for the island.

I may as well check it out now, Gryph thought. *I'm so close.*

He pulled himself up onto the island. It was twenty feet to a side. His mind fogged and the pain in his leg faded to a distant throb. The chest was close, and he knew, just knew it contained amazing treasures meant just for him. A shooting pain zipped through the haze as the spear grazed upon the stone of the island.

He grimaced and fell to his knees. Looking down he saw the barbed spear head pushed all the way through the muscle of his calf. Only a few inches of shaft protruded from the other side, broken off in a jagged splintery mess. Gryph grabbed the shaft below the tip and inhaled deeply. On the exhale he yanked the spearhead free drawing a gout of fresh blood. Gryph screamed and lost consciousness.

Sometime later he awoke, surprised the wound in his leg had healed. Residual effects of the healing potion, perhaps? He stood and the pain in his leg had reduced to a deep throb. His mind was foggy, reminiscent of a post bender hangover, but Gryph forgot his pain as he saw the wondrous chest.

He felt a longing like nothing he'd ever experienced. A child's obsession for a favorite toy or the alcoholic's need for a drink or the returning soldier's desire for his lover's touch. It was all these things and more.

He walked to the chest, his fingers trembling in anticipation. Energy flowed from the chest and as he got closer, he saw it was as much a work of art as a container. Aged wood that told a story with carved bas relief images, bolstered by bands of a green metal.

A mighty warrior, shining spear held aloft, stood by the open chest. Rays of radiant gold poured from surface of the chest, bathing the warrior in warmth and glory. His expression was the fulfillment of every promise Gryph now felt in his mind. Whatever was in this chest would change his life forever. The rest of the story told of the great adventures. Kingdoms united. Demonic beasts slain. Evil thrown from the

Realms.

Gryph's mind rushed to Brynn. *With this I can save her.* The echoes of his thoughts returning to him bolstering his surety. He had never been more confident of anything in his life. With trembling hands, he eased the chest open. A low click announced the mechanism had released, and the lid opened on well-oiled hinges.

Gryph looked down into the chest with awe. He was so distracted by the wealth in the chest he didn't notice the bubbles of rancid air break the surface a dozen yards behind him.

For the chest contained wonders unlike any Gryph had seen since entering the Realms. His *Identify* gift surged to life as he pulled each item from the chest.

You have found Elven Bracers of the Return.

(Light Armor)
(Air Magic)
Item Class: Base
Item Category: Active.
AC Bonus: +8 (+2 Base Item Bonus).

Active Powers.
Power (1): Magnetic Control of Thrown Weapons.

Mana Limit: N/A
Cool Down: 5 seconds.

Yellow elementum scrolling infuses these extraordinary quality leather bracers. Besides providing great armor bonuses, the wearer can use the bracers to summon thrown weapons back to them, allowing them to attack again. There is no cooldown for this power.

You have found Banded Leather Breastplate of the Moon.

(Light Armor)
(Life Magic)
Item Class: Major.
Item Category: Passive/Active.
AC Bonus: +18 (+5 Major Item Bonus).

Passive Powers.
Power (1): Health Regen +25%.
Power (2): Resist Death Magic: +25%.

Active Powers.
Power (3): Moon Flare: A surge of moonlight (Life Energy) explodes from the chest plate causing temporary blindness and 5 points of damage per point of mana spent to all creatures of the lower magics and healing 5 points of damage per point of mana spent to self and all allies within 50 feet.

Mana Limit: 20%.
Cool Down: 6 hours.

This extraordinary quality leather jerkin is covered in layered bands of green elementum and white mithril.

You have found Elven Boots of Deftness.

(Light Armor)
(Air Magic)
Item Class: Base
Item Category: Passive/Active.
AC Bonus: +10 (+2 Base Item Bonus).

Passive Powers.
Power (1): +2 Dexterity.
Power (2): -10% Stamina cost for Stealth.

Active Powers.
Power (3): Speed Doubled for 15 seconds per mana point spent.
These extraordinary leather boots are worn by elven warriors. Crafted from the hide of a strike lizard, the boots offer excellent protection and speed-based abilities derived from beasts.

Mana Limit: 10%.
Cool Down: 1 hour.

You have found Cowl of Elvenkind.

(Light Armor)
(Life Magic)
Item Class: Base.
Item Category: Passive.
AC Bonus: +6 (+2 Base Item Bonus).

Passive Powers.
Power (1): +5 Levels to Perception and Analyze while worn.

This soft leather cowl is made from the hide of a scout fox. It provides excellent protection and perception abilities derived from the animal. It is the traditional garb of wood elf scouts.

Mana Limit: NA.
Cool Down: NA.

You have found Elven War Pants.

(Light Armor)
Item Class: Non-magical.
Item Category: NA.
AC Bonus: +12.

A well-made pair of leather pants enhanced with thick hide pads that provides excellent protection.

You have found Bane of the Dark.

(Elvish War Spear)
(Staves/Spears)
(Life Magic)
Item Class: Base.
Item Category: Passive/Active.
Base Dmg: +11 (+2 Base Item Bonus).

Passive Powers.
Power (1): Double Damage to aetherial, chthonic, death or chaos creatures. The so called Lower Magics.

You have found Bane of the Dark. (Con't)

Active Powers.

Power (2): Banish (Undead or Summoned) Upon Strike a 2% per Mana point spent chance to sever the Undead or Summoned Being's connection to their natural realm, thus "killing" it. Capped at 80%.

This elvish war spear is made from a shaft of white alder wood tipped with mithril and sealed with starflower sap (a Life resin). The life energy in the weapon dispels undead.

Mana Limit: 5%.
Cool Down: 5 minutes.

You have found Empyrean Spider Silk Rope.

(30 feet)
Item Class: Base.
Item Category: Passive.

Passive Powers.

Power (1): Compel. Beings tied with this rope are compelled to answer all questions. Chance to resist is equal to twice the beings Wisdom.
Power (2): Animate Rope spells last twice as long.
Woven from the silk of an empyrean spider, this rope is nearly unbreakable and like the empyrean spider's themselves can compel truthful answers from other beings.

Mana Limit: NA.
Cool Down: NA.

The find was incredible and perfectly tailored to him. Part of his mind found this odd, but his excitement drove away all doubts. The chest also contained a sack of 135 gold coins, 235 silver coins, 432 bronze coins, five more *Health*, *Stamina* and mana potions and a small sack of glowing spell stones. He focused on the individual stones, receiving a slew of prompts.

You have found a Spell Stones.

You have found a spell stone for the Air Magic Spell
HALO OF AIR.

You have found a spell stone for the Life Magic Spell
MINOR HEALING.

You have found a spell stone for the Life Magic Spell
DETOXIFICATION.

He tucked the bag of spell stones into his inventory and pulled on the pieces of armor. He felt pulses of energy surge through his body as the various passive powers of the items enhanced him. He felt a boost of vitality as the breastplate kicked his *Health Regeneration* into a higher gear. He felt more agile and energetic as he pulled on the boots. He could sense the magnetic forces now at his command as he slipped the bracers onto his forearms. Finally, the fog in his mind cleared as the *Perception* bonus from the cowl became active. He hung the rope at his belt and hefted his upgraded weapon.

Life was good.

A second before pain erupted in his leg his upgraded *Perception* alerted him to a slithering noise behind him. He turned in panic, but even his newly enhanced *Dexterity* was not enough to evade the silent attack. A thick gray green tentacle wrapped around his left ankle and needle-like spines punctured his skin. Agony tore into his leg as he was dragged into the water.

25

Once, a long time ago, the Barrow was much larger. The physical space was unchanged. The same caverns and tunnels and ruins of barracks, storage rooms and ancient temples still existed and in the same places. The Barrow was no normal dungeon. It was alive, but it had been slowly dying for hundreds of years.

This is how Ovrym still lived. Had the Barrow taken him at the height of its power he would not have survived more than a few days, never mind the many years he had called this wretched place home. Some days he wondered if his existence was truly living. Perhaps it was his penance. He let these thoughts flow over him and their power dissipated like a wave breaking on a beach.

As Ovrym sat in his chamber meditating, he felt a ripple in the aether. The disruption that had so long ago sent him on this quest had come. The ripple became an explosion that flowed over him and pulsed outwards to cover the entire world. His eyes opened, pinprick coals of yellow light that pierced the darkness and living beings alike. The time he had foreseen was upon him. After years of waiting his purpose had revealed itself.

Ovrym was a xydai, perhaps the only one in this Realm. His gray skin was the color of spent charcoal, a dusky gray hue, that seemed more dead than alive. He was lean and tall. His shining silver white hair was long. Two thin strands of twined hair draped from the side of his head and past the pointed ears that were a daily reminder of his people's stolen heritage. A long thick braid draped to the middle of his back, clasped with rings of elementum. Badges of honor. Badges of office. Reminders of his betrayal.

He stood and walked to a small shelf against the wall. He

drank water from an ancient clay vessel and stoked the coals in the fireplace. The room that had been his home these last several years had likely once been a servant's quarters. Long before he arrived. Long before he'd gone into exile not once, but twice.

Now the small space was home. But as he urged the slumbering coals back to fiery life he knew today, everything would change. He placed a pot of too old mushroom stew over the fire. He willed the gurgles in his stomach from his mind and practiced his forms.

Ovrym had once been an Adjudicator, a warrior monk who had mastered his mind in the service of order. As he moved through the forms with practiced ease, his mind settled once more. He drew back from the negative thoughts that threatened to smother him and opened himself to the aether as sweat rose on his body.

The aether was ever present and had always been. The first of the spheres. To the uninitiated, the aether felt like an endless sea of sameness, but to one attuned it was a flowing ocean of current and potential. It was the most dangerous force in the universe, desperate to drag all of existence back into its primordial soup. But it was also the All from what all creation rose. He had been trained in *Thought Magic* as a defense against the aether.

Ovrym stilled his body, rigid as a statue, relaxed as water and sent his thoughts into the aether. His mind snaked through the tunnels and passageways like blood through veins. Pockets of light pulsed like organs as he traversed the body of the Barrow. He avoided the large glow in the depths and slipped around the wyrmynn camp. He slowed as he passed through the small outpost he had once called home but moved on before sentiment could grab hold of him.

He zipped and flowed and found what he sought. It was a man, a high elf, a race long believed to have abandoned this world as his own people had. He stretched himself around the newcomer and saw a mote of pure power at his core. Ovrym sent his thoughts into the mote and it pulsed with violent light.

Back in his cave Ovrym fell to the ground, stunned. Surges of all the spheres of magic bit into him sending cascades of pain into every cell. He opened his mouth to scream but nothing came out. After a moment, the pain disappeared and Ovrym regained control of himself.

"A *Godhead*. So, it is true," Ovrym said with fearful glee.

Ovrym sat and ate. The warmth from the stew brought comfort to his body as he tried to bring calm to his mind. After eating he stood and walked to a chest in the corner of the room. It was time to suit up. The Order had long followed a ritual of preparation. Patterns brought meaning to life and helped to shield the mind from the aether.

First, he pulled on breeches made from the spun silk of aether wyrms and felt a rush of wellbeing enhance his *Stamina*. His empyrean bull leather jerkin came next, and he felt a surge of *Health* pump through his veins. Arm wraps of treated celestial tree bark came next along with boots made from the hide of a prismatic serpent. His mind grew clear and his body grew stronger and more agile. He pulled his bow and quiver onto his back.

Finally, he took his *Bleed Metal Saber* from its pegs on the wall and strapped it to his waist. The traditional weapon of the Order was a razor-sharp curved blade made from elementum that had passed through a bleed zone, a place where the spheres of magic held no sway. The saber, like the Bleed itself, acted as a magical null zone, capable of dispelling all magics. In the hands of an Adjudicator it was a powerful weapon.

Ovrym exited his small cave and entered a larger one. The steady trickle from the stream that fed his garden helped ease his mind. Even here, in the depths of the Barrow life held sway.

He stopped at a wall of rough stone and gestured a pattern with his fingers. The stone flowed apart, its base structure altered by his thoughts. He stepped through, wrapped himself in *Stealth* and made his way towards the disturbance.

It took several hours to find the newcomer. During the journey, Ovrym felt ripples of pain, fear and triumph pulse through the aether. He passed many a beast on his journey. Wyrmynn and ridge worms, gnome and umber beasts. Once he was so close to his old companions from the Gray Company, he could hear their joking. He pushed back his feeling of loss and let them pass.

After a long search, he found him. The man with the *Godhead*.

Ovrym was at the end of a long unused tunnel, one blocked by an ancient cave in. Beyond he could feel the man. He was in a large chamber dominated by water. An underground reservoir. He raised his hand ready to ease the broken and fallen earth aside as he had the barrier that protected his home.

But then he felt something else. Something primal that dredged up ancient feelings of terror in all xydai. Something that should not, could not be here.

"An arboleth. The ancient enemy," Ovrym said in fear and disbelief. "How?"

His hand hesitated and shook. Ovrym pulled his attention away from the chamber and to his hand. He attempted to calm it, yet for long seconds it ignored his commands. Fear battled purpose. Ovrym knew he had to reach the man, but to face an arboleth was worse than suicide.

He closed his eyes and centered his thoughts. After long moments, he was back in control.

Ovrym sent pulses of *Thought Magic* into the dirt and stone in front of him. Slowly the rubble morphed and melted and spread open. There was just enough room for him to shimmy through, and he found himself on a ledge high above the water.

The cavern was huge, the largest he had seen so far in the Barrow. The man was far below on a small island in the center of the lake, standing in front of an open chest. He was pulling pieces of armor from the chest and donning them. From this distance, his *Identify* skill could not make out the items' stats, but their quality was exquisite.

As Ovrym turned his *Analyze* skill on the man with the *Godhead* an invasive feeling of longing flowed into his mind. He wanted what was in the chest. He had to have it. Before realizing it, Ovrym had taken several steps forward and his mind was calculating a dive into the water.

By Ymiir? Ovrym thought, shaking his head to regain control. He focused and flushed the toxic thoughts from his mind. The room was rife with powerful magic of a kind he had never encountered. Something that grabbed onto the core of his being and dragged him forward. It was only his stringent mental training and his skill level in *Thought Magic* that had allowed him to regain control. No wonder the man below could not resist the siren call.

It was the Barrow, Ovrym realized. It had to be. He'd known for some time that the Barrow had the ability to compel creatures of all kinds to enter its depths. That is how he and the Gray Company were snared. But this level of hold on the mind was much stronger than any he had felt even on that day so long ago.

The chest. The powerful magic was centered on the chest, drawing the man in like a vulture to carrion. The man must have awakened the arboleth. That was why Ovrym had never felt the stained thoughts of the aberration before now. It had been slumbering.

Ovrym snapped his head up, about to warn the man regardless of consequence, when a spiny tentacle twined around the man's ankle and dragged him into the water. Ovrym nearly jumped into the water, but fear took a hold of him. Ancestral memories rose in his mind. The arboleth had enslaved his ancestors, perverting their souls into a servitor race that had been a scourge on all the Realms.

He froze, unable to move. His thoughts fled into the past, back to the boy, the apprentice in the Order. An entourage had arrived that had struck fear and respect into his master. Ovrym was ordered to stay in his room, but he'd felt compelled by something he did not understand and snuck onto the balcony above the Grand Adjudicator's reception room.

That is when he saw them. Xydai like himself, but older, stronger and terrifying. Even the Grand Adjudicator had shown these men and women deference. He learned that they were called the Purity, hunters of aetherials.

The Purity had come for help, but the Grand Adjudicator refused. The Order were upholders of laws he said, not warriors and assassins. Ovrym had studied the Writs and knew the Grand Adjudicator spoke true, but he also knew the real reason he refused. The Grand Adjudicator was afraid.

The Mistress of the Purity, a tall woman with the same

yellow eyes and dusky skin as Ovrym, stepped forward hand held above her head. The Grand Adjudicator then saw what the Purity faced. Ovrym knew because he saw it too.

Ovrym was elsewhere. A small army of Purity stood on a blasted plain as several tall beings in flowing robes emerged from the mists. The squid like humanoids were illurryth, aetherial adepts of *Thought Magic*. Flashes of telepathic energy erupted from the illurryth and xydai fell. The Purity were fierce and would not go down without a fight. They struck back with magic and blade and the battle turned.

But the illurryth were merely servants and their masters were about to enter the fray. The arboleth, massive aquatic demons ensconced in hovering, water filled tanks of metal and glass, emerged from the mists. Terrific mental assaults poured from the arboleth and pummeled the Purity with waves of psychic pain.

Xydai fell screaming, and the arboleth pushed the Purity back. Yet, they did not kill their enemies. Instead, they took them as hosts for their young. These powerful enemies of the arboleth would be infected and reborn as illurryth. They would become Other.

Ovrym felt it all as if it had happened to him. In a way, it had happened to him.

Ovrym could still remember the psychic scream that tore from him that day. He had never felt such fear, such despotic evil as he did that day. The images halted and the tall xydai woman locked eyes with Ovrym. Sympathy poured from her and her thoughts soothed Ovrym with love and kindness.

He'd spent a week in the infirmary recovering, his master never leaving his side. The Grand Adjudicator visited, gazing on him with a kindness few had ever seen on the old man's face.

The Mistress of the Purity came to him as well and spoke in a soft voice. For the first time in his life he felt what most children in the Realms took for granted. He knew what it felt like to have a mother. He could still remember the warmth of her touch, the odd floral scent of her hair. She had taught him of his people and given him a gift.

"An icon to keep you safe," she had said of the intricately carved emerald held fast in a necklace of platinum and mithril. Ovrym kept it with him always.

Ovrym returned to the present, and he found his left hand had drawn the necklace from within his jerkin. Caressing the icon brought him comfort. He closed his eyes and banished his own fears.

He looked down at the still water.

"I am sorry I am weak," Ovrym said to the doomed man.

26

Once again, Gryph was drowning. It was becoming a habit he did not enjoy. The tentacle wrapped around his leg pulled him down fast and hard. He saw his *Stamina* bar plummet as the air in his lungs grew scarce. His *Health* bar also sank at a steady rate and his mind became foggy.

Debuff Added.

You have been poisoned with aetherial neurotoxin. This toxic substance causes surges of pain, mental confusion and if left untreated brain death. It does little damage as it incapacitates prey instead of killing.

Damage: 2 per second.

Well, shit, Gryph thought. He stabbed down at the tentacle with his spear, slicing into its spongy surface. The tentacle detached and disappeared leaving rivulets of black ichor that turned the water brackish. Gryph kicked towards the surface, but before he got five feet, another tentacle snapped from the depths and wrapped around his waist.

This tentacle was larger and stronger than the last one, covered in sticky cup shaped pads. Crustacean like nodules covered most of the exposed surface, acting as armor. It squeezed Gryph, forcing the little remaining air from his lungs and pulled him deeper into the darkness.

Panic took ahold of Gryph, heightened by the venom causing surges of confusion in his mind. There was something at the edge of his thoughts. Something tickling at his mind. Something he was desperately trying to remember.

He heard a voice in his head screaming and realized it was

his own voice. It was screaming, *Air, Air, Air!*

Well, no shit, subconscious Sherlock, Gryph raged at his inner voice. His lungs filled with water and his inner asshole continued to yell *Air, Air, Air* at him. Then, in a distant part of his mind, he understood.

Air Magic. Gryph shoved his hand into his inventory and extracted the *Halo of Air* spell stone. He held it tightly and tried to concentrate, but his mind was adrift, sinking with his body into the depths of the suffocating waters.

He was losing consciousness. As his mind went dark, a tingle of warmth throbbed in his palm. A torrent of air swirled around his arm and into his mind. The surge of power exploded into his mind, jarring him awake.

You have learned the spell HALO OF AIR.

Sphere: Air Magic.
Tier: Base.

Allows the caster to summon a bubble of continuously renewed air around his or her head. This is used for breathing underwater or anywhere else where fresh, clean air is needed.

Mana Cost: 30.
Casting Time: Instantaneous.
Duration: 5 minutes + 1 per Air Magic level.
Cooldown: None.

Gryph cast *Halo of Air* and the water exploded away from his head in a sphere that measured about two feet. He tried to gulp in the fresh, amazing air, but vomited up copious amounts of water instead. The halo siphoned the bile soiled water away from Gryph's face.

He was breathing normally, but his body still throbbed with pain from the neurotoxin. He pulled another spell stone from his inventory and soon knew *Detoxification.*

You have learned the spell DETOXIFICATION.

Sphere: Life Magic.
Tier: Base.

Allows the caster to cleanse themselves or another of the ill effects of poison, venom, spores, gases or other attacks that cause poison damage.

Mana Cost: 40.
Casting Time: Instantaneous.
Effectiveness: Reduces Poison Damage by 2 points per second per level. Poison is eliminated when the reduction per second is greater than the damage per second.
Cooldown: Five minutes.

You have learned the skill LIFE MAGIC.

Level: 1.
Tier: Base.
Skill Type: Active.

You can now wield the power of Life Magic. Life Magic allows the user to tap into the animating forces of life and sentience itself. Life Magic makes use of defensive and healing spells, but it also has some potent offensive spells.

Note: Users of Life Magic are beloved for their abilities to heal, to enable crops to grow quicker, and to make life better.

A quick casting of *Detoxification* cleansed his body of the toxin, but he was still being dragged deeper into the darkness. His eyes, perhaps shielded from the water by the halo, saw details of this watery underworld. Then he saw the beast that was dragging him downward and wished he hadn't.

Gryph screamed as the beast came into view. It looked like a primeval eel had mated violently with a squid. Its body was long and bulbous. It had a huge singular eye atop a swirling vortex of teeth that spun in concentric circles. Two large tentacles, one dragging Gryph down, protruded from the arboleth's underside. Four smaller tentacles emerged from its back, the underside covered in needle-like spines. One still bled from the wound Gryph had inflicted. He used *Analyze*, thankful for the boost given him by the cowl.

Arboleth.

Level: 42.
Health: 1004.
Stamina: 820.
Mana: 900.
Spirit: 0.

Arboleth are horrific aberrations. Natives of the aetherial realm, they are among the most ancient of all sentient races. They are highly intelligent, incredibly cruel and vastly dangerous. They are masters of both aetherial and Thought Magic, spheres normally incompatible in one being. This suggests that they were birthed in the earliest era of creation when the thought and aetherial realms clashed to give birth to the cosmos as we know it.

Strengths: Unknown.
Immunities: Unknown.
Weakness: Unknown.

The weight of impending doom threatened to crush Gryph's psyche. He was Level 7 and this offense to all sanity was level fricking 42. Fear and adrenaline built in his mind creating a cocktail of horror that Gryph wouldn't serve to his worst enemy.

The beast's mouth pulsed in an awful display of gyrating flesh and spinning teeth. Even with the sound dampening of the water, the roar hit Gryph like a fist. The arboleth's anger surged up the tentacle that continued to drag Gryph down, and despite the armor he felt a rib pop.

Gryph cast *Flying Stalactite* and watched as it slowly moved towards the arboleth's eye. The water slowed the missile's pace just enough for the arboleth to smack the stalactite aside with its other large tentacle.

The creature's eye pulsed with light and a wave of energy shimmered towards him like the waves of heat pouring off a desert highway. It passed over Gryph, and his brain exploded in a nova of migraines, one piled atop another in flashes of light and pain. Layers of sanity peeled back like a rotten onion, and he knew he was losing his mind.

The effect passed, but the damage was done. Not only was his *Health* plummeting, but the sea beast had dragged him closer. Its mouth gaped and the rings and rows of teeth spun. Gryph was being dragged into a massive, living garbage disposal.

Gryph thrust forward with his spear seeking to pincushion the arboleth's massive eye. The large tentacle was there again, moving much faster than Gryph thought possible. It smacked Gryph's spear thrust aside, the force of the deflection nearly tearing the spear from his grip.

Pain scoured both ankles again as the smaller tentacles gripped his legs, puncturing the leather of his boots and dumping more poison into him. He kicked his legs frantically but could not earn his freedom. Another tentacle grabbed onto his spear arm dumping more poison into him.

The arboleth brought him close to its mouth, and Gryph knew the end was nigh.

I'm sorry, Brynn. I've failed you, Gryph thought. He told himself he wouldn't close his eyes. That he'd face his death head on. But as the beast dragged him towards its mouth, all his bravado leaked from him, and with a whimper, he slammed his eyelids closed.

Nothing happened. The pain of the poison still burned in his legs, but he was still remarkably alive. He eased one of his eyes open to find the arboleth staring at him from its unblinking eye.

"WHAT ARE YOU?"

Gryph did not hear the creature speak but heard it in his mind. He blinked stupidly. "What?"

"WHAT ARE YOU? YOU ARE...DIFFERENT!"

The voice was getting louder, and his mind fogged. Whether it was from this psychic invasion or the poison spreading through his veins, or both, he did not know. He knew he had to do something. The arboleth was the most difficult opponent he'd yet faced in the Realms by several factors. He was only alive by the whim of the abomination's curiosity.

"**ANSWER!**"

The creature raged and wrenched Gryph's legs apart, threatening to tear him in two like a wishbone. He swung with his free hand and the golden glint of his bracers drew his eye. He remembered his new gear and a desperate plan formed in his mind. It would need timing and luck and still might end with him becoming arboleth shit. *Assuming this thing shits.* But he had no other choice.

He closed his eyes and focused on his core of mana. He pulsed it down three different paths at the same time. The concentration was near impossible with the poison clouding his brain and the fear boring into his soul, but then a warm calm settled over him. A blanket of hope enveloped him. Gryph wondered if it was his spec ops training.

Gryph squinted his eyes shut and three things happened in quick succession.

First, Gryph activated the *Moon Flare* ability of his breastplate. A flash of light erupted from his chest scalding the arboleth's eye. In the near blackness of the underground lake the pulse was brighter than a flash of lightning. The life energy burned at the arboleth's body for a massive 280 points of damage. A horrid mental scream raged from the arboleth as a surge of healing warmth flowed over Gryph. His pain eased and his *Health* neared 70%.

Next, Gryph activated the speed doubling power of his boots just as the arboleth's tentacles released their grip on him. They flailed wildly, striking Gryph with glancing blows. The newfound speed flashed through his nerves, and he avoided most of the beast's blind attacks.

Finally, he pumped more mana into his bracers activating their magnetic control and assigned the field to his spear. With a mental flick he launched the spear forward with much more force than he could ever manage with muscle power alone. The spear torpedoed through the water and found its mark, embedding itself in the arboleth's still blind eye.

You have scored a Critical Hit.
5X Damage.

The arboleth's *Health* fell by another 182 points. A mental scream unlike anything Gryph had ever felt erupted from the mind of the tortured beast, and he could feel the fear tear at its mind. Gryph had no sympathy and quickly chugged a mana potion. Power pulsed through his body, and he activated the bracers again, this time flicking his wrist, ensuring an extra eighty points of damage as his spear ripped from the beast's eye and flew back to his hand.

Despite the incredible damage Gryph had dealt the arboleth, the abomination still had nearly 50% of its *Health*, and he suspected with 900 mana, the creature could heal itself. He needed to keep it off balance. He pumped more mana into the bracers and shot the spear forwards again.

Another *Critical Hit* and another 182 points of damage as the spear punished the arboleth's eye again. More viscous fluid poured from the wound. The beast flailed. At first, Gryph thought it was trying to locate its tormentor, but then he noticed a pattern to the gyrations.

The damn thing is casting, Gryph thought in alarm.

Gryph tried to pour more mana into his bracers, but both the bracer's five-second cooldown and his dangerously low mana bar flared at him. The spear remained lodged in the beast's eye far out of reach. Gryph had just enough mana for one spell.

He cast *Animate Rope* and tossed his new spider silk rope towards the arboleth. It snapped forward like an eel and zipped around the beast's tentacles. On Gryph's command, they tightened, disrupting the beast's casting.

Gryph grasped the other end of the rope in his left hand and commanded the rope to pull him forward. He sped towards the beast hoping that his aim was on mark. If he was too low, he would end up inside the creature's thousand-toothed mouth.

But his aim was true, and he landed on the arboleth's head,

right above the eye. He grabbed the shaft of his spear with his right hand and twisted. With its tentacles entangled the arboleth could do nothing but try to buck Gryph off. But every jerk pushed the spear deeper and caused more damage.

"WHAT ARE YOU?"

The creature's terrified voice sounded small in Gryph's mind. Its immortal existence was ending, and it was desperate to understand how it had come to this end.

I am your death, Gryph thought back at it. Gryph yanked the spear from the arboleth's eye and thrust down with all his strength. The spear pierced the back of the eye, puncturing the thin layer of bone behind it. His arms sunk up to the elbows into the ichor of the abomination's eye. Gryph pushed harder.

The spear impaled the arboleth's brain and the creature's foul thoughts blinked out like a blown light bulb. The beast's body sank into the murk. Gryph opened his mouth to scream in triumph, but instead of yelps of joy a cacophony of air bubbles surged from his mouth. In the final moments of the battle, mind clouded by adrenaline and rage, he hadn't noticed the *Halo of Air* spell had expired.

His *Health* bar plummeted. Had he survived the arboleth only to drown?

Gryph's chest burned as his *Health* bar sank. He attempted to cast *Halo of Air*, but his blue mana bar blinked at him with the rhythm of laughter. Perhaps it was the last vengeance of the arboleth.

He dug for a potion. With no time to be selective he had to hope it was a *Health* or *Mana Potion*. Either would suit his purposes, but if he selected a *Stamina Potion*, it would mean his death. He popped the cork and crammed the vial to his mouth and sucked.

Drinking underwater was difficult in the best of circumstances, but when you are nearly drowning, it is orders of magnitudes more complicated. He tasted brackish water and wondered if the potion would be effective.

Stars popped behind his eyes as the pain in his lungs faded. He was dying. Then he felt a rush of energy through his body. A mana potion. As he passed out Gryph's fingers moved through the gestures of casting.

27

Gryph's mind was adrift, floating in a world of dim light and weightlessness.

I am dead, Gryph thought. There was no sound in this strange afterlife. No pearly gates. No endless hunting grounds. No field of honorable battle. Nothing.

Gryph drifted for an unknowable time before his back bumped against something large and spongy. He turned and forced his eyes to focus. A massive eye stared back at him. Gryph screamed, and a cough wracked his body. He vomited a massive volume of water and watched as it siphoned away from him.

In an instant, his mind was lucid. *Halo of Air* shimmered around him like its angelic namesake. He was alive. His last second casting had worked but his *Health* bar still pulsed crimson fury at him. He was alive, but only just.

He was about to reach for a *Health Potion* when he remembered the last spell stone. He grabbed the Minor Healing spell stone and held it in his palm, concentrating. A pulse of wellbeing surged from his hand up through his arm and settled in his mind.

You have learned the spell MINOR HEALING.

Sphere: Life Magic.
Tier: Base.

You can now heal minor wounds on yourself or others.

Mana Cost: 20.
Casting Time: 2 seconds.
Effectiveness: Heals 5 points of damage per level of Life Magic.
Cooldown: 30 seconds.

He cast the spell and warmth flowed through him. He still felt awful but considering the beast he had just slain was staring at him, the spear still protruding from its dead eye, he counted himself lucky. He waited for the cooldown period to end and cast *Minor Heal* again. His mana regeneration kept pace with the spell's cooldown period. So, given time he'd likely always be able to heal himself. After a few more minutes, his *Health* was back to 100%.

He rubbed his eyes and regretted it. His hands were covered in a thick slime that smelled like the insides of a dumpster that had been baking in the hot sun for a week. With a look of disgust, he realized that the clear slop covered most of his body.

He grumbled in disgust and his *Harvest* skill brought up a prompt.

You have found Arboleth Eye Ichor.

This incredibly rare and valuable ingredient has many uses in both Alchemy and Crafting. You feel as if it could make a Potion of Quick Thought and other unidentified effects. You also get the sense it could craft an item that blocks Scrying spells and Divination and other unidentified effects.

Gryph's eyes went wide. This disgusting stuff was amazing. Though he dreaded the idea of drinking something made from this foul ichor, he knew he needed to harvest as much of it as he could.

You have been offered the Quest: Harvest the Arboleth.

You have slain a Legendary Beast. Now take your reward. Harvest five vials of arboleth eye ichor, one arboleth toxin gland and at least one arboleth egg from the arboleth corpse.

Difficulty: Moderate.
Reward: Extremely rare Crafting and Alchemy supplies.
XP: 5,000.

The experience boost alone was well worth it, but he also felt a stirring of greed. What wonders could he craft with these ingredients? Then the naysayer in him brought attention to the word egg. The danger was obvious. The egg could birth another abomination. It had to have other uses, right?

He hesitated a mere moment before accepting the quest. Then he got to work.

He dug into his inventory and found his alchemy kit containing a variety of empty vessels for collecting ingredients and a siphon pump to collect liquids. He readied them all and replaced the kit.

He attached the siphon pump to one of the empty vials and watched in irritation as it promptly filled with water. He scowled at his own stupidity. Of course, that would happen. Perhaps that's why the quest was of moderate difficulty. He thought on the dilemma for a few moments and then grinned.

Once again, he cast *Halo of Air*, but this time he imagined the sphere around the hand containing the vial. Eureka. Another bubble of air formed around his hand, and he turned the vial upside down pouring the brackish water out letting the bubble of air siphon it away

He plunged the needle tip of the siphon pump into the arboleth's eye and pumped. Soon he had the five vials of ichor. Realizing he had many more empty vials, he kept siphoning If this stuff was half as valuable as it seemed he'd be a fool to leave any. When he'd filled the tenth vial, the pump stopped sucking ichor.

Gryph stashed his equipment and looked down on the dead beast's now desiccated eye. It looked like a balloon punctured by a massive pin. The pin being his spear, which he pulled free and stashed in his inventory. The beast was far less intimidating now, and Gryph wagged his middle finger, a posthumous up yours.

Now to harvest a toxin gland and an egg, but where the hell would he find either? It wasn't like he was an expert in horrid abomination anatomy. He swam back to get a better view hoping to get some clue. A dull blue light, like the glow he'd seen on the chest on the island above pulsed near the base of the arboleth's smaller tentacles.

Gryph swam down, taking a moment to refresh *Halo of Air* and realized that the glow was dull because it was coming from the underside of the massive corpse. Gryph frowned and attempted to shove the beast to gain access to its underside. His efforts were as effective as pushing a twenty-ton garbage bag filled with lard. His only reward for all his effort was a lower *Stamina* bar.

He swam back a few paces and thought. Gazing around he saw a few large stalagmites jutting from the lake bottom. A plan formed in his mind. He cast *Animate Rope* and commanded it to wrap around the base of the two smaller tentacles, careful not to tear the thin filament on the poison spines on the appendages' underside.

Satisfied he then ordered the rope to circle around the stalagmite and return to him. He braced himself and pulled with all his might. The beast's corpse shifted a tad as Gryph tugged, but a minute of straight effort did not get him access to his prize.

His *Stamina* spent, Gryph took a break. He cast *Halo of Air* again and considered his options. I need to be stronger, or smarter. As he thought on the dilemma, his eyes drifted to the glowing prompt icon in the corner of his vision. He sent a mental tap at the icon and prompts exploded into his mind.

You earned Experience Points.

You have earned 70,000 XP for slaying the Legendary Beast: Arboleth.

You have Reached Level (s) 8, 9, and 10.

You have 18 (15 Base and 3 Godhead) unused Attribute Points. You have 3 unused Perk Points.

"Holy Shit," Gryph sputtered. The arboleth alone had given him more experience than everything else he'd done since arriving in the Realms. "I should be dead," he said. Then a lesson he had learned long ago surged into his mind, and he heard the colonels' voice. *It is not power, but the intelligent application of power that wins the day.*

Evidently, that mantra was as true in the Realms as it was in the real world. He returned to his prompts.

Your Skills have Levelled.

You have reached level 12 in AIR MAGIC

You have reached level 4 in EARTH MAGIC.

You have reached level 9 in STAVES/SPEARS.

You have reached level 7 in THROWN WEAPONS.

You have reached level 9 in LIGHT ARMOR.

You have reached level 8 in DODGE.

You have reached level 7 in STEALTH.

You have reached level 5 in HARVEST.

You have reached level 9 in ANALYZE.

You have reached level 9 in PERCEPTION

Magic Skills: Level (Affinity) (Tier)

Fire: 0 (25%) (Base)
Air: 12 (75%) (Base)
Water: 0 (50%) (Base)
Earth: 4 (25%) (Base)
Chthonic: 0 (0%) (Base)
Empyrean: 0 (100%) (Base)
Chaos: 0 (50%) (Base)
Order: 0 (25%) (Base)
Life: 1 (50%) (Base)
Death: 0 (25%) (Base)
Thought: 0 (75%) (Base)
Aether: 0 (25%) (Base)
Soul: 0 (50%) (Base)

Martial Skills: Level (Tier)
Unarmed: 5 (Base)
Small Blades: 5 (Base)
Staves/Spears: 9 (Base)
Thrown Weapons: 7 (Base)
Stealth: 7 (Base)
Light Armor: 9 (Base)
Dodge: 8 (Base)

Knowledge Skills: (Tier)
Alchemy: 5 (Base)
Harvest: 5 (Base)
Analyze: 9 (Base)
Perception: 9 (Base)
Lock-picking: 5 (Base)
Traps: 5 (Base)
Perk Points: 3   **Divine Perk Points**: 0

Gryph's jaw gaped in amazement. His skills had surged during the battle with the arboleth. Now it was time to make use of his rewards. He had a dilemma. He could dump a bunch of his *Attribute Points* into *Strength* and muscle the corpse. But that seemed short sighted and even though Gryph was not a gamer, he understood how valuable *Attribute Points* were.

He took a moment to think. Strategy had always been one of his strong suits. It has served him well in the real world. It would serve him well in this one.

He dumped five points into *Intelligence* and his *Mana* increased significantly. He added five points to *Constitution* and his *Health* and *Stamina* rose. He placed another three into *Dexterity*. If he was to master the *Staves/Spear* skill, then being agile would prove much more important than overall *Strength*.

Gryph - Level 10	Stats
High Elf (El'Edryn) Deity: None Experience: 106,310 Next Level: 48,490	Health: 184 Stamina: 183 Mana: 168 Spirit: 136
Attributes	**Gifts**
Strength: 23 Constitution: 32 Dexterity: 32 Intelligence: 25 Wisdom: 10 Attribute Points: 5	Health Regeneration: +25% Mana Regeneration: +25% Night Vision: 120 Ft. Master of Tongues

He kept the last five points in reserve. Either to make better use down the road or as insurance. The game hack he'd discovered had saved his life once and his lack of foresight had nearly killed him. He'd learned his lesson and would do his best to never repeat that mistake.

Next, he decided it was time to spend some *Perk Points*. They were even more valuable than *Attribute Points,* so he knew he had to be strategic. He examined his skill trees and focused on his most used skills.

So far *Air Magic* had been his saving grace. Not only was it his highest leveled skill it was the one he used the most. However, as useful as *Air Magic* had been, he had no offensive spells in the sphere. *Halo of Air* had been a lifesaver, but he knew its use would be limited topside. He didn't plan to spend so much time drowning from here on out.

He chuckled to himself as he imagined what Lex would have said to that plan and found that he missed his NPC's sarcasm. He hoped the short hairy bastard was alive and well. He was likely sipping grog, eating mutton and flirting with barmaids while Gryph rotted in this dungeon.

He returned his focus to the task at hand and opened the

Air Magic perk tree.

Gryph had selected the *Base Tier Mana* perk after his battle with the baalgrath and knew that choice had saved his life several times. Unfortunately, he had to more than double his current level before he could unlock the apprentice tier perks.

The *Effectiveness* boost held some appeal, but he didn't jump the gun. *Resistance* wasn't too appealing since he had not yet faced another air mage. However, down the road such a perk could be invaluable, especially at higher levels.

His eyes went to the *Item Power* perk. Most of his current magic items relied on *Air Magic* so that perk would make all of them 25% more powerful, including his *Ring of Minor Air Shield*. A plan formed in Gryph's mind. He dumped one point into *Item Power*. The other two points he held in reserve.

Air Magic Perk Tree.				
Tier	Mana	Effect	Resistance	Item
Base	80%	+25%	10%	+25%
Apprentice	70%	+50%	25%	+50%
Journeyman	60%	+75%	50%	+75%
Master	50%	+100%	70%	+100%
Grandmaster	30%	+200%	80%	+200%
Divine	20%	+300%	90%	+300%

Gryph cast *Halo of Air* again and then set to work. He did some quick math in his head and smiled. In theory, his plan was solid. He inhaled and held his right hand out. He pumped a full 20% of his mana into the *Ring of Minor Air Shield*. Normally, he would just let the ring create the protective bubble of air around his own body, but this time he had a different plan.

He focused on the pocket where the arboleth's body met the smaller tentacles. It looked like an obese armpit and should, if Gryph's guess was right, be perfect for what he had planned. With a deep breath, Gryph unleashed the power of the ring.

A beam of solid air shot from the ring to his point of focus and built-up power. The blue-white vortex of air expanded, and the resultant explosion of water buffeted Gryph back several paces, spinning him head over heels. A moment later, he regained his balance to see that his plan had succeeded.

The arboleth's body had pushed upwards as if resting on an invisible globe, and Gryph could see the blue glow much clearer. It was time to test his second assumption. Gryph swam up to the barrier of air and paused. The blue glow of his prize was throbbing now, and better still he could see another, brighter blue glow further down the beast's abdomen.

The eggs, Gryph thought. A grin crossed his face as he stepped forward. If this didn't work, then he would fail this quest and maybe end up with a busted nose. His foot passed through the field of air with only the slightest of resistance. The rest of his body followed. He now stood in an invisible sphere under twenty tons of fish flab. It was time to get cutting.

28

He'd been sawing into the arboleth's corpse for nearly four minutes when the cooldown on his ring ended. He paused and formed another bubble, this one closer to the other blue glow Gryph hoped were the eggs. The current bubble had about a minute left before it would collapse, sending thousands of pounds of arboleth corpse thundering to the lakebed with him underneath.

One last rip and tear and he had the creature's toxin gland. He'd been incredibly careful not to cut into it. He had no idea if the toxin needed to be injected to be effective, but he was sure not planning to find out. The thing was the size of a large watermelon. Gryph wondered just how much poison he'd be able to extract from this treasure and just what he'd be able to do with it.

He cut away at the strands of flesh holding the sack in place, careful to tie off one that looked to be the poison delivery tube. With a rubbery snap that reminded Gryph of calamari, the sack came free. He looked up to see the air shield was now flickering at an alarming rate, and Gryph swam to the right into the second air shield and a few seconds later the first one blinked out. The blubbery flesh of the arboleth sagged down once again, flopping onto the spot he had just been standing. He checked the time and his current mana levels. So far so good.

You have found an Arboleth Toxin Gland.

This incredibly rare item can create a poison that could make enemies susceptible to Thought Magic and other unidentified effects. You also get the sense it could craft an item that could grant immunity to poisons and other unidentified effects.

He stashed the gland in his inventory, thankful not just for the satchel's auto organize feature, but also for its preservation feature. The last thing he wanted was a bagful of rotten toxic flesh getting all over all his stuff.

Gryph swam down towards the glow of the eggs and cast *Halo of Air* again. A moment later, the cooldown on the ring ended, and he created another air shield bubble. This one was further down and under the beast's body. By his count he had less than three minutes before the second bubble timed out and collapsed. If he wasn't finished by then, he'd be trapped and spend the last few moments of his life waiting to die by blubber smothering.

He hacked into the abomination's flesh once more and the dagger cut through a membrane with a snap. Inside he found three leathery sacks that resembled deflated footballs for giants. Umbilicals led up to the arboleth's body. As he moved to cut the closest umbilical, something inside the leathery sack moved.

Gryph jumped back in shock, his heart pounding madly. *Maybe this isn't the best idea I've ever had.* He watched for a tense few seconds as the thing inside the egg stopped moving. Then with a deep breath, he cut the umbilical.

He grabbed the egg and shoved it into his satchel, hoping that the stasis effects of the intra-dimensional folds would prevent the egg from doing something horrible, like hatching.

You have completed the Quest Harvest the Arboleth.

You have Harvested items from the arboleth corpse.

<u>Reward</u>: *Extremely rare Crafting and Alchemy ingredients.*
<u>Experience</u>: *5,000.*

Gryph took a deep calming breath and smiled. Mission accomplished. A quick glance told him he had another minute and a half before the second bubble collapsed. He had the time and got to work on the second egg. As he sawed through the umbilical, his mind wondered what good would come of harvesting these eggs? He sure as hell would not raise pet arboleth. The one had been enough of an abomination. Two could bring apocalypse.

The second egg came free, and as he tucked it in the satchel, he examined it with *Harvest*.

You have found an Arboleth Egg.

This insanely rare item is of both incalculable worth and incalculable danger. You feel as if it could create a potion that will give a permanent resistance increase to thought and aetherial magics and other unidentified effects. You also get the sense it could craft an item that will protect a large area from Thought and Aether Magic and other unidentified effects. It can also give birth to an arboleth, a species that has long been a scourge on the Realms. Use wisely.

"My word," Gryph muttered in shock. This thing was amazing and insanely dangerous. He placed the second egg into his satchel, sending a silent prayer that the stasis effect contained these seeds of destruction.

The second air shield blinked, a sure sign that time was up. Gryph knew he'd have to leave the third behind, but there was no way in the nine hells he would leave it alive.

He flexed his hand on the *Ice Dagger* and pumped a full charge into it. With a powerful thrust, Gryph plunged the blade into the egg sack. The thing inside the egg screamed in his mind, and he winced in pain. He thrust again, and the noise stopped.

The blinking of the air shield had grown critical, and Gryph kicked off the inside of the wall of solid air and emerged from under the massive body. A moment later, the second shield failed, and the bulbous corpse collapsed. Gryph smiled to himself, cast *Halo of Air* again and began a slow, steady swim upwards.

He was halfway to the surface when the fleshy body of the arboleth shook and rumbled. A second later, something lithe and fast shot out from an orifice near the arboleth's rear fin. It turned and darted towards Gryph.

29

Ovrym sat in meditation, his mind attempting to find ease. It was too late to help the man. All he could do was focus his own mind. The rock of the high shelf dug into him, but he did not feel it. He let his guilt and his fear and his weakness flow over him like the waves of a storm. Each breath brought relief. Each wave grew less toxic.

Eventually, he found peace again. His ancient demons chased back into the dark depths of his soul, for now. He reached out for the aether and spread his thoughts through it.

Then he felt the elf. Somehow the man was still alive. A shudder of shock and hope flowed through his body. Ovrym forced himself to focus. *Maybe I can still help,* he thought. He could feel the arboleth's stained and rancid thoughts, focused into a pinprick weapon.

Ovrym molded his thoughts into a field of warmth and life and hope and settled it down on the drowning man. It wasn't much, but perhaps it would be enough. Time lost temporary meaning as he became comfort and ease. He pulled his attention away from the battle. He was of no use if he could not remain calm.

The xydai became warmth and hope and strength flowing into the man. He was only a sprinkle of rain against a raging wildfire, but he was something. Ovrym let himself become one with the aether. He was no longer singular. He was part of the All. Heartbeats passed like centuries, breaths like ages. He was both always and never and still, he held to his task.

Then a pulse of shock and anguish flashed outward, a nova of rage that exploded before collapsing unto itself and disappearing. The arboleth was dead. Ovrym's eyes opened in shock.

He stood and stared down at the water as the last ripples of battle settled to calm. Where was the man? Had he succumbed? Ovrym reached through the water and found the barest pinprick of life distorting the calm of the aether. The man was alive but drowning. Ovrym shared his strength, hoping it was enough.

For a moment, Ovrym feared it was not enough. Then thoughts returned, and the spark became a fire. He stood, waiting to see the man emerge from the depths. Long minutes passed, and he did not surface. What was he doing?

Ovrym sat again and waited. Whoever this man was he was of an odd character. Was he friend or foe? The shock of the arboleth's presence had so overwhelmed Ovrym that he had not considered the man's nature. Was he a source of evil or a force for good? He possessed a *Godhead*. How was that even possible?

Was he wrong in aiding this latent god? Had his mind been so warped by his hatred and fear of the aetherial abomination that he had overlooked a greater threat? These were the thoughts that raged in Ovrym's mind as the man finally emerged from the depths.

He did not look like much, near drowned and so exhausted that he collapsed to his knees the moment he climbed onto the island. He swayed back and forth as he inhaled a lungful of air. He was shaking. Fear? Adrenaline? Cold? He seemed confused, disoriented.

Finally, he seemed to gain control over himself as a look of peace came over him. Then he screamed a scream few had ever heard. Ovrym knew that scream and fear stabbed at his soul. The man gasped and then fell forward onto his face. Ovrym saw the pulsating slug like creature as it sank spiny tendrils into the back of the man's head.

"Illurryth," Ovrym said in anguish.

The arboleth larva had infected the elf's brain. Soon it would feed upon it and replace his mind with an aetherial abomination, a sorcerer in service of the arboleth. The man was dead. Nothing could stop the metamorphosis, the process of consumption that resulted in a sentient being becoming the pure evil of the illurryth. He would be reborn as something else, a malevolence unlike any the Realms had ever seen, an illurryth in possession of a *Godhead*.

Before rational thought could stop him, Ovrym pulled his

bow from his shoulder. He knocked an arrow and drew back, focusing both *Mana* and *Stamina* into his shot. The arrow burned with the blue aura of *Thought Magic*. He closed one eye, and the *Stamina* flowed into *Viper Sting*, an *Archery* perk that increased both damage and the chance to hit.

"Shall you be reborn at peace," Ovrym said, putting his heart into the traditional prayer for the soul of the dead. He let fly and his aim was true. The arrow pierced both larva and man at the base of the neck, instantly slaying two minds.

3⊕

Gryph swam as his body and mind relaxed. He had survived. He had won. Above him he could see the dim light of the surface. He kicked his legs harder, relishing the thought of feeling fresh air on his face again. Even if fresh was a matter of degree.

He laughed aloud as his exhalations pushed through the halo to become bubbles of air. He imagined that when they broke the surface, the sound of his laughter would echo around the chamber like they did in the cartoons he watched as a kid.

The surface was close now, and Gryph kicked harder. He was exhausted and wanted to be free of this watery prison. He pumped his arms and legs again as ease flowed into his mind. Then something punched into the back of his head with a wet thud.

Waves of pain erupted in his mind, and he lost control of his body. Psychic threads of hate, anger and hunger delved into his mind. Part of him was aware of a debuff, but it felt as if it belonged to someone else.

Debuff Added.

You have been poisoned with Arboleth Larval Toxin.
Thought resistance reduced by 80%.

Possession: Your body is no longer your own. You are now controlled by an outside influence.

Cooldown: 5 minutes.

Gryph filled with terror, but his mind could find no focus. He was an observer. He felt drunk, ecstatic, without a care in the world. As he breached the surface of the water an oily stain of incomprehensible thoughts flowed over him. He tried to focus on them, but they tasted of acid. Through the rancid spiraling a thought came to him. *This is for the best. You are becoming greater. You are becoming Prime.*

Inky fingers of wrath oozed from the Prime, grasping and tearing at Gryph's mind. Slowly bits of him were being flayed and consumed. Gryph was becoming something else. He tried to find himself, some core of who he was to cling onto, even if it were for a few moments, but he felt his light dimming. Soon he would be Prime.

What was it doing to him? Fear bit into Gryph, and he could feel the alien presence rejoice. Gryph began to disappear. Alien thoughts spread through him, replacing his own. He knew that he should be terrified, but his thoughts were distant as if he were being summoned to a permanent sleep. The Prime was consuming all that he was.

What is fear? the colonel said from the deepest recesses on his memory. His mind found some measure of calm as the memory of one his father's earliest lessons came to him. The colonel despised intellectual sloth and believed in the power of books to expand the mind. He had given Finn a well-worn copy of Frank Herbert's *Dune* on his tenth birthday and made him memorize the famous litany against fear.

He turned his internal gaze to the Prime and showed the alien entity what it meant to be a Caldwell. He rushed the Prime, fury and purpose beating the infection back into the deepest part of his mind. Somehow, he knew he couldn't exorcise it, but he could lock it away. He sealed the mental prison, and the alien presence howled in rage. It beat itself against the fortifications of Gryph's mind, slowly chipping away at their protection.

A spike of pain exploded into the back of his head and a terrible scream erupted from his throat. It was both his own voice and the Prime. His body pitched forward, but his mind departed before the body hit the ground. An arrow pierced both the larva and brain stem and the distant part of him that still existed sped down the tunnel of light.

As Gryph's lifeless body hit the sand of the island, a distant voice spoke.

Thank You.

31

Gryph's mind returned with a surge of shock and pain. He hit the ground hard, his lungs exploding. *Not again*, Gryph thought as he struggled for breath. Agony throbbed through him as he assessed the damage. He was hurt, but alive. What was happening?

Debuffs blinked in his vision.

Debuffs Added.

You have died and respawned.
All attributes reduced by 25% for two hours.

Short-term paralysis.
Cooldown: 2 minutes.

Died? Gryph's mind surged with panic. *Respawned? What the hell is going on?*

He looked around and realized he was in the small cave where he'd killed the barrow rat. He was back where he'd started. His mind struggled to remember what happened. The last thing he remembered was the Prime and the pain. He reached for his neck but could not move.

Fucking debuffs, Gryph thought. *Is that thing still on me?* Fear threatened to drag him back into the darkness of the lake, into the maw of the arboleth. His memory of the Prime surged back. Fear crawled into him again, and he sought a safe harbor for his mind.

As if answering a prayer, a gold prompt unlike any he'd yet seen called to him. With nothing else to do while he waited for the paralysis to wear off, Gryph tapped the prompt with a mental flick.

A Prime Godhead is a Mote of Creation.

It is a nexus of ultimate potential, but that potential must be earned. You have survived a Legendary Trial and slain a Legendary Beast (Arboleth).

Your Godhead has evolved to Tier 1.

There are 10 Tiers that can only be achieved by completing Legendary Trials.

Each Tier will provide 1 Divine Perk Point and Tier specific bonuses.

Congratulations, your Prime Godhead has evolved to Tier 1.

The nascent mote of creation inside you has awakened.

You now have 100% Affinity for all spheres of magic.

You are awarded +50 to Health, +50 to Stamina, +50 to Mana and +50 to Spirit.

You are also granted +5 to all attributes.

All skills (including those learned in the next 24 hours) are increased by one level.

You now have access to the Divine Perk Tree.
+1 Divine Perk Points.

You have chosen to worship the Deity Gryph and have unlocked the Incantations associated with your deity. As long as you stay true to the tenets of belief set down by Gryph you will keep access to your Incantations.

Gryph – Level 10	Stats
High Elf (El'Edryn) Deity: None Experience: 116,310 Next Level: 43,490	Health: 234 Stamina: 233 Mana: 218 Spirit: 186
Attributes	**Gifts**
Strength: 28 Constitution: 37 Dexterity: 37 Intelligence: 30 Wisdom: 15	Health Regeneration: +25% Mana Regeneration: +25% Night Vision: 120 Ft. Master of Tongues

"Holy Crap." The Godhead had just given him an incredible surge in power. Not only was the +5 bonus to each *Attribute* like getting an instant six levels, the +50 bonus to all four *Stats* was insane. And 100% *Affinity* for every sphere of magic. His body surged with power and warmth. *What the hell are incantations?* Gryph wondered. He suspected that they made use of *Spirit*, but he had no idea where or how to acquire them.

Gryph turned his focus to the *Divine Perk Points*. If he understood the prompts, then they were exponentially more valuable than normal *Perk Points*. He could acquire a maximum of ten, so he would have to spend them wisely. In his excitement Gryph had forgotten about the paralysis debuff until he received the prompt telling him he was no longer paralyzed. He reached a tentative finger up to the back of his neck and found nothing. No parasitic slug, no wound, no scar, nothing.

Gryph sat cross-legged and laughed out loud. He could barely contain his excitement and joy as he opened his *Divine Perk Tree*.

<table>
<tr><td colspan="1" align="center">Divine Perk Tree Tier 1</td></tr>
</table>

Inspire
Imbue
Assimilate
Resurrection

<table>
<tr><td align="center">Divine Perk Tree Tier 2</td></tr>
</table>

Information Currently Unavailable.

<table>
<tr><td align="center">Divine Perk Tree Tier 3</td></tr>
</table>

Information Currently Unavailable.

Well, that's annoying. He'd made educated choices based upon an understanding of available factors. Without full knowledge of the downstream perks, how could he make a wise choice? *Guess it is time to have faith,* Gryph thought, fully understanding the irony of the statement.

More frustrating was that each level required more *Divine Perk Points.* Level one needed one. Level two required two. Level three required three. That meant that even if he maxed out the *Godhead,* he still wouldn't be able to acquire every perk on the Divine Perk Tree. He would have to choose wisely.

DIVINE TIER 1 PERKS.

----- Inspire -----
This perk enables the god to Inspire his followers. Once a day the bearer of a Godhead may Inspire all of his followers. Inspire gives followers +5 to all Attributes, +50 to all Stats and +25% to all Regenerations for one hour. Followers are those who select you as their deity.

DIVINE TIER 1 PERKS (CON'T).

----- Imbue -----
This perk enables the god to empower the weapon of a follower with incredible power. Once a day the god can imbue an item, temporarily turning it into an artifact level magical item for 24 hours. The artifact is determined by those that the deity has owned, used or encountered. The bearer of the artifact must be a follower of the god.

----- Assimilation -----
Once a week, a god can Assimilate a skill from a defeated opponent. The skill becomes a permanent part of the god's skill set. The level gained is equal to ⅓ of the opponent's skill level. For example, if the bearer of a Godhead defeats a wizard with level 60 in Fire Magic, he will reach level 20 in Fire Magic.

----- Resurrect -----
Once a week a god can return a fallen companion to life for 24 hours.

The perks were amazing. Each one was vastly more powerful than any other power he currently possessed. But which one to pick?

Inspire sounded amazing although Gryph was still seriously uncomfortable about the idea of being a 'god.' The whole concept went against his personal philosophy of self-determination and personal responsibility. He was enough a student of Earth's history to know how easily religious beliefs could be twisted to zealotry.

Imbue also sounded badass. He wasn't sure what an artifact was, but he imagined it was a vastly powerful magic item. Would he be like the Lady in the Lake, gifting Excalibur to Arthur? He didn't have an Arthur at this point. He didn't even have a friend, much less a sidekick.

Assimilation appealed to him. Gryph knew in this world, knowledge was power. If he could take knowledge from his enemies and use it for his own purposes, he could increase his chances of saving Brynn.

Resurrect made him uncomfortable. Gryph had long ago abandoned any religious beliefs, but a Catholic woman who hadn't been much of a Catholic had raised him. Despite this, he felt raising the dead skirted into the realm of blasphemy.

Gryph thought about the perks for a moment. He'd always believed that true power came from the intelligent application of knowledge, thus gaining more knowledge would make him more powerful. Plus, he didn't currently have any followers and wasn't sure he wanted to be worshipped as a god. This made *Assimilation* the obvious choice.

He clicked onto the perk and spent his *Divine Perk Point*. He expected some massive rush of energy or warmth, but he got nothing. Guess he'd just have to wait until he could use the perk.

He closed his sheets and stood. He'd played around enough. It was time to find a way out of this dungeon. Gryph triggered the secret door and walked into the outer room. There he found a dusky skinned man pointing an arrow at him. The man's cat yellow eyes widened, and he pulled the bowstring taught.

Gryph felt a tingle in his head as the man's eyes bore into him. Gryph raised his hands and stood still. The last thing he needed after his day was to be robbed by some strange elf. Gryph used *Analyze* on the man and got a most unusual prompt as a reward.

Analyze is Blocked.

"Don't waste your time. You are not capable of analyzing me."

Gryph's eyes widened. Not only was the stranger right, but the man knew he was right. His mind scrambled through available options. "Who are you?"

"How are you still alive?"

"What do you mean?" Gryph asked, his eyes drawn to the man's bow. Realization hit Gryph like another arrow. "You killed me."

A moment of shock widened the strange elf's eyes, before his incredible control dampened the surprise. Gryph knew he was right.

"You did. Did you know that I would respawn?"

Another flash of surprise. The man's confidence wavered.

"You didn't, but you did it anyway." Gryph raised his hands up higher and pumped mana into his ring. Somehow the man knew what he was planning and released the arrow.

The *Air Shield* was a split second too late, but Gryph had already initiated *Dodge*. The arrow sliced his cheek as it zipped past his face, siphoning a few points from his *Health* but otherwise doing no harm.

Another arrow shot at Gryph, but this one bounced harmlessly off his shield. Gryph cast *Flying Stalactite*, but the man had lightning reflexes and spun out of the rock missile's path. He dropped his bow and drew a fantastic red sword. Its slight curve reminded Gryph of a katana.

The man swung the sword in a series of intricate forms and plunged the tip of the sword into the air shield. The magic barrier pulsed, and Gryph could see the mana, his mana, flowing into the blade.

Gryph pulled his spear and got into a defensive stance. A moment later, the shield collapsed with its characteristic *pop*. The sword flew at him like a cobra. He had never seen anyone move so fast. The respawn debuffs were kicking his ass. He felt like a guy trying to run a marathon the night after a bender.

Gryph used *Parry* to deflect the attack, but only just. He heard the sword *clang* against his spear, the blade an inch from his face. The blade had sunk halfway into the wood, despite its toughness. The man brought considerable strength to bear as he pushed, buckling Gryph's knees.

Gryph dropped and spun and the man's momentum took him past. The shaft of the spear smacked into the back of the dusky elf's calves, rewarding Gryph with a grunt of pain. Gryph spun again, standing behind the dusky skinned man.

Gryph activated both *Impale* and his bracers and his spear launched itself at the man's exposed back like a bullet. The stranger arched his back in a feat of gymnastic skill that would put Olympic medalists to shame and brought his sword into a defensive position.

The spear's trajectory was altered, but the tip still found

purchase in the man's side. What had been a sure killing blow had only delivered a flesh wound. With a small grunt, the man spun again and flashed his blade at Gryph.

Gryph fell back, summoning his spear back to him with the bracers. He tried *Parry* again, but only redirected the sword from his neck to his shoulder. The razor-sharp metal found a small gap in Gryph's armor and bit into his shoulder. His *Health* went down by 30%.

Gryph grunted in pain and made a clumsy *Counter Attack* that failed to find his mark. Gryph's breathing turned ragged. His *Stamina* was about to bottom out. He needed a new tactic. He tossed his spider silk rope and cast *Animate Rope*. The man stepped over the silver white coil and brought his sword down again.

The viper of living rope snapped around the man's wrist and then slithered to his neck. At Gryph's command the rope tightened, and the man smashed the hilt against the side of his own head. He stumbled, more from shock than pain, but it gave Gryph the time to get to his feet and retrieve his spear.

The yellow-eyed elf wasted no time struggling against the rope but dropped his sword from his bound hand into his free one. Then he eased the tip against the silvery filament and the rope went limp. Whatever spirit of air had given the rope life was banished by the mana draining blade.

The man advanced, pushing Gryph back to one of the massive mushrooms, coating him in a shimmering haze of spores. *This is all too familiar*, Gryph thought. His spear spun to and fro, but the elf warrior was just too damn good. Gryph's spear clattered to the floor, and he felt the tip of the red blade draw a bead of blood from his jugular.

"How are you still alive?" the man said, his breathing even and steady.

"I do not know," Gryph said, raising his hands. "I'm as surprised as you."

"Are you illurryth?"

"I'm Gryph. I'm a player from Earth."

"Are you illurryth!" the man demanded louder, and Gryph could see the fear at the back of the man's eyes.

"You mean the Prime?"

The dusky man cocked his head and his eyes glazed over.

Gryph almost made a move when he felt another mind in his head. It was this man. He could feel him inspecting the infinite corridors of his mind. The strange elf opened his eyes and focused on Gryph. He eased the tip of his blade from Gryph's throat.

"How are you here? How did you respawn?" the man asked in amazement.

"I don't understand it either," Gryph said, hands still raised. "It has something to do with being a player. Evidently, if I die I respawn."

The odd elf with the eyes of a demon stared at Gryph for a long moment. The man was capable and terrifying. His hands fell to his side as the man lowered his blade.

"I sense no deception in you." The elf inhaled and with a flash of motion sheathed his sword. He held out a hand. "I am Ovrym."

Confused, Gryph hesitated, before easing his own hand forward. The man took it in a forearm grasp, and Gryph could feel strength pulse through the man's grip.

"Gryph. Good to meet you. I think." His knees went wobbly, and he fell to the ground. Now that the adrenaline of the fight had worn off, the full power of the debuffs came rushing back in all their nauseous glory. Ovrym caught him before he fell to the ground.

"We must be quick. The Barrow King knows where you are. He is sending wyrmynn to capture you. That cannot happen."

"What the hell is a Barrow King?"

"A disembodied spirit of evil and hunger. It is ancient, older perhaps than the Old Gods themselves. He is not only the master of this dungeon; he is the dungeon. Surely you have felt him?"

"I have, but I still do not know what he is."

"An ancient lich of formidable power. He was once a powerful wizard. An adept of the sphere of *Soul Magic*." Ovrym hesitated. "*Soul Magic* is powerful, yet seductive and dangerous." His gaze moved to the walls of the Barrow. "This place seethes with the residue of his horrid acts, done in the name of power and immortality. His existence is a wretched half-life, and he wants what you have."

"The *Godhead*."

Ovrym nodded. "Make no mistake, the Barrow King wants you more than he has wanted anything in his long existence. He will use every method at his disposal to get you. If he does, the world will know misery unlike any it has seen in millennia."

"So, what's the plan?"

"We need to get you out of here, but we could use some help."

"I know a guy."

Ovrym nodded and without another word, Ovrym marched towards the tunnel descending into the Barrow.

"Damn. I wish Lex were here," Gryph whispered to himself.

As they left the chamber, they passed the headless corpse of the baalgrath. Ovrym gave it a glance and spoke. "Nice work."

"Thanks," Gryph said, his eyes moving from the corpse to the strange warrior monk. Then silence overtook the motley pair as they dipped into *Stealth* and made their way down the tunnel.

32

The High God Aluran was under attack. Blow after blow came from multiple directions. Multiple attackers doing their best to kill a god. Clangs of weapons bouncing off his plate armor thundered across the courtyard of The Dragon's Nest, the keep that was Aluran's home.

His attackers were among the best of his private guard. Men and women who had served him faithfully their entire lives. Ordered to give it their all, they were doing their best to kill their god. If they held back, it would mean their death. The High God Aluran had decreed it and his decrees were holy writ.

An ebony war hammer careened towards Aluran's head. Quicker than the eye could follow he made the slightest of moves and sidestepped the skull crushing blow. The hammer pounded into the ground shattering the polished marble cobblestones and the man grunted in pain as shock waves thundered up his arms.

A lithe woman leapt at Aluran, spinning a double-ended spear at her god. Aluran raised his gauntleted hands. He bore no weapon, but he was hardly unarmed. A fast strike from each hand shot outwards one disarming the woman, the other sending her flying back into the wall of the courtyard. She fell in a broken heap and several Life Masters rushed to her side and cast healing spells.

Aluran took the spear from the fallen woman and spun it in a blur of death. A lighting fast whip of his arm plunged the spear into the stomach of a massive man wielding a war hammer. The spear impaled the man on a nearby wooden beam, a scream of agony burbling from his mouth before he lost consciousness. Once again, a cadre of Life Masters rushed up to him.

Aluran sidestepped the swipe of a two-handed sword so

large that most mortals were incapable of lifting it, much less wielding it effectively. The strike was close and Aluran felt the blur of wind pass his face. He spun and his left leg surged forward taking the sword bearer in the gut. As had the woman before him, this massive fellow crumpled to the ground. His grunt of pain silenced by the snapping of his spine. More Life Masters moved to the fallen man's side.

As the battle raged, a hooded man entered the courtyard and stood at the edge of the combat arena waiting for his master to finish his morning workout. The High God did not look up, but the Hooded Man knew his master sensed his presence. The Hooded Man was patient.

In mere moments the other three combatants lay broken and defeated. Life Masters were at their sides and then helped them exit the arena. Cheers rose from the audience. The High God's training sessions were always popular entertainment for the pilgrims who had journeyed to prove their love and adoration of the High God.

The High God removed his helmet and held it out to his steward. Aluran took a clean cloth from the man and wiped the few drops of sweat from his brow. The Hooded Man swallowed trying to ease his nervousness as his god walked towards him.

"Your Eminence," the Hooded Man said, bowing so low his head was near parallel to the ground.

"Have you found him?" the High God asked.

The Hooded Man leaned back to his full height. He was a tall man, but his god was a full head taller than he. The Hooded Man brought his gaze up to his god's face. Few could perceive the Hooded Man's true nature, but his appearance was neither a surprise nor a shock to the High God.

"No, Your Eminence. None of my eyes or ears have reported seeing him. And my *Divinations* have also turned up nothing."

A small frown crossed Aluran's lips. "Then it is as we suspected?"

"Yes," the Hooded Man said. "If I may, I suggest that we retire to a more private location."

Aluran nodded and placed his hand on the Hooded Man's shoulder. Reality bent and blurred, and they were elsewhere.

The High God, now clad in robes of burnished gold and emerald, walked to a tall window and gazed down upon the Shining City. They were at the top of the tower known as The Fang that soared several hundred yards above the courtyard of the Dragon's Nest.

"Then it is a true *Prime Godhead*?" Aluran queried without turning his gaze from his city.

"It is the only explanation, Your Eminence. At first, I suspected that someone had altered one of the *Godhead's* you constructed for the Pantheon, somehow making it immune to your influence."

The Hooded Man paused.

"But?" Aluran said with a note of impatience.

"Even if someone removed the domination protocols, they could not erase the beacon. It is part of the base code upon which you layered the new *Godhead* matrices. Despite several exhaustive searches, I could not divine his location."

"I was under the impression that the location of all the *Prime Godheads* had been accounted for?"

The Hooded Man cringed. That responsibility had been his, and he had been certain that the location or fate of all the *Prime Godheads* were known. Yet, somehow, he had missed one. The High God had a well-known reputation for benevolence among the peoples of Korynn, but the Hooded Man knew better. He knew ancient paranoia still raged in the soul of his master. Even the Hooded Man, the most loyal of the High God's servants, knew he could be sacrificed on the altar of those ancient fears.

"I am sorry, Your Eminence. I have sent spies to all corners of Korynn. They will find him. And I will continue to *Divine* as well." The Hooded Man lowered his head as he heard Aluran turn and walk towards him. Every second ticked by in an age and the Hooded Man wondered if this moment would once again be his last.

"Look at me," the High God said, and the Hooded Man raised a fear-filled gaze to his master.

The High God stared at his minion with an unknowable expression. Had the Hooded Man still possessed a living heart he knew it would be near bursting. Yet, he did not and so he had no biological mechanism to track time.

"Finding this man, this heretic is your only purpose," the High God commanded. "You will do nothing else until he is found."

The Hooded Man knew better than to say anything when his master was in such a mood. He watched as the High God buried his rage. It did not disappear. It never disappeared.

Aluran gazed down on the map and spread his hands wide. The map moved in to settle on a town near the Myrric Mountains a mere thousand miles from where they now stood.

"This heathen who bears the power of a god may shield himself, but his banner NPC is here. Find him. Bring him to me. Alive."

The Hooded Man hung his head low in humility. "I will send my best agent."

"See that you do," the High God said, his powerful grip clasped the base of the Hooded Man's thin neck. A mere flick of the wrist would mean another death. With no warning, the High God released him and turned.

"Steward, attend me," Aluran said in a measured voice and a thin pop of air announced his steward, the same squat man who had taken his helmet in the courtyard.

"You called, Your Eminence?"

"Bring me something to kill."

"At once," the steward said with a bow and disappeared, and the High God turned to the Hooded Man.

"Someone gave this man a *Prime Godhead*."

With a sudden shock of realization, the Hooded Man understood his master's words. "You believe there is a traitor in our midst?"

The High God whipped his head towards the Hooded Man and a slight twinge of anger burbled to the surface before Aluran buried it. He turned back towards the window and gazed to the south.

"There are always traitors," the High God said.

33

Wick had found the small set of rooms on their third day in the Barrow and it had been home since. An ancient cave-in blocked the entrance, but after a long day's work the group had cleared the rubble away to find a hidden door. The rooms had contained a small armory of rusted weapons and armor and a dozen beds. Hugarn thought it was a barracks, a secret guard room from the long-ago days when the Barrow had been more fortress than dungeon.

The six members of the party had found the small space cramped. Now that it was just Wick and Tifala, the place felt cavernous. Once again, the guilt wormed into him. They were all dead. Hugarn, Zelyanna, Thaardik, and poor sweet Jebbis missing these last three days. He had no idea what he would tell Rehla if they ever got out of this hellhole. She would blame him for his cousin's death, and she would be right.

His thoughts so troubled him that he did not hear Tifala come up behind him and he jumped when she lightly touched his shoulder. She handed him a cup of steaming liquid. She saw his troubled thoughts painted on his face and smiled.

"The potion?" he asked bewildered. She had been crafting a potion from the ingredients Wick had collected after his encounter with the player called Gryph. A potion that would increase his *Stamina, Constitution,* and *Dexterity.* Why would she give him this? To test it?

"Tea," she said with a smile that told him he could be dim, but that she found it endearing.

Wick smiled grimly and nodded a salute to his own foolishness.

"You're thinking about them again."

Wick nodded, embarrassed and ecstatic that she knew him so well. "Jebbis is still missing. I should be out there looking for him."

Tifala took his face gently in her small hands and turned him towards her. The look in her eyes was pure sympathy layered in love. "Jebbis is dead. We both know it." She pulled him to her as his eyes brimmed with tears.

"What will I tell Rehla?"

"We will figure it out together," Tifala said, holding his face in both hands and forcing him to look her in the eyes. "We will get out of here together." Wick's mood lifted, if only slightly. He knew the truth of the words Tif spoke, at least on an intellectual level. He knew in his mind that he was not at fault. Every member of their party had chosen to adventure into the Barrow. Their deaths were not on his conscience. He knew that in his mind, it was his heart that disagreed, and his heart had always held sway over him.

She held out her pinky finger to him, her smile growing warmer and brighter in a place bereft of both light and warmth. After a few seconds he smiled and nodded. He held out the pinky finger of his right hand. She raised hers, curling it around his.

"Together forever," he said.

"Together forever," she replied.

The slight smell of sulfur filled the room, and Wick's mood went from content to on edge. A moment later, a small flash and the pop of air announced the arrival of the imp Wick referred to as Xeg, since his true name, the name used to summon him from the chthonic realm, was both incredibly difficult to pronounce and extremely taxing on the vocal cords.

"Things come," the imp sputtered in a voice that sounded like lava melting ice.

"What kind of things?" Wick said, attempting to keep the anger from his voice. Xeg wasn't the most cooperative servant. Chthonic beings loved getting away from their hellish plane of existence, but they despised having to serve mortals like Wick. Mortals who were inferior to Xeg and his kind.

"Xeg know not. Things. Walk on two legs. Wear clothing." This last bit featured a forward thrust of its crotch, only instead of genitals Xeg's groin was blank. Wick had often wondered in moments when his mind went idle how imps reproduced. Sometimes he was not a fan of his mind.

"Are they wyrmynn or other?"

"Other. Not stinky cold vermin. Warm and tall with pokey ears."

"Pointy ears," Wick corrected.

"Pffft," was the imp's only response.

"Elves?" Tifala asked in a curious tone.

"How far?" Wick asked as the mechanism that hid the door to their room *clicked*. Wick and Tifala both whipped their hands towards the door. Hers covered in a warm halo of golden light. His in a roiling pulse of inky blue black.

"Now," the imp responded, amused by his not so helpful warning. Summoned imps were required to obey the commands of their masters, but they would always look for any loophole. Wick cursed himself for speaking too vaguely when he'd laid out his commands.

"Wick," said a voice. "You there?"

Wick exchanged a frantic glance with Tifala. Through the thick wall of rock, it was difficult to tell who the voice belonged to and for a moment, hope dug into Wick's heart. Was Jebbis somehow still alive?

"It's Gryph. You know the one you forgot to designate as friendly. Let's not make the same mistake twice, okay, buddy."

Wick's heart sank as he calmed himself. *Jebbis is dead,* Tifala's face said. He looked to her and her eyes showed sympathy, somehow knowing what he was thinking. He knew his cousin was dead. His hope was a paltry attempt to soothe his guilt. His mind raced. What was Gryph doing here and how the hell had he found them?

"What do you want?"

"I think we may be able to help each other."

Wick glanced at Tifala in uncertainty. He had told her about his encounter with the strange player. A silent debate raged between them and, finally, with a simple nod, she agreed to open the door.

Wick moved to the door, glancing back at Tif, who raised her arm, ready to send a *Life Blast* into any face that was not Gryph's. Wick unhitched the lock and eased the door open. Gryph stood there, looking awful and supported by a dusky skinned man with yellow eyes.

"A Fallen," Wick exclaimed in horror and moved to slam the door.

"See, Things. Xeg told you they were things."

"Wait, he is a friend." Gryph said. "Please."

"Tif?" Wick said without looking back. The glow on her hand morphed as she changed her casting. The glow flowed up her arm and into her eyes where the golden energy turned her pupils into stars of pure light. She kinked her head to the side and stared at both men.

"He speaks the truth," Tifala said, and then her eyes went wide. "An Adjudicator."

Wick spun back to look at his beloved. "A what?"

"A warrior monk that uses aether to serve order," Tifala said, gold eyes staring.

"What the heck does that mean?" Wick asked, eyeballing Ovrym. "You sure?"

"She is sure," Ovrym said. "I am an Adjudicator. Or more accurately, I was."

Gryph looked between the three of them, a confused look on his face. "I've got no damn clue what the hell any of you are talking about, but we had to avoid several wyrmynn patrols to get here, I recently died, and I feel like complete shit. So, can we please come in?"

"Dead? So, you are a player?"

Gryph looked at Wick in shock and remembered the odd parting words Wick had spoken during their first encounter.

"I told you, I'd see you in your next life," the gnome said with a mirthless grin.

"You could have warned me."

"Where's the fun in that?"

Tifala pushed Wick aside and held out her hands. She looked at Gryph with a gentle face, and he knew she meant for him to kneel. He did, and she took his head in her hands. Warmth spread from her fingers and deep into him.

"Try to relax," Tifala said to Gryph. The voice and manner reminded Gryph of his childhood doctor back in New Hampshire. In fact, take away the purple frock of hair and the fact that she was the size of a child, and she could have been Doc Verril. He did as she bid and felt at ease in the presence of this diminutive life mage. A glow surrounded her, and then his entire body grew warm as if he was being scanned by the loving eye of God. He calmed, and he felt at ease.

"Sweet Mother," Tifala said, her hands jerking back from Gryph. "There is something inside you. Something ancient and filled with potential."

"It's called a *Godhead*," Gryph said. "It's why we are here." Gryph told the two gnomes the little he knew about the divine artifact. Their eyes went wide in disbelief. Fear mingled with purpose in their eyes as he finished his tale. Ovrym chimed in with tidbits that fleshed out the group's understanding of the dangerous artifact.

"The Barrow King can sense the *Godhead*. I have been able to shield him from the revenant's sight, but I fear it is only a matter of time before the Barrow King finds him."

"Yet you brought Gryph here? You endanger both of us," Wick said.

"There is no safe place in the Barrow," Ovrym countered. Wick's scowled, but he said nothing further. He knew the man spoke the truth.

"We need to get him out of the Barrow," Tifala said.

"And how do you plan to do that? It's not like we've been sitting idle here," Wick said.

"The Barrow King controls the only way out," Ovrym said.

"Then we take the fight to him," Gryph said.

Wick opened his mouth ready to protest, but he knew Gryph's words, however unwanted, were the truth. "Maybe Jebbis was the lucky one."

Mention of Jebbis brought the dead gnome's journal to the fore of Gryph's thoughts, and he considered giving the journal to Wick. But Gryph did not wish to add more despair. It could wait.

Gryph became dizzy and nearly fell. Ovrym caught him and Tifala rushed to his side. They eased him onto one of the stone slabs that doubled as a bed. Someone, likely Tifala, had persuaded a soft moss to grow across the hard stone surface. Just enough to provide some comfort.

"You need rest."

"There is no time," Gryph said, attempting to rise. He felt Ovrym's strong hand holding him down.

"She is correct. In this state you will probably get us all

killed. We will wait."

"Adjudicator," Tifala said to Ovrym. "How long can you shield our location from the Barrow King?"

"An hour, maybe two."

"It will have to be enough." The life mage placed her hands upon Gryph's head and closed her eyes once more. "There is nothing I can do about the debuffs, but I can help you sleep until they wear off."

Gryph was about to protest when his mind drifted and the other's conversation became a dull hum. Before he knew it he was fast asleep.

Wick felt like a third wheel at the summer solstice and gave them space to work. "I'll go keep watch," Wick said. Tifala gave him a sweet smile and, once again, Wick fell in love with her. He geared up and exited their hideout.

"Report Xeg," Wick said to the imp, growing irritated. The chthonic creature always soured his mood, as if he exuded some kind of invisible, but malevolent aura.

"No things about, save for this rat," Xeg said offhanded as he smashed the squealing rat against the wall with a bone crunching thud. "Rat is mine. No share." With that he crunched the still twitching rat's head off and chewed happily.

Wick held his hands apart to show that he was more than fine the imp was unwilling to share his raw rat. He sat down on a boulder and tried to calm his stomach.

He closed his eyes and attempted to ease his mind, to bring it to a state of nothingness. A slight tweak in the back from sleeping on hard rock made it difficult to find calm, much less the disgusting squelch of the hell beast eating vermin. Then there were the smells. His own ripeness and the sulfuric stench of the imp. He grumbled to himself as his eyes snapped open.

"This isn't working."

"Xeg much better at meditation than tiny blue hair midget.

Cuz Xeg am smart and brilliant and very smart."

"I'm at least three times your height," Wick said. "And you meditate?"

"Have you ever been to Bxrthygaal? Very nice. Very relaxing. Easy close eyes listen to screams and relax."

Wick eyed the demon with a sideways glance. He knew that his mastery over the creature was complete, but he still did not trust it even slightly. He tried to ease his mind, but images of massive pitchforked demons and tortured souls filled his mind.

Wick sighed in frustration and stood, checking his equipment again. His movements were slight and nearly silent, but evidently still irritating to the imp.

"Xeg relaxing. Very, very good at relaxing. But stomp, stomp, stomp of your big clumsy feet very distracting."

"Okay, enough relaxing, let's go," Wick said, standing and readying a spell. "Go forward a way and tell me what you see. Our friends said they encountered several wyrmynn patrols on their way here. We don't want to be caught off guard."

"Xeg does. Xeg thinks it funny when small blue head gets killed by stinky lizard things."

"Just do what I say," Wick said. "Exactly what I say. Look for things, stay silent, report back to me the moment you find something."

Xeg grumbled something under his breath in his native language that could have been an insult or could have been 'I love you' if his species had such a concept. Their language was so ugly that every word whispered or yelled, made Wick suspect the tiny beast was plotting his murder.

Yet, the imp obeyed, bounced down the tunnel and soon disappeared. To make the time pass, Wick pulled out his journal. He had been writing since the day they had left the village. He had dreams of publishing his tales as a great epic, like Gersham the Adventurer. Wick hoped that his tale would rival his hero's book, but he now suspected Gersham had never been on any adventures. Adventure brought only death, and death was no glorious thing. Wick became lost in his reverie, staring at the blank page that had seen no words in days. Not since they had lost Jebbis. Poor, sweet Jebbis. Always so eager to please, always so easy to talk into things.

They'd been in the Barrow for a few weeks and their numbers had dwindled. Hugarn had been first. Big, dumb, loyal and brave, poor Hugarn had saved them all from the undead horrors in the lower Barrow. Ancient wights and revenants controlled by some unseen master. The same kind of creature that had commanded the wyrmynn.

Zelyanna, the tall regal and feisty sea elf had been next. She was not built for the under realm and her mind and her spirit had declined within days of being sealed in the Barrow. She claimed to hear voices and see things in the corner of her eyes that were never there when a full gaze was turned on them. Unknown to the rest of the group, she had decided to end her life instead of facing the daily horrors of the Barrow with no end in sight. Wick could still see her jump from the high ridge and into the raging waters of the river that moved through the Barrow.

Thaardik had felt most at home inside the Barrow until the voice of his god faded. There was something about the Barrow that interfered with his daily prayers and it got worse each day. Eventually Thaardik could hear his god no longer and desperate to return to him, he snuck away in the middle of the night and ambushed a camp of wyrmynn alone. The next day when Wick found his body. It lay in the middle of a dozen of the cretinous lizard folk. He had gone out fighting.

It was poor Jebbis that he was most guilty about. Perhaps because he had no idea what had happened to his jovial cousin. They had been mapping a new part of the Barrow when a deadfall trap separated the two. His cousin had been calm, even joking about their situation. Even as Wick promised to find Jebbis, a part of him knew he would never see his kin again.

Wick wiped away an unbidden tear and clutched his staff in anger. The black, gnarled wood of the staff held incredible power, but it made Tifala, a master of the nature side of *Life Magic*, nervous, even though she never said so. So lost in his own guilt was Wick that the sudden sulfurous appearance of Xeg nearly made him fall from his rocky perch.

"Run, blue-haired midget. Things come. Lotsa things." Xeg said and ran, not bothering to wait for Wick.

34

A slap to the face dragged Gryph back from the peace of nothingness. He struggled to focus and finally, the kind face of Tifala came into view. "Hi," he said like a drunken man grinning at a friend.

"Yes. Hi. Time to get up, sweetie. Now. This should help." Tifala cast a spell and the sounds around Gryph came into sharp focus as the fog in his head cleared.

Ovrym handed Gryph his spear and nodded, a grim smile crossing his face. "It's good to see you, but the wyrmynn have found us," Ovrym said. Gryph nodded and stood.

"Ready?" Ovrym asked.

"Yes," Gryph said and Ovrym opened the doorway. Outside the sound of yelling and clashing weapons rang. The two warriors were calm and controlled. An outsider would likely believe that these two men had fought alongside each other for years. A true testament to both of their training.

You have been invited to join a War Party by Ovrym.

Gryph agreed and was greeted by a buff.

Buff Added.

You have been granted Adjudicator's Boon. Health, Stamina and Mana regeneration are increased by 25% for the duration of the battle or until Ovrym is killed.

Wick stood behind a rocky outcropping firing volley after

volley of oily black energy bolts at a large cadre of wyrmynn. Most missed, as the lizard folk were not dumb enough to give him an easy target. Several reptilian bodies lay in the space between them. Victims of his surprise attack. A trickle of blood leaked down his face. The arrows zipping over his head told Gryph that at least one had grazed his diminutive friend.

Ovrym leapt over the boulder shielding Wick and spun into battle. His red and black metal blade flashed from its scabbard and sliced cleanly through the neck of the closest wyrmynn, a look of stupid shock still on its face as the head bounced to a stop at Gryph's feet.

Gryph quickly assessed the force arrayed against them. They had chosen their defensive spot well, which told Gryph that their commander was no fool. There were at least a dozen of the scaly beasts. A quick use of his *Analyze* skill told him that they were mostly scouts and skirmishers, ranging from levels six to ten. Yet it was the two robed wyrmynn in the far back, chanting and mumbling that drew his eye. Gryph *Analyzed* them. One was a [Wyrmynn Death Priest; Level 12] and the other was a [Wyrmynn Chthonic Mage; Level 13].

Gryph cast *Animate Rope,* and it slithered towards the mage. He had seen the horrors that Wick could summon, and he had no interest in seeing if this lizard could repeat the trick. To buy his animated minion some time he also kicked the head at his feet. The head soared over the line of wyrmynn and smacked the mage in the face, disrupting his casting. Gryph grinned, pleased that he still possessed his skills despite not having seen a soccer pitch since his West Point days.

Ovrym nodded in appreciation at the successful distraction and barreled into the first line of defenders, a spinning blur that made Gryph think of a Whirling Dervish. Green blood and screams of pain splashed across the tunnel.

"You okay?" Gryph said to Wick as he neared his friend.

"I am," Wick said, grunting through the pain of the deep cut on his head. "You?"

"Your woman is a miracle worker."

"That she is," Wick smiled.

On cue Tifala leapt over them, flipping and landing with the grace of a cat. She brought her small green bladed sword point down into the hard-packed earth of the floor and shouted a word of command.

A rumble surged from the point of her sword and an array of vines exploded from the ground. They slithered and spun at the first line of wyrmynn attackers and twined around ankles and legs. They screamed in alarm at the sudden lack of movement, but barked orders from their commander brought their discipline back. Several unleashed arrows. Most missed, but Gryph took one in the arm.

Debuff Added.

You have been poisoned.
5 points of damage per second for 10 seconds.

"Their weapons are poisoned," Gryph yelled as he finished casting *Flying Stalactite*. The missile of rock took the nearest wyrmynn in the eye. Gryph earned a *Critical Hit*, and the wyrmynn collapsed, the body held upright by the twining vines.

Ovrym spun several more times, both inflicting and avoiding wounds. The man's *Dexterity* must be off the charts. Wick sent several more bolts of oily energy into the crowd of saurians, earning many a satisfying grunt of pain.

"Wick, can you summon that demon?" Gryph yelled.

The gnome shook his head no and gave him a look that screamed 'you don't think I thought of that already.' Gryph was both relieved and disappointed. Avernerius could have made quick work of these wyrmynn, but Gryph had seen few more terrifying sights in his life.

The death priest finished casting and an aura of deepest black exploded from him and roiled like incoming surf. It flowed over everyone. As it touched Gryph, he instantly felt sick. His head spun, his stomach hurled and sweat poured from him.

Gryph collapsed to the floor and vomited a thin stream of bile and drool. He felt as weak as he had when the flu had kept him in bed for a week as a child. A quick glance showed that the others were suffering as well.

The wyrmynn commander ordered his second line of troops, those that had avoided Tifala's vine attack, into battle. They leapt over their kin and brought sword and spear to bear on Ovrym and Gryph.

Ovrym parried several attacks before a spear took him in the side, and he fell to one knee. Wick sent a volley of chthonic blasts into the faces of the two lizards about to slay the injured xydai. Both went down.

"Cover Tifala," Wick yelled as he leapt from cover to stand next to Gryph. He could hear Tifala's melodic chanting behind him. He did not know what she was casting, but he was determined to buy her the time.

Several wyrmynn rushed them, and Gryph knew in their weakened state they would be quickly overwhelmed. Ovrym's *Health* and *Stamina* were dwindling fast as the front-line warrior fought off attacks from several wyrmynn.

"Close your eyes!" Gryph yelled and pushed mana into his armor just as a wyrmynn raised his sword to remove his head. In one of the most difficult mental acts of his life, Gryph forced his mind to ignore the incoming shard of death and squeezed his eyes shut. He activated the chest plate, and the world exploded with light.

Hisses of pain pulsed through the cavern as the blast of life energy not only blinded the subterranean creatures but pummeled them with damage. Simultaneously, Gryph and all the members of his team were both healed and rejuvenated. It was not enough to remove any of the debuffs, but it gave them a surge of life and power.

As the light faded, Gryph saw his entire team leap back into action. Wick tossed volley after volley of bolts into the blinded wyrmynn. Ovrym spun and swirled. Most important of all Tifala finished her casting.

A wave of flowing golden light flowed from Tifala's body. As the blessing crested over Gryph, he instantly felt better and was even more thrilled to see his debuffs disappear. However, they had done their work well and his *Health* bar sat at barely 50%. He took a moment to down a *Health Potion* and his *Health* popped back up to near 80%. Not perfect, but good enough for now.

The flowing wave of *Life Magic* poured over the wyrmynn, and they howled. Their skin blistered and charred as if ten hours of sun exposure pummeled them all at once. Several of the lead wyrmynn, those who'd faced the brunt of the attacks died instantly. The wave moved on and it passed over the wyrmynn commander who stood unmoving as his skin crisped. His eyes bored into Gryph's and a snarl crossed his face, pulling the jagged white scar that bisected his face taught.

Gryph cast *Flying Stalactite* at the beast's face. His aim was true, but at the last second the beast raised his shield and the shard of rock stopped short. The beast grinned, and Gryph realized the staring match had been a ploy. Scarface had distracted Gryph enough to allow the chthonic mage to complete his chanting.

A rift to another place opened, and Gryph's eyes went wide in fear. It was the same place that Wick had summoned the demon from, in their last battle against the wyrmynn, and Gryph knew that this time there was no chance that he would be marked as a friendly. Too late to stop this casting, Gryph's rope entwined the mage. At least he'll be out of commission for a while.

A massive wolf the color of cooling magma leapt from the portal and sprinted directly towards Ovrym. The Adjudicator bled from a half-dozen small wounds and was unaware of the approaching hell hound.

Hell Hound.
Level: 19 *Health*: Unknown. *Stamina*: Unknown. *Mana*: Unknown. *Spirit*: Unknown. *Hell Hounds are a demon's best friend. These massive canines are the literal guard dogs of hell. Ferocious carnivores who love feasting on mortal flesh.* *Strengths*: Unknown. *Immunities*: Unknown. *Weakness*: Unknown.

The beast ran through Tifala's field of light, grimacing as its fur singed. Gryph sprinted towards Ovrym and leapt over the quick warrior, pumping mana into his spear and activating *Banish*. The spear plunged into the beast's side and both it and Gryph toppled heavily to the ground.

The life energy erupting from his spear caused the hell hound to howl in pain and it shimmered. Gryph held his breath in hope. *Please work, please work, please work,* he begged. The beast shook its head as it phased in and out of this realm and finally with a deep growl of primal hatred it became solid once again.

"Shit," Gryph said, yanking the spear from the beast's side. *Banish* may have failed, but the spear strike had done massive damage and, better yet, prevented the monstrosities rabid jaws from crushing down on Ovrym's neck.

"Thanks," Ovrym said as he went back to back with Gryph. They were surrounded and cut off from their friends. Wick was tossed aside by a club swing from a skirmisher and lay pinned away from the others. Tifala was, if possible, even worse off. While she was unhurt, she was the furthest away from the rest of them and face to face with both the death priest and Scarface. In a small miracle, Gryph's rope still entangled the mage.

The hell hound got back to its feet and charged Ovrym and Gryph again. Gryph snapped his right hand up and activated his ring. A bubble of solid air exploded just in time to push the bear sized dog back, but Gryph could tell that it had caused significant damage to the shield's integrity. It could take one, maybe two more hits like that.

Surprisingly, Ovrym sat down in the middle of the sphere of calm and closed his eyes. Gryph was about to ask the nimble warrior what the hell he was up to when he heard a low chanting coming from the xydai.

"Make it a good one, buddy," Gryph muttered as he sent a volley of throwing knives through the barrier accentuated by the power of his bracers. They bit into demon dog flesh and with a twist and a tear Gryph summoned them back to him. The beast howled, but its *Health* bar barely moved. It lunged at the barrier again stealing more of the shield's dwindling power.

Ovrym finished his casting. He hadn't moved and his eyes were still closed, but Gryph knew his spell had been successful, because one of the larger wyrmynn skirmishers turned towards one of its fellows and swung its two-handed sword in a wide arc, separating the shocked wyrmynn's head before it could wonder what the hell had just happened.

Watching the lizard slay his fellows brought a smile to Gryph's face and then something better. His eyes snapped over to the chthonic mage to see that while he struggled, he was still wrapped tightly by Gryph's spider silk rope. Gryph decided that if he ever met one of the mysterious spiders, he'd have to give it thanks. *The Realms are a very weird place*, he thought, and he reached out to the rope and activated its *Compel* ability.

Gryph felt his thoughts meld with those of the wyrmynn mage and made a vow to never, ever do so again. The beast's mind was a fetid swamp of hatred and pain. This creature enjoyed torture and murder the way perpetually single women loved walks on the beach.

"Send it back," Gryph commanded through the mind meld. The mage resisted, but Gryph could tell it was a strain.

"Send it back," Gryph commanded again. The mage snapped his eyes onto Gryph's and grinned as it used its powerful willpower to resist him.

The hell hound pummeled against the air shield again and it shimmered with its last bit of strength. Ovrym turned his possessed wyrmynn against the fiery wolf and was rewarded with a significant hit. The hound collapsed and raged in pain. It turned and launched itself with vicious speed at the traitor lizard. Its jaws sunk into the wyrmynn's neck and it belched a torrent of flame outward. The possessed wyrmynn screamed for a few seconds before the hellish flames charred its face and it collapsed.

Gryph's battle to compel the mage was not going well, and he was running out of time. He changed tactics. Perhaps he could not force the mage to banish the creature but there were other ways to tame the beast.

"What is its true name?" Gryph commanded through the link.

The wyrmynn's eyes went wide as it tried to battle the command, but this ability of the empyrean silk rope was far harder to resist than direct mind control. A guttural and harsh sentence of horrid syllables flowed into Gryph's mind.

He turned to the hell hound and began the litany of words that comprised the beast's true name. As each word erupted from Gryph's tortured throat like vomit, the beast grew more furious. It bashed its head and forelimbs against the air shield, finally reducing its power to zero.

The beast prepared to leap, just as Gryph finished saying it true name. It spasmed, trying to resist, but Gryph's will was a vice grip that the foul creature could not escape. A moment later, the battle was over, and the hell hound lowered its head.

"Kill," Gryph ordered, sending a mental image of the death priest and the chthonic mage into the hell hound's brain. The two-ton creature spun with a grace an animal so large should not have possessed and charged its onetime master.

Gryph did not waste time watching his new pet's slaughter. He and Ovrym were still surrounded by angry wyrmynn. Ovrym spun up and about, his blade slicing through limbs and necks with ease and grace.

A wyrmynn hit his shoulder, but Gryph activated *Parry* and turned the attack. Gryph dipped, spun and plunged the spear up and into the wyrmynn's neck, scoring a *Critical Hit* and killing the beast instantly.

Gryph spun again to discover he had no enemies to face. Then he saw why. While the hellhound had distracted them, Scarface and his minions had surrounded Tifala. She had taken out several as evidenced by the wyrmynn corpses at her feet, but a massive blow from the flat of Scarface's blade knocked her unconscious.

"No!" came a scream, and Gryph spun to see Wick, cornered by several more of the saurians, frantically trying to reach his woman. The diminutive gnome was so focused on the plight of his love that he failed to see the wyrmynn strike coming at him. The blade took Wick in the side, and he fell out of sight.

Gryph shot his arm forward and cast *Flying Stalactite* as the wyrmynn drew his sword over Wick's head for a killing blow. The jagged rock spear caught the beast in the throat and the life left his eyes instantly.

"Ovrym, to Wick," Gryph commanded as he spun and ran towards Tifala and her captors. He sent a quick glance towards the hell hound to see it tear off its onetime master's left arm. The mage fell, screaming, and the hell hound turned its attention to the death priest.

But the other magic user had not stood idle and a lance of black energy tore from the priest's outstretched hands and impaled the fiery canine as it lunged. Gryph's hellacious minion's own weight carried it further down onto the spear of death. In a flash of red-black light, the hell hound disappeared.

Gryph turned back to Tifala's captors. They had her bound and one skirmisher tossed her up on the leader's shoulder. Scarface pointed directly at Gryph and said attack in its putrid tongue. Then he turned around and disappeared into the tunnel with Tifala.

The remaining four wyrmynn rushed at Gryph. He sidestepped the first attack and activated his *Counter Attack* perk, dipping low and dragging the blade of his spear along the creature's hamstring. It toppled to the floor.

Gryph turned and parried another blow. The wyrmynn lifted its blade to try again, but Gryph punched the shaft of the spear upwards and into the beast's face. He heard a crack of bone and blood exploded from its nose.

He ducked under another attack, his left hand holding his spear straight up. As the wyrmynn flew past, Gryph pushed some mana into his bracers and released the spear. It tore upwards like a rocket, lifting the lizard off its feet as it punctured its heart. *Critical Hit.*

The beast's momentum tore the spear from Gryph's grip, and he had to throw himself aside to avoid the final wyrmynn's attack. Gryph tucked and rolled and pulled his ice dagger as he rolled up. He was breathing heavily. The constant movement and use of his perks had seriously drained his *Stamina*, and it was barely holding at 10%. He backed away to gain breathing room, but the wyrmynn was smarter than it looked and with a grin, it charged.

Gryph attempted to block the burly lizard's strike, but neither his *Stamina* nor his dagger was up to the task. He felt the rusted metal dig into his shoulder blade and his *Health* sunk by nearly 40% as the dagger fell from his hand. A gush of blood erupted from his mouth, and he collapsed.

The wyrmynn took a second to gloat, growling the wyrmynn equivalent of 'soft weakling' down at Gryph. In pain, without a weapon and about to be killed, Gryph let instinct take over. He pushed with all his remaining strength and launched his head upwards. It impacted the wyrmynn in the crotch, and Gryph learned a truth he never thought he'd seek. Yes, wyrmynn do indeed have balls. Gryph felt the soft, egg like spheres turn to pulp against his skull and as the wyrmynn collapsed in agony Gryph hoped that would be the last time he experienced that sensation.

Gryph got to his feet, collected his spear, and thrust the tip deep into the beast's chest. Gryph thought he saw a look of relief in the saurian's eyes as its life ended.

Gryph spun in search of enemies, but there were no wyrmynn standing. Or so he thought, until a ragged strand of black energy whipped around him, pinning arms to body. Gryph screamed as the death tendril drained his life. Again, he fell to his knees as the agony ripped into him.

Then it stopped. Gryph looked up to see Wick's hand outstretched. He followed the gnome's arm to see the death priest collapse, a hole charred into its chest. He looked back at the gnome and nodded thanks. Wick collapsed, supported by Ovrym's lean, powerful arms.

Wick wept as the solemn adjudicator held him.

35

Wick was inconsolable. He wanted to rush after the wyrmynn to save his love, but Ovrym convinced him that none of them were in any shape to pursue them.

"But she'll die."

"We'll all die if we go now. We need to heal, to recover. And she'll be fine for a while, at least," Gryph said.

"How can you know that?" Wick demanded, his face red from rage and fear.

"If they wanted her dead, they would have killed her here. So that suggests they want her for something else. Whatever that something else is, it buys us some time. Time we desperately need."

"I agree," Ovrym said.

Desperate fear waged a battle with logic on Wick's face. After a few moments he found calm. "You're right." He pulled a chain from his neck on which hung a ring. A ring very like the one Gryph had stashed in his inventory. Wick concentrated on the ring for a moment and then choked back tears. "She's alive. Scared, but alive."

Ovrym squeezed his shoulder, and Gryph kneeled down next to Wick with a grimace of pain. "We will save her." Gryph said. Wick locked eyes with him and nodded.

"Help me up?" Wick said and Ovrym hefted the gnome to his feet. With a grimace Gryph also got to his feet. "What a sad trio we make," Wick jested, and a small smile crept across his face. "Let's go back to the hideout. Tifala should have something there we can use." The mere mention of her name brought worry back to his face, and Gryph added his hand to the gnome's other shoulder.

"We will save her." Ovrym said. Wick nodded.

The trio entered the hideout to find Xeg digging through a chest.

"What the hell do you think you're doing?" Wick demanded.

The imp tore its face up and glared. "Shiny. Want. For Xeg."

Ovrym walked up and tried to grab the irritating imp, but he bounced aside and whipped Ovrym across the face with his tail. Xeg landed atop a high shelf and stuck his tongue out at them. He looked at the three warriors with worry in his eyes.

"Where pretty lady? Pretty lady promise Xeg shiny."

Wick grumbled under his breath in gnomish, and while Gryph had not heard enough of the diminutive man's native language for his *Master of Tongues* ability to translate the language, he was pretty sure the tirade was laced with profanity.

Wick walked to a leather case and opened it, revealing row after row of potions. He searched through and found three red *Health Potions* and tossed one each to Ovrym and Gryph.

"*Potions of Major Health*. Should get us all back up to snuff," Wick said, upending his.

Gryph and Ovrym did the same and a rush of healing heat surged through Gryph's body. If a minor *Health Potion* felt like a cup of coffee, this thing was like a triple espresso.

"Damn," Gryph said in appreciation.

"Told you my girl is good."

Wick walked over to the chest Xeg had been rummaging through and dug out a small mirror. He tossed it up to Xeg, and the imp squealed in delight and looked at himself from all angles. He grinned like some kind of horrid fashion model doppelgänger and spun to see himself in different positions. When he checked out his own ass, Gryph checked out of the scene and looked back at Wick.

"Tif always insisted we be nice to Xeg. Promised it a mirror just like hers if it helped us out."

"Then where was it during the fight?" Ovrym asked.

"He no say fight. He say look. Xeg look, find things, tell short ugly man about things," Xeg protested.

Wick sighed and rubbed his forehead with his hand. "Technically, it is right. Damn imps are always so literal."

"Is it always here?" Ovrym asked.

"Thankfully, no," Wick said. "I can summon him for up to 24 hours before he returns to the chthonic realm. Then I need to wait another 24 hours before summoning him again. I'd estimate I have him for another half hour at most."

"Can he track the wyrmynn?" Gryph asked.

"Given the time, yes. Since he can port pretty much anywhere he has seen. But it takes time, and that is something we don't have."

"Lies. Always lies about Xeg. Lying, liar, short, ugly man's pants on fire." Xeg snapped his fingers and Wick's pants smoked. Wick slapped the small flames away with practiced ease.

"I thought you said he wasn't allowed to attack you," Gryph said.

"No attack. Make joke. Ha, ha, ha, Xeg funny. Hilarious. The most funny," Xeg said and then chortled lightly to himself as he posed in the mirror more. "Plus, Xeg find pretty lady. You say Xeg can no find. You lie. Pffftt."

All three of the men stared at Xeg.

"What do you mean?" Gryph asked.

They waited for Xeg to respond, but it just stared with a sleepy expression at them.

"Oh, mean Xeg. Why you call Xeg You? You no know Xeg's name tall, pokey eared goober?" Xeg asked quizzically.

"Goober," Gryph scowled, which earned a small grin from both Ovrym and Wick. He now understood Wick's frustration and even felt sympathy for the gnome. His affinities had sent him down the path where frequent interactions with the obnoxious imp were common. Gryph imagined Lex would love the little devil.

"You said you can find Tifala?" Wick said. But Xeg was once more admiring his reflection. "Xeg. Hello Xeg."

"Yes, find pretty lady can Xeg, but Xeg need one something."

"What is that?" Wick said.

"Promise can have and Xeg tell."

Gryph was no expert on demons, but he suspected that agreeing to any deal with one before knowing the terms was a bad idea. He looked from wick to Ovrym and shrugged. "Not sure we have much choice." Both men nodded.

"Fine Xeg, you can have one something," Wick said.

"Whoooop," the imp said and jumped and danced and spun. It then leapt from its perch atop the shelf, bounced off Gryph's head and then onto Wick's back.

"Hey, get off," Wick said, trying to slap the imp off his shoulder and failing. Xeg bounced and sang and then reached down the back of Wick's shirt and tugged. A gold chain popped out and Xeg tugged harder, choking Wick. After a moment, the chain snapped and Xeg pulled it free. Dangling from the chain was Wick's *Bond Ring*.

Wick coughed and sputtered for a minute before regaining his breath. He then ran after the imp who bounced from shelf to bed and onto Ovrym's back. "Give that back," Wick finally said through coughs.

"You said any something. This something Xeg need."

"Anything but that," Wick said with deep anger. Gryph held him back, earning a glare of ire from the gnome.

"Just watch," Gryph said. Wick calmed somewhat, but he eyed Xeg like a father glaring at his daughter's prom date. Xeg closed its eyes and mumbled a chant.

An oily glow pulsed from Xeg's palm and into the ring. The ring drank in the energy like a dry sponge tossed into a full sink. Wick grumbled, and Gryph couldn't blame him. This was much more than a symbol of his love for Tifala, it was an actual magical connection. Whatever the imp was doing was a violation. Then it got worse.

Xeg tossed the ring into the air and caught it on its long, very slimy tongue. It then moved it around its mouth in a manner that would make a stripper blush. It even gargled the ring at one point before finally jumping down. It grabbed Wick's hand and spit the ring onto the gnome's hand. The ring landed with a sickening slop and mucus, spittle and various other viscous and cloying semi liquids bubbled on his palm.

"Well, I can go the rest of my life without seeing that again," Ovrym said.

"Trust me, you got off easy," Wick said as the slime slithered and burned his skin. Wick wiped the ring as best he could on a spare rag and returned it to its place under his shirt.

"Okay, Xeg and uglies go now," Xeg said.

"Aw, too bad Xeg. Your twenty-four hours are up. Looks like it is time for you to go," Wick said with a small look of triumph.

"No, Xeg stay."

"Wait, what? It's been almost a day. I thought you said you could only stay in the mortal realm for a day?"

"You speaks. Xeg agreed. Don't mean true."

"Wait, you don't have to stay here for twenty-four hours every time I call you?"

Xeg shrugged and picked at his teeth with a wickedly hooked nail.

"Xeg, answer me," Wick demanded.

"Xeg come you say. Xeg go you say or when Xeg bored. Xeg don't even know what hour is."

Both Gryph and Ovrym had to laugh at Wick's shocked expression.

"You and I will have a long speaks if we get out of this," Wick grumbled. "Now go and find Tifala. Then come right back. Do you understand?"

Xeg grumbled and shook its tiny, crackless butt at Wick.

"Say you understand," Wick repeated.

"Course understand. Xeg no dummy head. Xeg have more gooder idea. Xeg say give ugly pokey man to soul wizard. Xeg want pretty lady back."

"We all do you creepy red monkey," Gryph said.

"Xeg no monkey," the imp blurted in anger before sticking his tongue out at Gryph. "Wait, what is monkey?"

"Xeg. Go. Now," Wick commanded in a tight voice.

With one last grumble, the imp disappeared in a flash of sulfur and flame.

Wick inhaled deeply and pulled the ring from under his shirt once more and cradled it gently in his palm. Worry painted his face.

"We will save her," Gryph promised.

"I'm gonna hold you to that," Wick said, eyes red with tears and fear. He looked at Gryph, and Gryph knew that, in that moment, he would trade the world for Tifala. *Would I do the same for Brynn?*

"That is not the way," Ovrym said. I know you want it to

be, but you know it isn't the way."

Wick turned his eyes down and shame and fear gripped him. Gryph walked up to him and pulled him close. Wick resisted for a moment before giving in. He looked up with a strength that belied his small size.

"So, what's the plan?" Wick asked.

"We need help," Gryph said.

"Yeah, and where are we going to find that? This place isn't exactly brimming with friendly faces," Wick grumbled.

"I know some people," Ovrym stated in a tone that suggested it was the last thing he wanted to consider.

"Friends?" Gryph asked.

"Not exactly. They're called the Gray Company. I used to be a member."

"Used to be?"

"Let's just say, we didn't see eye to eye on a few things."

"And they'll help us find Tifala?" Wick said in a voice near begging.

"If we pay their price."

"And what is their price?" Gryph asked.

"Me."

36

Ovrym led them down a tunnel that hadn't seen use in years. Dust and cobwebs clung to every surface. The tunnel twisted and twined and turned back on itself. Several times they had to squeeze through thin cracks, but Ovrym pushed them on. Once they had to jump across a crevasse and the floor dipped at an odd angle. While they walked, Gryph checked his prompts.

You have received Experience Points.

You have received 15,637 XP for slaying Wyrmynn X 10.

You have received 11,666 XP for slaying Hell Hound.

Impressive, Gryph thought.

"Did you know that the Barrow was once on the surface," Ovrym stated in a tone that made Gryph think of the bored tour guide the time when the colonel took him and Brynn to see the Washington Monument.

"It was a tower that stood taller than the tallest trees. Then, some cataclysm occurred, and the earth swallowed the tower. Eventually, a hill of grass grew over the entrance. Locals told tales of ghouls and revenants, saying the Barrow was haunted."

"Looks like the locals were right," Wick said. Gryph could tell the gnome was attempting to jest away his fear over Tifala.

They rounded a corner and Ovrym stopped. "Do either of you have any affinity for *Thought Magic?*"

"I don't," Wick said.

"I have 100% affinity in every sphere," Gryph said in a low

voice. Wick and Ovrym stared at him in shock. "The *Godhead*."

"You may want to keep that information on a need to know basis," Ovrym said intently. "People fear power and you could someday grow to be very powerful."

Gryph's mind immediately went to Aluran, and he knew the Adjudicator spoke true.

Ovrym stepped up to Gryph. "I will teach you something." He held up his hands. "May I?"

Gryph hesitated before nodding. Ovrym placed his hands on Gryph's head, feeling the power of the man's grip.

"Close your eyes and try to ease your thoughts."

Gryph closed his eyes and breathed in deeply several times, inhaling through the nose and exhaling through the mouth. Then he felt, or perhaps heard, a low hum as unseen energy built around Ovrym's hands. The humming increased and then waves of warmth pumped from Ovrym into Gryph. Tendrils of thought whorled their way through the fog that clouded Gryph's mind and then suddenly he knew.

You have learned the spell MIND SHIELD.

Sphere: Thought Magic.
Tier: Base.

Allows the caster to shield his mind (or the mind of another with the proper leveling).

Mana Cost: 50.
Casting Time: 2 seconds.

For purposes of resisting metal attacks, Mind Shield temporarily allows the user's Wisdom to mimic their highest Attribute.

Duration: 10 minutes per level. Each tier of mastery allows the caster to shield another mind. At Grand Master level, all allies of the caster are shielded.
Cooldown: Ten minutes.

You have learned the skill THOUGHT MAGIC.

Level: 1.
Tier: Base.
Skill Type: Active.

You can now wield the power of Thought Magic. Thought Magic allows the user to tap into the power of the sentient mind. Advanced users can tap into The Source itself, the organizing intelligence behind the formation of The Realms and perhaps the only true God. Thought Magic makes use of spells that enable one to see other's thoughts, manipulate the minds of others and affect the world with their thoughts. Users of Thought Magic are rare, and most do not advertise their abilities. For obvious reasons, they are mistrusted.

Gryph's eyes popped open, and he nodded wryly to himself at the last comment of the prompt. Having just had his mind nearly shredded by *Thought Magic* he understood the mistrust all too well. He would endeavor to learn all he could about this magic. If nothing else, it would help protect him from creatures like the arboleth.

They rounded another corner and a break in the masonry of the wall revealed a deep shaft. Gryph stuck his head through the broken wall and looked down. An immediate sense of vertigo gripped at him and his knees buckled. The shaft disappeared deep into the ground much further than Gryph's night vision could pierce. The shaft was uneven and had the bulbous texture that reminded Gryph of cooled magma. Had this shaft melted? Is this where the earth swallowed the tower?

"You want us to go down there?" Wick said with trepidation.

"It's how I got up here," Ovrym responded as if that helped.

He ignored Gryph and Wick's exchanged glances and tugged on a metal piton set into the masonry.

"You hammered these in?" Gryph said. He could see the faint metal glint of several more descending into the darkness.

"Yes."

"There has to be another way," Wick complained again, his face blanching as he looked down the shaft of endless black.

"There is, through the wyrmynn camp and then through the under lake where Gryph had so much fun and then through the Warrens and then through the Grove. At least Gryph killed the arboleth for us."

"Well, that doesn't sound so bad," Wick said. "The Grove sounds lovely."

"It's the home of a dark dryad and her army of wolf spiders."

"Oh, well maybe the death shaft is all right then," Wick said and once again stared down into the unknown depths. Gryph knew Wick was covering his fear with sarcasm and knew that fear wasn't only about the chasm below them, or the wyrmynn or even a troop of wolf spiders, but a deep fear for his missing love. Gryph grabbed his shoulder and squeezed.

"We'll find her," Gryph said.

"How can you be sure?" Wick said, his mask falling away and his eyes pleading.

"Because the Barrow King doesn't want Tifala," Gryph said. "He wants me."

Gryph cast *Animate Rope* and ordered his rope to secure itself to the piton. Ovrym nodded as Gryph spun around and dropped. For a sickening moment gravity tugged him down into the unknown, but then the rope held, and Gryph's feet came to the wall.

"Just like old times," Gryph said.

"You and I have very different old times, buddy," Wick said. Gryph gave one last glance up and thought he saw a look in Wick's eyes. A look that said, 'I'll give you to him, if it saves her life.'

Gryph reached the next piton and secured his rope to it before moving on. Ovrym picked his spots well, suggesting he had some caving experience. As Gryph descended, ancient fears built inside him. The deep dark shaft was a scary place on Earth, in the Realms it was downright terrifying.

"Is there anything in here we should be afraid of?" Gryph

said in a whisper when the group had gathered on a large outcropping to rest.

"A dose of healthy fear helps one survive."

"Yeah, that is the worst way you could have answered that question," Wick said in a low voice, his eyes moving to and fro.

"Just stick to the path and we should be fine. But it is best if I lead."

"Should be?" Wick said. "I'm pretty sure I hate you."

Ovrym said nothing as Gryph helped him over the edge, but Gryph could see a buildup of apprehension as the man eased himself down. Despite the thundering of his heartbeat they traversed three more rope lengths before the terrain changed.

This latest stop was on a small rock bridge that traversed from one side to the other as if it was some kind of support beam. As Gryph's feet hit the bridge, Ovrym brought a finger to his lips, requesting silence. Gryph's eyes scanned the area, but the darkness was too great and even his night vision couldn't make out any details.

Gryph helped Wick down and motioned for his silence as well. The gnome didn't exactly have a track record for being quiet. Wick nodded and likewise cast an apprehensive look. Ovrym hung over the side of the bridge and pointed his hand straight down. Silent chanting resulted in a pulse of purple energy firing from his hand. It travelled about a hundred yards, where it hung in the air, illuminating the area.

Gryph noticed how much slimmer the shaft became and a dread feeling of claustrophobia built up inside him. Then he saw that the walls were moving.

Gryph snapped his gaze up to Ovrym, whose grim look did not ease Gryph's fears. Wick clapped a hand over his own mouth to prevent his natural outburst. A moment later, he pulled his hand away and mouthed "What the hell" to the other men.

Ovrym eased himself over the edge and clipped his rope to a piton sunk in the underside of the bridge. Then as gently as a mother caressing a babe's brow, the tall warrior moved down. Wick went next with Gryph bringing up the rear.

About a dozen yards down, a rough horizontal line

bisected the entire shaft. Gryph realized that it was a vein of silver. It shone a dull purple in the light of Ovrym's spell and whatever horror clung to the walls seemed incapable of passing the silver barrier.

Gryph pushed back a feeling of panic as he lowered himself past this barrier and into the maw of the pulsating shaft. A sickening sensation dug into his gut.

Ahead of him both Ovrym and Wick had stopped. About two yards below Ovrym's dangling feet another stone causeway bisected the shaft, but this time instead of naked stone, this bridge swarmed with roiling motion.

Gryph found his eyes drawn to the inky movement. Gryph had no real-world equivalent for what he was seeing unless crude oil somehow learned how to pulse with some wretched mockery of life.

Ovrym eased his satchel open and removed a flask of silver laden liquid. He thumbed the top open and poured the contents in an even swath along the bridge. When the silver solution touched the ooze, it reacted as flesh to fire and retracted as it burned. Tendrils rushed away from the burning liquid and the smell that reached Gryph's nose forced him to hold back a retch.

Gryph *Analyzed* the retreating blob.

Behemoth Black Ooze.

Level: 66.
Health: 2,200.
Stamina: 4,044.
Mana: 0.
Spirit: 0.

Black Oozes are sentient aberrations born from the misuse of Soul Magic. They start off small, but over time they can grow to be incredibly large and deadly. They are intelligent, but incredibly alien and have no sympathy for any other beings in the Realms.

Strengths: Unknown.
Immunities: Unknown.
Weakness: Unknown.

Gryph's mind reeled in horror. This thing was one massive organism, and it completely surrounded them. Its total *Health* dwarfed even the arboleth. Below him, Gryph could hear Wick's breathing become erratic as panic invaded the gnome's mind. Ovrym's eyes snapped up at Wick, which only caused the gnome to breathe heavier.

The ooze seemed to sense the noise and stretched out tendrils from the surrounding walls. First one then another, then dozens, then hundreds. Above and below them tentacles searched. Wick was about to lose it. Gryph quickly cast *Mind Shield* on Wick, hoping that it would ease his fear.

After a moment, Wick got his breathing under control, but the tendrils of ooze continued to search, and they were getting closer. Ovrym reached into his bag again, but this time he threw the vial against the wall a dozen feet below the bridge. It exploded and cast a silvery wave of liquid in all directions. The ooze spasmed in pain again and pulled back from the spot of the attack. Better yet, nearly all the tentacles grasping towards the party retracted and reemerged around the point of the attack.

Ovrym dropped silently to the cleared bridge and motioned for the others to do the same. Soon all three crouched on the bridge. Ovrym pointed down and the ball of violet light barely illuminated another bridge about thirty feet below. Ovrym tied another length of rope around the bridge and motioned for Gryph to take point on the next leg.

Gryph eased himself over and climbed down. A few feet above the next landing, Gryph paused and tossed his own silver grenade onto the pulsating mass of ooze. Once again, the ooze instantly retreated allowing Gryph to land softly.

He looked up to see Wick easing himself over the edge and down the rope. Wick was barely halfway down when Gryph saw the ooze advancing once more. Ovrym was running out of space. He shot a quick glance down at Gryph, who nodded in understanding.

Hurry, the look said.

Gryph tossed a frantic look at Wick and motioned for him

to hurry. The gnome nodded and increased his pace, seeming to control his fear. Above him, Ovrym slipped over the edge and moved down the rope by alternating tight and loose grips.

Wick dropped into Gryph's waiting arms, jumped down and pulled two of the silver grenades from his pack, eyes trained in all directions. The tendrils came close a few times, but Wick ducked under them, keeping his cool.

Gryph looked back up to see Ovrym about halfway down. Despite the speed of his descent, Gryph could see that the ooze had reached the rope and was eating through it. *He will not make it.* Gryph realized. He pulled his rope from his side and cast *Animate Rope*. The length of spider silk twined itself around his waist, and then around the bridge he was standing on.

Ovrym slid down the rope again, but this time when he gripped the rope to slow his descent, the force on the acid damaged rope proved too much and it snapped. To his credit, Ovrym did not scream as he fell. Gryph moved to catch him, but Ovrym hit the bridge mere inches from his grasp.

Ovrym's head smashed against the stone with a wet thud. For a moment it seemed as if he'd be able to hold on to the stone trellis, but the impact caused him to lose consciousness. His grip went slack, and he fell over the edge.

Without hesitation, Gryph leapt off the edge. He dove at the tumbling man, arm outstretched. Just as Ovrym was about to pass the limit of the rope's length Gryph grasped him by the ankle.

Gryph held on with all his might and was happy he'd tossed a few points into *Strength* the last time he leveled. He felt his shoulder nearly dislocate and Ovrym's ankle break as the rope arrested their downward spiral.

Ovrym's eyes snapped open as the pain awoke him. He nearly gasped but refrained. They swung in a loose parabola back and forth, coming closer and closer to the spasming sides of the shaft with each motion, before their spin calmed and eased. A small grunt of pain pushed through Ovrym's lips and tendrils reached out and towards him.

One entwined itself around Ovrym's waist, and Gryph could hear the dull sizzle as the acid ate through the warrior monk's armor. Then another reached towards Ovrym's face. It slid across the man's exposed skin and ate at his flesh. Tears streamed down the xydai's face and blood oozed from the corners of his mouth where he had bit his tongue to hold back from screaming.

But soon the pain was too much and Ovrym howled. The ooze reacted with hunger and tendrils whipped out from the walls. They twined around both men, and Gryph felt himself burn. He too screamed. His *Health* plummeted.

Debuff Added.
Acid damage. 20 points/second.

Gryph was being eaten alive and knew he had mere seconds. Then there was a pop and another and another and plumes of silver laden water covered him. The ooze instantly retreated, and the solution counteracted the acid attack, easing Gryph's pain.

He looked up to see Wick tossing a few more of the silver concoctions clearing most of the bridge. He then pulled his silver dagger and swiped at a tendril that came close. It cleaved through the gloppy ooze with a sizzle and a hiss. Three more tentacles met the same fate before the assault stopped.

"We need to get back up to that bridge," Ovrym yelled through gritted teeth. "There's a tunnel we can use to escape this hellhole."

Gryph nodded and commanded his rope to pull them to safety. Wick held guard as Gryph pushed Ovrym up onto the bridge. Both men downed a *Health Potion*. Ovrym pulled a few silver potions from his pack and advanced on the ooze-covered wall. He held the potions high and stared in silence at the pulsating blob. His eyes closed as if he were attempting to communicate with the beast.

After a moment's pause, Ovrym fell to one knee. The tendrils withdrew their attack and the ooze in front of Ovrym sluiced open, revealing a tunnel. "We have come to an agreement."

"You can't be serious. You trust this giant blob of acid snot?" Wick said as he eyed the now smooth surface of the ooze.

"Its mind is very alien, but it understands pain as well as any other living creature. I promised it far more pain if it did not let us pass in peace."

"Will it keep its side of the bargain?" Gryph asked, eyeing the long tunnel ahead.

"I believe it will but hold your silver solutions in your hands and be ready to run."

Gryph reluctantly nodded and watched for a moment as Ovrym entered the tunnel. He had a flash of being stuck in the digestive tract of a massive beast and felt himself panic slightly. He breathed a few deep breaths before stepping in as well.

"I hate this fucking place," Gryph muttered.

The party moved slowly through the tunnel as it turned and weaved. As they walked, the ooze parted like the red sea as they approached and flowed back in as they walked past.

"The walls are moving. The ceiling is moving. The floor is moving." Wick grumbled as he forced back another bought of claustrophobia. "Absolutely nothing about this is okay."

"Quiet," Ovrym said in a calm but deadly tone.

As they rounded another corner, it dawned on Gryph that without Ovrym's parlay there was no way they'd have been able to force their way through this length of tunnel. Had this been a part of the plan?

Ovrym turned another corner, and Gryph heard the man say, "Almost through," in a calm voice. Gryph breathed heavily and tried not to run as he rounded the bend and light from the end of the tunnel came into view.

Ovrym passed through unscathed. He smiled at Gryph and nodded, pointing his attention to the ground at the tunnel's exit. Gryph saw a perfect crescent of silver embedded in the floor. As he crossed over the barrier, he craned his neck. The thin silver band crested the entire entrance way like the line of a magic circle. As his foot hit solid ground on the other side he realized he'd been holding his breath. The exhalation was as big a relief as any he'd ever experienced.

Ovrym motioned Gryph to stand behind him. "Keep those solutions ready."

As Wick turned the last corner a huge grin crossed his face, and he ran. The sudden motion caused the ooze to flutter and pulse. "Slow," Ovrym warned, but Wick would have none of it. Panic had taken him.

Wick was near the end when his toe caught a ridge on the floor, and he went down. The vial in his left hand skittered across the floor before bouncing up and onto the wall where it burst. The ooze at the point of contact sizzled and disappeared, burned away under the power of the silver.

Wick struggled to get to his feet as the rest of the ooze pulsed in what may have been anger. Gryph could hear a deep rumble akin to the sound of water gurgling deep inside a network of pipes, but this was a hundred times louder.

Ovrym didn't hesitate and lobbed several of the silver grenades into the tunnel. This opened a path for Wick who scrambled to his feet and ran again. This time tendrils erupted from the sides and the roof of the tunnel, tripping Wick.

Terror crossed the gnome's face as he jerked to a stop and the noise from further down the tunnel grew to a cacophony. More tendrils lashed out, enveloping Wick. He screamed as the acid dissolved his skin.

Gryph drew his ice dagger and rushed back in the tunnel, hacking and slashing at tendrils that came his way. The daggers did not slice through the thick liquid the way the silver did, but the freeze damage seemed to stop them in their tracks for a few moments.

Unfortunately, he still felt the burning pain of dozens of tendrils latching onto his limbs and biting into his face. The cloying black ooze could just muster up more tentacles than he could cut. The world turned to black as the ooze sealed off the entrance, entombing them.

Gryph heard Wick's low moans ahead and knew his friend was near death. If only he could get to him. Another tendril gripped him around the arm, and another around the neck. Deep, burning pain dug into Gryph. Death was coming for him.

37

Safe in the antechamber, Ovrym howled as the tunnel sealed with a plug of bulbous ooze. He tossed his last few vials of colloidal silver at the rancid beast, but only succeeded in burning the edges away.

His friends were trapped, and they would soon be dead. Then a glow began to rise deep inside the tunnel and the ooze bubbled and boiled off like water sputtering off a newly forged sword. Rancid steam and bits of burning ooze erupted from the tunnel like over shaken champagne and Ovrym dove aside.

✵ ✵ ✵ ✵ ✵

Inside the tunnel, the world went quiet as the ooze enveloped Gryph. He was in agony, but his outstretched arm found Wick. He found the gnome's head and cradled it in his arms. Gryph then drew every ounce of mana he could from deep inside of him. When it had built up in his mind to bursting, Gryph fed it into his breastplate and ordered it to explode.

The burning stopped instantly as the healing light ravaged the black ooze, burning it away like the desert sun to spilt water. Gryph could hear a deep rumble and a splintering of stone as the black ooze tried to force too much of itself into too small a space, desperate to get away from the scalding light. Gryph opened his eyes as the healing warmth of the light eased his pain.

He looked down on Wick who was inhaling deep ragged breaths. He was alive, but only just. His blue hair was shorn by the deadly acid and his skin was raw and blistered. Gryph upended a *Health Potion* into Wick's mouth, again amazed at the healing powers of the Realms.

A moment later, he heard Ovrym's voice. "Keep a hold of him. I got you both." Gryph gripped both arms around Wick's child sized body and cradled him as Ovrym's strong arms pulled them both into the light and airiness of the cavern beyond the tunnel.

Wick was alive but unconscious. As Ovrym tended to him, Gryph downed another *Health Potion*. The warmth flowed through him, eased his pain and smoothed out the acid burns that covered much of his exposed flesh.

Ovrym carried Wick and led them to another tunnel at the opposite end of the small chamber. "The ooze shouldn't be able to get past the vein of silver, but I'd rather not test that theory."

"Seems rather convenient," Gryph said. "A silver vein in exactly the right place to keep that monster at bay."

"It is no accident friend. It is the will of the Barrow," Ovrym said as if that explained anything. They moved through the tunnel and came to what appeared to be a dead end. A slab of granite blocked the way forward. Ovrym nodded to a small lever. Gryph eyed it a moment before turning it. A grinding of stone on stone rose as the slab of stone eased aside on a well-oiled track.

"What do you mean the will of the Barrow? You act as if this place is alive."

"It is," Ovrym said as he slipped through the opening left in the wake of the grinding slab. He eased Wick down and checked on him again.

"I don't understand."

"Long ago, something happened here. A battle between two powerful users of magic. I believe it was that battle that sent this tower plummeting into the depths of the earth. I think that battle not only made the Barrow but the Barrow King."

"How can you possibly know that?"

Ovrym helped Wick to the ground and placed the gnome's pack under his head. Wick groaned in his sleep but did not wake.

"My Order are experts of *Thought Magic,*" Ovrym said. "It

helps us uncover truths and better enforce the Accords. I am particularly gifted in the art. Perhaps that is why they tolerated a xydai." The already melancholy man seemed to descend deeper into the darkness of his past for a moment before coming back to the present. "It is difficult to explain, but a powerful mind infuses the Barrow. Whatever the Barrow King once was, it is now a disembodied mind whose will can alter the very fabric of the dungeon. The Barrow King is weaker than he once was. He is hungry and his ability to alter the Barrow is waning. Good for us. Had we fallen into its trap in his prime, we would have long ago been consumed."

"Consumed?"

"Yes, I don't know how exactly but the Barrow feeds on life. It lures prey into itself with the promise of treasure and glory and once it has killed them it absorbs their remains."

"A Venus flytrap," Gryph muttered.

Ovrym gave him an odd look.

"There is a plant where I'm from that uses a sticky, sweet sap to lure insects into itself. Then it traps and consumes them."

"An apt analogy."

"And I'm the juiciest of flies," Gryph said.

"Whatever happens my odd immortal friend, you must not let the evil in this place take you."

Ovrym locked eyes with Gryph, and he knew that to prevent the Barrow King from attaining the *Godhead*, the Adjudicator would kill him again and again.

"Rest if you can. Wick will be unconscious for a few more hours."

Gryph nodded and glanced around the small chamber for a place to lie down. Near the far wall was a small alcove covered in worn runes. Curiosity tugged at Gryph, and he walked to the niche. The runes were too faded to make out, but the spot had the feel of an ancient altar. There was something warm and inviting about the spot and before he realized it Gryph had placed his hands on the small altar. A prompt floated into his vision.

> ## Respawn Point Discovered.
>
> *You have discovered a nexus of power that can be designated as a respawn point. Do you wish to change your respawn point to this location?*

Gryph jumped back in alarm. He already knew that he was functionally immortal but having his ability to return from death so casually tossed in his face was jarring. He let his heart rate cool and then placed his hands back on the altar.

> ## Do you wish to change your Respawn Point?

Gryph toggled the **YES** icon. At the very least, if he died again, he wouldn't have to traverse the pit of horrors where the black ooze lived. A pulse of warmth flowed from the altar through his arms and into his body. The warmth was relaxing, and Gryph found his mind eased somewhat.

> ## Congratulations.
>
> *You have changed your Respawn Point.*

Gryph tried not to dwell on the casual nature the game dealt with death. His eyes drifted over to Wick and Ovrym, and he knew that neither of his companions was blessed with the same gift. They had one life, which made them more precious. He was starting to wonder if he'd selected the right divine perk.

What is the point of all this? Gryph thought to himself. Brynn's face popped into his head again. She'd been terrified, so why had she entered the Realms and where was she now? Whatever part Brynn had wanted him to play, this was not it. He calmed his mind and tried to focus on the task at hand. The plan still hadn't changed. He needed to get out of the Barrow. Only then could he find Brynn. For now, his greatest chance at success seemed to be with the two men next to him.

It was time to spend his two saved *Perk Points*. He was sick of being so easily damaged. Not only did this increase his chance of dying, but it really damn hurt. Gryph opened up his *Light Armor* perk tree.

LIGHT ARMOR PERKS.

----- *Set Bonus* -----
The bonus to AC when a complete set of light armor is worn.

----- *Agile Defense* -----
It is easier to move in light armor, thus making it more likely to avoid attacks. The % bonus to AC for light armor.

----- *Silence* -----
The increase to Stealth while a complete set of light armor is worn.

----- *Damage Reduction* -----
The reduction to damage when a full set of light armor is worn.

This choice was a no-brainer. He put one point into *Agile Defense* and another into *Damage Reduction*.

Light Armor Perk Tree.				
Tier	Set Bonus	Agile Defense	Silence	Reduction
Base	20%	25%	20%	20%
Apprentice	30%	40%	30%	30%
Journeyman	40%	60%	40%	40%
Master	50%	80%	50%	50%
Grandmaster	60%	100%	60%	60%
Divine	75%	200%	75%	75%

Gryph and Ovrym came up with a plan and then Gryph laid down for some much-needed rest. Several hours later, Ovrym shook Gryph awake. He nodded towards Wick who was sitting up and eating. Gryph stood and went over to Wick, who smiled up at him grimly. The gnome's skin was still raw and red, but the deep scarring of the acid had healed. His hair was a different matter. Gone were most of the long, flowing azure locks that had once graced the diminutive man's head. What remained reminded Gryph of the time five-year-old Brynn had given "my dolly a haircut," a mohawk styled by a drunk blind man. But Wick's smile remained.

"You look good," Gryph said.

"Liar," Wick said and grasped Gryph by the forearm. "Thank you," he said. In answer, Gryph nodded. Gryph felt the strong grip on his arm, he saw the intense look in Wick's eyes and knew that the gnome was a true friend.

Gryph told Wick the plan he and Ovrym had conceived while Wick had been resting.

"Your plan is insane."

"You have a better idea?"

The gnome thought for a moment before nodding his head no. "Guess we go with insane."

Ovrym helped Wick to his feet. "Time to visit some old friends."

The men geared up and walked to the secret door that kept this room hidden. They took a moment to ready themselves. Once they opened the door, they would be in the province of the Gray Company.

"Ready?" the yellow-eyed man asked. Wick and Gryph nodded grimly.

Ovrym eased his hand into a small crevasse and with a small click, the door slid open, exposing stone steps carved directly into the rock. They climbed the stairs and emerged into what appeared to be an ancient storeroom. Massive stone urns that likely once held the water supply when the Barrow had been a tower lined the room.

After they climbed out, Ovrym twisted an old faucet and two halves of another ancient urn moved with a low grinding noise. Gryph admired the handiwork as the secret passageway sealed itself shut, leaving no trace that this urn was any different from the rest of its brethren.

"I was wondering when you'd show up," a deep voice tinged with amusement and danger said and a group of men wielding bows and swords emerged from the shadows.

38

"Hello, Dirge," Ovrym said, only mildly surprised. "Long time."

The man named Dirge emerged from the shadows. He was wiry but held a deadly grace that Gryph had seen in many men. A grace that not only suggested an ability for deadly violence, but a love of it.

He was nearly a head shorter than both Gryph and Ovrym, with a shaggy mop of unkempt hair surrounding a dark-skinned face. Ice-blue eyes pierced the distance between them like a laser. A thin scar traced down his left cheek from jaw to cheekbone. As he eyeballed the tall xydai, the man known as Dirge traced the scar with an idle thumb, almost as if he wasn't aware he was doing it.

Gryph saw Ovrym tense and knew that the warrior monk had been the one to give Dirge the scar. Gryph got ready for action as this encounter was unlikely to go any better than that one.

"Been wondering these last few months if you were still alive," Dirge said as he picked at his fingernails with a wickedly sharp dagger. "But part of me knew you were still around. Part of me knew all I had to do was wait for the sign. I didn't know the sign would be such a little prick."

"No squeeze Xeg, fat hairy thing."

A heavy man emerged from the shadows, his sausage fingers clasped around Xeg's thin neck. When Xeg saw them, it grinned. In anger or joy, Gryph could not tell.

"Stupid blue-haired midget. See what trouble get Xeg into."

"Of course," Wick grumbled, gripping his staff harder. "I bet you didn't even try to keep your mouth shut."

"Fat hands want crush Xeg's neck. Xeg like neck just fine. No want crushed. Xeg tell thin ugly scarface what want know.

Xeg's neck stay no crushed."

Gryph felt the tension rise as Xeg laid out insults without care of consequence.

"We have somewhere we need to be," Ovrym said in a steady voice, his eyes never leaving Dirge's.

"At first I wondered what would bring you back down here," Dirge said. Then his voice changed to a mockery of Xeg's. "Pretty lady need save," Dirge squeaked before the strain of the tone caused him to cough and clear his throat. "Damn, how do you talk like that?" Dirge said, glancing at Xeg.

"Sound nothing like Xeg," Xeg pouted.

Dirge chuckled to himself at the imp's irritation, but then brought his focus to Gryph. "You are new to the neighborhood, aren't you? How are you liking the accommodations?"

Gryph said nothing.

"Oooh, the strong, silent type. My favorite. What's your name, sugar?"

"Gryph, and I have no quarrel with you."

Dirge walked up to Gryph, running a thin hand along Gryph's chest and then down his arm and along his back. It was all Gryph could do not to flinch at the man's predatory attention. This Dirge was skilled in the art of psychological warfare. He was trying to make Gryph uncomfortable. After a moment, sensing that Gryph was no easy target, Dirge gave up on the tactic.

"You're the one who stirred up this hornet's nest aren't you? The vermin and the dead have been all aflutter these last few days. That's when you arrived, isn't it? What makes you so interesting?"

"Nothing. I've been here for weeks," Gryph said. "So, if you could point the way to the exit, I'll gladly get out of your hair."

Dirge laughed what seemed to be a genuine laugh. "Amusing and attractive," Dirge said, taking Gryph's chin in his hand.

Gryph did his best not to flinch and stared back into the man's eyes.

"But I do not think so. You're new to the Barrow. Your

eyes don't have that sunken desperation the rest of ours do. You still think there's a way out, don't you?"

"There's always a way out," Gryph said. "You just have to do what is necessary to find it."

"You may be right, my tall friend. And just what will you do to find it?" Gryph felt an odd twinge in his mind as Dirge stared at him. Without thinking he cast *Mind Shield*. Dirge jumped as the shell snapped around Gryph's mind.

"Well, that was rude," Dirge said. "But there are other ways of seeing truths." Dirge studied Gryph's face, twirling his knife almost casually as he did. Gryph stared back with an unflinching gaze. He'd faced more skilled interrogators in his day. After a few moments, Dirge understood he would get nothing from Gryph and chuckled slightly.

"I wouldn't trust this one, Ovy, he has the look of a man who will stop at nothing to achieve his goals, even if that means tossing you and wee mohawk boy aside like last week's fling."

Wick glowered at the comment, even as Xeg chuckled at the insult. Dirge looked down on Wick. "This one's yours if I'm not mistaken?" Wick said nothing. "A gnome chthonic summoner? I'm sure that went over well with the family."

Wick tensed and gripped his staff tighter. Ovrym extended a hand to the gnome's shoulder, warning him with a calm grip. Dirge's hand whipped up to Ovrym's neck and a small bead of blood pulsed from the xydai's jugular.

Gryph tensed, ready to move, but with a last motion, Ovrym warned Gryph off. A moment later, he collapsed to one knee and then fell onto his side, muscles knotted in paralysis.

"That was a long time coming," Dirge said with a satisfied sigh.

Gryph walked to his fallen friend and felt for a pulse. Ovrym's heart was beating at a normal rate and the xydai's eyes were alert. "What did you do to him?"

"A little gift," Dirge said, holding the index finger up. A thin needle protruded from a thimble like apparatus on his right hand. "He'll be fine in a few hours." The rogue moved his hands with a flourish, and the thimble disappeared somewhere in the folds of his clothing.

251

Dirge kneeled down and traced a line on Ovrym's face as if willing a matching scar to appear on the monk's face.

"Did Ovy here tell you about me? We used to be the best of pals. Thick as thieves as the saying goes. Which was proper because we are all of us thieves." Dirge stood and spread his hands around his assembled men. "We were brothers in blood. It broke my heart when I learned he no longer wanted to be buddies. I tried to talk some sense into him, but he wouldn't have any of it. Even left me with a parting gift." Dirge rubbed the scar on his cheek with the thumb of his right hand.

"I'm afraid he didn't mention you," Gryph said, causing the wiry man to pause. Dirge did a good job of hiding his irritation, but Gryph saw it still. Dirge smiled and turned away.

"No? Too bad. We had some good times, Ovy and I. But enough reminiscing about old times. What can I do for you my new, strapping friend?"

"I want an alliance." Gryph noticed that several of the men lurking around the cavern were eyeballing Ovrym in a way that suggested they didn't quite approve of Dirge or his methods. "With the Gray Company."

"Interesting. To what end."

"I already told you. I am leaving the Barrow."

Dirge laughed again. "I think he just insulted us boys. Apparently, without the great and wonderful Gryph, we're too weak and stupid to figure a way out. Now that he's here things will be just grand. Soon we'll be having garden parties and singing songs and frolicking through the trees."

Forced laughter spread through the assembled men, and Gryph knew that every one of them pictured that very thing in their minds now. Dirge didn't have quite the control over his men as he thought.

"I'm leaving the Barrow, but I need your help."

"Okay, I like riddles and games. How?"

"We're going to kill the Barrow King."

A silence descended upon the room as the audacity of the idea wormed its way into every mind present. Even Dirge looked taken aback for a moment. But then, like a practiced actor getting into character, the thief smiled once more.

"Good plan, with just one minor issue. You know the Barrow King is already dead, right?"

"Doesn't mean he cannot be killed. If the Gray Company will help."

Several of the assembled men exchanged glances. It was clear to Gryph that while they still had their lives in the Barrow, they all knew that they were prisoners. For men like these that had to be the worst torture.

Dirge must have sensed the tide in the room and was desperate to return to the status quo. "It isn't so bad here. Our little corner of the Barrow is quite nice. It's easily defensible, has plenty of water, a farm, sure it's a fungus and root vegetable farm, but still fresh food. We even have our own tavern courtesy of Runveld over there." Dirge indicated the burly sausage fingered man clutching Xeg.

Runveld grinned at the praise. Xeg took that moment to kick the brute in his stomach, a motion that earned an annoyed glance from the large Ordonian.

"No offense to Runveld and his fine fungus brew, but what I'm offering is a chance at life again. It won't be easy. Some of us may not survive, but at least we'll retain some control over our own lives."

A pulse of anger surged through Dirge as the Aegtyptian sensed the tone of the room turn. He sidled up to Gryph, whispering in his ear.

"What's your game friend?"

"No game," Gryph whispered back, staring directly down into the thief's blue eyes. "All I want is to get out. I have somewhere to be." Gryph leaned in close. Lowering his voice. "And I know what happened between you and Ovrym. I know the truth."

Panic surged into Dirge's eyes, and Gryph knew that Dirge's grip on the Gray Company was tenuous. After a long moment where Gryph could feel Dirge's thoughts testing his mental defenses, Dirge finally grinned. "You know, maybe you are onto something." He turned back to his fellows and opened his eyes wide. "What say you fellas, feel like getting out of here?"

A lukewarm cheer rose among the men and many of them gripped their weapons, ready for action.

"I just have one condition," Dirge said. "And it is non-negotiable."

"Name it."

"This one stays behind. Locked up and left." Dirge nudged Ovrym with a toe. A small grunt came from the xydai's mouth and his eyes locked onto Gryph's. "He betrayed the Code. None of us will fight alongside him."

Every man of the Gray Company nodded in agreement. Whatever this Code was it apparently held sway over these men. Gryph wished that Ovrym had told him the truth of his banishment, but if Dirge's moment of panic was any clue, then it was likely Dirge had been the one to betray this Code.

Gryph inhaled deeply and pretended to be deep in thought. After a moment, he turned to Dirge. "Fine by me," Gryph said in his most casual tone. Dirge smiled. Wick reacted a little worse.

"You bastard. He got us down here and you're just gonna leave him to this psycho?"

Dirge turned on the gnome. "You want to join him? The well has enough room for two if you don't move around too much." Wick's eyes went wide in panic.

"We need him," Gryph said. "I've seen the things he can do."

Dirge thought for a moment and then waved his hand idly. "Fine! But keep him under control or my next sting will be for him." Dirge nodded his head towards Ovrym and one of the larger men hefted the fallen xydai onto his shoulder.

Without another word, Dirge exited the room. Some of his men filed out after him. Others eyed Gryph and Wick warily, waiting for them to leave. Wick glared anger at Gryph before leaving.

39

Dirge led them on a circuitous path through the Barrow. Gryph knew the thief was doubling back on purpose in an attempt to prevent Gryph from gaining an accurate feel of the terrain. It would have been a smart tactic, but Gryph's map auto updated. *I wonder, does that only work for players?*

Eventually, they emerged into a large cavern. Gryph imagined that in the days when the Barrow had been a tower, it had once been some kind of reception hall. The ceiling was at least thirty feet above their heads. Luminescent moss covered the walls casting a pleasant glow across the small village that dominated the chamber.

The efficiency of the setup surprised Gryph. Several neat lines of tents filled the cavern. A small brook babbled from the wall and skirted the wall where it fed a small field of plants before disappearing into the far wall. It wasn't paradise, but one could do worse inside the Barrow. No wonder the Gray Company seemed somewhat content here.

The men carrying Ovrym left the main group and brought the paralyzed xydai over to a well in the center of the chamber. They tied a rope around his chest, and none too gently dumped him over the side where they lowered him down. Gryph paid only the slightest attention, feeling Dirge's eyes on him.

A small grin crossed Dirge's lips as he led them into a large tent where rows of dilapidated chairs butted up against stone blocks used as tables. He hadn't been lying. They had their own pub, and while it wouldn't make any Travel and Leisure top ten lists, it had a certain hominess to it.

Dirge snapped and held up three fingers. A barman poured two draughts of some brackish amber liquid and placed the gourd cups on the stone bar. Dirge picked up one, and Gryph grabbed another. Wick sat unmoving, silent and fuming. Gryph knew that fear was eating at his friend.

Gryph placed his hand on the gnome's shoulder. "We'll find her, but we need a plan."

Wick shrugged Gryph's hand off and stood. "Make your plans and make them quickly. I will go it alone if I must." Wick picked up his gourd of beer and threw it across the tent where it smashed against another table spilling the contents. Then he stomped out, came back in and grabbed a wineskin full of the rancid stuff that the barman was pouring.

"What the hell? You little bastard," the barman said, but Dirge held up a hand to stop his complaints.

Wick stared at Gryph with a look of anger and hate that made Gryph's veins turn to ice. Finally, the gnome turned and stomped out of the tent.

Dirge laughed, and Gryph felt an intense need to punch the wiry man in the face. Instead, Gryph raised his glass to the man in salute.

"To new friends," Dirge said, hefting his cup high.

"To getting out of here," Gryph countered and clapped his gourd against Dirge's. The thief nodded and grinned.

Both men drank, but only Gryph's face screwed up in distaste. The liquid may technically be beer, but it was unlike any brew Gryph had ever tasted. Peaty, earthy and sour, the liquid burned as it went down. The aftertaste wasn't any better, reminding Gryph of rancid meat.

Dirge laughed. "It takes some getting used to, but it packs a punch." Dirge indicated a table and waited for Gryph to sit.

"So, tell me about this plan of yours," Dirge said taking another swig.

Gryph held out his hand palm up. "First, I need to know the lay of the land." Dirge stared at Gryph's hand and then up at him. Gryph could see the man's mind working. Knowledge was power down here, but there was no logical reason for Dirge to withhold any. After all, they were allies now.

Reluctantly Dirge placed his hand on top of Gryph's and Gryph's mental map expanded with knowledge. Gryph took a moment to examine the map. They seemed to occupy most of the tenth level of the onetime tower. According to Dirge's information the Barrow King occupied the lowest level, three levels down. The twelfth level was a warren of passages and dead ends filled with red trap icons and numerous enclaves of creatures Dirge had marked as the Dead.

"The Dead?"

"As in undead," Dirge said, questioning Gryph's blank look. "Where the hell are you from that you haven't encountered the undead?"

"I'm new to the area. Can they be killed?"

Dirge eyed him suspiciously before speaking. "Sure, same as anything else. Hit them hard they'll eventually go down. Lower level undead like skeletons and zombies are pretty easy. Revenants, spectres, wraiths and the more ethereal dead need silver or magic weapons."

"Now, the Barrow King is something different altogether. Technically he is some kinda lich." Dirge saw Gryph's blank expression and shrugged. "I'm going to regret this."

"Just do your part and we'll stay pals."

"Anyway, a lich is the spirit of a powerful magician who has stuck around after death. Kinda foolish if you ask me since every sentient being in the Realms has an immortal soul that reincarnates after death as something new. Why get stuck as some half-life monster when you can just come back as a newborn babe."

"Power," Gryph said.

Dirge nodded in assent as if he had never thought of it before but knew it to be true.

"What's on the next floor down?"

"Nothing really. Rats, some random monsters, but no organized force."

"Seems a little odd."

Dirge eyed Gryph a moment before answering. "It was part of the deal we negotiated."

"Some deal."

Dirge leaned forward, anger taking hold of him. "Judge me all you like my new friend, but all of us are still alive because of the deal. It has held for the last two years."

Gryph realized that timeline likely matched up with Ovrym's exile from the Gray Company. "Then why agree to my plan?"

"Like you said, some deal," Dirge said and took a sip of his beer, never once taking his eyes from Gryph.

Their talk turned to the casual. Dirge told him about his home. A small town on the shores of the Gypt River, a massive waterway that stabbed through the desert lands to the west and gave rise to some of the most fertile lands in the Realms. "The most advanced civilization on Korynn," Dirge boasted.

"Sounds lovely. Why'd you leave?"

"Let's say a powerful noble and I didn't see eye to eye on a few things."

Dirge gave Gryph a smug look. "I may have bedded his daughter," Dirge said, raising his gourd. Gryph nodded in understanding. "And his wives."

Gryph spit up his drink in amusement. "Wives?"

Dirge held up three fingers as he took another sip from his gourd. Gryph laughed.

"What can I say? I have a particular skill with alchemy and my wares were popular with men of a certain age." Dirge held his forearm up in an unmistakable gesture. Dirge had made magic Viagra. "This noble was a longtime customer. Even introduced me to his wives." Dirge winked, and Gryph laughed again, a true belly laugh this time. "That isn't the worst of it. Pretty sure the last straw on the camel's back was the bedding on his favorite son."

Dirge looked at Gryph, searching for judgment, but an even larger smile crossed Gryph's face.

"I'm starting to like you, Dirge."

"Watch out for that. I'm a rogue who can't be trusted. Say, you don't happen to have a sister, do you?"

Gryph choked on his beer and while thoughts of worry turned to Brynn, he found that he was enjoying himself for the first time since he'd entered the Realms.

"Get me out of here and maybe I'll make an introduction," Gryph said.

"I think this will be the beginning of a beautiful friendship, sir elf." Dirge hoisted his gourd in salute. Gryph did the same.

"You bastards," came a voice swimming in the deep depths of inebriation. Both men turned to see Wick stumble into the tent. The empty wineskin dangled from his hand as he stumbled. Bleary, red eyes stared out from underneath the gnome's acid shorn frock of lightning blue hair.

Gryph had to stifle a laugh. Wick looked like an angry drunk toddler whose big sister had tried to "pretty him up" and failed. Dirge felt no need to hold in his laugh, earning the immediate ire of the angry little man.

"Fridckkfr Yuuf" Wick mumbled. Gryph's *Gift of Tongues* failed to translate the gibberish, but Dirge and Gryph still took the meaning. Wick strained to focus on the wiry man and dark purple chthonic energy pulsed and dissipate in his eyes. Dirge's demeanor instantly shifted.

Gryph jumped to his feet, nearly falling over. Damn this horrid root beer was strong. Gryph rushed up to Wick and kneeled in front of him. He forced the diminutive man to turn towards him.

"Wick. We will find her. We will save her."

Rage and doubt and fear battled on the gnome's face and finally, the fear won. Tears poured from his eyes as the magic faded. "Promise?"

Gryph held out his pinky. For a moment Wick just stared before finally grasping the extended finger with his own pinky. The bond sealed, Wick stumbled back out of the tent.

"I...sleep," the gnome mumbled and pushed past the flap of the tent. Gryph eased the flap open to watch as his friend weaved his way through the camp. He bumped into an old chest and then into a burly man who pushed him none too gently.

Gryph felt Dirge come up next to him. "Is he going to be a problem?"

"No," Gryph said, never taking his eyes off of Wick.

His friend walked past a small cage and a tiny, three-fingered red talon lashed out and tripped the gnome. Wick stumbled and fell, face planting onto the hard-packed dirt of the cavern floor. The imp's laughter followed. "Fall on face, go boom," Xeg grumbled and then spat on Wick.

The gnome stumbled to his feet and kicked the cage. A yelp of anger piped up from inside the cage and Wick flipped the small demon off before stumbling towards a dilapidated old rope ladder that clung to the wall of the cavern.

Gryph watched with apprehension as his small, drunk friend climbed the ladder. After several anxious moments and a few close calls, the gnome made it to a small alcove carved into the rock of the cavern wall. There he plopped down and pulled a ragged set of old blankets over him.

"He'll sleep it off," Gryph said. "I think I'll do the same." Gryph hoisted his gourd to Dirge, drained the last bit of rancid liquid and walked off with a stumble. The cold eyes of Dirge followed him every step and then an even colder grin crossed the wiry Aegyptian's face.

40

Gryph felt the tiny prick and his eyes snapped open. Dirge stood above him, grinning down on him like some maniacal circus clown. The thief wiggled his finger, taunting Gryph with the poison-filled thimble. Gryph moved his hands through the gestures to cast *Flying Stalactite*. His arm grew heavy as the power of *Earth Magic* flowed through him. The stalactite flew from his hand, but his aim was off, and it sailed past Dirge's head to impact against the wall with the *thud* of stone on stone.

Gryph's hand flopped uselessly to his side. Dirge mounted him with ease, straddling Gryph like he was a prize-breeding stud.

"Well, that was rude," Dirge said and punched Gryph in the face. The blow hurt his pride more than his body as only a small fraction of his red *Health* bar disappeared. The pain faded as his body became numb.

"Hello, pally. Did you sleep well?"

Gryph attempted to tell the wiry man to screw off, but he could not speak. What came out was a pathetic moan of droll and gibberish.

"So, as you may have figured out, I've reneged on our deal. His decrepit majesty the Barrow King has offered me a better one. My freedom from this hellhole in exchange for you."

Gryph mumbled again, and Dirge feigned shock and irritation.

"Did he just tell me to screw off?" Dirge asked turning to one of the burly men that stood behind him.

"Sounded more like fuck off to me," said the giant goon.

Dirge looked to the other man. "What do you think?"

"No idea, but it didn't sound friendly."

"No, no it did not," Dirge said and punched Gryph again.

"You should behave, sir elf. It'll go much easier for you."

Gryph grumbled more nonsense insults.

"Or we can do it the fun way." Dirge punched him once, twice, three more times. Each shot barely doing any damage. With each punch, the Aegyptian's faux calm faded, and Gryph could see the psychotic anger the small man otherwise masked so well. Dirge leaned in and whispered into Gryph's ear.

"I so wish Ovy hadn't told you about our falling out. I could have maybe worked with you, but I don't think the rest of the crew would take kindly to discovering the truth. Foolish of them really. Do they think that we're allowed to stay here without cost? The Barrow King may be weaker than he once was, but he could still wipe us out. What's the life of one man every few months compared to the lives of all of us?"

"Ovrym just couldn't see the wisdom of it, and he wasn't willing to make the sacrifice when it was his turn. Sure, I may have cheated a tad. Rigged the game to get rid of him." Dirge rubbed the scar on his face. "It would have been so much easier if he'd just gone quietly."

Gryph's focus locked on the debuff cooldown. Dirge was a talker. Maybe, just maybe, he'd keep blathering long enough to give Gryph a chance. Gryph mumbled and drooled, but nothing intelligible came out.

"You know I just can't understand you. It's as if somebody injected you with a paralytic. Oh wait, that was me." Dirge chuckled at his own jest. He punched Gryph once more and hopped up. He sauntered almost casually around the room, puffed up with the bravado and cockiness only small men can muster. He nodded to the two goons, and they tied Gryph. Gryph tried to struggle, but his body refused to respond.

"We will play a little game called Truth or Slice," he said as he pulled both daggers from their sheaths and spun them artfully. He sat back on Gryph's chest and placed his blade a mere inch from Gryph's left eye. "Now, let's play."

"Why does the Barrow King want you so badly? He insisted that I bring you to him alive."

Gryph again mumbled something that may have been a suggestion about inserting vegetables somewhere they weren't meant to go.

"Oh, tease of teases. I so wish there was time for that," Dirge said and brought his knife closer to Gryph's eye. "But, unfortunately, time is not on our side. More on mine than yours, but we all have deadlines to keep so to speak."

The knife tip was so close to Gryph's eyes that he could no longer focus on it. Even paralyzed by Dirge's sting, Gryph put immense effort into remaining still. Dirge had the steadiest hands he'd ever seen, but he trusted neither the thief nor himself at this moment.

Seeing that he'd made his point, Dirge pulled back a fraction of a hair. Gryph blinked and a muffled "I don't know" chortled from his throat.

"You know what, I believe you. Too bad." Dirge eased back, flipped his daggers around and sheathed them as gracefully as a dancer. He spun off Gryph and nodded to his two burly companions. "Gag him and toss him in a sack. It's time to go."

Gryph was gagged, hoisted up, and tossed into a rough spun sack that could use some serious laundering. It smelled of sweat, vomit and old blood. Gryph knew that he wasn't the first person to face the end of his days in this bag. He tried to struggle with his bonds, but his body refused to obey commands.

One brute tossed him over a shoulder, and they left the tent. The brute adjusted Gryph's weight several times as they walked, seeking the most comfortable position to carry his hogtied prisoner. The movement pushed Gryph's face up flush against a small hole in the sack's thin, scratchy surface. He could now see a small, jagged part of the world.

They stopped, and Gryph could see Dirge staring upwards. It was amazing what details the human mind could extrapolate from the tiniest bits of information. The other brute nocked an arrow and drew the bowstring. The upward trajectory of his shot combined with their location meant there could only be one target. He was aiming at the place where Wick had climbed to sleep.

With a low twang, the arrow zipped, and Gryph heard the sound of the arrow impact the mound of blankets. The brute knocked and fired again and was rewarded with another thump.

The group snuck towards the old well they'd tossed Ovrym down. He saw Dirge nod to the hooded guard that sat in the shadows near the well. Then he looked down with a grin and spat. The rogue nodded to the bow carrying brute again and two more quick twangs ended a life. Dirge nodded to the hooded guard, who returned the gesture. In silence, they moved through the camp and entered a tunnel that descended deeper into the Barrow.

"Hold up," Dirge said and suddenly Gryph's whole world was filled with the effeminate rogue's face. "Hello," he said with a winning grin of white teeth. "Goodbye." Dirge brought the pommel of his dagger down hard onto Gryph's head and the world went black.

41

Gryph woke with a start. He didn't know how long he'd been out. It could have been seconds or days. His head pounded, and he fought to stay awake as the steady, even steps of the brute that carried him nearly lulled him back to sleep.

From what he could see, they were walking down a wide corridor, lined with green flames that burned directly from the sconces set into the wall. He didn't see any torches nor smell burning. This was magic.

He felt the brute carrying him tense up and then heard Dirge's voice. "Easy." Gryph could tell by the strain lingering under the surface of Dirge's voice that he was far from calm. Then he saw why.

Spaced midway between two points of green light was a vertical alcove set back into the wall. Standing inside was an armored corpse, the skin of its face pulled tight across its teeth giving it a feral grin. It held a massive two-handed sword point faced down. The creature's black eyes snapped open and watched as the party moved past, but otherwise, it did not move a muscle.

Though Gryph couldn't move his *Analyze* skill still worked just fine. He almost wished it hadn't.

Dread Knight.
Level: 22.
Health: 350.
Stamina: 420.
Mana: 0.
Spirit: 250.

The undead creature was high level and formidable and as they drifted down the hallway, Gryph saw that it wasn't alone. He saw four more on his side and assumed that the same number lay ensconced on the other side of the corridor.

This is a bad plan, Gryph thought.

They walked a few more feet before stopping. Gryph could not see why they had stopped, but the chill of evil crept into his bones. Dirge cleared his throat attempting to force courage into it.

"Let us pass. We are here at your master's invite."

The chill expanded and bit into Gryph's cramped muscles, and he was certain that his life would end, again. Then he heard Dirge exhale. A scrape of metal on stone followed as the sound of massive doors creaking on ancient hinges came to Gryph.

The party moved in, and Gryph saw the doors they passed through. They were 20 feet tall and emblazoned with scenes of death and battle. As they crossed the threshold, the creaking began again, and the doors sealed with a thud.

The brute carrying him shook in fear, but he walked forward on Dirge's command. A few moments later, they stopped again and tossed Gryph to the ground.

An oily hiss crept over the party, and Gryph heard Dirge say, "Easy." The brute mumbled an apology and propped Gryph up on his knees and pulled off the sack.

Gryph blinked a few times to clear the fog from his mind. As his eyes focused, a horror came into his field of vision. Sitting on a throne made of bone was a spectre of rancid fog and malevolent darkness. Glowing embers of green fire peered at him from behind a cowl of animated smoke. A gnarled hand that was neither bone nor flesh emerged from the ever-flowing robe that the creature didn't so much wear as exude.

Without meaning to Gryph's *Analyze* skill jumped to the fore.

Barrow King.

Level: 67.
Health: 1,245.
Stamina: 1,578.
Mana: 1,574.
Spirit: 0.

The Barrow King is the disembodied soul of an ancient wizard. It is a Legendary Opponent whose skill with magic is near unparalleled.

Strengths: Unknown.
Immunities: Unknown.
Weakness: Unknown.

Fear dug deep into the core of Gryph's being. He felt tendons seize and his blood turn cold. Bones felt as if they were splintering under the gaze and his muscles seized. His eyes could not focus on the foul creature as if it was phasing in and out of existence. With an incredible effort, Gryph forced himself to break eye contact. Instantly, the phantom pain brought on by the creature's gaze abated.

The Barrow King leaned forward, and a guttural grumbling flowed across the room. "Who are you?" said a voice of cracking stone and burning oil.

"Before we get to that," Dirge said. "I believe you owe us payment."

The spectre's eyes snapped up to Dirge. To his credit, the rogue barely shivered, one foot easing back a bare millimeter. The Barrow King' gaze bore into Dirge's soul, but the man stood his ground.

It's too bad he's proven to be an enemy, Gryph thought, impressed with the traitorous man's courage.

The Barrow King made the slightest motion, and two of the dread knights moved towards Gryph and Dirge. The two brutes tensed in uncertainty and fear, clutching weapons in suddenly slick hands.

Dirge never took his eyes off the Barrow King as he pulled a dagger from its sheath and spun it lightning quick. Gryph felt the tip bite into his neck. The point pulsed with each beat of his heart.

"There's no need for that," Dirge said with an eerie calm. "We can both get what we want and part as friends." The Barrow King snapped its head in an almost insectile manner, a sure sign of anger. "Or as temporary chums who never have to see each other again."

Another deep rumble emanated from the very stone of the throne room. Gryph looked around as much as he was able without skewering himself. The room was massive. Along the sides were balconies that Gryph imagined at one time, when the Barrow King had still been living, had held supplicants and underlings. Now, Gryph just hoped that the ancient stone held and did not come crashing down on him.

Gryph felt the tip of the knife push harder against his jugular and his gaze snapped back to the Barrow King. The rail thin creature's shoulders moved up and down as if the Barrow King were breathing to calm itself. But Gryph knew this creature had not taken a breath in millennia. What kind of terrible will kept this creature alive?

After a few tense moments, the Barrow King waved his hand in an idle backwards motion at an intricately carved stone archway to his right. A point of light came into being in the center of the arch, a singularity of all and nothing. It pulsed and then expanded filling the archway.

Gryph's heart both leapt and sank at the vision through the portal. It was a verdant valley. Sun streamed down through the branches of dappled trees, and he could hear the singsong of birds. Gryph had not realized just how detached from nature and life he had felt since arriving in the Realms. If the place beyond the singularity was real, then perhaps the Realms held some good after all.

Dirge yanked Gryph's head back, adjusting his blade again. "Now call off your goons and you'll have what you want."

The Barrow King stood, a flowing motion more serpentine than mammalian. As he flowed upwards, Gryph realized just how tall the creature was. It topped seven feet, and it flexed its shoulders backwards expanding before their eyes. It took a step forward on heavy booted feet, which had until a moment ago, not existed.

"Eh, eh," Dirge warned, and Gryph felt the knife pierce his skin. Blood flowed in a rivulet down Gryph's neck.

The Barrow King paused and sniffed. A keening noise, akin to the desperate hungry cry of a bird rose from inside the Barrow King's ever flowing shawl. Gryph sensed a craving like a junky smelling his next fix cooking.

Tense moments passed and after a glacial age, the Barrow King waved his hand again. The dread knights backed away, clearing a path for Dirge and his buddies to move towards the portal.

Dirge dragged Gryph to his feet and slowly moved towards the shimmering gateway. With each small step, he repositioned himself, always keeping Gryph between him and the Barrow King. The two brutes took up flanking positions, weapons at the ready, eyes on the dread knights.

Gryph flexed his fingers, working feeling back into them. *Now or never*, he thought.

Now, came a mental reply.

Chaos erupted.

42

Back in the cave where Wick had recovered from the black ooze, Gryph laid out his plan. According to Ovrym, Dirge was the leader of the Gray Company, a group of mercenaries, thieves and killers. Ovrym had taken up with them while searching for his onetime mentor, Zyrrin.

"Zyrrin was searching for a *Godhead*. He had found an ancient text that suggested one existed on Korynn, left unclaimed. I didn't believe it. *Godheads* were mere legends. And coming to Korynn violated the Accords. The Outer Realms may not interfere with this Realm. So, by joining him I sealed my fate."

The xydai fell silent. Both Gryph and Wick gave him time.

"Without him...I," Ovrym hesitated again. "I should have stopped him. But he'd become obsessed, and the quest drove him mad." Emotion surged into Ovrym. "In his madness he suspected me. Claimed that I would take the *Godhead* from him. Even then I didn't believe he would do it. Even then I thought there was hope. But he was too far gone. We battled, and he defeated me. He could have killed me, but he left me wounded, dying. A farmer woman found me, and she nursed me back to health. Me, a demon from the old tales. It was then that I realized what I had to do, no matter what the cost. If this woman could risk her life for a stranger, then I must do the same for the man who raised me. I tracked him to a city a few days ride from here and learned that he had gone to the mountains to the west. Legend told of an ancient city, long abandoned by the Thalmiir, the High Dwarves. It was said to contain a great treasure, an ancient weapon."

"The *Godhead*?" Gryph asked.

Ovrym eyed Gryph. "Zyrrin thought it to be true. He was lost, but no fool."

Ovrym explained how he had met up with the Gray

Company, convinced them of the wealth to be had. En route, they had become seduced by the Barrow.

"We fought and died, and the Barrow King came for us. Then after several days, the attacks just stopped."

"Dirge?" Wick asked.

Ovrym nodded. "He'd somehow made a parlay. None of us asked questions, not even me."

"It turned out that the parlay came with a cost. Dirge had broken the Code of Brotherhood by offering members of the Gray Company as a sacrifice. Every three months, he'd select a member he felt was a rival to his power or otherwise expendable and would take them on patrol. Invariably, the group would return with one less member and the Barrow King would leave us be for a time."

"I suppose I didn't want to know how he had done it. The men who he sacrificed are on my conscious as much as Dirge's, yet I did nothing." Ovrym said. "Until Dirge decided it was my turn."

"Dirge has a strong mind and could shield his intentions. But his two cohorts did not," Ovrym said. "Byrrck, the uglier of the two couldn't stop thinking about what he could kill once he had his hands on my saber. That's how I knew, I felt his thoughts. I would have killed them all, but Dirge sensed my intent and I only just escaped. I left him with a parting gift, though."

"The scar?" Gryph asked.

Ovrym nodded and a thin smile curled his lips. "We will use his own nature against him."

It had taken some convincing, but Xeg had finally agreed to the plan. The imp disappeared in a puff of sulfur and flame. Ovrym made an antidote to the paralytic that Dirge favored. Then they waited. When the time came, they downed the antidote, suited up and opened the secret door.

The Gray Company was waiting.

Wick stumbled from the tent where Dirge and Gryph were

getting chummy. Feigning anger at Gryph was easy for Wick. Despite the logic of the plan, fear bit at Wick's soul. He turned the fear to anger and feigned drunkenness. After his last confrontation with Gryph, he'd climbed up to the old guard spot and snuggled under the blankets. To all peering eyes, he was fast asleep. He waited an agonizing hour before peering out from his hiding spot.

Down below, he could see the back of the hooded guard keeping watch over the well they'd tossed Ovrym down. His eyes scanned the rest of the cavern. From his perch, Wick could see the entire village. Nobody was looking his way. He had played the role of angry drunk perfectly.

Wick eased himself over the edge and dropped to the ground. He skirted by several tents with stealth born of his small size. Snores and grunts popped here and there, but he encountered no one.

Soon he slithered up behind the lone guard. Ovrym had not known if this man was part of Dirge's group of traitors or not, so he had insisted that Wick keep him alive. The same poison Dirge favored coated the tip of Wick's blade. He snuck up behind the man and like a cobra striking from the shadows nicked the man's exposed hand.

"What the..." was all he managed, before the poison did its work and the man slumped. Wick tossed a rope into the well. A moment later, Ovrym pulled himself over the lip of the well and landed as silently as a mouse next to Wick.

They bound and gagged the man and eased him down into the well, making sure to hide his features. Then Ovrym took his place and Wick hid.

Soon, Dirge and his minions emerged from Gryph's tent with a man-sized sack. Two arrows sailed up to Wick's onetime hiding spot, slaying the pile of rags. Then the traitor came over to the well. Ovrym tensed but kept his cool as Dirge looked into the well.

"Goodbye, old friend," Dirge said in a low voice. He nodded to his cohort, who sunk two arrows into the bound form at the bottom of the well. For a moment, Ovrym felt a pang of guilt but then realized if Dirge was so casual about murder, then the guard Ovrym was masquerading as was part of Dirge's crew. Perhaps this was justice.

Dirge and his crew moved out.

"It's time," Ovrym said. Wick emerged from the shadows. They stopped at the cage that held Xeg and Wick nodded. The small demon grinned a mouthful of needle-sharp teeth and disappeared in a puff of rancid smoke. They dipped into *Sneak* and followed the three traitors.

Ovrym had no idea how Dirge had parlayed with the Barrow King, but the way to the depths of the Barrow was clear of enemies. No wyrmynn rushed them from hidden corridors. The dead stayed dead. So far, both sides were keeping the bargain. When Gryph suggested this plan, Ovrym thought it had a slim chance at success. While he still had his doubts, he now believed they at least had a fighting chance.

They kept to the shadows and always a turn or two behind Dirge and his cronies. Eventually, they came to the massive door that marked the entrance to the Barrow's inner sanctum. They stopped.

"You realize that this entire plan relies on a demon of the chthonic realm, right?" Wick said.

"That's why Gryph called it a Hail Mary. I do not know what kind of god this Mary is, but if she helps us get through this, I'll make whatever sacrifice she desires."

Wick nodded, and then they waited. Seconds felt like hours but, soon, their patience was rewarded.

"Pssst. Stupid ugly things. Look up. Xeg here."

Ovrym and Wick looked down the corridor where Xeg's head hung upside down, dangling through a small square hatch.

"Thank you, Mary," Wick said as the two men rushed to the hatch, careful not to disturb the undead sentinels in their receded alcoves. Ovrym boosted Wick. Wick held his hand down, but the warrior monk just nodded no and jumped into the small crawlspace.

Wick nodded in appreciation and closed the hatch again. They moved down the thin shaft scattering a few rats, spiders, and things with hundreds of legs. Soon, they came to a grate that overlooked a balcony. Below they could hear Dirge and something much, much worse.

Ovrym closed his eyes and his fingers moved as if unbidden by the conscious mind. The four points that held the grate to the wall parted, and the grate fell forward. Wick grabbed the grating with his right hand before it could fall to the ground.

The weight of the grate pulled at Wick's fingers. Gnomes weren't known for their strength, and he panicked. Ovrym's eyes snapped open, and a hand lashed out to grab the grate before the heavy iron could smash to the ground.

Wick breathed a heavy, silent breath and Ovrym gave him a sideways glance of apology. They eased the grate against the wall and clambered out. Ovrym pulled his bow from his back. Wick admired the intricate scrollwork that ran up and down the fine weapon. The buzz of potential inside its taut length was palpable.

Wick pulled on his *Maker Goggles* and prepped himself. A wet squelching crunch caused both men to snap their eyes down to Xeg. The tiny demon had a fat spider clasped in its hands and was tearing off its legs. Each leg pulled free with a wet tear and then stuffed into the demon's mouth. Then came the unpleasant crunch.

Xeg was in a world of his own, thoroughly enjoying his disgusting treat. Wick nudged the imp with his knee, and Xeg nearly cried out in irritation before scowling up at Wick. Wick gave the universal 'shut the hell up' look and for once Xeg seemed abashed. As if making up for the faux pas the imp offered Wick a leg.

Wick shook his head in disgust, earning a silent chuckle from Ovrym. Xeg shrugged and tossed the half-chomped spider aside. The poor creature pulled itself away on half legs. Xeg saw the spider slime on its hands and grimaced before looking from Wick to its hands and back to Wick. Realizing what was about to happen, Wick reached out to stop the imp, but he was too late, and a mélange of spider guts joined the other muck staining his clothes.

Wick felt the urge to punch the imp but knew they still needed its help to save Tifala. He could not see her, but Xeg had told them she was in a cage somewhere against the wall below the balcony on which they now stood. He could feel her through their bond and forced his will into the ring at his throat. *I'm coming my love*, he thought.

Ovrym cast another spell and Wick felt other minds inside

his own. It wasn't like he was sharing one mind, but more like these other voices were hovering right out of his perception. He heard a calm voice in his head.

Xeg, once we attack you go free Tifala and get her to safety, Ovrym said inside Wick's head.

Xeg will save pretty lady, tall demon eyes. Wick's mind recoiled at the oily slipperiness of Xeg's mind. The imp was most assuredly not of this realm.

Wick felt a schematic of the room pop into his mind, and he knew Ovrym's plan. They would hide on opposite ends of the balcony and would take out the dread knights closest to Gryph, giving him the time to get free.

Wick nodded and moved silently to his position. Down below he could see Gryph on his knees with Dirge's dagger at his throat. A portal to a wondrous place of green shimmered in front of them. Then there was the Barrow King.

Wick's mind and soul told him to flee. Fear bubbled up inside him at the sight of the revenant whose nature was so unnatural as to make Xeg seem like the fairest of elf maidens. Whatever the Barrow King was, he had perverted not only nature but his immortal soul. Wick forced his fear away.

Eight dread knights lined the walls along with the two at the Barrow King's feet. Shoving his fear away with a deep breath, Wick summoned chthonic energy around his hand and waited.

Eons passed until a single word pulsed into his mind. *Now.*

43

A flash of red-black energy exploded against the nearest dread knight's face, searing desiccated flesh and exploding the creature's skull.

An arrow zipped down and caught another of the undead creatures in the eye. Whatever animated the beast must have still considered the brain important because, like its fellow, it dropped to the ground dying for a second time.

Gryph's right hand moved the second the mental call had come through and as the blast tore the first dread knight's head from its shoulders, the rope binding Gryph snapped up and coiled itself around Dirge's wrist.

The thief yelped in surprise and attempted to thrust the dagger home, but the serpentine rope's strength was too much. The rest of the rope disentangled from Gryph and flowed around Dirge and squeezed. Gryph poured his will into the rope and activated the spider silk's compel ability.

Drop the blade, he ordered Dirge. The Aegyptian's face contorted, but he held onto the blade. Ovrym was right, the man had a strong mind.

"Betrayers," the Barrow King bellowed in a voice that tore at Gryph's bones. The revenant leapt from the dais with incredible speed and raised his staff on high. As the Barrow King landed, he brought the tip smashing down onto the stone floor. A wave of raw energy exploded from the impact point, knocking everything in the room from their feet.

The Barrow King spun his staff and pointed its gnarled tip at Gryph. Tendrils of inky black shot from it and flew at Gryph. He rolled and spun, avoiding the lithe streams of smoke and darkness. He pulled his spear from his inventory and pushed mana into the tip. There was little time to load the spear before he arced the weapon down. It sliced through several tendrils near to enveloping him. Gryph spun again, slicing through another reaching tendril.

Then one and another, and then a half a dozen grasped a hold of Gryph and squeezed. The spear fell from his grasp as his body immobilized. The tendrils squeezed harder and stretched him. Gryph imagined this what was being drawn and quartered felt like.

Debuffs Added.
Immobile. *Health Drain: 5pts/sec.* *Mana Drain: 5pts/sec.* *Stamina Drain: 5pts/sec.* *Spirit Drain: 5 pts/sec.*

Gryph screamed in pain as his life essence siphoned from him and into the Barrow King. He couldn't grab his spear, couldn't down a *Health Potion*. He couldn't move, but he didn't need to. Gryph poured mana into his chest plate and released it. The room exploded with the light of a newborn sun. The tendrils burned away under the intense glare, and Gryph could almost hear them scream in otherworldly pain.

Dirge, his thugs, and every dread knight in the room roared in pain as the searing light bit at their eyes, blinding them. The Barrow King staggered. Gryph was surprised that the brightness did not blind him.

Gryph threw his left hand out and poured mana into his bracers. His discarded spear flew to his hand just as the Barrow King drove downward with his staff. Gryph parried the blow, the power knocking him to his knees. For an ethereal spirit with no real physical form, the Barrow King packed a wallop.

Gryph spun, adding mana into the spear and slashed at the Barrow King's ankle. The tip passed right through the ethereal limb, leaving flashes of brilliant light in its wake. The Barrow King's leg buckled, and he fell to one knee. He turned towards Gryph and roared.

Viscous black liquid vomited towards Gryph as he once

again spun and rolled out of the way. It landed in a heap and the floor beneath it sizzled. Gryph poured more mana into his spear and struck again, this time triggering the weapon's *Banish* ability.

The Barrow King shimmered as the spear interrupted the connection to the netherworld that sustained him. Gryph used the time to regain his footing and catch his breath. Gryph pleaded with the universe for aid, but his prayers fell on deaf ears as the shimmer of light assaulting the Barrow King faded.

"Shit," Gryph muttered as he backed away from the shadow-cloaked revenant. With a quick glance borne from intense training, Gryph surveyed the battle.

Ovrym had leapt from the balcony and his red saber was a blur of crimson energy, slicing and dicing through the desiccated limbs of several dread knights. The xydai's grace and power amazed Gryph. Two of the undead warriors lay dead, and a third was not long for it.

Dirge and his cronies had pulled together into defensive positions. Back to back to back, they held their own. The ugly one, Byrrk screamed in agony as the black ooze enveloped his leg. The same black ooze that the Barrow King had vomited at Gryph.

Holy Shit, Gryph thought. *The black ooze is an undead vomit baby?*

Gryph watched in horror as the baby ooze leached itself up Byrrk's body, consuming him. The brute swung his sword down in panic, doing as much damage to his own leg as to the ooze. Soon, he collapsed, and he was enveloped. The large man's horrific screams were muffled and then ended. The smell of dissolving flesh reached Gryph's nose, spasming him from his momentary shock.

Wick was nowhere to be seen. Gryph smiled. That was part of the plan. The gnome conjurer's power did not lay in hand-to-hand combat, but in his ability to summon. A powerful ally was about to join the fray.

Xeg was at the cage holding Tifala, struggling with the lock. Gryph couldn't hear what the gnome woman was saying, but he knew that her gentle voice was encouraging the imp. She made eye contact with Gryph and nodded.

Gryph turned back to his own fight as the Barrow King

launched a lightning quick strike of his staff. The gnarled wood caught Gryph in the chest and a pulse of black energy smashed him backwards. Pain erupted and for a moment Gryph feared his heart had stopped. But soon, he felt the beat and a deep breath pushed a shard of icy pain into his chest. He had broken ribs and his *Health* bar had dropped by a quarter.

The Barrow King swung again, and Gryph knew he couldn't take another shot like that. He thrust his right hand out and activated his ring. The bubble of solid air shimmered as the staff struck. A corona of black energy flowed around the sphere, but it held.

Gryph fired *Flying Stalactite* through the shield and grinned as the spike of stone bit into the Barrow King's shoulder. The undead lord screamed and tore the shard of earth from its body, whipping it back at Gryph with incredible force. Once again, the air shield deflected the attack, but its shimmer told Gryph it would not hold much longer.

Gryph double fisted a *Health* and *Mana Potion* and rolled back to his feet just as the shield failed. Gryph put himself into a defensive stance and poured mana into his spear. He activated his bracers and threw the spear with all his might. The blazing missile surged towards the shadowy form of the Barrow King and thundered into his chest. The force of the blow pushed the creature back, and it fell to one knee. It shuddered as if in pain, and Gryph took a quick glance at the wraith's stats.

The thing's *Health* was still at 75%, but its *Mana* was bottoming out. Gryph grumbled. He'd been pounding the wraith with everything he had and barely made a dent to the revenant's life.

The Barrow King pulled himself back up to his full size. It pulled the spear from its body and held it in a shaking hand. A pulse of power flowed down the Barrow King's arm, and Gryph's spear disintegrated into ash.

"Shit." Losing good spears was becoming a bad habit for Gryph.

Then things got worse.

The Barrow King's dead eyes filled with eldritch green energy and it spread both arms wide. Its mouth opened far wider than it ever could have in life and a piercing scream, like the sound of some demonic bird calling allies to arms, erupted from its throat.

Around the chamber, the fallen bodies of the dread knights and Byrrk shook as if seething maggots were trying to burrow free. Pulsing blobs of green energy erupted from their mouths and flew into the waiting maw of the Barrow King. The revenant's body spasmed and all of his stats surged to 100%.

The Barrow King had just used their souls. As casually as Gryph would use a healing potion. He advanced on Gryph with terrible speed.

44

Disarmed and facing the onslaught of a rampaging bull, Gryph made a desperate gamble. He forced mana into his boots, and he felt every fast twitch muscle fiber in his body flush with energy.

With his speed doubled, he dodged the Barrow King's clumsy onslaught. He dove to the side, drew his *Ice Dagger* and flipped over a sideways swipe of his enemy's staff. The power of the boots boosted his leaping ability as well, and he came down behind the Barrow King, thrusting the dagger into the base of the creature's neck where skull met spine.

Gryph was rewarded with a dry snap as the dagger buried itself into the top vertebrae. He filled the dagger with mana and the frigid field expanded, crumbling already brittle bones. The Barrow King wailed in agony and spun to and fro, trying to dislodge Gryph, but he held fast.

"AVERNERIUS!" boomed a voice that both was and was not Wick's, and a point of crimson light appeared a dozen feet in front of the Barrow King. The point expanded into a vertical line, and then the line widened into a door to hell.

This time, when Gryph saw the horrid devil rushing towards the door, he did not fret. He smiled. His momentary glee distracted him enough for the Barrow King to grab his arm in a cold, skeletal embrace. Iron strong fingers of bone dug into Gryph's forearm, and he heard bones crack.

Gryph yanked the dagger free with his other hand and tried to thrust it into the side of the ancient skull, but the Barrow King's other arm spun in its socket in a way no living arm could and grabbed his wrist. Now trapped Gryph could only watch as the Barrow King's head twisted 180 degrees, his gaping mouth mere inches from Gryph's face.

Gryph's entire world became that gaping maw of death and the horror it was about to spew forth.

✳ ✳ ✳ ✳ ✳

Wick chanted the final word of the summons, nearly tearing his mortal vocal cords to shreds. The gnome collapsed to one knee as the infernal portal tore a slice in reality. The strain of summoning hell's lieutenant made him dizzy and weak. He willed himself to get to his feet just as the massive demon crossed the threshold into this realm.

Frantic eyes searched for Tifala, and he smiled when he saw her exiting the cage. She gave Xeg a quick pat on the head, eliciting a smile and a coo from the imp. Her eyes darted up to his, and he sent the thought *run* through the mental link Ovrym had given them.

She grinned up at him, shook her head no and his mind filled with her voice. *No, my love, I am here with you to the end.* Wick scowled but knew there was no talking her out of it.

Tifala summoned blinding white energy to her hands. She unleashed two life bolts at the nearest dread knight, taking the creature unawares from behind and blowing its head from its shoulders.

Avernerius swung his tree length sword of flame back and forth in slow, almost lazy arcs. Each swing decapitated or bisected the torso of a dread knight. Dirge, who had been fighting the dread knight the demon had just bisected, back flipped away from Avernerius' third swing. The arc of flame just missed the thief as he thudded hard to the ground.

Wick couldn't help but laugh. Apparently, he'd forgotten to name the traitor bastard as friendly. "Whoops," Wick said aloud.

A little help here, came Gryph's frantic mental call, pulling Wick from his temporary glee. He saw his friend being stretched by the Barrow King's misaligned limbs as the revenant's head spun.

Wick jumped from the balcony and slid down a support column. As he landed, he threw his arms out to the side and pulsed mana into them. Two short swords of blazing crimson darkness appeared in his hands, and he ran towards the

Barrow King's back. He leapt up, just as the cloaked shadow's shoulders hunched and buckled like a child about to vomit.

Wick brought both summoned swords down on the Barrow King's shoulder. The chthonic metal sliced through shadow and bone and severed the arm. Wick landed with agile grace as Gryph brought both feet up to kick the Barrow King in the head.

The wraith's head was knocked to the side as a stream of black ooze erupted from its mouth. It covered both the Barrow King's arm and Gryph's wrist. Gryph screamed in agony as his arm burned, but the revenant's skeletal arm was immune to the acidic damage. The creature's head turned back to Gryph, ready to hurl another volley of black death.

Gryph was injured, but he was a warrior born. He lifted the Barrow King's severed skeletal arm with his left hand and crammed it with tremendous force down into the Barrow King's open mouth. The arm blocked the torrent of black ooze allowing only a trickle to bubble forth.

Gryph landed on his feet and tossed several of his throwing knives at the Barrow King. They didn't do too much damage, but he recalled and tossed them again. The small blows slowly whittled at the lich's *Health*.

Wick doused the taller man's arm with the last of his silver solutions. The acid dissolved under the metal's onslaught, and Gryph's pain abated. Gryph nodded his thanks and was about to say something when the Barrow King screamed again.

Gryph pushed Wick aside as several more globes of silver soul energy flew from the defeated dread knights and down the Barrow King's throat. In an instant, the creature was again at 100%. Even the severed arm regrew.

He snapped the new arm out and the fallen staff flew to its hand. With a dramatic two handed thrust, the Barrow King smashed the staff into the floor.

The massive doors at the far end of the room opened.

"He's summoning reinforcements. Send the demon," Gryph yelled.

Wick nodded and sent a mental command to his demonic minion. *Block the door. Kill anything that enters.*

With a final backward swing, Avernerius decapitated the second of Dirge's cohorts. Alone among enemies, Dirge turned his attack to Ovrym. As if predicting Wick's question, Ovrym's voice filled the communal channel.

I have this. Help Gryph.

✳ ✳ ✳ ✳ ✳

"So, this is how it ends," Dirge said, his dagger held forth. Ovrym knew the skill with blades possessed by the leader of the Gray Company. He had seen it many times before and faced it once. The blades Dirge held were not so much tools as extensions of the wiry man's deadly intent.

But Ovrym was an Adjudicator, and he would dispense justice. The xydai settled his mind and his body eased like water. He sent an invocation into the aether and felt spirit energy flow down his arm into his saber. While Dirge's weapons may be extensions of his body, Ovrym's weapon was an extension of his will. And it wasn't his only weapon.

Ovrym lashed out with his thoughts, attempting to stun Dirge into submission. The dagger-wielding thief threw up a barrier. For an assassin, the smaller man was an adept thought mage. Dirge grinned at Ovrym.

The Aegyptian slashed with his left dagger, an obvious feint meant to distract Ovrym from his mental assault. Another opponent would have succumbed to the stunning mental bolt Dirge sent. But few could overcome the defenses of a fully trained Adjudicator.

Ovrym let the aether in and his mind expanded. Dirge's mental attack flowed over him like river water over a stone and Ovrym parried the dagger strike with ease. He pushed his momentum into a kick to Dirge's stomach. Pain and surprise tore across the smaller man's face before a cruel grin replaced them.

"Oh, Ovy, you've been holding back on me darling."

"You are a traitor Dirge. And I am here to pass judgment on you."

"You sanctimonious jackanapes. Who are you to pass judgment on me? I know all about your Order and the Accords and how you've spit on them both."

Shock crossed Ovrym's face. Few people on Korynn even believed in the Outer Realms existence, much less the laws and powers that governed them. How had this thief learned of these things?

Dirge grinned and launched a flurry of attacks. Ovrym barely avoided the poisoned whirs of death. Dirge would know that Ovrym was immune to the paralytic. He wasn't playing any longer. He was here to kill.

"You see it, don't you?" Dirge said. "You sense the death dripping from my blades. Well, let me tell you a little story."

Dirge danced left, then right and spun and stabbed. Ovrym blocked the attacks, but only just. His counter attack sliced through cloth, but left flesh untouched.

"Deep in the desert of my homeland lives a spider. A tiny thing, so easily missed. Not like the giant monstrosities that the dark forests harbor. No, the Mother of Death is barely the size of a thumbnail, but it bears a gift unlike any other. A poison made of the distilled essence of all spheres."

Dirge lunged again. Ovrym ducked and rolled and felt the blade zip by his ear.

"Most poisons can be countered by their antipathetic magic. Life can cure death, death life," Dirge said with a grin at his witticism. "But the mother of death mixes all spheres in her tiny crystalline body. A single drop of *Mother's Milk* will bring the full power of every sphere to bear. No immunities can counter it. No antidote exists. You will feel as if you are on fire while you are drowning. Your breath torn from your lungs as your blood turns to dust."

Dirge spun and threw a dagger at Ovrym. A pulse of aether took control of Ovrym's body tossing him aside before his mind was even aware what was happening, so attuned to the aether was Ovrym.

"Impressive," Dirge said in surprise. "Now I won't bore you with what the rest of the spheres do, save one. Those who succumb to *Mother's Milk* lose their immortal soul. The poison eats away at the core of your being, feeding he who delivered the killing blow. This is how I knew what power the Barrow King possessed. This is how I knew what bargain to make."

The man's impossible knowledge stunned Ovrym. The Aegyptians had long claimed ancient and secret knowledge, but most of the mystery schools were shams feeding power to charlatans. *Soul Magic* was a rare affinity with even fewer practitioners.

Dirge backed Ovrym up further, and he stumbled over the desiccated corpse of a twice killed dread knight. The warrior monk went down, and Dirge jumped putting weight and momentum into his deadly knife. Dirge came down hard on Ovrym's sword hand, snapping his wrist. His sword fell from his hand, and he barely caught the arm, arresting the dagger's deadly intent.

Normally, Ovrym was much stronger than the thief, but he was on his back, one arm immobile. Dirge had the superior position, and he leaned his entire body weight onto his knife arm. Slowly the blade came closer. Ovrym could see a milky white sheen on the blade and knew that the Aegyptian had not been lying. Death was mere millimeters away and coming for him.

Dirge pushed all his weight down and eased his face near Ovrym's. In a low voice full of malice and hatred, Dirge whispered, "Dearest Mother, I offer you a gift."

Desperate, Ovrym pumped his mind full of spirit energy and the aether took ahold of him. He could feel every mote in the room. His friends facing off against the Barrow King. The summoned demon raging against a horde of dread knights. Tifala firing life bolts in and around the giant devil, potshots that found their target more often than not. Only Ovrym was near death.

Then his mind found salvation, and he grinned.

"What are you grinning at, you madman?" Dirge asked as the knife tip came ever closer to Ovrym's face.

"I think you dropped something."

Ovrym's mind grabbed onto Dirge's other blade, another blade soaked in death, and called it. A flash of metal flew past Dirge and embedded itself in the wall behind Ovrym. The movement startled Dirge, but then he laughed.

"Missed."

"Did I?" Ovrym said as a single drop of blood welled on Dirge's cheek.

The thief's eyes went wide, and he backed off of Ovrym like a man bitten. His hands trembled as his fingers came to his face. They pulled away, marred by a small dot of crimson.

"You bast…" Dirge began, but then his body seized. He fell back, choking and burning. Boils and pustules erupted from his skin. His eyes turned crystalline, and his skin glowed a warm yellow light. His skin sloughed off as if ten years of decomposition had occurred in mere seconds. Dirge stopped moving, and his body turned to dust.

Ovrym reached out with his mind and felt the small man's soul die. A sin of the highest order and Ovrym was responsible. A tear rolled down Ovrym's cheek as he stood. "Forgive me for the unforgivable."

Then he heard Tifala scream.

45

Once again, Gryph faced a fully powered Barrow King, this time without a weapon. Sure, he had throwing knives and a very nice dagger, but against this self-healing, soul sucking perversion of nature that was worse than David with his sling.

He fired several volleys of *Flying Stalactite* at the spectral monster, but the Barrow King set them aside with almost casual waves of his staff. Wick got into the game, tossing several chthonic bolts. One hit the Barrow King in the side, earning an angry snarl that exposed rotten teeth.

The Barrow King held his staff in both hands and murmured. A shimmering semicircle of energy pulsed around him, giving off an oily haze, like a polluted puddle in a parking garage. Wick's next several bolts bounced harmlessly off the shield and the Barrow King floated towards them.

"Behind you," Gryph heard Tifala yell, and he spun just in time to see a dread knight swing a broad headed axe down at him. The heavy metal blade bit into the stone where it stuck. Gryph kicked the legs out from under the undead warrior and it hit the ground with a sickening *thunk* as its head pounded onto the stone of the floor.

A living creature would have lost consciousness. Being dead had advantages. The dread knight rose to its knees and wrapped long, skeletal fingers around Gryph's neck. The strength in the dead fingers was incredible, and Gryph could not breathe.

He punched up into the dead beast's face, once, twice, three times. The third blow took the knight's jaw off, but apart from a slight dip in *Health* seemed not to faze the creature.

Debuff Added.
Suffocation.

Well, it isn't drowning, technically, Gryph thought as he continued to punch. Each blow having less and less strength as his life faded. As his vision blurred, and the colors melded, he noticed a familiar sparkle moving to the beat of his ever-weakening punches.

One last rush of adrenaline cleared his mind enough to realize the sparkle was from his ring and in his head, he laughed. With the last of his life petering away Gryph pumped as much mana as he could into the *Ring of Air Shield*. He punched again, but this time he fully sank his fist into the dread knight's mouth. Its rotten teeth bit into his knuckles as his fist pushed down the creature's throat. Then he sent the command.

The air shield expanded, and the dread knight's head exploded. The hands around his throat stopped squeezing and the air shield blinked.

Oh, not this again, Gryph thought, and he scrambled to the left as the air shield collapsed raining gore and rotten bits of brain down upon him. He sucked ragged gasps of air into his lungs and coughed. He lay there a few moments, trying to recover.

Then he heard Tifala scream.

Wick saw Gryph go down, but there wasn't much he could do about it. He now faced the Barrow King alone. His mana was near depleted, and he couldn't spare a single second to chug a potion.

He fired the last few chthonic bolts he could muster and then pulled his summoned swords from their netherworld sheathes. They had a few more minutes of potency before they too would dissipate back to the chthonic realm.

Wick spun and ducked, using his superior agility to avoid the Barrow King's attacks, but the revenant still cowered behind its shield. Wick reached out to summon Avernerius to help but felt the last of the demon's *Health* disappear. A quick glance showed that at least the demon had collapsed the tunnel. The Barrow King would get no more aid.

Tifala was holding her own against one final, wounded dread knight. Ovrym was battling the traitor Dirge.

Wick realized he was on his own. If he didn't stop, or at least delay, the Barrow King they were all dead. Then a crazy idea popped into his head. An idea that just might work, but one that would likely end up with him dead.

He glanced once more at Tifala and poured waves of love at her. She danced and spun, pulses of white life light shredding the dread knight's *Health*. He smiled grimly and returned his attention to the Barrow King. He got into a fighting stance and then ordered his summoned weapons to blink and disappear.

The Barrow King grinned in triumph as it saw Wick's weapons disappear, and it advanced upon him. Wick took a few fearful steps back before forcing himself to stand his ground. Fear ate at his mind as he felt the outer edge of the revenant's energy field pass over him. He felt stained by a residue of hateful evil and nearly vomited.

But he was where he needed to be. The Barrow King reached out with one of his arms and grasped the small gnome by the throat. He hoisted Wick off his feet and brought him close to his face. This close, Wick could see the Barrow King was only partially physical. A human face seemed to phase in and out of existence over desiccated flesh pulled taut along the creature's skull. Wick was seeing the face of the man who had become the Barrow King, and he looked oddly common.

Then the Barrow King spoke, "You are a fool, gnome. I will feast on your soul and its power will enable me to take the *Godhead* from your pathetic companion. He does understand what power he possesses, does he?" The Barrow King laughed.

Wick summoned his short swords and drove them down and into the Barrow King's shoulders. The lich buckled but did not let go. His hand squeezed Wick's throat tighter, forcing Wick's mouth open.

This isn't going to plan, Wick thought as the Barrow King breathed death into his mouth. Wick's body seized, and he felt energy drain from him. Through his goggles, he could see that it was the same silver color as the energy he'd seen stolen from the wyrmynn. That seemed so long ago now.

Wick felt his soul leave his body.

Then he heard Tifala scream.

It was the last sound he heard.

46

Tifala's scream tore through the room, and all eyes went to her. Then all eyes went to where her gaze fell.

Gryph saw his small friend in the grasp of the Barrow King. The revenant was feeding on his soul. Gryph summoned the last remaining bit of mana he had and fired a stalactite at the unholy nightmare, but it clattered harmlessly off the revenant's shield. Desperate, Gryph searched for any kind of weapon.

"Gryph!" he heard Ovrym yell. His head whipped towards the warrior monk who stood, arm held at his side. He was too far away to do anything but hefted his red saber and tossed it towards Gryph.

"Go!" Ovrym yelled as the sword flew towards Gryph.

Gryph sprinted, easing himself under the blade like a wide receiver running under a quarterback's pass. He caught the blade in mid-run and rushed to the barrier separating him from Wick.

Gryph gripped the saber with both hands and forced the point into the shield. A surge of mana rushed into him as the elementum blade drained the shield's power. He pushed harder, and the tip forced itself deeper into the shield. More power rushed into him, and still the blade sunk deeper.

Gryph saw his friend's head loll back just as the shield collapsed.

"No!" Gryph screamed as the Barrow King let Wick's limp body fall to the floor.

The noise seemed to catch the spectre off guard, and Gryph jumped forcing every bit of the stolen mana back into the blade. The Barrow King's eyes flared emerald as the tip of the sword bit deep into its neck.

With a twist of the blade, Gryph severed the head from the spine, and the Barrow King went down. Its robes and body dissipated like smoke in high winds, leaving only a wretched skull.

Gryph cradled his friend's lifeless form.

Death is nearly always silent. That's one thing they don't tell you. Perhaps it is the shock. Wick's death was silent.

Tifala was the first one there. The imp perched on her shoulder. Her eyes were stained by tears, but she held a simple grace in her. Ovrym limped up a moment later. Neither could help Gryph as he looked from the lifeless eyes of his friend to their grief-filled ones.

Tifala knelt down and brought a gentle touch to Wick's face. She smiled through her tears. "So brave. So foolish. My love." A look of odd calm came over her face as if she realized she'd forgotten something at home.

Shock, Gryph thought. But then her other hand came to the chain at her neck, and a small smile came over her face. She held it in her palm and closed her eyes. Gryph wondered if it was a gnomish ritual and had no idea what he should do. Then her eyes snapped open.

"He is still alive," Tifala said.

Gryph looked at Ovrym with doubt. He couldn't imagine the pain she was feeling. It had to be a state of shock. Gryph placed a hand on her shoulder and she looked up at him, startled as if she'd forgotten he was there.

"He saved us all," Gryph said, feeling as if it was not near enough to ease her suffering.

Tifala smiled. "Yes, he did. Now it is our turn to save him."

An odd look crossed Ovrym's face as he struggled to kneel. He picked up the skull of the Barrow King and turned it towards him like Macbeth holding his father's skull. Ovrym closed his eyes and concentrated. It was a surreal moment more at home in a London theater than the depths of this dungeon.

"She is right," Ovrym said, his voice tinged with surprise. "I am feeling … something. Wick's soul is still here. As is the Barrow King's. There is…" His eyes opened in shock, and he stared at Gryph. "I am holding a realm in my hand. A small one to be sure, but a real place nonetheless."

Gryph motioned to Ovrym, and the xydai handed him the

skull. A prompt popped into his vision as soon as his fingers closed on the wretched sphere of bone.

You have discovered a Nexus of Power.

You have discovered a Respawn Point.

You have discovered a nexus of power that can be designated as a respawn point.

Do you wish to change your Respawn Point?

"You're right," Gryph said as an insane plan took root in his mind. "I think I can save him."

47

The group knelt around Wick's body. Now that the shock of his small friend's death had abated and his plan had formed, Gryph was calm. He could see the small rise and fall of Wick's chest as his body's autonomic functions continued despite the lack of higher brain functions.

"This plan is insane," Tifala said.

"And dangerous," Ovrym added.

"Plan stupid," Xeg said. "Xeg have better one." The diminutive demon jumped from Tifala's shoulder and landed on Wick's chest. He grabbed Wick's cheeks in his thin hands and tugged and shook the gnome's face. "Wakes ups, smelly blue hair."

Ovrym, his arm repaired by Tifala's *Life Magic,* reached down and grabbed the imp who got in one last kick before being pulled away.

"Not helping," Ovrym said, scolding the small creature.

"There is no other way," Gryph said. "If Ovrym is right, and Wick's soul still exists in this mind verse, then I am the only one who can get to him."

"Assuming your assumptions are correct," Ovrym said. "You know what they say about assumptions?"

"They make an ass out of you and me," Gryph said.

The xydai looked confused but nodded. "Sure, that works."

"He's saying it is too dangerous. If what you suspect is true, then you are putting not only yourself but the *Godhead* at risk."

"The evil that lives here cannot, must not get this kind of power. Ever." Ovrym stated.

"Xeg agree. Smokey skull man is real jerk and Xeg knows jerks when Xeg sees jerks."

"He'd do it for all of us." Gryph looked from Tifala to

Ovrym to Xeg. "Well, most of us."

A scowl crossed the imp's face. "Short, ugly man do for Xeg. Xeg knows he would." Tifala stroked the small demon's head, and Gryph almost believed that the imp cared for Wick.

The Realms are a very weird place, Gryph thought.

"Then you must do it alone," Ovrym said, crossing his arms for extra emphasis.

Gryph inhaled deeply and then grabbed both of the yellow eyed man's shoulders. "I understand your fears. You seem to know more about this thing than any of us and normally I'd defer to your judgment here. But we both know that Wick doesn't have long."

This earned a small sniffle from Tifala.

"And if the Barrow King consumes him and reforms in this realm, then all of this starts again." Gryph waved his hands about in dramatic fashion, encompassing the bodies, both human and undead.

"And if he consumes yours, he'll have the power of a god," Ovrym countered. "Who knows what evil he could wreak with such power?"

"I know you don't know me. I know you cannot possibly comprehend where I come from. But I am asking you to trust me. I can do this. I've trained for this."

Ovrym stared into his eyes, and Gryph could feel more than the man's eyes on him. If they survived this, he would ask the man to show him what he knew. Ask him very nice like.

Finally, the xydai exhaled. "Fine, we'll do it your way. But first, you need new weapons and new skills. Time to assign your points. Tifala and I will teach you what we can." He looked down at the imp. "Xeg, see if you can find any weapons or magic items that Gryph can use."

The imp just glared at the tall warrior monk.

"Please?"

Xeg grinned and rushed off.

"That is one weird imp," Ovrym muttered.

Over the next few minutes, Gryph learned new skills. *Thought Magic* spells from Ovrym.

You have learned the spell TELEPATHIC BOND.

Sphere: Thought Magic.
Tier: Base.

Allows the caster to form a telepathic bond with one or more other beings. It is easier to establish a telepathic bond with willing participants.

Mana Cost: 100.
Casting Time: Instantaneous.
Duration: 5 minutes + 1 per Thought Magic Level.
Cooldown: None.

Water Magic and spells from Tifala.

You have learned the spell WATER BLAST.

Sphere: Water Magic.
Tier: Base.

Allows the caster to shoot a torrent of water from their hands that will impact opponents like a firehose. Base Damage: 20 points of water damage +2 points per level of Water Magic mastery. Double damage versus fire-based beings. Can cause drowning.

Mana Cost: 40.
Casting Time: Instantaneous.
Duration: 10 seconds +1 per level of Water Magic mastery.
Cooldown: 2 minutes.

You have learned the skill WATER MAGIC.

Level: 1.
Tier: Base.
Skill Type: Active.

You are now able to wield the power of Water Magic. Water Magic allows the user to manipulate liquids of all kinds.

WATER MAGIC. (Con't).

Water Magic is primarily used for offensive and defensive purposes but can also be used to summon or create creatures made of water. Water Magic is also capable of changing one liquid into another. Spells that make use of ice and cold are the province of Water Magic.

And surprise of surprises, *Chthonic Magic* and spells from Xeg. The mischievous imp hadn't asked Gryph's permission. He'd just jumped onto Gryph's head and forced the knowledge into his mind.

You have learned the spell DEMON SCALES.

Sphere: Chthonic Magic.
Tier: Base.

A tough and scaly demonic hide will form over the caster (or target's) skin, providing a +10 bonus to AC +1 per every 3 levels of Chthonic Magic mastery.

Mana Cost: 50.
Casting Time: 1 minute.
Duration: 10 minutes +1 per level of Chthonic Magic mastery.
Cooldown: 2 minutes.

You have learned the skill CHTHONIC MAGIC.

Level: 1.
Tier: Base.
Skill Type: Active.

You are now able to wield the power of Chthonic Magic. Chthonic Magic allows the user to tap into the energies of the Chthonic Realm.

Gryph's mind expanded with all the new knowledge and his training parsed the new skills and abilities into tactics. He had just scratched the surface of what he could do in the Realms. *What will I be capable of when I master the Godhead?*

Gryph closed out all of his interfaces and returned his attention to the real world. In his absence, Xeg had been busy. A large pile of loot lay at Gryph's feet. Ovrym was already searching through it.

Most of it was junk. Ancient rusted weapons and armor from the dread knights. Ovrym handed Gryph a few potions to restock his inventory. "Is this it?" Gryph asked the imp.

"Yes, nothing else. Xeg no find better shiny things."

"Xeg," Gryph said. "What did you find?"

Xeg scowled and looked away, avoiding the question.

"Xeg, my brave friend, we need your help," Tifala said in a soothing voice. "Did you find something?"

Xeg huffed and puffed and finally sighed. "Xeg find box with shiny pretty."

"Where?" Gryph asked.

A moment later, they were in a small hidden room behind the Barrow King's throne. It had all the bearings of a royal treasury and if the contents told the tale, they belonged to a king.

"Whoa," Gryph said.

"Um, yeah," Ovrym agreed.

(Staves/Spears)
Item Class: Artifact.
Item Category: Passive/Active.
Base Dmg: 18 (+8 Artifact Bonus; +12 Adamant Tip).

Passive Powers.
Power (1): +20% Total Mana.
Power (2): Store 200 pts of Mana.
Power (3): +3 to all Attributes.
Power (4): +20% immunity to all Spheres of Magic.

Active Powers.
Power (1): Penetrating Strike (Damage added to strike).

Mana Limit: 20% (+Option for Stored Mana).
Cool Down: 10 min.
Icons Slotted: 0 of 6.

This magnificent weapon was constructed by three grandmasters; an El'Edryn Smith, a Nimmerian Imbue Master and a Thalmiir Artificer with a gift of ultra-rare Prismatic Elementum from the Raal Zanaag (Orcs), to commemorate the Alliance Against the Dark Ascendency.

To create the War Stave of the Elven King, four ingots of White Mithril to construct the stave itself, one ingot of Prismatic Elementum (a mix of Black, Blue and White Elementum) entwined throughout, 6 draughts of Aether Worm Blood (to etch/burn the slots for 6 Icons), an ingot of Adamant to make the adamantine spear tip, and four Blood Diamonds (diamonds infused with the blood of powerful beings; in this case a willing offering from the four racial leaders of the Alliance).

"Well, this will come in handy," Gryph said as he hoisted the *War Stave of the Elven King.* He felt a powerful surge explode into him as he held the perfectly balanced spear. He took a few moments to familiarize himself with the weapon. The *Mana Store* ability was incredible, and Gryph filled the reservoir. If he planned well, just carrying this spear upped his mana limit by 200.

Below the spear was an intricately carved metallic disk. It was six inches across and bore the visage of a powerful and wise dwarf. Gryph picked it up, and his mind filled with a new prompt.

You have found Seal of the Dwarven King.

Item Class: Artifact.
Item Category: Passive/Active.

Passive Powers.
Power (1): This seal enables the bearer to take ownership of the ancient Thalmiir city of Dar Thoriim.

Active Powers.
Unknown.

You have been offered the Quest Reclaim the Dwarven City.

The ancient Thalmiir city of Dar Thoriim was long ago sealed to prevent a powerful evil from infesting the world. Rid the city of the infestation and claim the city as your own.

Difficulty: Epic.
Reward: Control of Dar Thoriim.
XP: 1,000,000.

"Holy shit," Gryph muttered. The XP award for the quest was insane. Ovrym eyed Gryph oddly, so Gryph passed the seal to him. His eyes also went wide before he passed the artifact back to Gryph.

"Looks like we'll be busy if we ever get out of here."

Gryph nodded and tucked the seal into his *Inventory*. There were more pressing concerns. Gryph gripped his new spear again. Hopefully, he could take everything with him into the Barrow King's mind verse. If not what he had planned would be near impossible. They returned to the throne room.

Tifala had made a makeshift bed out of discarded cloaks and old bits of cloth and laid Wick's empty body on top of it. She was gently washing the dirt and grime from his face and eased his *Maker Goggles* from his head.

She walked up to Gryph and handed the goggles to him. "Perhaps this will aid you in your quest."

Gryph shook his head. "They belong to your husband."

"And they will help you find him. Give them back when you both return."

Gryph nodded his thanks and placed the goggles over his head, leaving them to dangle at his neck. Ovrym shook his hand and wished him luck. Even Xeg seemed genuine when he told Gryph he "no want you go dead."

Ready as he would ever be, Gryph picked up the skull, and a prompt popped into his mind.

Do you wish to change your Respawn Point?

Gryph tapped the **YES** icon.

Congratulations. You have changed your Respawn Point.

"I'm ready," Gryph said and pulled down his cowl, exposing the back of his neck.

Ovrym drew his saber and walked up behind Gryph, the point settled at the base on his skull. "See you soon, my friend."

Tifala stood in front of him, her smile trying to hide the worry in his eyes. Behind her Xeg sat on the throne, chewing on something that may have been a foot.

"Do it."

With a smooth, quick motion, Ovrym pushed the tip of his saber into Gryph's spine. Death was instantaneous.

48

Gryph only felt the pain for a second before his soul left his body. Once again, he stretched thin and was pulled through a singularity. He was energy, and he was descending fast. As he approached the pinprick of light, he knew to be his *Respawn Point* he brought all of his focus to bear. If he was right, this was the critical part of his plan.

The point of light expanded from a single star into a swirling cloud of interstellar gas. Within the endless nebula were two single points of light. Gryph focused on them. There had to be a way to tell which one was which?

The first orbited near the edge of the nebula and shone an intense white. Looking upon it, Gryph felt longing and comfort. This was where his soul wanted to be. A realm of life and wonder.

The other point was a dark mass of seething blue and black. It stood out not due to its brightness, but due to the hole it produced in the light of the nebula. It was a place of rage and anger and every photon of Gryph's being spasmed away from it.

This is where he would find Wick. He turned himself towards the darkness and zipped faster and faster towards it. His soul screamed at him to turn away, but his mind was the master here.

The blue-black sphere was all of reality now, larger than the largest star in his own universe. It now was the universe. A universe of anger, hate, fear and pain. Gryph doubled down and surged forward.

As he got close, he eased back. This time, when he landed he would land softly. He could not risk the painful entries he'd experienced the last two times.

He hit the surface of the seething black star and passed through with a snap. His mind receded from the universal to the local and, once again, he was in his own body. His landing wasn't pretty, but he stayed on his feet. The surrounding energies dissipated, and he looked about.

What he saw stunned him. His expectations had been that the mind verse would be some kind of hell realm, like the one through the portal Avernerius came from. But this place was not. This place was a wonder.

He was in a grassy clearing in an ancient forest that reminded him of the old woods of Europe. In the distance, snowcapped peaks kissed the sky and mountain streams fed down into a thin alpine lake. A tower shot upwards from the far shore of the lake, piercing the morning like a beacon.

He pulled his new spear from his inventory. This place was just too normal, too nice. Why would the Barrow King's mind create such a place?

Gryph did a slow circle, keeping his weapon ready. Everywhere he looked he saw more wondrous nature. Woodland animals hopped and grazed, birds chirped, and brooks babbled.

He walked towards the tower in the distance. He wondered if this was what the Barrow had looked like all those millennia ago when it had existed on the surface, but doubts crept into his mind. This spire was tall and elegant, a natural extension of the surroundings as if it had grown directly from the land. It sure did not feel like the hellhole he'd spent the last several days in.

He ran and sent mana into his boots, doubling his speed. Normally, he'd opt for *Stealth*, but he had no idea how much time Wick had left. He didn't plan to waste any more time.

The world zipped by and he refilled the power of his boots twice. After a time, he came to the edge of the forest and the edge of the clearing that sprouted the tower. It was hundreds of feet tall and made of shining white stone. A circular wall surrounded it, creating a massive green courtyard. An open set of gates led into the courtyard.

Gryph dipped down into *Stealth* and made his way through the gates. He saw nothing and no one. Was this the right place? Had he chosen wrong when he was floating through the nebula? Had he sentenced Wick's soul to permanent death with his error?

He refused to let himself wallow down that path. If he had chosen wrong, there was nothing to be done now. He had to move ahead with faith. Wick was here. He had to be.

Gryph ducked low and sprinted across the sward of green between the gate and the tower itself. If hidden snipers lurked, this would be their chance to strike. Gryph forced himself to focus and soon his breathing relaxed.

He came to the base of the tower and crouched at the left side of the heavy wooden doorway. A glance back and forth told Gryph he was still alone. Was it going to be this easy? Was the Barrow King so sure that this private realm, this pocket universe, was secure that he had no guards, no security?

Still in *Stealth*, Gryph reached his hand towards the large handle on the door. A moment before his fingers touched the metal ring, the door eased open on well-oiled hinges. Gryph jumped back startled and held his spear in a fighting stance. Almost more unnerving than the door's movement, was the complete lack of noise. How could such a massive door be so silent?

The door opened, and Gryph saw a humanoid figure back lit by torch-bearing wall sconces. His hands gripped the shaft tighter, and he sent mana into the tip.

"Oh, you're here," said a high-pitched voice that cracked as if its owner were on the cusp of puberty. "I've been waiting so long."

Of all the things Gryph had expected to emerge from the tower, a fourteen-year-old boy had not made the list. But as the figure emerged into the light that is exactly who greeted Gryph.

"My name is Simon," said a sandy-haired boy with the thin, gangly limbs that made the early teens a time of clumsy nervousness. "Would you like to come in?"

"Um?" Gryph said, standing at his full height and clutching the spear tighter.

For the next several moments, man and boy just stared at each other.

"Are you slow or something," Simon said in the typical tone of the irritated adolescent. "Great, alone all these years and I get an idiot as my first friend."

"Who are you?"

"Oh good, you do talk. I'm Simon, but we already covered that, didn't we?"

In an almost comical way, Gryph backed up, looked up and down the tower, and turned around in a 360-degree circle. Something just wasn't right. Simon stared at him in a way that was both curious and condescending. Finally, the kid snapped, bringing Gryph's attention, and annoyance, back to him.

"Hello, sir knight, would you like to come in?"

Gryph gave the kid a look that suggested he shut up, and Simon pouted. "You're here to see *him*."

"*Him*?"

"His Majesty, the great and powerful Ouzeriuo."

"I don't know who that is. I'm here to find a friend. He was taken here against his will by an entity known as the Barrow King."

"Yup, that's him, but I always thought that name sounded stupid. I mean of all the names you could choose you go with the Barrow King. Seriously?"

"Kid," Gryph said, moving to grab the annoying adolescent by the arm, "time to focus."

Simon lurched away from Gryph's grasp. It reminded Gryph of a childhood friend who never liked being touched. Years later, Gryph had learned that his friend had suffered abuse.

"Sorry, I won't touch you. I don't have a lot of time. Is he here?"

Simon harrumphed with such drama that Gryph was surprised the kid didn't pull something but, eventually, he tossed his head back in a 'follow me' gesture and walked into the tower.

"Okay," Gryph muttered to himself and looked around one last time. He was almost certain he was being punked, but further surveillance proved fruitless.

Knowing that he would regret it, Gryph stepped over the threshold and into the tower. The inside looked exactly as one would expect. A large circular room with a ceiling that reached a hundred feet or more dominated the ground floor. A few doors led off the main chamber and two large staircases circled upwards.

Gryph felt as if he were in some ultra-modern skyscraper. Something you'd see in Dubai or Singapore. Instead of technology, archaic magics adorned the place.

"So, he is here, your master?"

"He's not my master," Simon spat. "But yeah, his majesty is here. Just got back, too, so your timing is impeccable. He has a guest and told me not to disturb him except to bring dinner."

"Dinner?"

"Yeah, yah know the meal, lamb, potatoes, turnips, and jellies." Once again, Simon eyeballed Gryph as if he were talking to a moron.

"Have you brought it yet?"

"What?"

"Dinner?" Gryph said, his voice rose in ire.

"No, I was just about to. Why you wanna help?"

"Yes. Yes, I very much do," Gryph said.

"Okay." Simon shrugged in a way that said he didn't care either way. "Follow me."

Simon led him through one of the side doors to a small room that was unadorned save for a circle of engraved metal in the floor. Simon stepped into the circle and waited for Gryph to do the same. With some apprehension, Gryph put one foot then another over the circle. He could sense the power that lay in the ring.

"I'd stand still if I were you," Simon said. Gryph became rigid, like a statue, but gripped his spear. A moment later, the world folded and popped. His guts shuddered, and nausea poured over him, and then the world folded again, and they were in a nearly identical room. Gryph's ears popped, and he nearly toppled.

"What the?"

"*Port Circle*," Simon said with a grin. "Guess I could have warned you."

Simon didn't wait for Gryph to respond and exited the room. Gryph forced himself to recover. As annoying as this kid was, he couldn't risk losing him. The kid was just entering another door when Gryph exited the *Port Circle* chamber. He clutched his spear as he lost sight of the kid and stumbled down the hall.

The door led to a large kitchen. Inside was a wonderland of automation unmatched even on Earth. Food items prepared themselves. Moving about, in and out of ovens and pots, as if unseen hands were carrying them. The smell was fantastic, and Gryph's stomach grumbled. It was then that he realized that the last real meal he had eaten had been the food Doc had brought him the day before this entire nightmare had started.

Gryph resisted the urge to scarf some food. For all he knew this Simon was the Barrow King, and the food was poisoned. That would be an ignominious way to die and lose his *Godhead*, poisoned by a bratty teenager because he was hungry.

Simon snapped, and the food all drifted over to a silver serving cart. A cover slipped over the food to keep it warm and a jug of wine slid over and landed next to the food.

"Ready?" Simon asked.

"Hold on just a second. You need to answer some questions."

Simon crossed his arms in the condescending way that all teens had of showing displeasure. Some things did not change no matter what universe you were in. Simon stared at Gryph and the stare said 'fine, let's get this over with.'

"Who are you?"

"I'm Si..."

Gryph cut him off with raised palms. "I know you're Simon. But who are you and how did you get here?"

The look of irritation fell from Simon's face as he thought. "Um, sometimes I'm not sure anymore. It's been so long. I've served Ouzeriuo for so long I can't remember." The memory seemed to touch something painful inside Simon and his cocky demeanor returned. "Why are you asking me this?"

"Because there is something off about this place."

"Yeah, it's boring."

"Yeah, it is," Gryph thought as his mind worked. "You said your mast...Ouzeriuo, just got back?"

"Yup."

"From where exactly?"

Simon shrugged. "I don't know. He goes away and comes back. He usually brings a friend. I bring meals for a few days.

Then the friend goes away, and for a while, Ouzeriuo is happy. Then he isn't, and he goes away again. He doesn't bother telling me his schedule."

Gryph was piecing together the odd logic of this realm, but he needed to ask more questions. Wick's life, his soul, might rely on the answers this brat provided.

"How many meals have you served him this time?"

"This is the first."

"Good. And how many do you normally serve before he goes away again."

Simon shrugged. "It varies."

"Well, take a guess."

"Sometimes one. Sometimes a few. I never know until I bring up dinner and he's just gone." Simon shuffled his feet in a way that told Gryph he was hurt by it but didn't want to admit it.

"Okay, that's good. Now, why don't you tell me about yourself."

"Whatcha wanna know?" Simon said, excited for the interest but also fearful that it was some kind of trick or joke.

"How did you come to be here?"

Simon screwed up his face as if the memory was painful, and he didn't want to remember. After a moment, he shrugged. He stayed silent.

"Come on, kid. You help me, maybe I can help you. Take you from this place."

Simon's eyes snapped up, an odd mix of fear and excitement in his gaze.

"I have to bring dinner," Simon said, shunting the hope aside.

Gryph held back a sigh. This kid had some serious trust issues. He walked over to the cart and pushed.

"Let me help you."

Simon nodded but said nothing as they exited the kitchen into a long hallway. After a dozen steps, Simon spoke up in a small voice.

"I don't remember much. It was a long time ago."

"It's okay just tell me what you remember."

"Morrigan brought me. I think I was his manservant. Not a bad gig, all things considered."

Gryph wasn't sure why, but the name Morrigan made his skin crawl. Was it a name he'd heard Wick say, or maybe Ovrym? He didn't know. He knew he had to ask and hoped that the question didn't set this sullen teen down the wrong path.

"Who is Morrigan?"

Simon's gaze snapped up at Gryph, an incredulous look painted across his face. The boy stopped and fidgeted back and forth as if wanting to run but fearing the consequences.

"It's okay, buddy. I'm kinda new to the Realms."

Simon's eyes went wide in excitement.

"You're from the Outer Realms? Wow."

"Something like that. Regardless, I'm not up on current events. I promise, someday I'll tell you about my home."

"Okay," Simon said and nodded in excitement. "Well, Morrigan is one of the gods. Soon, he will be the High God. That's why we came here. Ouzeriuo is a very powerful wizard. He knows secrets that nobody knows, not even Morrigan. Morrigan wanted to learn and for a while, Ouzeriuo taught him. Then…" Simon stopped as if the next part was painful.

"Then?" Gryph prompted.

"Then they got in a big fight." Simon held his head as if hit by a sudden migraine. "It's hard to remember sometimes. I think they fought. Then Morrigan went away and left me here with Ouzeriuo. I think that was a long time ago." He stopped again, almost falling over in a feint.

"Whoa, I got you," Gryph said, lunging out to catch the kid. Simon jerked from his touch again, and Gryph released him. After a moment, Simon seemed to regain his composure and pushed the cart onwards.

"You know," Simon said in an odd voice as if he had drifted light years away. "I'm not even sure my name is Simon."

Gryph felt tension rise in him as they got closer to the doors at the end of the hallway. "Well, it's a good name."

"Yeah?" the kid said as he pulled the cart to a stop and moved to open the doors.

Gryph pulled mana into himself and clasped his spear. Whatever lay behind these doors, he would be ready.

49

The doors were fifteen feet tall and made of pale amber wood. Simon pushed them open with practiced ease and returned to the cart. As his gaze passed over Gryph, his eyes grew distant, almost glazed, as if he was no longer present, but just an automaton fulfilling a task.

He pushed the cart into the room, and Gryph followed.

"Ah, Simon," said a voice that reminded Gryph of a kindly grandfather from a candy commercial he'd seen as a child. "I was wondering where you'd gotten yourself to, lad. I am famished."

Gryph eased around the cart, muscles tensed for action. What awaited him was both stunning and expected. An old, white-haired man sat at one end of a long dining table. You know those tables you see in movies that rich folks use. The kind that circumvents any chance at real conversation.

The elderly man, who Gryph guessed had to be Ouzeriuo, the Barrow King, looked at Gryph, and a smile both genuine and confused crossed his face. He reminded Gryph of his own grandfather the last several years of his life. They were not the eyes of a soul-consuming revenant.

"Why, Simon, who is your friend?"

Simon said nothing as he pushed the cart forward. Gryph eyed Simon warily. Something wasn't right here. He backed away but kept pace with the thin boy. As they fully entered the room Gryph got his first look at the guest Ouzeriuo was entertaining.

Wick sat at the table's far end, as healthy as Gryph had ever seen him. The gnome's skin looked as if he'd spent the last few months in the sun and not the dour darkness of the Barrow. The blue shock of hair was lustrous and undamaged by acid. A jovial smile split his face. It was only when Gryph saw his friend's eyes that he realized something was very, very wrong. They were the eyes of the dead, listless and lacking light.

Wick's gaze fell on Gryph, and the gnome said, "Hello."

Ice dug into Gryph's veins. There was something going on here that he wasn't seeing. On a whim, he pulled Wick's goggles up over his eyes and toggled the lenses to see magic. He almost jumped. The place was rife with tendrils of all colors, moving to and fro. His head began to pound just trying to differentiate between the strands.

He closed his eyes and forced his mind to focus and to calm. When he opened them again, he centered his gaze on Wick. Sure enough, a silvery tendril of magic pulsed from Wick directly to the food Simon was serving Ouzeriuo.

The old man pulled a tender bit of lamb free with his fork and shoved it past trembling lips, where he chewed. Each movement of his jaw brought a pulse of light into the strand leading from Wick to Ouzeriuo.

Gryph's eyes widened. He was consuming Wick's soul. Gryph spun his spear around and dipped the tip into the stream moving from the gnome to the old man. Maybe the spear's ability to store magic would interrupt the flow. The tip punctured the flow and energy shot up the spear and into Gryph.

Pain exploded into every cell in Gryph's body as he flew backwards impacting the wall and knocking the wind from him. His *Health* bar dropped by nearly a third.

He stood, wobbling back and forth on unsteady legs. The old man continued to chew, and Simon continued to set more dishes in front of him.

"Simon, this is quite delicious," Ouzeriuo said. "I'm not sure I've ever had the like. What is it?"

"It's called gnome, sir," Simon said.

"Gnome. Hmmmm, quite tasty. So tender and full of vitality."

Gryph shook his head, trying to clear away the cobwebs. He advanced on Simon and pushed the lad away from the serving cart. Then he tried to push the cart, get it as far away from this soul cannibal as possible. But his hands phased right through it. It was incorporeal.

"I don't like to be touched," Simon said as he stood, dusted himself off, and returned to his duties.

Gryph panicked. Ouzeriuo was consuming more of Wick's soul and it was taking a toll on his friend. His skin had turned sallow and strands of gray had wormed their way through his hair.

He rushed to his friend and tried to tear him away from the table, but his hands phased through as if Wick was not there. This close he could hear his friend's wheezing breath. It was as if his lungs no longer inhaled enough oxygen to fuel him.

Gryph turned and raised his spear. He poured mana into the spear, adding it to that stored in the weapon. The adamant tip glowed as bright as the noonday sun, and Gryph hurled it at Ouzeriuo with every ounce of strength he had.

His aim was true, but the weapon passed harmlessly through the old man and hit the wall behind him. A cacophonous explosion tore outwards, smashing a massive hole in the wall. A breeze drifted into the chamber, bringing the sweet smell of spring with it.

Ouzeriuo didn't seem to notice as he took another bite, this time it was some kind of custard. More pulses of Wick's soul oozed down the tendril with each cycle of the old man's jaw.

Gryph rushed to Simon and grabbed the kid by the arm, tugging him backwards before he could deliver another dish to his soul eating master.

"Let go. I told you I don't like being touched," Simon screamed, struggling to pull free of Gryph's grasp. But Gryph refused to let go. Fear dug into the boy's eyes and tears streamed down his cheeks.

"How am I able to touch you, but not the others?" Gryph screamed at the frightened boy. Simon said nothing, just tried harder and harder to pull away. "How?" Gryph screamed.

"Because I have no body," Simon screamed, and his eyes widened in realization. Gryph knew, right then, that until that very moment, Simon had forgotten this terrible truth. More tears poured down his face, and a cold calm came over the boy. "I am stuck here because Morrigan gave me to him." Simon pointed an angry finger at Ouzeriuo. "Gave me to him to be a sacrifice. I watched them experiment on me, slowly killing my body as they sought to understand my soul."

Simon shook as the terrors of his past came rushing back.

"No, no, no, it is all my fault. It's because of me that Ouzeriuo and Morrigan understand how to feed on souls. I was the first."

Gryph knelt and shook the boy. "Listen to me, Simon. It is not your fault. They used you. They abused you."

"They murdered me," Simon said, "but they did not consume my soul. They used … used me, it to build this place."

Simon walked over to the hole in the wall that Gryph's spear had made. A small smile came to his lips. "This was my home. Long ago. It's why I made it again. I wanted to go back home."

Gryph knelt by the boy, pain fighting against compassion at the thought of what he'd suffered. "How can I help?"

Simon looked up at Gryph with sad eyes. "I do not know if you can, but I may be able to help you." He looked at Wick. "And your friend."

"How?" Gryph said in a voice full of desperate need.

"You must kill me."

50⊕

Gryph backed away in shock. Every fiber of his being recoiled at the idea. But he was also desperate to save his friend. There was no training that could help him make this decision.

"I thought you said you were already dead?"

"Yes," Simon said. His demeanor had changed. He was no longer a scared child but a being who had existed for untold millennia. "My body died so long ago that I'm not even sure that this is what I looked like."

"I don't understand. If you are already dead, how can I kill you?"

"You must kill my soul. It enables this place to exist. Without it, the Barrow King cannot survive, and he will cease to be. You must sacrifice me to kill him. While he is still weak."

"No."

"It is the only way to save your friend. And I no longer want to live this half-life."

Gryph paced back and forth in anguish. He could not destroy a soul even to save one. He looked from Simon to the Barrow King, and then to Wick.

"Think. Think. Damn you." Gryph bashed the palm of his hand against his forehead. Something tickled at the back of his mind. Then it came at him, like a tsunami wave, and he knew what he had to do.

"I may have another way, but I need you to do something for me," Gryph said.

"What?" Simon asked.

"Stop feeding this old fuck."

"I'll try," Simon said. "But he is able to compel me."

"Try. That is all I can ask."

Gryph turned to Ouzeriuo, the ancient evil that had

destroyed countless lives. He was already looking younger. Gryph had no idea how much longer Wick could hold out, but Gryph suspected he did not have long. "Hey, old man, your days are done."

Gryph built up mana and cast *Telepathic Bond*. He reached out with his mind and found the wisp that was the mind of the Barrow King. It was a tainted, oily pond of scum and sewage. It's rancid taste nearly made Gryph vomit, but he would not fail.

Their minds touched, and Gryph showed the Barrow King his *Godhead*. The spectral creature pulsed and morphed, rushing at Gryph with a hunger unlike any it had ever felt. Gryph held fast as Ouzeriuo's mind swam into his own, burrowing to the deep recesses where the *Godhead* resided.

Gryph pushed forward, digging deep into the foul center of the Barrow King's mind. He was gambling all and knew that if he didn't find what he sought, then all was lost. Gryph pushed through memories of atrocities, nearly drowning in their pain and the utter joy Ouzeriuo had taken in inflicting them.

It was like swimming through toxic mud. He burned and suffocated under the wretched onslaught. But he kept swimming. He knew what he sought was there. He kept moving.

He was getting close. He could feel it like a blind man felt heat. He dove deeper, and the world became blacker. It was down here, the knowledge he needed. The knowledge the Barrow King had guarded for millennia.

Then he saw it. A mote of silver light puncturing the black crud. He swam deeper and deeper and reached out. At his touch, the world exploded in silver and he stood in some kind of laboratory.

He looked down and saw arms clad in an arcane robe. He looked up and saw a reflection looking back at him from a mirror of burnished silver. He was Ouzeriuo. A younger Ouzeriuo, for sure, but the man all the same.

There was another man with his back turned from Gryph. He was sharpening implements.

"We are close, my friend," the man said, and the voice was familiar. Like something from a distant dream or an often-heard radio commercial.

But the man did not turn around, and Gryph discovered he had no control over the body he now inhabited. He was living a memory.

He felt himself look down and there, tied to some kind of operating slab was the boy Simon. A gag stoppered the terrified boy's mouth. Some skin on his torso had been flayed and burns and sliced flesh dotted other parts of his small, quivering body. As Ouzeriuo moved to his side, the boy shivered and shook his head in a desperate no. Tears poured from his eyes. Gryph could feel what Ouzeriuo had felt that day, and it made his blood turn to ice.

The man had felt nothing that could be deemed a decent human emotion. No pity. No shame. No hesitation. Just anxious excitement.

Gryph felt himself smile down on the boy and he lightly pet his forehead. "Everything will be alright," he lied. "Soon, it will all be over."

"Would you like a turn," the familiar voice asked.

"Why not, Morrigan," Ouzeriuo said. "After all this will be my crowning achievement." He lightly stroked Simon's head, and the fear exploded in the boy's eyes. Ouzeriuo looked up at the man holding out a scalpel like a device of torture, and Gryph knew why the voice was so familiar.

"Alistair Bechard," Gryph said in horrified wonder.

"Yes, yes it will be," Morrigan, the man those of Earth knew as Alistair Bechard, the god worshipped by millions across Korynn as the High God Aluran, said. "Yes, I will remember this day forever."

Then Gryph felt this body that he could not control torture Simon until the boy died. As a small part of his own soul died, Gryph's reached out with *Assimilation*. He had defeated the Barrow King in the Realms. Now it was time to claim his prize.

Gryph dug into the mind he shared with Ouzeriuo and grabbed the pulsing silver beacon. His mind exploded with knowledge. It was as if a thousand hands made of acid, rotting death, plague, and pestilence dug into his mind and forced the knowledge to stick.

```
┌─────────────────────────────────────────────────────────────┐
│        You have learned the skill SOUL MAGIC.                 │
├─────────────────────────────────────────────────────────────┤
│                                                               │
│                      Levels: 1 – 25.                          │
│                      Tier: Apprentice.                        │
│                      Skill Type: Active.                      │
│                                                               │
│   You can now wield the power of Soul Magic. Soul Magic is    │
│   the rarest and potentially the most powerful of all the     │
│   spheres of magic. Soul Magic taps into the essence of the   │
│   immortal soul for a wide range of abilities.                │
│                                                               │
│   Note: Soul Magic, while powerful, is also easy to abuse.    │
│                                                               │
└─────────────────────────────────────────────────────────────┘
```

Gryph would have vomited had he been in his own body, and the fact that neither Ouzeriuo nor Morrigan did, told Gryph everything he needed to know about these two men.

"Congratulations, master," Morrigan said as he eased himself as fluid as a snake around the slab where Simon's body lay to face Ouzeriuo. "You are truly the greatest mage alive." Gryph felt a smug smile form on Ouzeriuo's face as he drank in the praise. Then, Morrigan moved with incredible speed, and Gryph felt a dagger puncture through the underside of his neck and up into his brain.

Ouzeriuo died.

Armed with the knowledge he'd come for, Gryph pulled from the Barrow King's dying mind and swam towards the surface. Compared to the vileness of the last scene, the acidic sewage he now swam through felt like a dip in a pool on a hot day. He slogged and swam, all the while desperate for release from Simon's terrible despair and pain.

He saw light above and emerged from the recesses of Ouzeriuo's foul mind and back to the lighter realm of his own mind, when a piercing agony, worse than Morrigan's dagger exploded in his head. He squeezed his eyes shut trying to force the feeling to abate. Then, suddenly, it did.

Gryph opened his eyes, and he was somewhere else. It was dark, and he was running. A gunshot rang out behind him, and he dodged to the right, rushing around a corner. Ahead, in the distance, he could see an illuminated tower. He recognized the memory that Ouzerio had dredged. One that he had desperately tried to bury.

He was in Seoul. The place where he'd been left for dead.

More gunshots rang out as he sprinted, and one caught him in the leg. He tumbled to the ground as a gasp of pain spat from his mouth. He got up and hobbled. He took a quick turn into an alley and moved as fast as he could.

But it wasn't fast enough. Another shot took him in the back, high near the shoulder blade and he went down, tumbling over. He tried to scramble back behind a rot-filled dumpster, but the man with the gun caught up with him.

Gryph held his hands out, but he did not plead. The man grinned, raised his pistol and took aim.

"Hold," came a voice that could not possibly be there. The man lowered his gun to his side. A dark shadow moved up behind him and gently eased the gunman aside. The man came into a halo of light from an overhead bulb, and Gryph gasped.

"Hello, son."

"Colonel," Gryph heard his former self, the man named Finn say.

"Still can't call me Dad?"

"You were always the Colonel and never my father."

The Colonel took off his hat and passed it to the gunman. His aged face was determined, and Finn could see a future he would never live in the man's eyes.

"I wish this wasn't necessary," the Colonel said.

"I suppose we always knew this was how things would end up," Gryph said.

"I suppose we did," the Colonel said as he pointed a gun and fired.

The muzzle flash tore Gryph back to the tower. He looked down on Ouzeriuo, who now grinned at him with full awareness. The man was no longer old nor decrepit but as young and vital as he was in the torture room with Morrigan and Simon.

Gryph's eyes snapped over to Wick, slumped over and aged near beyond recognition. He didn't move.

"No!" Gryph screamed, and his mind summoned up his newfound knowledge. He poured the power of his own soul into his hands and launched himself at the Barrow King. He was unsure what he wanted to do, but knew he had to.

"Your own father betrayed you. Left you for dead. Forced you into hiding. Oh, the torture you must have gone through. The need to know why? An answer you never received." Ouzeriuo laughed at him. "Well, I know what you won't admit. He shot you, tried to kill you because you were a failure. You failed then and you will fail now. I will take the gift you have brought me, and then I will take all of Korynn."

Ouzeriuo flashed at Gryph and sunk a spectral hand into his chest. He felt fingers twine and dig and branch into him, seeking to extract the *Godhead*, the gift, the curse, the burden he bore.

"And what's more, I will find … Brynn." Ouzeriuo cocked his head to the side. "Your sister."

"You bastard," Gryph said through gritted teeth and a burst of spittle.

Gryph arched his head back in pain as the revenant dug into his body. He felt small bits, strands of the *Godhead* being ripped from their roots deep in his mind, his body and his soul. The Barrow King was dragging them back to him like a fisherman pulling nets from the sea. Gryph could feel their paths and see them enter the mind of Ouzeriuo.

Then he knew what he had to do. He focused his will and flashed up the tendrils, burrowing deeper and deeper. As he passed a threshold between his mind and the foul mind of the Barrow King, he found the one point of light and pushed towards it.

The pain in his chest and in his mind grew to blinding, and Gryph collapsed to his knees. With one final burst of effort, he reached out gently with both hands and curled them around the glowing cocoon like a father with a newborn babe. Inside, curled in a fetal position, was a small, glowing figure. This was Wick's soul. Black tendrils of oily darkness fired from the surrounding nothingness and borrowed into Gryph's body worming their way towards the soul he protected.

The pain was excruciating, and Gryph knew he would soon succumb. There was a way to survive. He could consume the soul he held and use its power. But that was an eternal death for Wick, and there was no coming back from such an act.

Gryph closed his eyes and curled his body around Wick's soul. "I am sorry. I am so sorry. I have failed."

A brightness built up, one that burned through the paltry defenses of Gryph's eyelids. Yet the light did not bring pain, but hope. Deep in the darkest of pits, Gryph discovered something that neither Morrigan nor Ouzeriuo could ever know. A soul given freely is far more powerful than one consumed.

Wick's soul enveloped Gryph, and the light expanded, burning away the stain of darkness. Gryph stood and launched himself upwards and outwards. He reached superluminal speed.

The Barrow King grinned as his extraction of the *Godhead* neared completion. Soon, he would be all powerful. "I am coming for you, Morrigan," the Barrow King said, and he began the maniacal chortle of the truly insane.

The sound was like stone crushing flesh, horrid and unnatural. Then it suddenly choked off as a blazing light flowed from Ouzeriuo's mouth. He released Gryph's body and brought his hands to his throat. The blazing light was choking him, and it was growing brighter.

Ouzeriuo would have screamed if he'd been able, but the light prevented him. It grew and pulsed and then exploded from the mage's mouth, twined and spun into the air above him, and then flashed downwards and into the center of Gryph's forehead.

Gryph's eyes snapped open, and they burned bright like two rising stars. Gryph stood and eased the Barrow King's clawed hand from his chest. Ouzeriuo swung his other hand, but his strength was failing, and Gryph caught and snapped the wrist with ease. The tendrils disintegrated, and the *Godhead* settled back into him.

The Barrow King struggled. Long bereft of life and with no stolen soul to sustain his long dead spirit, the Barrow King's true form was exposed, a desiccated corpse dry as tinder. The Barrow King's mouth opened in a final silent scream, and then his body disintegrated to dust and fell silent as the grave to the floor. Gryph toed the pile of ash at his feet.

"He is truly dead," said a voice that was both Wick and

Gryph.

Gryph turned and walked to the slumped body of his friend. He gently took the gnome's head in his hands and opened his eyes. Gryph's hands glowed as he transferred Wick's soul back to his body.

The glow faded, and Gryph fell to his knees, weakened beyond any weariness he had ever felt. He considered taking a nap right there, but then he felt small hands turn his face upwards. Wick, young and vibrant and grinning like a dick, was looking down on him.

"Laying down on the job?" Wick asked.

Gryph said nothing. He laughed. He laughed like he had not laughed since entering the Realms. He laughed like he had not laughed since he was young. A vision of Brynn and he laughing so hard that breath would not come infused his mind, his soul.

A deep rumble built in the tower and dragged Gryph from his reverie.

"What is happening?"

"This place is going," Simon said.

Gryph turned to see the small, ancient boy standing. A look of sad resignation painted his face. Gryph walked up to him and knelt, taking his shoulders lightly in his hands. For once the boy did not flinch from his touch.

"What do you mean?"

"It may have been my memories and my soul that powered this place, but it was his will that kept it together. Now, it will fall, and I will fall with it."

"There has to be a way out," Wick said, coming up to stand behind Gryph.

Simon lowered his gaze to the floor as tears welled up in his eyes. "For you maybe. You both have bodies waiting for you. Mine has long since turned to dust. There is nowhere for me to go. When this place dies…"

Simon looked out the gaping hole in the side of the tower, drawing Gryph and Wick's gazes along with him. The world was disappearing, the edges of the mountains and the forests were melting like the edges of a Polaroid photo tossed into flames.

"I will die with it."

322

Gryph's mind flailed. "I will not let this be."

"There is nothing to be done," Simon said, looking up at Gryph. "But I thank you. At least I am free."

The white nothingness encroached further, eating at the fabric of the tower itself. Gryph's mind floundered. There had to be a way. He felt Wick's gentle touch on his shoulder, and he knew his friend was telling him they had to go.

Simon walked over to the pile of dust that had once been Ouzeriuo and toed it with his left foot.

"At least he has nowhere to go either."

Gryph's eyes widened. "But he does." Simon and Wick both looked at Gryph. "Or more accurately, you do, Simon."

Simon's face went grim as millennia of lies and mistrust flashed through his mind. It was as if the boy was angry at hope. Gryph could not blame him. He'd been betrayed and abused in a way that was inconceivable.

"Can you trust me?" Gryph said, hand extended.

Simon hesitated as the whiteness ate away the world behind him. It had taken the walls and was now eating at the floors. Wick's grip on Gryph's shoulder intensified, but Gryph ignored his friend.

"Please," Gryph said. His eyes locked with Simon's and time stretched. Finally, a small smile curled the boy's lips, and he ran forward taking Gryph's outstretched hand.

Gryph closed his eyes as the whiteness became the world.

51

Gryph awoke with a start. His body was sore, and his mouth parched. He coughed and hacked as a set of hands helped ease him up. His eyes opened to see a haze of motion and shapes. He blinked and muttered and finally, the world came into focus.

Ovrym held him and smiled down. "You okay?"

"Ugh, I feel like total shit."

"You look like it," Ovrym said with a grin. He helped Gryph up into a sitting position.

"Wick?"

Ovrym grinned and moved aside. A few paces away, Tifala was forcing a *Health Potion* down Wick's throat. As expected, the gnome was grumbling at all the fuss. "I'm fine. I'm fine," he said, pushing her away.

Tifala smacked him lightly across the face, and his eyes darted up in indignation. "That's for being the stupid hero," Tifala said. She smacked him again. "And that's for almost leaving me alone." She drew her hand back again and Wick flinched. Instead of another smack, the pretty gnome eased down and kissed Wick on the lips. "And this is for coming back to me."

"Always," Wick said.

Xeg jumped down from his perch on the back of the Barrow King's throne and landed lightly on Tifala's shoulder. He curled his tail around her neck and nuzzled her. Tifala smiled up at the imp and scratched it behind the ear.

"Great, you're still here," Wick said with a frown.

Xeg smacked Wick across the face. "That for being stupid hero."

Wick's shock was such that he didn't see the imp's second smack either. "That for leaving Xeg," the imp said. Xeg then leaned in. "And this…"

Wick grabbed the imp by the neck. "You kiss me, and I'll send you back to the chthonic realm permanently."

Xeg frowned and crossed its arms in a teen girl pout. "Xeg only joking. Stinky blue hair wishes Xeg want kiss him." He jumped back up on Tifala's shoulder.

Gryph exchanged grins with Ovrym before walking to Wick. He extended a hand, helping the gnome to his feet. Wick gave him an abashed smile of thanks. Gryph gave him a nod that said all the gnome needed to hear.

"So, it is over?" Tifala asked, clutching her man.

"It's over," Gryph said with a nod.

"Going to explain what happened in there?" Ovrym asked.

"Over a very large beer when we get out of this hellhole," Wick said.

Behind them, a clatter of bone said otherwise as the Barrow King's skull shook. A white glow grew from the depths of its empty eye sockets and flared. The skull floated upwards and gazed down on the group.

Ovrym was the first to move, swinging his crimson saber towards the skull. Right before it impacted, Gryph's spear parried the blow. Ovrym looked at Gryph in shock.

"Wait," Gryph said. He also held a hand out to Tifala, who had pushed Wick behind her and emblazoned her hands with white *Life Magic*. Wick lightly grabbed Tifala's wrist and eased her palm down.

Both companions stared at them as if they had gone mad, but they held their attacks. Satisfied that he had bought some time, Gryph turned his attention back to the skull.

"Whoa, this is really weird," the skull said in Simon's voice. The skull hovered off kilter as Simon adjusted to his new existence. After a few moments, it balanced, and a spectral essence flowed from the skull, and Simon made an ethereal body in the image of his long dead physical one.

"You okay, kid?" Gryph asked.

Before Gryph could answer, a rumble shook the Barrow. It was centered on Simon. "Um, what is happening to me?" Simon's skull began to glow and burn from inside and the undead kid began to scream.

Gryph ran to him, shielding his eyes as he approached. But something stopped him and then began to push him back.

Ovrym, Wick and Tifala all prepped weapons and spells, but then a wave of energy exploded from Simon's skull.

Is the Barrow King back? Gryph thought in alarm.

The wave knocked them all to the ground and flowed through the solid rock of the chamber and up into the Barrow. The wave disappeared, and the group got back to their feet. Once again, Gryph held up a hand, halting their attack.

"Kid, what was that?" Gryph asked.

"Whoa," Simon said and looked from his hands up to Gryph and smiled.

"You okay kid?"

"I think so. This is a little weird. Feels like my old body, but more, much more. I can feel…" he looked around, but his eyes seemed to be looking past the stone walls of the chamber. "This entire place."

"You can feel the Barrow?" Wick asked.

"I am the Barrow," Simon said. Then his mouth turned into a frown.

"What?" Gryph asked, nervousness creeping into him.

"This place needs a serious redesign and better tenants."

Gryph and Wick grinned and laughed. Ovrym and Tifala exchanged confused glances, but both eased back on their attacks.

"Somebody please explain what is going on," Ovrym said.

Wick took his friends aside and explained. Gryph held his palm out to Simon, who placed his spectral hand up against it. Warmth flowed into Gryph's body. Simon smiled and then wandered off, exploring his new home, his new body.

Gryph walked away from his friends and sat against the wall. Prompt alerts had been flashing at the corner of his vision since he'd woken up. He brought them into focus.

You have earned Experience Points.

You have earned 120,000 XP for slaying The Barrow King.

You have earned 45,000 XP for slaying Dread Knight (x10).

You have earned 55,000 XP for slaying Thieves of the Gray Company (x3).

Gryph's mind was at peace for the first time since he'd arrived in the Realms. He was still worried about Brynn, but he knew that, at this moment, there was nothing he could do for her. *You need to take care of yourself before you can tend to others*, he heard the voice of his long dead mother say.

To reward himself, he opened his *Character Sheet* and did some shopping. He still had the five points he'd saved from the last time he'd upped his *Attributes*. He'd been so engrossed in battle he hadn't even considered using the game hack. Well, that meant more to spend now.

He decided to put five points into *Strength, Constitution, Dexterity,* and *Intelligence*. The last four he dumped into *Wisdom*. Now that his *Spirit* was available, he figured it was time to up the *Stat*. He didn't yet know what an *Incantation* was, but he hoped to find out soon enough.

There was one last prompt blinking in the corner of his vision. He knew it was the *Godhead*, and while part of him was excited to see what amazing things, the prompt would reveal, another part of him was terrified by the divine artifact. He took a deep breath and clicked the prompt.

Congratulations, your Godhead has evolved to Tier 2.

Due to your completion of the Legendary Quest Cleanse the Barrow in which you slew a Legendary Adversary (The Barrow King)

The mote of creation inside you has increased in power.

You are awarded +75 to Health, +75 to Stamina, +75 to Mana and +75 to Spirit.

You are also granted +5 to all attributes.

All skills (including those learned in the next 24 hours) are increased by 2 levels.

+1 Divine Perk Points.

Once again, Gryph was stunned. He was growing in power quickly, and he suspected that it would not go unnoticed. He decided to hold his *Divine Perk Point* in reserve alongside his regular *Perk Points*. He needed to consult with Ovrym about the best way to proceed. The xydai seemed to be the most knowledgeable of the strange artifact that had bonded to him. Gryph inhaled and closed out his interface. He took a quick peek at his *Skill Sheet*.

Magic Skills: Level (Tier)
100% Affinity in All Spheres
Fire: 0 (Base)
Air: 15 (Base)
Water: 3 ((Base)
Earth: 6 (Base)
Chthonic: 3 (Base)
Empyrean: 0 (Base)
Chaos: 0 (Base)
Order: 0 (Base)
Life: 3 (Base)
Death: 0 (Base)
Thought: 7 (Base)
Aether: 0 (Base)
Soul: 27 (Apprentice)

Martial Skills: Level (Tier)
Unarmed: 7 (Base)
Small Blades: 7 (Base)
Staves/Spears: 13 (Base)
Thrown Weapons: 10 (Base)
Stealth: 10 (Base)
Light Armor: 14 (Base)
Dodge: 12 (Base)

Knowledge Skills (Tier)
Alchemy: 7 (Base)
Harvest: 7 (Base)
Analyze: 17 (Base)
Perception: 13 (Base)
Lock-picking: 7 (Base)
Traps: 7 (Base)
Perk Points: 4
Divine Perk Points: 1

Gryph was wowed by the 100% *Affinity* in every sphere of magic. That could sure come in handy. Now, he just needed to find people willing to teach him. He suspected that magical knowledge was an incredibly valuable coin in the Realms, and he doubted everyone would be as free with the knowledge as his companions in the Barrow had been. The need to survive made people do odd things.

Gryph opened his *Character Sheet*.

Gryph - Level 14	Stats
High Elf (El'Edryn) Deity: None Experience: 452,303 Next Level: 182,697	Health: 347 Stamina: 342 Mana: 325 Spirit: 280 **Secondary Stats** Morale:
Attributes	**Gifts**
Strength: 38 Constitution: 47 Dexterity: 47 Intelligence: 40 Wisdom: 24 Attribute Points: 5	Health Regeneration: +25% Mana Regeneration: +25% Night Vision: 120 Ft. Master of Tongues Identify

Wick's tale ended by the time Gryph finished inspecting his interface. Ovrym walked up to Simon and chatted with him. Wick and Tifala were inseparable. Even Xeg seemed chipper as it gnawed on one of the Barrow King's arm bones. Gryph had to smile at the motley crew of companions he'd assembled around him.

Is this what life in the Realms will be like? he thought. *If so, I could do worse.*

Not long after, Simon activated the archway opening a

portal to the outside world. Gryph was worried that the expenditure of energy would drain the spectral teen too much, but Simon said he had some ideas about how to sustain himself and fix up the Barrow.

"That's something Ouzerio never discovered, never could discover," Simon said. "A willing soul is far more powerful than a consumed one. Give me a few weeks and you won't even recognize this place."

Gryph promised to return when he was able and walked through the shimmering portal. The sensation was much more pleasant than the last several portals he'd walked through, and he felt a cool spring breeze blowing on his face.

He stood in a grass clearing in the middle of an ancient forest. Beyond the trees were tall mountains. Birds chirped and flew in lazy circles. Insects buzzed. Life was everywhere.

He closed his eyes and inhaled deeply. The smell of fresh air brought tears to his eyes. Somewhere near he could hear a babbling brook.

"I will say one thing, Dinkwick Flintspanner, you sure know how to show a girl a good time," Tifala said. She hugged Wick fiercely as the gnome's body tightened before his head snapped back at his taller friends.

"So..." Gryph began, a smirk splitting his face.

"Don't say it," Wick grumbled.

Gryph stifled a laugh but kept quiet.

"Your name is Dinkwick?" Ovrym asked.

Gryph erupted in laughter to the horror on Wick's face.

"It's a family name," Wick said, head hung low.

"It is a good name," Ovrym said, with no sense of irony or humor. "A strong name, a warrior's name."

Gryph couldn't help himself as he laughed out loud. Tifala smiled, and Xeg barked what may have been a laugh. Ovrym looked confused.

"Am I missing something?" Ovrym asked.

Even Wick had to smile at that one. "You really aren't from around here, are you?"

"I am confused," Ovrym said again.

"I'll explain it over one of those beers," Gryph said, clasping the tall xydai by the shoulder.

The group walked down a small trail, laughing and

smiling.

Then the world shifted, and Gryph was somewhere else.

52

One moment, Gryph was in a forest walking next to Ovrym, and the next, he stood on a massive balcony overlooking a wondrous, blue ocean. Gryph spun in a panic, moving to draw his spear. But he had no access to his inventory. In fact, he was no longer dressed in his armor but wore a flowing robe of white and gold.

The patio was massive. Columns held a half moon roof above the back part of the massive outdoor space. Arrayed in a matching half-moon pattern were thirteen stone chairs. The space was familiar, and Gryph remembered the Chamber of the Pantheon from his entry to the Realms. It wasn't identical, but the similarity was too close to ignore.

"Welcome," a voice that was both sure and serpentine said.

Gryph spun to see a tall man clad in a hooded robe that shrouded his features. On instinct, Gryph prepped *Flying Stalactite*, but the magic sputtered like an engine stalling.

"My apologies, Your Eminence, but magic does not work here," the Hooded Man said with a slight bow of apology. "And as you have already discovered, weapons are also prohibited."

"Where am I?" Gryph asked, his fists clenching and his body relaxing into a defensive pose. He may have no magic and no weapons, but he was hardly unarmed.

"This is the Agora, Your Eminence. The meeting place of the gods." The Hooded Man walked past him.

Gryph tensed, reaching a hand out to grab the tall, hooded figure. His hand pushed through the man as if he were a ghost or a hologram. The Hooded Man looked at Gryph.

"No harm may be dealt or received while in the Agora."

"Why am I here?" Gryph asked.

"Because you are a god. And a Quorum has been called."

Gryph's eyes went to the thirteen stone chairs. The central throne was larger than the twelve that ringed it, six to a side.

"Called by whom?"

"By me," came a powerful and familiar voice. "I felt it was time that we met face to face, so you could meet your brothers and sisters."

Gryph turned, not at all surprised to see the High God Aluran standing behind him. He wore the same simple robes as Gryph, but he was no less imposing than he had been in his golden armor. He stood, arms clasped behind his back with a beatific smile that would have been at home on the Pope's face.

Gryph attempted to use *Analyze* on the High God but got nothing but his grandiose titles. The High God Aluran, Arche of the Pantheon, Prime of the Realms. Father to all.

"The others will join us shortly, but I felt it proper that you and I had a chat." The way he said *chat* suggested that casual conversations were beneath him. Aluran turned to look down upon the wondrous city.

Gryph recognized Aluran's attempt to put him at ease by exposing his back. *He knows that I cannot hurt him,* Gryph thought. Gryph walked up next to the man and took in the city below. It was a stunning view. If the most wondrous of magical cities existed on Italy's Amalfi Coast, it would still pale compared to the wonder of this place.

"The Shining City," Aluran said. "My home."

"It is amazing," Gryph said.

"Thank you. I have worked very hard, over many long years to build it and make it my home." He turned his gaze to Gryph. "And I am very protective of what is mine."

"As you should be."

Aluran smiled and gave a small bow. "But how rude of me, I have not introduced myself. I am the High God Aluran, Arche of the Pantheon, the Ruler of this Realm. But I suspect you already knew that?"

Gryph nodded.

"And you are?" Aluran asked.

Gryph stared at Aluran, mulling over the dangers of letting him know his name. "I am Gryph."

"Just Gryph?"

"I have yet to acquire any fancy titles," Gryph said with definite snark.

"Well, you have just arrived," Aluran said, a verbal jab back at Gryph.

"Still getting my feet wet, as they say."

"And performing quite admirably. Your *Godhead* has already evolved."

Gryph tensed. *How could he know that?*

"Well, my father instilled a strong work ethic in me."

"As all fathers should. If it is acceptable, I will dispense with the small talk."

Gryph nodded.

"You are an enigma, Gryph. You are not supposed to be here, and you are not supposed to possess … what you possess. I do not know who you are, or where you come from, but I dislike unknowns."

"On that, we can agree," Gryph said.

"Excellent, you are a civilized man. I believe that we can come to an accord."

"What is it you want?"

"Straight and direct. I appreciate that."

Aluran turned and walked away, hands clasped behind his back. Gryph knew it was another ploy, designed to make him feel comfortable. It was failing. Gryph tensed.

"I ask that you join me. I ask you to join the Pantheon. I ask for your fealty," Aluran said, turning his potent gaze on Gryph. "In exchange, I will teach you. Help you achieve your ultimate potential."

He truly doesn't know who I am, Gryph realized. *If he did, then he'd use Brynn to threaten me. Which means my presence is no threat to Brynn, yet.* Waves of relief surged through Gryph. To hide this joy, Gryph smiled a wry smile.

"I've always been more of a solo kinda guy."

Aluran's expression soured as a deep anger surged from the depths of his being. Gryph got the smallest of peeks at the high God's true nature before it was buried.

"That presents a problem. I brought the Pantheon here to restore justice and order to a world long infected by corruption and evil. I have built a better realm for all who reside here, and I will let no power threaten my world."

Gryph's mind flashed back to the ancient scene he'd experienced in the Barrow. *I know you, Morrigan*, Gryph thought. *I know what you truly are.*

"I'm just a man trying to get by in a strange world," Gryph said. "I have no plans to throw a wrench into your gears."

Aluran smiled. "Ah, so you are a player then. I suspected as much."

Shit, Gryph thought. *I need to watch what I say. Damn colloquialisms. What else have I given away?*

"Tell me, how do you still have access? Or are you trapped? Do you have loved ones who miss you? I could send you back."

"Like I said, I've always been a solo kinda guy."

"Too easy, I suppose," Aluran said with a smile. "Well, Gryph, I suppose if you behave I can let you stay." He gazed into Gryph's eyes. "It is time to meet your brethren."

Twelve other figures materialized on the stone chairs arrayed in front of Gryph. As they coalesced, Aluran took his seat on the central throne.

"Welcome, gods of the Pantheon," the Hooded Man intoned.

Gryph took an involuntary step back as he saw the deities before him. He saw Aluran smile. Gryph's eyes scanned the arrayed gods. Several were female. He had already met Heleracon and Zeckoth, but neither showed any sign that they recognized him.

Just recordings after all, Gryph thought in relief.

He scanned the other goddesses, and his eyes settled on one, a few spots to the left of Aluran. She was tall and regal, with a warm face that did not look like Brynn, but it felt like her. Gryph used *Analyze* on her.

Ferrancia, The Messenger Goddess of the Travelers and Guests.

Ferrancia noticed his attention and leaned forward in her chair and grinned at Gryph. The small uptick of the mouth that Gryph had seen a thousand times on his sister when they were kids.

This is *Brynn.*

Gryph almost stepped forward, almost outed Brynn, but then his instincts took control. *An amateur move if there had ever been one.* He buried his fears and turned back to Aluran.

"I have called you here so you could all meet Gryph. I have offered him a place at our side, but he is reluctant." Aluran leaned forward ever so slightly. "I wanted him to meet you so that he understood exactly how things work here."

The threat was obvious. If Gryph stepped out of line, Aluran would bring the full power of the Pantheon down upon him. Gryph wouldn't be fighting one god, but thirteen, including, it seemed, his own sister.

"What say you, Gryph, I ask you one last time. Will you join us?" Aluran boomed.

All eyes were on Gryph, and he flashed back to his childhood. The time as a teen when he'd stolen a car and gone on a joyride. The cops had not scared him. They were nothing compared to the Colonel. As Aluran's gaze drilled into him, Gryph realized that the Colonel was nothing compared to this god.

Fear ate at him, but he pushed it down and stared back at Aluran. Aluran's gaze and body knew Gryph's answer before the words came from his mouth. Had the Agora allowed for it, Gryph knew he'd be dead this very moment.

"I appreciate the High God's most gracious offer, but I believe I will make my own way in this realm."

To his credit, Aluran held in his rage. With no further ceremony, Aluran stood. "Then this Quorum is at an end."

Aluran flicked his hand in a petulant and dismissive manner and, suddenly, Gryph was back in the glade with his friends. He stumbled, and Ovrym caught him.

"You okay?" Wick asked, seeing the fear in Gryph's eyes.

"I'm in a world of shit," Gryph said.

The End of Barrow King - Book One of the Realms.

**Continue your journey into The Realms with
The Lost City - Book Two of The Realms.**

Acknowledgments.

I couldn't have made this book what it is without the help of numerous people.

Thanks to Erica, my first reader, and the love of my life. Thank you for being you.

Thanks to my mother Kathy for always believing in me, and my sister Melissa, for never letting me forget I was a dork.

Thanks to Charlie and Mary Lou Adams for so generously letting me house sit their home in Colorado. Without your roof over my head I'd still be slogging away at this book.

To my awesome Beta Readers, including Erica Rasborn, Robert Petersen, Ben Evans, Jennifer Haviland, A.J.P., Jo Hoffacker, Wade Tiberius Pena, Florian Cadwe, Zach Goza, and the others who gave me feedback. Without you guys, Barrow King would be a shell of what it is today. Thank You.

And thanks Lou Harper for the awesome cover.

Printed in Great Britain
by Amazon

20583306R00202